The Preservation Series! – Book 1

<u>BROKEN UNION</u>
War in the West

Eldon H. Kellogg

ISBN: 9781079902990

https://www.eldonhkellogg.com/
contact@eldonhkellogg.com

The Detonation Series:

FIFTY (2018)

HARRIS (2018)

FIRE & WATER (2019)

Available at Amazon.com

ACKNOWLEDGEMENTS

To my wife, Patty: my editor and best friend, whose critiques, and valuable insight into human motivation and the nature of women (an enormously complex subject) continues unabated.

To Katherine Koerner, who, at age 100, read my first series of three novels in less than a week. I hope she is pleased with my latest work. May she continue to read for many years to come.

To our cats, Abby and Sophie, for their contribution of an endless supply of cat hair for my keyboard!

"Received as I am by the members of a legislature, the majority of whom do not agree with me in political sentiments, I trust that I may have their assistance in piloting the ship of state through this voyage, surrounded by perils as it is; for if it should suffer wreck now, there will be no pilot ever needed for another voyage."

— Abraham Lincoln

"The death of one man is a tragedy. The death of millions is a statistic."

— Joseph Stalin

PROLOGUE

Brisket BBQ
15 Smolensky Boulevard
Moscow, Russia
September 30, 1030 hours MSK (Moscow Standard Time)

"A strange place to find you, Mr. President," said General Grigory Gerasimov, as he strolled into the nearly empty barbecue restaurant.

His security team and those of the President of the Russian Federation glared at each other as the two men greeted as old friends.

"What can I say? I developed a taste for American barbecue the last time I was there," said Russian President Vladimirovich Morozov, as he and the general exchanged hugs.

"If this is truly American, then you can get the food to go, Mr. President. I would suggest that you make it a takeout order," the general said, as he removed a chair and sat across from the president.

"So, Grigory, my old Russian bear who is now a fox . . . what is the hurry?"

"Vladimirovich, my friend of so many years, I told you a few weeks ago that my little birds would find out for sure what the Chinese were up to in America. I just received a report that they will be detonating our two RDS-220s in less than six hours. One will impact the East Coast . . . the other the West Coast. If they are successful, the United States will be crippled . . . permanently. I would recommend that you move to some place a little more . . . secure."

"And what do your little birds tell you of their chances for success?"

"Better than 50/50. If either one succeeds, the Americans will lose most of their military assets on that coast. The impact on the civilian populations will be devastating. If both succeed, the United States will no longer be a factor on the world stage. We need to be prepared to move immediately. I would suggest that we prepare to invade Alaska, as previously discussed, and move our fleet into the North Atlantic. Either way, we will be prepared to take advantage of the situation as it develops."

"And if neither Chinese operation is successful?"

"Then we have been conducting field operations . . . training."

"You have my blessing, Grigory. Move your chess pieces. But I will stay and enjoy my meal."

"As you wish, Mr. President!" General Gerasimov said, as he stood up to leave.

"Grigory, one more thing! Do not activate our nuclear forces beyond their current state of readiness. Understood?" President Morozov said, as the waiter stood nearby with his 'Texas Mix' order of brisket, coleslaw, corn bread and a large sweet tea.

"Understood, Mr. President! Enjoy your meal!"

. . . .

Ranch of the Tres Mezquites
Mexicali, Baja California, Mexico
September 30, 0408 hours UTC-7

One minute after detonation of the 100-megaton 'Fire Dragon' 4.6 miles below the northern end of the Gulf of California.

Alberto Mota sat on the front porch of his ranch house. He rocked gently back and forth in the chair that had been his father's.

The scent of the morning's first cup of coffee reminded him there was work to be done.

"Papa would have been in the barn by now. He would have told me, 'Alberto! You are a lazy boy! The sheep do not milk themselves! No milk, no cheese. No cheese, no money! No money, we starve!' Yes, Papa! I'm on my way, Papa!" Alberto said, and laughed at the memory of an exchange he had heard throughout his youth.

"Papa, I am now 'el hombre cabeza' (the head man). The sheep will wait for a few more minutes," Alberto said, as he glanced under the grouping of mesquite trees that surrounded the family cemetery.

"Three years, Papa! Over three years, and I still miss your wisdom, your love, and yes . . . the bark of your voice. But . . . at least, Mama has company now," Alberto said, as he raised the full mug of coffee to his mouth.

The coffee splashed and burnt his lips. He cursed, jumped up and stared as the dark liquid began to ripple in the mug. The house began to shake as he leapt off the porch and ran away from his home. A hundred sheep began screaming in the barn as the ground began trembling. He turned and stared, as his ancestral home began to crumble.

"Charo!" he yelled, as he threw the mug aside, and ran back toward the house, and his sleeping wife and children.

He was thrown off his feet by a sharp jolt. The ground began violently rolling. Alberto sat bouncing on the dry soil, his hands covering his ears, as the sound of a hundred storms erupted from the earth. He could only stare as lightning rose from the countryside south of the ranch, lighting the early morning sky.

The shaking stopped for a few brief seconds. As he began crawling toward his home on hands and knees, the earth dropped, then rose, tossing him into the air. He crashed to the ground, rolled to his side, and stared as the soil 50 yards to his right disappeared.

"The trees . . . the cemetery . . . they're gone!" Alberto said, as yard by yard the ground began to fall away.

Over everything else, he heard the thunderous sound of rushing water. His last thoughts were of his wife. His last words were, "Papa! I'm coming . . ."

. . . .

91 Avenida Galaxia
Mexicali Industrial Park
Mexicali, Baja California, Mexico
September 30, 0409 hours UTC-7

Site Director Jorge Alvarez sat at his computer staring at numbers. Chromalloy had significant contracts with the United States military, but all that was now in jeopardy.

"Canada? Why would they go with Canada? Their labor costs are ten times ours. The maquiladoras (duty-free factories) here can't be matched. They send us parts, we put them together and ship them back. Our quality control is excellent. It doesn't make any sense!" Jorge said, as he began calculating how much of a price cut he could take and still make a profit.

Mexicali was the capital city of the Mexican state of Baja California. Tucked up against the U.S. border, its highly educated and skilled population provided low-cost labor that dozens of major US companies utilized to maximize their profits. Over a million people were crammed into 40 square miles. The city was 80 miles northwest of the Gulf of California, but only 27 feet above sea level . . .

"The meeting with the US Defense Department representative is in less than three hours. This is our biggest contract. If I lose this, I'll lose my job. I'll wind up selling insurance and used cars in Tijuana."

Small quakes were common in Mexicali. After all, the San Andreas Fault ran directly under the city. Jorge felt a small tremor, but ignored it. The second tremor was more significant. His monitor began

4

dancing across his desk. He stood up when a pane in the window in front of him cracked. His last thoughts, as he ducked under the heavy oak desk, were not of his family, but the delay this might cause in his upcoming meeting . . .

.   .   .   .

Aviation Enforcement Flight 32
Elevation 1000 feet above
Jacumba Hot Springs, California
0412 hours PST

Stacy Thomas had been an Air Interdiction Agent with U.S. Customs and Border Protection for seven years. The Beechcraft King Air 200 was cruising at 250 mph. In another hour he'd be landing at the small airstrip outside Jacumba Hot Springs for refueling, and more importantly, breakfast.

"Nice to have a quiet shift for a change," said Agent Cristy Davis, from the co-pilot seat.

"Yeah, I can't remember a flight when we didn't see someone trying to cross the border illegally. Must be a holiday or something."

The sunrise wasn't due for another two hours. Cristy was still glued to the infrared monitor mounted between them. Anything alive that moved through the empty spaces by the border, glowed like a furnace.

"What the hell was that?" Stacy asked, as he stared to the south.

"What? Did you see another aircraft?" Cristy asked, as her head popped up from the monitor.

"No, look south. It was some kind of weird lightning."

"I don't see . . . whoa! What is that? There's a bunch of them! It looks like it's coming from the ground. It must be an illusion! That's impossible."

5

"Well, the illusion is getting worse, and it seems to be heading this way!" Stacy said, as he pulled the nose of the aircraft up and turned to the north.

"Never thought I'd see you spooked by a little lightning!"

"The sky is perfectly clear . . . no clouds. That lightning is coming from the ground. I've heard about this phenomenon. I even saw a few videos on YouTube. Shit! Look at that!" Stacy said, as fingers of lightning leapt from the ground.

"What causes it?"

"Earthquakes . . . real big earthquakes! Scientists aren't sure what causes it. Contact Boulevard Border Patrol Station. Tell them there may be a big quake in Mexico!"

The lightning grew more violent and seemed to be marching northward toward them at a rapid pace, as Cristy contacted Boulevard Station.

"They haven't been notified of anything and . . . shit! What was that?" she yelled, as the cockpit lit up.

"Ball lightning! I've heard about it, but I've never seen it before!"

"There's another one! It just hovers . . . then disappears."

The sky and the ground below were lit up by the constant lightning rising from the earth.

"Turn the plane to the south!" Cristy said.

"We're too close to the border. We don't have permission to cross."

"Turn south and go lower! Look!"

The full moon had almost set, casting long shadows on the terrain below.

"Look there!" Cristy said, while pointing to the southeast.

Stacy pointed the nose of the aircraft in that direction and began decreasing altitude. They continued south as the aircraft leveled off at 500 feet. The ground below was moving. They could see ripples and huge cracks appear in the surface. Behind it all came water. As the ground sank, a wall of water began flowing northward toward the border. The bright lights of Mexicali glistened below them, unaware of the approaching doom.

"Oh, God! What's happening?" Cristy asked, as the city began to disappear into the ground, to be replaced by an expanding body of water.

"The ground is splitting! Something has triggered the San Andreas Fault! Look! The cracks are passing the border and heading northwest. Find an emergency channel! There are a dozen cities up that way! El Centro, Imperial, Brawley . . . then the Salton Sea. After that, it's Palm Springs, San Bernardino . . . then right through LA!" Stacy said, as he turned the aircraft and began following the disaster northward . . .

.   .   .   .

Headquarters Building
Naval Amphibious Base Coronado
3632 Tulagi Road
Coronado, California
0415 hours PST

"Admiral! We just received a comm from the Pentagon! They say the mission failed. They expect the device to detonate at . . ." Captain Harold Turner began, as the building began to shake.

"Sir?"

"I think we know when the device detonated, Captain. I would suggest that you hold on to something," Admiral Turner said, as the room lurched to one side, hurling books from a nearby shelf.

The two officers stared at each other, then the building around them, as the shaking grew more violent. The sounds of cracking masonry and shattering glass increased as the ground beneath them continued to move.

"This isn't just the bomb. The detonation is 100 miles from here. They were right! The San Andreas . . . it's opening . . ." Admiral

7

Turner thought, as the brick building around them began to collapse . .
.

.   .   .   .

Ryan Powell lay in bed dreaming of a basketball game from long ago. North Carolina State was playing someone, but it was all a blur. Then a man walked on the court and everything stopped. Everyone in Reynolds Coliseum was silent . . . 12,400 people transfixed, as Coach Valvano began to speak. Then he paused and pointed at Ryan.

The old coliseum began to shake as Coach Valvano said, "You better wake up! You must leave! Now!"

Ryan's eyes popped open. He felt the bed shaking. Anita was oblivious, tucked tightly against his side.

"This is a pretty good one. Over ten years living here, and I haven't felt one this strong," Ryan said, as he lay in the dark, listening to things falling off the shelves and dresser of the bedroom.

The shaking continued, growing steadily more violent. Their young daughter began crying down the hall in her bedroom. Anita grabbed his arm.

"Ryan . . . what's happening?"

"Earthquake . . . bad one! I'll go get Beka!" Ryan said, as he jumped out of bed and began staggering down the hall.

Beka met him at the doorway and jumped into his arms.

"Daddy! Make it stop!"

She was shaking as he clutched her tightly and ran back to the bedroom.

"Ryan, this isn't stopping! What should we do?"

"It'll end in a few seconds. They never last very long," he said, as he tossed Beka into the bed beside her mother and climbed in after her.

But the shaking didn't stop. It grew more violent. The bed began dancing across the wooden floor. Flashing lights could be seen through the windows as transformers began exploding across the vast city of Los Angeles. When the bedroom window shattered, they all screamed.

"Get up! Get dressed! We're getting out of the building. Move! I'll get her clothes!" Ryan yelled, as he ran back down the hall.

The sound and the shaking grew ever more violent as the family dressed in the darkness. There was no electricity. Car alarms, awakened by the earthquake, began to add to the chaos. They fled outside and sat together in their small front yard. Beka sat in his lap, her arms wrapped around him. Anita clung to his side as the ground began to roll and tilt.

"Ryan, the 'bug-out' bag!" Anita yelled.

"Hold her!" Ryan said, as he bolted back into the ground floor apartment.

The walls began cracking as he pulled open the front door and ran to a storage closet in the rear of their home. He grabbed the backpack and ran for the front door, only to feel the building lurch, slamming the front door in his face.

"Dammit! It's jammed!" he said, as he yanked on the door handle.

The ceiling began to crumble as he turned, threw the backpack on, and ran for the bedroom. Climbing over the bed, he threw himself out of the broken window and onto the grass outside. Beka was crying hysterically as he ran over to his wife and daughter. They clung to each other as the disaster unfolded around them . . .

.   .   .   .

Fire Station 31
San Francisco, California
0430 hours PST

Jamar swore as he sat bolt upright in bed. He had been dreaming of Las Vegas. The casinos had gotten together and thrown him a parade. No one had ever broken the bank at five major casinos on five straight days. He was surrounded by beautiful women while cruising in a red 2019 Dawn Drophead Coupé Rolls Royce convertible filled with $1000 bills. The money blew out as they sped down South Las Vegas Boulevard. He didn't care. It was only money, and he was filthy, stinking rich! Thousands of people were screaming his name as they fought over the flying bills . . .

"Damn! That was sweet!" he said, as he stared around the dimmed interior of the second floor of the firehouse, the fire alarm still ringing in his ears.

"Jesus, Jamar, you're getting slower than Tom! Move your ass!" Heather Moore yelled, while pulling the suspenders of her turnout gear pants up over her shoulders.

"Remind me not to get drunk before I go on shift," Jamar said, as he swung his legs off the bed, and inserted his feet into his fireman's boots.

Heather was heading for the fire pole when she was thrown to the floor by a sudden jolt. She lay sprawled, then turned her head and stared at Jamar.

"Yeah, girl . . . that was a bad one!" Jamar said, as he stood up and pulled up his pants.

They were both thrown across the room as the old brick fire station tilted, then split in half. They huddled together and stared up at the night sky. Bolts of lightning leapt upward. The sounds of buildings being shattered, gas lines and transformers exploding, were overshadowed by a deep rumble that rose in intensity until they both screamed in fear.

Jamar's last thought, as he clung to Heather, was . . . *"Why do I smell the ocean?"*

CHAPTER 1

Raptor Flight Charlie-2
15,000 feet above the Bearing Sea
October 2, 0330 AKST (Alaska Standard Time)

The ongoing disaster on the West Coast had come as a shock to both F-22A pilots. Tidal waves from the massive series of quakes had reached Alaska six hours after the initial detonation in the Gulf of California. Damage along the coast had been extensive. Reports, a few hours later, of an attack on the People's Republic of China, was as an even greater shock. The world had slipped into war and chaos . . . and they were still on routine air patrol over the Bering Sea.

They were an odd pair, an exceptional pair. Captain Julia "Flash" Jamieson, a graduate of the Air Force Academy, was the first female pilot to qualify in an F-22A Raptor. Major Paul "Turbo" Knowlton, an ROTC graduate of North Carolina Agricultural and Technical State University in Greensboro, North Carolina, was the first African American to qualify. Both were outstanding pilots and close friends.

"Turbo, look to the south. It's just a wall of dust being blown across the Pacific," said Captain Jamieson, the moon above and on their starboard side.

"Flash, that 'wall' looks like it reaches up to 50,000 feet. I flew through shit like that over Iraq in an F-16. It messes with everything and eats up your turbine blades. Lots of down time for maintenance," replied Major Knowlton.

"That wall is what's left of China. Do you think the rumors are true? We have some kind of space plane that could do that?"

"If we do, I'd sure like to fly it!"

"Always something different for you. Combat wasn't enough. Now you want to fly in space."

"Like you wouldn't jump at the opportunity?"

"Of course! But then . . . wait! Turbo, I'm picking up something below us . . . way below us," Captain Jamieson said, as she began studying an alarm on her AN/APG-77v1 radar.

"Yeah, I see it. What the hell! That's down on the surface . . . just above the waves, and it's moving fast."

"Multiples! They're incoming across the Bering Sea. Chinese?"

"Don't know . . . running recognition now!"

"Holy shit! Russian! Those are Tu-160s, long-range bombers. I'm getting 17, but the numbers keep going up."

"Seventeen . . . two more . . . now three! That's 20, all flying nap of the earth . . . or in this case, ocean. That's dangerous as shit for a plane like that!"

"Roger that! Turbo . . . that is an attack. No bomber flies that low on a training mission. They're either heading for Alaska or they're going to skirt down the Pacific Coast. I see five waves . . . four bombers in each wave."

"I'm transmitting data back to Elmendorf. I'm requesting permission to attack," said Major Knowlton, then switched over to a different radio channel.

"Roger that!"

Captain Jamieson could feel herself break into a sweat even inside her pressurized flight suit. She had never flown in combat. It was something she had dreamed about since she was a little girl. Her father had flown an F-4 Phantom II over Vietnam during the last two years of the war. When she was older, he had told her of the abject fear of being shot down as missiles and tracers filled the sky around him. He had tried to talk her out of going to the Air Force Academy, but she was in love with flying. She had soloed in gliders when she was 14 years old and powered aircraft at 16. A private pilot's license at 17 was a mere formality. Now she was in it for real. Combat was minutes away.

"Flash! We have been instructed by Elmendorf to get on their six and warn them off. If they ignore or take any hostile action . . . we start taking them down. You copy?"

"Roger that, Turbo! Warn them . . . wait . . . kill them!"

"Follow me in. We'll stay 500 feet above them and two miles behind."

The F-22A Raptor was a fifth-generation, single-seat, twin-engine, all-weather stealth tactical fighter. Its combination of power, maneuverability and lethalness made it one of the most formidable aircraft in the world.

The two Raptors dropped from the sky, leveling off 600 feet above the surface of the Bering Sea. The sky had turned black as they flew into a storm front headed for the Alaskan coast. The last of the trailing Tu-160s was just visible in the distance. The Russian bombers mounted four Kuznetsov NK-32 afterburning turbofan engines, the most powerful ever mounted on a combat aircraft. The engines were throttled back as the swept-wing bombers fought to maintain control so close to the ocean's surface.

"Flash, something just happened. I lost my link with Elmendorf."

"Turbo, maybe they aren't all bombers. The Tu-160PP is an electronic warfare variant. My locks on the forward aircraft are starting to blink out. We're going to lose them."

"Bombers with a jammer, heading toward Alaska during a storm in the middle of the night. We're already at war with China. Throttle up . . . check Master-Arm hot! I've got the two on the left. You take the two on the right. Get in close before firing your AMRAAMs. They may be able to jam them. Then we power through into the next set."

"Turbo, you sure about this?"

"Yeah, Flash . . . I'm sure! In a few days you'll get to talk to your dad about air-to-air combat. He got two Migs, right?"

"Yeah . . . I'll get to talk to him!"

"Throttle up . . . Master-Arm hot!" Turbo ordered, as the distance between the two Raptors and the bombers closed.

There was another variant of the Tupolev series of aircraft . . . the TU-161, a long-range interceptor carrying a dozen R-77 air-to-air missiles. It was flying 20 miles to the north of the main group, paralleling their course when the Raptors were first detected by the TU-160PP jammer. It immediately turned toward the pursuing American aircraft. When the American Raptors fired four AMRAAM at the Russian bombers, it released four R-77 AAMs at the Raptors.

"Turbo! Incoming!"

"Punch it, Flash! Follow your missiles in. Mix with the blast and debris! Countermeasures when they get close!"

The last flight of bombers broke away when the American missiles were detected. The TU-160 was a fast aircraft, capable of Mach 2.5 when at 35,000 feet. But a sea level, with its wings swept forward to enhance stability, it was relatively slow.

Despite evasive maneuvers and countermeasures, the trailing group of four TU-160 bombers became fireballs erupting above the Bearing Sea. The two Raptors flew by the explosions. The trailing missiles from the Russian interceptor nearly on them.

Captain Julia Jamieson had always hated the moniker 'Flash'. She had received it at the Air Force Academy during her freshman year, when she was a 'Doolie'. She had just stepped out of the shower into her spartan living quarters, when two upperclassmen had accidently barged into her room. She had screamed and run back into the bathroom, 'flashing' the upperclassmen as she fled. They had been disciplined. She received a nickname that had followed her through four years at the academy and through flight school.

Both R-77 air-to-air missiles that were on her six, detonated in the fiery explosions of the two bombers she had killed. For one second, she thought of her father. She had equaled his combat kills.

She flew so close to the ocean that she felt like she was flying between the waves. Everything was now instinct and training. The next flight of Russian bombers disappeared in the darkness, but her radar showed them eight miles ahead . . . same heading . . . same speed as before. She accelerated the raptor toward her next set of targets.

"Turbo, I'm onto the next flight. I'll get close again like you said. I got two, Turbo!"

There was no reply . . .

"Shit! Turbo, I can't see you on radar. I'm trying other channels. Give me a click. I know you're still there . . . you have to be there!"

There was no reply . . . no signal. She flew on into the darkness, sensing . . . knowing, that she was alone.

"The mission . . . the mission first!" she told herself, as she focused on the enemy aircraft ahead of her.

"Damn . . . two AMRAAM left . . . then the cannon!"

During the Vietnam War, F-4 American pilots had suffered losses at the hands of North Vietnamese Migs. They had become dependent on technology and forgotten the art of the 'dogfight'. All fighting between aircraft had become long-range missile duels. Early F-4's didn't even have a cannon for close-in defense. The Migs had shown the American military the fallacy of that reasoning.

The F-22A possessed an internally mounted M61A2 Vulcan 20 mm rotary cannon embedded in the right wing. The rate of fire was 6000 rounds per minute. But the aircraft only held 480 rounds, or less than five seconds of firing time.

She silenced the alert alarms as more missiles were detected heading toward her Raptor.

"*Shit! Four missiles!*" she thought, as she closed on the next set of Russian bombers.

They were flying line abreast. The coastline was just under 100 miles away. Her attempts at contacting Elmendorf had proven futile. She was alone and knew that these bombers would head for Elmendorf . . . all her friends.

"*Twenty seconds to impact. They have me bracketed. I have to go right through them,*" she told herself, as she swung her aircraft to the right, knowing that all the Russian missiles would follow her course change.

"Ten seconds!" she said, as she jerked the Raptor back to the left and cut underneath the first Russian bomber.

Her cockpit lit up as the bomber exploded, struck by one of the pursuing missiles. The second detonated nearby. Shrapnel perforated the skin of the Raptor. Onboard alarms began screaming in her ear. Her Heads-Up-Display showed damage to flight control surfaces. She silenced the alarms as she approached the second bomber. Her radar had lost track of the remaining two Russian missiles.

The TU-160 appeared before her, ghostly white. A huge plane, 177 feet long and 183 feet wide, with its adjustable wings spread outward. One cannon burst . . . two . . . three, and she flew through the exploding bomber, hoping that the pursuing missiles would be caught up in the explosion.

"*Three, Dad . . . I've got you beat . . .*" she thought, while lining up on the remaining two Russian bombers.

The two AMRAAMs were away when the fourth Russian missile found her. Two fireballs billowed ahead of her . . . two more Russian bombers that wouldn't make it to Alaska.

The last thoughts of Captain Julia Jamieson were of her father.

"*Daddy . . . five kills . . . I'm an ace!*"

Her F-22A Raptor, shorn of one wing, spun into the cold waters of the Bering Sea and disintegrated.

The remaining 12 Russian bombers, and their escort, continued on course, for Alaska . . .

CHAPTER 2

"Received as I am by the members of a legislature the majority of whom do not agree with me in political sentiments, I trust that I may have their assistance in piloting the ship of state through this voyage, surrounded by perils as it is; for if it should suffer wreck now, there will be no pilot ever needed for another voyage."

Abraham Lincoln, February 21, 1861

The United States of America had never really suffered during a war. From 1775 to the Chinese Conflict only 1.3 million American combatants had died. The number seemed significant to Americans, but to the global community it was a trifle. The total global deaths from World War I and II alone were over 80 million. Times had changed for the United States of America. Over 24,000,000 American citizens were killed after the detonation of the Tsar Bomba beneath the Gulf of California. The psychic shock on the American people was unprecedented. The great oceans on either coast had been a barrier that had protected them for over 250 years. This wasn't supposed to be possible. That time had ended!

.   .   .   .

Seven days later and the aftershocks just kept coming. The initial series of quakes had been theoretically impossible. The Richter

Scale of earthquake measurement was logarithmic. A level 3 was ten times greater than a level 2. A Level 4 ten times greater than a Level 3. The West Coast of North America was torn apart by a series of Level 10 convulsions. Three volcanos in the Cascades were now erupting.

The East Pacific Rise dominated the boundary between the Pacific Plate and the North American Plate. Like the mid-Atlantic Ridge, it was a place of tectonic growth. For the last eight million years it had been slowly increasing the northwestward march of the Gulf of California at two inches per year. That sedate pace disappeared in one instant. The tectonic zipper had been ripped open, and the planet wasn't happy. Over 3,865 linear miles of crust had been displaced by a 100-megaton nuclear detonation at a depth of 4.6 miles. The entire planet vibrated and continued to do so as the fractured crust tried to settle . . .

. . . .

The White House
The Oval Office
Washington, DC
October 7, 1130 hours EST

Acting President Clarisse Beaumont had been massaging her temples when the note arrived. She stared at the cryptic message, tears in her bloodshot eyes, then read it again. She threw it aside and continued massaging her aching temples.

"How did I wind up in this position? I never wanted this job. I was just a placeholder until the next election. Then I could step aside and let them select a proper Vice President. Now look at me! The migraines won't go away. They just . . . won't . . . stop . . ." she thought, as the door to the Oval Office opened.

"Madam President, we have to talk," said Speaker of the House Carla Jacobson.

Senate Majority Leader Bob Marker stood at her right shoulder.

"Please, come in, have a seat," Clarisse said, while smiling and gesturing toward a pair of ornate 18th Century chairs placed before the Resolute Desk.

"This is the last thing I need. They'll want answers . . . solutions. I've got nothing to give them, and now I'm stuck here!"

"I know why you're both here. I just received the same information. The doctors don't expect President Miller to live much longer."

"Madam President, it's uncomfortable to discuss, but we have to proceed under the assumption that he'll be dead by tomorrow. His brain . . . the blood clot . . . they can't . . ." Speaker Jacobson began, then looked away.

"Madam President, we're at war. The nation is crippled. Tens of millions are dead. Our military forces on the West Coast are either destroyed or rendered ineffective. The Russians are moving on Alaska. They've massed troops on their borders with Eastern Europe. Their fleets are in the North Atlantic. The Middle East is preparing to explode. Scientists are predicting the ecological effects of a nuclear winter because of your attack on China. Somehow . . . you must stabilize things!" said Senator Marker.

"If you're looking for a magic wand, I don't have one. What must stop are the constant attacks on this administration by your party, and I'm addressing this to both of you!" Clarisse said, as she began massaging her temples once again.

"That is completely uncalled for! As was your declaration of Martial Law! You went to war without our permission!" shouted Speaker Jacobson, as she leapt to her feet.

"Speaker . . . the West Coast is gone! Every major city in this nation has seen riots of unprecedented ferocity. We have lost control of much of our country at a time when we could least afford it. The Mayor of New York . . . of frikin' New York City . . . called me and begged for Federal troops . . . begged! He has over 60,000 police officers, but it's not enough. And he's not the only one screaming for help! The Chinese did this! What about this situation does not justify Martial Law? The war was justified!" Clarisse responded.

"You didn't come to us! You should have come to us and gotten the permission of Congress before acting!"

"And do what . . . sit on my hands while you debated for the next six weeks? There wasn't time. That is why the Founders placed Article 1 Section 9 Clause 2 in the Constitution! President Lincoln was forced to do the same thing in 1863, and Congress was pissed then! Get over it! If you wish to fiddle while Rome burns, have at it! Someone had to act, and that is what I have done. The Chinese had to be dealt with once and for all! I did that!"

"Carla, please sit down . . . please! This is getting us nowhere," said Senator Marker.

The three most powerful civilian officials in the country sat and stared at each other, seemingly afraid to restart the conversation.

"Oh, Konrad! Damn you for leaving me with this mess!" Clarisse thought.

"Speaker Jacobson . . . Carla . . . I apologize for my outburst. I'll admit that my fuse has been rather short lately," Clarisse said, as she consciously placed her hands on the desk and kept them there.

"During the few hours of peace that I've had, I've been reading about Abraham Lincoln. In 1862 he said . . . and I've memorized this part, 'We of this Congress and this administration, will be remembered in spite of ourselves. No personal significance, or insignificance, can spare one or another of us. The fiery trial through which we pass, will light us down, in honor or dishonor, to the latest generation.'"

Clarisse paused, glancing from Congresswoman to Senator, as she chose her next words carefully.

"We must stop fighting each other. Just like back then, the survival of the Union is at stake. If all you want to discuss is my impeachment, then you will preside over a dead nation. I'm not a dictator, even during a declared National Emergency. I want your approval of my going to war and my declaration of Martial Law. The people of this nation deserve no less. They must see that our Republic, based on the Constitution and the Rule of Law, is still intact. I'm speaking to the country at 9 PM Eastern. If you agree, I'll bring up the fact that Congress will soon begin discussing my declaration of Martial Law and defending ourselves against the Chinese."

"It's possible . . . probable, that the President will be dead by then," said Speaker Jacobson.

"If that's the case, then I'll praise him as an American patriot who gave his life in defense of the Union. He once told me that the President was no more than a caretaker. Benjamin Franklin is credited with saying, 'We must, indeed, all hang together or, most assuredly, we shall all hang separately.' We must show 'We the People' that their country will survive. Right now, they're not sure . . . and neither am I."

"I've been told that the Russians have landed troops in Alaska," said Senator Markle.

"It's like they are daring us to attack them!" added Speaker Jacobson.

"The Russians have so many nuclear warheads, on so many different delivery systems, scattered across so much of the Earth's surface, that they feel we don't dare attack them with nukes. They're correct. I'll never authorize their use unless the Russians use them first. We have one Space Carrier, the USS Kraken. It expended almost all its non-nuclear kinetic weapons during the strike on China. Those kinetic weapons were built at a secret facility in California. That facility no longer exists. The industries that supplied the spare parts for the space planes and carrier . . . no longer exist. It will take months, if not years, to reconstruct those facilities at another location."

"Are the Russians aware of this?" asked Speaker Jacobson.

"I don't know. Probably . . . maybe? We had far too much data storage, resources, suppliers and irreplaceable people, located on the West Coast. We've been gutted! That was the term that the Chairman of the Joint Chiefs used when I talked to him this morning . . . gutted!"

"Are we defenseless?" asked Senator Marker.

"As defenseless as we've been since Pearl Harbor, and our oceans are no longer much of a barrier," Clarisse replied.

"So, what do we do?" asked Speaker Jacobson.

"We listen to Ben Franklin and stand together," Clarisse said, as an idea formed in her mind.

"We'll back you, Madam President. I can't speak for Carla, but the Senate will start the approval process tomorrow morning."

"I agree. I'll start pushing for a vote in the House as soon as we leave here," Speaker Jacobson said.

"One more thing . . . when I said, we will stand together, I meant that literally. When I address the nation tonight, I want both of you with me . . . one on either side. That visual will say more than anything else. That's what the people will see. Their government standing together . . . united," said Clarisse, as she looked at both, waiting for a response.

"She's correct, Bob. It's the right thing to do," said Speaker Jacobson.

Senator Marker thought for a moment before saying, "Well, ladies . . . it looks like we have a date tonight!"

They were all walking toward the exit from the Oval Office when the room began to sway . . .

CHAPTER 3

US Geological Survey Headquarters
12201 Sunrise Valley Drive
Reston, Virginia
October 7, 1140 hours EST

Dr. Janice Wolf, Advanced National Seismic System Coordinator, felt her cell phone vibrate against her right cheek as she lay sprawled across her desk. She chose to ignore it. She had averaged three hours sleep per day since the Great Quake on September 28. She had bypassed total exhaustion two days ago and kept on working. The voice and the shaking blended into the nightmare she was having. Her eyes snapped open when she was pulled upright in her chair.

"Janice! It's happening! Just like you predicted!" said her assistant, Brenda Carson.

"What? The West Coast? More earthquakes and volcanoes?"

"No! Worse! It's the New Madrid Fault. We just recorded a 7.2, and it was south of the known seismic zone. The center was 12 miles northwest of Memphis. You could feel it here!"

"Does Dr. Latham know? How bad is the damage in Memphis?" Janice asked, as she blinked sleep from her eyes and rubbed her face.

"Bad! It's not just Memphis. There are reports of damage as far away as Little Rock, St. Louis and Nashville. And we're getting indications that it's going to get worse."

Janice sat up and activated the screens on her PC. She had three upper and three lower screens. Each gave her pieces of data she used to assess a seismic situation.

"Get me some coffee . . . lots of sugar, no cream. I'll look at the data and then contact Dr. Latham. No! Add some cream. My stomach is killing me!"

"Yes, ma'am!" Brenda said, as she hurried away.

Janice reached for her glasses and sighed as she began studying the seismic data on the multiple screens.

"7.2 . . . 14 miles down, six minutes ago . . . that's really odd," she said, as two more indications appeared 100 miles to the north of the original quake.

"6.0 and a 6.8! That's 40 miles north of the New Madrid Seismic Zone. Now two more . . . even further north! What the hell is going on?" she asked, as Brenda appeared with a steaming mug of hot coffee.

"Oh, my God! There's more? What's happening?" Brenda said, as she studied the data on the screens.

They both stared at each other as the building began to tremble. Coffee sloshed from the mug, causing Brenda to yelp and set the mug on the desk.

"It's the Reelfoot Rift . . . pieces of ancient continents were thrust together 750 million years ago. What we call Rodinia. It was a merger that never fully sealed. North America is welded together at the Rift. The continent almost split apart 500 million years ago. We aren't sure why it didn't. Now, the artificial shearing of part of the continent in California has left a weakness. It's like . . . a cantilever. Part of the continental plate is now hanging loose. No, not loose, but the stress on the West Coast is far less than it's been in millions of years. The stress on the continental plate must be unbelievable! It may compensate by cracking along the weak spot . . . the Rift . . . the New Madrid Fault . . ." Janice said, as she turned and stared at her assistant.

"What does that mean?" Brenda asked.

"It means that the country may crack in half! Where the hell is Dr. Latham?"

CHAPTER 4

US Highway 1, the Coast Highway
Rock Point Beach, California
October 7, 1000 hours PST

"Crap! I still can't get a signal!" Lihwa Yan said, as she stood at the peak of the small hill overlooking the Pacific Ocean, her cell phone held above her head.

"You may never get a signal again," Tom Jackson said, as he lay back on the hill amongst the yellow flowers and stared into the murky haze that drifted above them.

"What the hell does that mean?"

"It means that we both assumed that when we walked away from the mess with the nuclear bombs we discovered, the federal government would take care of things and protect the nation! Based on what's happened during the last week, they pretty much screwed the pooch!"

"Tom, we didn't walk away. Homeland captured us after we discovered the third weapon. They told us we'd be in prison if we kept looking," Lihwa replied.

"Well . . . there is that, but they failed. Our city is gone!"

"I can't believe that. My family is in San Francisco! They have to be safe!" Lihwa said, as she lay beside Tom and leaned against him.

"Babe, if we were still there . . . I don't think . . . from everything we've heard . . . that we'd still be alive. There's nothing left."

"I don't believe it! It's all bullshit! I don't believe that California split in two. You're a sci-fi nut. I'm a lawyer. I believe in facts, not fantasy."

"You felt the quakes, the same as me. You talked to your brother before the cell towers all went down. You think he was exaggerating when he said that the ground was collapsing beneath him and all the buildings were falling?"

"This is California. There are always quakes. This was just a big one. I have to . . . I just have to believe they're all still alive," Lihwa said, as she wrapped her hand in his, and stared into the darkening clouds swirling above them.

"We still have a quarter tank of gas. We'll head north. It'll be better there. We'll get some more gas, something to eat, and hopefully some news," Tom said, as he pulled her close.

They had been in the mountains when the quake struck. The cabin had collapsed, but they had dragged themselves from the ruins with only bumps and bruises to show for it. His old '67 Camaro had not been designed for travelling across rough terrain, but landslides and fallen trees had forced them off-road, down hillsides and across meadows. It had taken two days to reach a paved road, and all they found was devastation. The food and water from the ruined cabin had run out a day ago.

"It wasn't supposed to end this way. First, North Carolina, and now this. It's the nightmare you feared after you found the first bomb behind my father's restaurant," Lihwa sighed.

"Yeah, it sucks being right!"

"Tom, I can't go north. We're going back to San Francisco. I have to know!"

"Babe, you know I love you . . . that I'd do anything for you. But I don't think that's a good idea. People will get crazy after this. There won't be any law enforcement. It won't be safe. Remember the couple we met yesterday? They had just left the area. They said San Francisco's gone. It sank into the Bay."

28

"I don't believe it! We must go back home. I have to see it for myself. Otherwise . . . otherwise, I'll always wonder if I abandoned my family. If there's something I could have done. Tom . . . we have to go back!"

.   .   .   .

They travelled south on US 1. What little traffic they passed was heading in the other direction . . . north. They reached the Salmon Creek Ranger Station, just north of Bodega Bay, and found the bridge crossing Salmon Creek blocked by three abandoned cars.

"Tom, pull in here. The rangers may have some information," Lihwa said.

He pulled into the parking area. There were only four other vehicles. All had Ranger markings. The ground shuddered as Tom pulled into a parking space. Strong aftershocks had become so commonplace that they barely noticed them anymore.

"You wait here. I'll go talk to them," Tom said, while opening his door.

"What? After all we've been through, I'm still the little woman needing protection?" Lihwa asked, as she hopped out of the Camaro.

Two men stood on the porch of a nearby cabin. Both clutched the railing as another tremor shook the area. Tom stopped ten feet away from the cabin and stuck out his arm to keep Lihwa from going any further. The men were passing a pint of some liquor back and forth. Both wore the uniforms of Rangers.

"Hey, the bridge is blocked. Is there any way we can get through? We're trying to get to San Francisco," Tom asked.

Both men stared at him and then started laughing.

"Pal . . . there ain't no San Francisco! A half mile past the bridge US 1 is gone and the land along with it. When I say gone, I mean that it's gone all the way down to San Jose. There is no San Francisco! It went like Atlantis and sunk into the sea!" one ranger said, as he yanked the bottle from the other man and drained the bottle.

"You're wrong! It can't be gone! My family lives there . . ." Lihwa said, brushing aside Tom's arm and approaching the two men.

"Lady . . . don't mind him. His family's dead. They were in San Francisco visiting his wife's mother . . . three kids and his wife. We were both at a Ranger convention in Sacramento when it happened. The power was still on then. I saw it on TV. The whole city, all of San Francisco . . . it just slid into the ocean . . . all of it!" the other ranger said.

"What don't you get, Lady? They're all fucking dead!" the first ranger screamed, while pulling his 9mm from his holster and placing it against his temple.

Tom grabbed Lihwa and shielded her as the shot rang out. When they glanced at the porch, the first ranger lay in a pool of blood. His friend stood speechless, spattered with gore, staring at his friend's twitching body.

"We're leaving! We're going back north!" Tom said, as he grabbed Lihwa, and began dragging her back toward the Camaro.

"No! Tom, I have to see!"

"What did you not hear! It's gone! There is no damn city!"

"I don't care . . . I have to see it. I have to say goodbye! If you won't go with me, then I'll walk there," Lihwa said, as she pulled herself free from his grasp.

Tom just stared at her, then glanced back at the porch. The second ranger was sitting in a rocking chair, seemingly oblivious to the corpse lying beside him. His eyes were glazed over, unblinking, as the slow squeak of the rocker began on time with another tremor.

30

CHAPTER 5

Ministry of Defense Building
22 Frunzenskaya Naberezhnaya Avenue
Moscow, Russia
October 7, 1930 hours MSK (Moscow Standard Time)

President Vladimirovich Morozov was growing impatient, and when his patience ended, people would begin to disappear.

"General Gerasimov, I trust you do not intend to keep me waiting much longer!" President Morozov said, while glaring at the senior military officers seated around him.

"I apologize, Mr. President. We are waiting for one last satellite feed. The American attack on China has left the atmosphere in the Northern Hemisphere . . . disturbed. We have a few items of interest to discuss. The images we are about to present will be worth your wait, I promise you. While we are waiting, I will update you on the status of our conventional forces," replied General Grigory Gerasimov, Chief of the General Staff of the Armed Forces of Russia.

President Morozov sighed as he glanced around the interior of the Information Hall of the National Defense Management Center. They were 300 feet below the streets of Moscow, encased inside 30 feet of steel-reinforced concrete. The steel entry door weighed 25 tons and took two minutes to open. The room was circular, 90 feet in diameter. The walls were 20 feet high and lined with interlocked monitors along the entire circumference. The impression was of sitting inside a movie theater and being surrounded by the screen. In the center was a raised platform containing a large circular table. The platform was surrounded by three rings of workstations. Technicians and soldiers were constantly updating displayed information from all over the world.

"First, Mr. President . . . the monitor to your left," said General Gerasimov, as he pointed.

"I see a satellite view . . . and what? I do not recognize that coastline."

"That is because that coastline is brand new, Mr. President. The American West Coast now has a new island . . . a very long one. The separation of California from North America should have taken a few million years. Our friends in Beijing accelerated the process. That island is over 1200 miles long. The new Gulf of California, or whatever it will be named since it is no longer a gulf, is 130 miles wide at the south and two miles wide in the north . . . where San Francisco used to be."

"I appreciate the geography lesson, General, but we are now at war with the Americans. What do you really want to show me?"

On a signal from General Gerasimov, the image began to zoom in until it halted above open ocean. The ocean was not empty. An additional signal and the image settled over numerous vessels . . . very large vessels.

"American aircraft carriers?"

"Yes, Mr. President . . . two of them. Specifically, the USS Carl Vinson and the USS Theodore Roosevelt. There are other vessels floating about, but these two are of primary interest."

"I don't understand."

"The San Diego Naval Base was destroyed during the massive quakes caused by the RDS-220 that the Chinese planted in the northern Gulf of California. Over 40 ships were anchored at San Diego when the quakes struck. Many of them tore free of their moorings and are now floating free on the ocean."

President Morozov began laughing, then slapped the table in front of him.

"You want to steal the American carriers?"

"They seem to have been abandoned, Mr. President. Two of our Akula Class attack submarines are enroute to the area. Each is carrying an assault team of Spetsnaz and technicians," said Admiral Viktor Masorin, Commander of the Russian Navy.

"The Americans are not completely defenseless. They must have numerous attack submarines in the Pacific."

"They do, and they have been actively hunting and sinking Chinese war ships. But all their Pacific bases are gone or under assault. Pearl Harbor was hit by three waves over 200 feet high. Their bases in the State of Washington are now landlocked. It would seem, that the four-mile-wide waterway previously used to enter the Pacific is now closed. The land has risen. It will take them many years to dig a new passage. They have a few bases in the western Pacific, but they are being destroyed by our forces as we speak. If they wish to resupply, they will have to go to the American East Coast," replied the Admiral.

"General Gerasimov, what of their space planes? Specifically, that damned space carrier! That one vessel destroyed the People's Republic of China!"

" That is the second . . . and primary reason . . . that I invited you here. Yes . . . the space carrier . . . the USS Kraken. The Chinese tried to destroy it . . . but failed. Our question was . . . how did they find it? One of my little birds told me the Chinese discovered that this space vessel leaves a trail of ionizing radiation in its wake. That is how they located it. They attempted to destroy it with satellite nukes . . . but failed. The technology . . . the rate of acceleration . . . is quite amazing, Mr. President."

"I think I like you better when you've been drinking. You don't ramble. Get to the damn point!"

"The point, Mr. President, is we have been in the 'space game' as long as the Americans. We don't have their technology, but we have hundreds of satellites in orbit. Many of them can detect ionizing radiation. We, also, have found their space carrier. We have even managed to break their communications security. They are now toothless . . . almost."

"Define toothless!"

"It is a unique vessel in many ways. If we just focus on its combat capabilities, it is a hybrid . . . part battleship and part carrier. It has four banks of mass drivers. Each bank has five launch tubes. Based on intercepted communications, they fired almost everything they had on board during the attack on China. I can barely imagine such power. Our scientists estimate the mass of the kinetic projectile at 10,000 kg. The launch velocity is over 95,000 kph. Nothing can stand before such a weapon system."

"You have five seconds . . . and then, old friend, I will be talking to your replacement. Define toothless!"

"They are now like a battleship with no ammunition, Mr. President. Their resupply bases were in Southern California. Those bases no longer exist. The Americans have a saying . . . too many eggs in one basket."

"Why didn't you just say they were out of ammunition?"

"As I said, Mr. President, it is a hybrid vessel. It also contains four flights of the fighter version of this technology. They call them TR-4a Dory's."

"First a 'Kraken' and now a 'Dory'. The Americans have fallen in love with Greek mythology. How many of these craft are aboard the Kraken?"

"Four flights of three, Mr. President. They are formidable, but not a game changer in such small numbers. Their home base was located near Area 51, in Nevada. It is believed to have been made inoperable during the many quakes and volcanic eruptions that have struck Southern California," said Colonel-General Andrei Yudin, Commander of the Russian Aerospace Forces.

"So how do we destroy this thing?"

"A difficult question, Mr. President. The Chinese tried to bracket it with satellites armed with nuclear weapons. The Kraken was

34

too quick. We would suggest another ploy . . . a different weapon system," replied Colonel-General Yudin.

"Educate me, General."

"We have publicly demonstrated the 'Peresvet', Mr. President. It is a laser weapon system capable of shooting down drones and low flying aircraft. But it is only a toy. The energy output is too low. However, we do have another system the Americans know nothing about. The Kop'ye Molnii, what the Americans would call 'Lightning Spear', has been under development for over ten years. We have three systems operable. One in the far east on the Kamchatka Peninsula. The other two are further west."

"General Yudin, if I was not aware of where billions of rubles were being spent, even in a 'black budget', I wouldn't be a very good president, now would I? Your predecessor started this . . . I love American slang . . . 'money pit'. I had him replaced for lack of progress. So, will this Lightning Spear catch me a big space fish or not?" asked President Morozov, as he leaned forward and stared at Colonel-General Yudin.

"Mr. President . . . this weapon could punch a hole in the Moon!"

"Perhaps, but if the system is land based, then the target must be on our side of the planet. Where is it presently located?"

"You are correct, Mr. President. Kop'ye needs 'line of sight'. At this time the Kraken is located above the United States at an altitude of 160 kilometers. It is far below the horizon. We aren't sure why they are above the US. Perhaps an attempt at resupply?"

"Colonel-General Yudin . . . Andryusha! Unlike your predecessor, you have shown me that you are at least competent. Plus, you do not cower like a dog when I raise my voice and ask difficult questions. You have courage, but not arrogance. Keep me informed of the whereabouts of the American carrier. And . . . make sure that you are prepared to kill it!"

CHAPTER 6

The Cave
Island of La Palma
Canary Islands, Spain
October 8, 0955 hours UTC

"Shit! Eight frigging days to get that thing out of the hole!" CIA Agent Amanda Langford said, while staring at the massive nuclear antique from the Cold War.

"Considering everything that's going on right now, I'm surprised we got any support. The original cable was undersized for the weight of the RDS-220. To safely pull that thing out of a hole that deep, we needed a better margin of safety," replied Kate Williams, still wearing her matt black Mark IV exo-armor.

"So now what? Take it back to the States?" Amanda asked, as she walked beside the 26-foot-long, 30-ton hydrogen bomb.

"I'm not sure. All the Chinese devices we found inside the US were taken to our base in Nevada. We disassembled them and turned the fissile material over to the Department of Energy for storage. But now . . . my base, all the equipment, resources, people . . . people I've known for 20 years . . . " Kate began, then sat down at a bench near a series of tables set up for the work crews.

"Kate . . . if you hadn't disarmed this damn thing . . . while hanging upside down in a 3000-foot-deep hole . . . with your suit almost out of power . . . we wouldn't have a country."

"I wasn't upside down, and David was the one who figured out which wire to cut. He also linked me to his own exo-armor so I wouldn't run out of power. You know . . . I really did think I was going to die down there. That didn't bother me. What bothered me was that I thought I was going to fail. I was going to die, and then my country was going to die because I couldn't figure it out. David looked at the interior of the weapon and knew which wire to cut. I don't know how, but he just knew. The inside was a mess. The Chinese had added multiple false devices inside. Wires went everywhere."

"Well, he was your mentor back in the day."

"I hate that phrase. 'Back in the day'. It makes me sound like an antique. And yes, he was my mentor . . . and then some."

"So, how did he know?"

"He wouldn't tell me. He just laughed and said if I came to visit him in Israel, we'd sit outside his home in the evening, drink some wine, and he'd tell me how he knew which wire to cut. One damn silver wire! It was that simple. A three-stage, 100-megaton Hydrogen bomb, designed in the '50s . . . no known records or blueprints . . . and he knew which wire! Bastard!" Kate said, and smiled at the memory of their time together, hanging beside the huge weapon, deep inside the earth.

"Oh . . . one thing I forgot to tell you," Amanda said, as she stood up and pulled her cellphone out of her jeans.

"What? And please, don't take a selfie with the device."

"Too late, I already did. What I wanted to show you was this. Communications with the West Coast are still intermittent, at best. But I was sent a report about the other device . . . the one that detonated. Your son was on the Seal Team that was sent to disarm the device."

Kate turned and stared at Amanda. Tears began to well up in her eyes as she steeled herself for more bad news.

"Kate . . . don't cry! He's alive! I don't have all the details, but he's on a nuclear sub and he . . ."

Kate swept Amanda up in her arms and hugged her as tears ran down her face.

"Damn, Kate! You're breaking my ribs!"

"Sorry . . . sorry! The little bastard didn't tell me he was going on a mission. Wait until I see him!" Kate said, as she set Amanda down, and began laughing and crying at the same time.

"Kate, there were losses. Jim Padenko didn't make it. I guess it got rough on the sub when the bomb detonated. He was killed."

Kate sat back down on the bench and stared at her armored hands. Then she began to cry again.

"Oh, Jim . . . we were close. He was like a brother to me. He was the one person I could really confide in. I was older than him, but he was one of these people who seemed older than his years. Stubborn, set in his ways . . . brilliant, hard working . . . he was my No. 1. The company was his life. Nathan O'Malley was with him . . ."

"Kate, Nathan survived. He was with the assault team. He was on the oil rig and survived when the device detonated. I was told they commandeered a Chinese helicopter to make their escape. Jim stayed on the sub. I don't want to seem insensitive, but I've been through a lot of shit in the last year. I've had people I was standing beside die. I've come to believe that when it's your time . . ."

"What? Fate controls our destiny? Maybe you were just lucky. Maybe you were skilled enough," Kate replied, as she jumped up and began to pace back and forth.

"Maybe . . . maybe God still has things for me to do in this life."

"God? Millions of Americans are dead . . . millions of Chinese. None of these people wanted to die. I don't see it! I was raised in California. My parents weren't church people. They raised me to believe in me."

"It gets pretty damn lonely, doesn't it? I was raised a Southern Baptist. I'm not a Bible thumper, but I do believe in God."

"Yeah? Well, you tell God I said thanks for not killing Brandon, but I'm pissed at him about Jim! I need some fresh air!" Kate said, as she began walking toward the cave exit.

CHAPTER 7

The Chicken Creek Café
Airport Road
Chicken, Alaska
October 9, 0040 hours AKST

Company A, 1st Battalion, 5th Infantry Regiment, 1st Stryker Brigade Combat Team, 25th Infantry Division, had been on maneuvers over 100 miles east of their base at Fort Wainright, when the Russian invasion of Alaska began. Their orders from Brigade Headquarters were to hold fast until notified. Additional orders never came. Now the officers of Company A were sitting in the Chicken Creek Café, which sat beside the Chicken Creek Saloon, liquor store and Chicken Emporium. All were 'thriving establishments' in a town with only seven permanent residents.

Chicken was established by gold miners in the late 1800s. Huge, rusted gold dredges were left abandoned when the gold began to peter out. A few stores, a few homes scattered about, were all that remained.

The five US Army officers sat in the darkness at a large round table. The enticing smell of brewing coffee almost concealed the smell of their unwashed bodies. The only light was from several MX-991/U Army flashlights with red filters installed.

"Sir, from everything we've heard, the Russians are going to make a run down the Alaska Highway to Dawson Creek in British Columbia. Then they'll head for the Lower 48. Two thousand miles, and then they're driving down US highways. We may be the last combat-effective Army unit left in Alaska. We have to stop them here!" said First Lieutenant Deion Daniels, as he placed his finger on the map spread out on the table.

"You're out of your mind, Deion! Captain, we're just one Infantry company . . . 180 men, 21 Strykers. Before the transmissions were jammed, we heard that Russians were coming into Anchorage by the thousands. What can we do against that?" asked Second Lieutenant Baskin Morgan.

"What the hell, Bask! You don't want to fight?" asked First Lieutenant Rico Castillo, leader of the M1128 Mobile Gun System platoon.

"Screw you, Rico! I'm not into suicide!"

"At ease, both of you!" ordered Captain Dothan MacLynn.

"If the Russians go by land, there is only one way south. That's on the Alaska Highway. Obviously, we don't have the personnel or firepower for a direct assault on them. What we do have is the terrain. Southern Alaska is not tank friendly. Lots of mountains, lots of rivers and marshy land everywhere. That means that they must stay on the roads, and more importantly, on the bridges. If they wait two or three months, then everything will freeze up and they'll be able to go off-road. But I don't think they'll wait that long. From everything we've heard, the West Coast is a wreck. All our military bases are gone or ineffective. They must move now before we have a chance to recover," said Captain MacLynn.

An old man sat quietly in the corner of his store, sipping whiskey while the five officers discussed their plans on how to fight the Russians. Jeremiah Jones was 69 years old and felt every year of it. He had lived in Alaska all his life, except for four years. He was 18 when the draft notice came and had wanted to see what the rest of the world looked like. Being an avid hunter and a dead shot, the Army made him a sniper. Two tours in Vietnam had cured his wanderlust. All he wanted was to live out his life in peace. Now another war had come after him. He sighed as he rose from his chair and approached the officers.

"You know, you boys are just going to get your asses shot up. You go heading down Highway 5 in those big old Strykers and the Russkies will be on you quicker than shit. You're used to having air superiority so you can go where you want, when you want. You don't have that anymore," Jeremiah said, as he stared down at the map spread across the table.

"Mr. Jones, we appreciate your hospitality, but this is US Army business. We know what we're doing," said Second Lieutenant Branson.

"Son, they teach you any military history at OCS? You're where the Germans were at the end of WWII. Every time they moved their armor during daylight they got jumped by our fighters. Now it's even worse. Every modern military can see in the dark. You head down there all together . . . to Tetlin Junction on Highway 2, and you'll be lucky if half your vehicles survive the road march."

"Listen . . . old man . . ."

"At ease, Lieutenant Branson! Mr. Jones, Strykers are eight-wheeled, 20-ton, armored vehicles. They don't fly. This time of year, our travel routes are limited by soft terrain. We have to take Highway 5 south, unless you know of another way," said Captain MacLynn.

"Yeah, son, I'm older than dirt, and I'll be settled six feet down before too much longer, but I'm not stupid. Charlie was smart. He knew that if he sent big units down the Ho Chi Minh trail that our aircraft would spot him. So, he broke his units into small parts, travelled separately. Then they would meet up at a location just prior to attacking. You better do the same . . . just sayin'," said Jeremiah.

"That was 50 years ago. You lost your war!" replied Second Lieutenant Branson.

"We didn't lose shit. Every time Charlie or the NVA massed, we kicked their ass. Even the Tet Offensive was a disaster for them. The politicians in Washington and the left-wing media lost that war, not the people who fought it!" Jeremiah replied, as he turned away in disgust and returned to his chair in the corner.

"Captain, the old man has a point. We go down there at night, one platoon at a time. Four vehicles . . . spread out. We assign fighting positions in advance. We dig in and camouflage our vehicles," said First Lieutenant Castillo.

"I'll agree with that. Mr. Jones is correct, but I've got a better idea. We must split up, but each unit is going to a different location. We're going to set up a series of ambushes. Look at Alaska Highway 2. There are four bridges between Big Delta and Tetlin Junction. It's risky, but 1st Platoon will head to Big Delta and make a stand at the first bridge. If you can block the bridge with wreckage, that will buy you time to fall back. This time of year, we get misty rain and heavy fog. Use that to your advantage," said Captain MacLynn.

"Too bad we can't just blow the bridges. That would really slow them down," said Second Lieutenant Morgan.

"Good idea, Baskin! I'll just call up Battalion Headquarters and ask for an EOD team. Maybe some hot chow while I'm at it," said First Lieutenant Castillo.

Baskin just glared at Castillo.

"Fine set of leaders you got there, Captain. Looks more like a nursery school," Jeremiah said, from his chair leaning against the wall.

"I've about had it with you, old man!" Second Lieutenant Morgan said, as he rose from his chair.

"You're just scared, son. You'd be crazy if you weren't. Different men handle it different ways. I've seen them all."

"Sit down, Lieutenant Morgan! Mr. Jones, do us all a favor and find another place to drink. We have some planning . . ." Captain MacLynn began.

"You know, I bet you boys could use some dynamite right about now," Jeremiah said, and let the words hang in the air for effect.

"Mr. Jones . . . do you have access to explosives? If this is a joke, I'll have you . . ."

"No joke, Captain. There's still a fair bit of mining that goes on around here when the roads are open. I used to do some mining myself. When I came back from 'Nam, I got a job with my brother-in-law. He used to own the Crow Creek Gold Mine down near Alyeska. I worked for him for over 20 years until the government shut us down. I reckon too much runoff and pollution. One of the things I learned early on was explosives. I know my way around dynamite. Not as powerful as C-4, bit it'll blow shit up."

"Mr. Jones . . ."

"I don't leave this place anymore. I like being alone. So, the local miners have me look out for all their stuff while they vacation in Vancouver for the winter. That includes all their explosives. Not the kind of stuff you want to drag back and forth on our fine highways," Jeremiah said, laughed at his own joke and took another sip of whiskey.

The five officers just stared at him, wondering what to believe.

"If you go about five miles north of Chicken, up past Jack Wade, you'll come to a dirt road that leads up a valley and into the hills. Nobody around for miles and miles. That's where they keep their explosives. It's a big cinderblock building with a metal roof. Nice and dry inside . . . no electricity though."

"Mr. Jones, how much dynamite are we talking about?"

"They restocked last summer. All the material is brand new fresh. Which is a good thing. Dynamite gets a little unstable when it ages . . . kind of like me."

"Captain, this is bullshit! That old man . . ." Second Lieutenant Morgan began.

"Fifty-two boxes. Each box contains 100 sticks. Blasting caps, wire, detonators . . . it's all there. No bullshit!" Jeremiah said, as he screwed the top back on the pint bottle and slipped it inside his coat pocket.

"Mr. Jones, take your chair and join us at the table. We have some things to discuss," said Captain MacLynn.

CHAPTER 8

USS North Carolina (SSN-777)
The California Straight
October 9, 1115 hours UTC

For eight days they had cruised the polluted surface of the new body of water known as the California Straight. Contact with COMSUBPAC (Commander Submarine Force Pacific) was non-existent. Pearl Harbor, the command structure, the facilities, and many of the US Navy warships and sailors that had been stationed there, were gone. The USS North Carolina now reported to COMSUBLANT (Commander Submarine Force Atlantic).

Their present mission was search and rescue. They had saved 811 people either floating in the open water or clinging to wreckage. Survivors had been dropped off at refugee camps scattered up and down the new coastline. The dead in the water were so numerous that lookouts on the sail were switched out every hour. The sight of so many dead men, women and children was more than many of the sailors could take. The morale of the young crew had plummeted after seeing what had been done to their country.

On the morning after the Great Quake, the brilliant blue of the California air had been filled with soot, acrid fumes and the smell of death. On the fourth day, the sky to the west had turned brown as the massive amounts of debris blown into the upper atmosphere by the kinetic strikes on the People's Republic of China began drifting across the Pacific. By Day six, a yellow pall had settled over the entire West Coast. Visibility was less than a mile.

Captain Augustus North stood alone with his thoughts on the sail of the SSN-777. His original crew of 134 was down to 87. Eighteen had died when the submarine was rolled in the shallow waters of the northern Gulf of California during the quake. Another twenty-nine were injured and unable to stand watch at their duty stations. The detonation of the 100-megaton Chinese weapon deep below ground, near the San Andreas Fault, had thrown the sub around like it was a toy. Technically, they were combat-ineffective and should return to port. But the city of San Diego, and Naval Base San Diego, no longer existed.

"Captain, we just received a message from COMSUBLANT. New orders!" said Lieutenant Commander Gail O'Teul, Executive Officer of the USS North Carolina, as she entered the observation deck atop the sail.

"Orders? We've got half a crew and a banged-up boat. They better be sending us to a shipyard," Captain North said, as he began reading the message.

"They've got to be kidding! We had 17 fast attack boats stationed in Hawaii, and they want us to go protect two aircraft carriers floating in the middle of the Pacific Ocean? We're still repairing equipment all over the boat. Our stealth capabilities are shit. Half of our hull coating has been skinned away."

O'Teul stood quietly, letting her Captain vent. She knew that he would never say such things in the presence of any other crew member.

"XO, we haven't even submerged in the last week. I'm not sure I trust the hull anymore. We were tossed around like a piece of driftwood and wound up on the side of a cliff. The crew is banged up, and . . . what's their mental state?"

"I talked with Master Chief Ingeram a couple of hours ago. He and the remaining Senior Chiefs have had to counsel a lot of sailors. A lot of them are from the West Coast. They want to know who's alive, who's dead . . . what happened to their families. They lost a lot of friends onboard. I'd say PTSD is the norm onboard right now."

"And yet we have orders to proceed into the open ocean and protect carriers that are dead in the water. For those ships to break moorings and float away . . .the city . . . the base . . ."

"Sir, I try not to think about it. I must believe that my family is safe. If I stop believing that . . . I don't think I'll be able to function."

"I feel the same way, Gail. If you need to vent or cry or just talk, you can do it with me. The crew must see their Captain and Executive Officer as pillars of steel. They can't see that we're as shaken as they are. We're going to ask them to go way above and beyond normal expectations. The Russians are taking up where the Chinese left off. There is active combat in the western Pacific. No one will want to be the first one to use nukes. This could be a conventional war."

"What are your orders, Sir?"

"Plot a course . . . no, we'll have to find our way to open ocean and deep water. Our charts are useless. Satellite images that we've received from COMSUBLANT show a narrow passage at the north end of this new island. We'll be exploring new coastline in our own country. Sonar needs to start mapping everything we pass. This is all new ocean bottom. We can't assume anything, even when we reach the open ocean. The bottom must have changed . . . new ridges, mountains and canyons. When we reach deeper water, we'll try a few shallow dives and see how the boat holds up. Sorry . . . I'm thinking out loud. Get us to open water, XO!"

CHAPTER 9

The Chicken Creek Café
Airport Road
Chicken, Alaska
October 10, 0140 hours AKST

"Well, they may live out in the middle of nowhere, but they keep their sense of humor," said Sergeant Bart Jacobson, as he stood smoking a cigarette beside the 'Cracked Egg' sign outside the café that read 'I Got Laid in Chicken Alaska'.

"Yeah, I'm tempted to take a selfie and send it to my girlfriend in Tennessee," said Specialist Collin Elkins, as he began searching through his coat pockets for his cell phone.

"Collin, you take a flash picture out here and the LT will put a boot up your ass."

The fog had settled in again and it seemed to get thicker each night. Company A was scatted throughout the thick pine woods that surrounded Chicken. The Strykers were camouflaged and silent. Heat and light security were strictly enforced. The two soldiers could hear the screen door to the café squeak as it opened and slowly shut. A figure walked off the porch and approached.

"Sergeant Masterson, walk with me!" said First Lieutenant Daniels, as he turned and walked away.

"What's up LT?"

"Sergeant, what don't you understand about light security? The CO looks out the window and sees two red points of light identifying our location. To anyone with infrared sensors, you might as well have started a frikin' fire! We're not fighting Jihadis. The Russians have the same tech we have, and they know how to use it!"

"Yes, Sir! Sorry, Sir!" Sergeant Masterson said, as he stomped out the cigarette.

"This isn't about me being a dick, Sergeant. This is about you doing something stupid that could get us killed. Understood?"

"Yes, Sir! Won't happen again, Sir!"

"Collin! Put that damn thing out!" Sergeant Masterson said, as the lieutenant walked back toward the café.

Inside the Café

"Sorry, Captain! They've been calibrated," First Lieutenant Daniels said, as he sat back down at the darkened table.

"Gentlemen, you have to make sure that your men understand what's going on. We don't have the time or the resources for a learning curve. We split up and start moving into our assigned positions in less than an hour. No lights, no smoking, no unnecessary talking. The fog tonight is thick as hell, and we're going to need it. GPS is still working, so don't get lost," said Captain MacLynn.

"Sir, I still don't like splitting up my MGS (Mobile Gun System) platoon. They're more effective when you can concentrate their firepower," said First Lieutenant Castillo.

"Pardon the pun, but we can't afford to have all of our best eggs in one basket. Those 105mm guns are the only real firepower we've got. But remember, it's not a damn tank! This operation is not a shootout. This is an ambush. No matter how tempting it is, no one opens fire until I order it. Is that understood?" asked Captain MacLynn.

When his officers all confirmed they understood, Captain MacLynn turned to Jerimiah Jones.

"Mr. Jones, are the explosives ready?"

"Yep, I've trained six of your boys how and where to install the dynamite, the blasting caps, and hook them to a detonator. Most of these bridges are pretty old, but they won't come down easy. Bridges are made tough up here because of the climate, but if your boys do like they were taught . . . they should go down."

"Are you sure, Mr. Jones? If the bridges don't fall, then this whole plan falls apart," said Captain MacLynn.

"When are you planning to start?"

"We move tonight to get into position at each bridge. Then we lie low and wait for the Russians."

"You ever do any hunting, Captain?"

"I used to hunt deer when I was younger."

"Well, you're hunting bears this time. It's real easy for the hunter to turn into the hunted. Your boys better be quiet and still. Your heat signature will be what gets you killed. No smoking, no heating up food, no walking out into the woods to take a dump. A man walking in the woods looks like a roadside flare on infrared. The Russians aren't stupid. The Afghans shot the shit out of them back in the '80s. They learned all about ambushes. I'll bet it's a routine part of their training. You might even see a Hind attack-chopper or two on overwatch as they travel."

"Our TO&E (Table of Organization and Equipment) includes six Stingers. Each platoon gets two. If the Russians have helicopter support, we'll deal with it. Gentlemen . . . remember . . . this is an ambush. We wait until their lead vehicles start crossing the bridge over the Robinson River. That's the third bridge in our target area. Then we blow the first bridge and the shooting starts. Then First Platoon mounts up and flees to the south. After they cross the second bridge, over the Robertson River, you blow that one, and First and Second Platoons head south to the third bridge, the one across the Johnson River. Then you blow that one and you all meet up back here. Then we blow the fourth bridge and head for Canada. Remember, if they have tanks, take them out first!"

"Captain, that first bridge is steel and it's new. It's going to be really hard to take down. I'd like to go along and help your boys place the explosives. If I see the bridge . . . how it's built, I'll know the best place to put the dynamite," said Jeremiah.

"Mr. Jones, you're a civilian. I can't allow . . ."

"Captain . . . I used to be a civilian. The Russians have invaded my country. I may not have a uniform, but I'm going to fight these bastards, and that makes me just as much a soldier as you are. Let me go with 1st Platoon."

Captain MacLynn glanced at Lieutenant Daniels, the commander of First Platoon.

"We could use his help on placement of the explosives. Without him we're just guessing," said First Lieutenant Daniels.

"Okay . . . Mr. Jones, pack your shit. You're going with 1st Platoon. Kickoff starts at . . . 0230. Gentlemen, get back to your platoons for a final mission brief. And . . . good luck! Let's go kill some Russians!"

CHAPTER 10

US Geological Survey Headquarters
12201 Sunrise Valley Drive
Reston, Virginia
October 10, 0540 hours EST

Dr. Janice Wolf was asleep on a cot jammed into the corner of her small office. She'd only been asleep for three hours, but it was the most rest she had managed in over a week.

She was lying face down on the hot sands of Myrtle Beach, in South Carolina. Her husband, Hank, lay beside her. There was a stiff breeze, and the windblown sand was stinging her sunburned back. She could hear the wind, the screech of gulls, and the joyful screams of her children playing in the surf. Matthew, her 10-year old son, walked up, dripping wet, and sat beside her blanket. He had a hammer in his hand. She stared at him as he began to pound the sand as hard as he could.

"Matthew, what are you doing?"

"Stopping the crack, Mommy . . . stopping the crack!"

"What crack?"

The scene shifted . . . front row seats, the aroma of roasted chicken. She could smell the horses and the steel armor of the mounted knights as they rode past, colorful banners waving. Medieval Times was a must see every time they came on vacation at Myrtle Beach. Both Amelia, age 12, and Matthew loved the pageantry, the color and the excitement of the mock battles. Matthew would wear the paper crown, for a week after they went back home . . . home . . . and the scene shifted once again.

She stood on a precipice. She could feel the ground tremble and shake beneath her feet. She wanted to turn and run away . . . but couldn't move. The ground crumbled. She screamed as she began falling into a deep abyss . . .

"Dr. Wolf! Are you okay? You were screaming!" Brenda said, while staring down at her boss.

"What? Was I yelling? It was just a dream . . ." Janice said, as she threw off the blanket, swung her legs off the cot and tried to stand up.

"Whoa! Take it easy! Sit back down. That must have been a bad dream. I could hear you out in the hall," Brenda said, as she steadied her boss.

"Brenda, please get me some coffee . . . the usual . . . no, more sugar, lots of sugar. Go on. I'm fine," Janice said, while shaking off Brenda's hand.

Brenda stared at her friend, nodded, then turned away. Janice sat back down on the edge of the cot. The final scene of the dream still fresh in her mind. She knew that the abyss was the Reelfoot Rift ripped open, and the country split in half.

"Crap! Why did I dream that? The tremors have subsided. It looks like the North American Plate is adjusting to the quake in California. It's stabilizing! Am I missing something?" she thought, while rubbing the sleep from her eyes.

"Here's your coffee, boss!"

"I hate being called 'Boss'. Why can't she just call me Dr. Wolf?"

"Just put the mug on my desk. I'm going to wash up and then look at the latest data," Janice said, as she stood up and headed for the small restroom attached to her office.

"How about some food? Somebody brought in doughnuts."

"Any bagels . . . fruit? Anything remotely healthy?"

"I think there are some leftover bagels from yesterday. I could warm one up in the microwave?"

"Please! That would be great!" Janice said, while walking past her desk.

She glanced at the mug of coffee. The tan surface began to ripple. Then she felt the vibration in her feet. The mug began to dance across the flat surface, sloshing coffee, as she grabbed the edge of the desk with both hands. The sound of screaming could be heard from other offices and cubicles as the tremor intensified. Then it was gone . . . as quickly as it had started.

She turned around. Brenda was standing in the doorway, tears running down her face, both hands tightly gripped on the doorframe.

"It's okay, Brenda! I think it's over. We've had worse. I still need that bagel and some paper towels."

Brenda nodded, released the doorframe, and hurried away.

After using the bathroom, Janice walked back into her office. She found Dr. Bill Latham sitting at her desk. All six flat screens, mounted on the wall above, were filled with data.

"So, how is it that you know my password?"

"Just a guess," Bill said, as he picked up a framed picture from her desk and showed it to her.

"The Blue Knight! Renowned as Champion of the defenseless! Your password had to be 'Blue Knight'," he said, as he stared at the photo of Amelia and Matthew posing with the handsome blonde knight in armor with a golden fleur-de-lis on his chest.

"I guess I'm going to have to be more creative. So, what's the rush?"

"Close the door. You were right. The Reelfoot Rift is trying to open. Look at this map. This data is accurate up to 30 minutes ago. We're still analyzing that last little shake we had."

"It's moving south, but it's not as deep," Janice said, as she pulled a chair over and sat beside Bill.

"I think it's starting to unzip, but from the top down. This may take years, or it may take a few weeks, but it is happening . . . and quickly! I'm arranging a meeting with FEMA. I want you there to help explain the data."

"What are we going to recommend?"

"That's not our job. We give them information so they can decide what to do."

"But they have to evacuate . . . all the people."

"If this opens like your models suggest, we're talking about a rift that runs from the St. Lawrence Seaway all the way to the Gulf of Mexico. This could start draining the Great Lakes!"

Janice sighed and picked up the half empty mug of lukewarm coffee. She closed her eyes as she sipped the sweet liquid. More of her dream slid back into her conscious mind.

"*The hammer* . . . Bill, my father was a furniture maker. He used to go out in the country and hunt for old piles of timber. People used to cut down trees and have them milled for lumber. I went with him a few times. I remember him finding a huge walnut slab. The figure and grain were beautiful, but it was cracked. He kept studying the wood, talking about what he would do with it. I asked him about the cracks. Wouldn't that make it useless? He just smiled and said that he would put a butterfly there, to relieve the stress, and the crack would stop . . ." Janice said, as she started running a program that would estimate the future path of the Reelfoot Rift.

"What the hell are you talking about?"

"A hammer, Dr. Latham! I'm talking about a hammer. When is our meeting with FEMA scheduled?"

"It's not. I haven't called them yet."

"Better make it today. We may not have much time . . ."

CHAPTER 11

The White House
The Oval Office
Washington, DC
October 10, 1130 hours EST

"Rick, is this some kind of a bad joke? After everything that's happened, some crackpot is predicting that the country is going to split in two . . . literally?" President Beaumont asked.

"No, Madam President, it's not a joke . . . and it doesn't come from a 'crackpot'. Dr. Latham is the Senior Science Advisor for the USGS. An employee of his . . . a Dr. Janice Wolf, predicted this after the Great Quake. Evidently, the quakes we've been feeling here are part of that. There is a meeting scheduled today at FEMA Headquarters, over on C Street, Southwest," replied Rick Dunlevy, the new White House Chief of Staff.

"When?"

"In about 90 minutes. I just found out about it . . . sorry!"

"Contact FEMA! The meeting is getting moved to the Situation Room. Make it for this afternoon. No media . . . essential personnel only. The country's panicked enough without another 'chicken little' meeting with the press in attendance."

"Do you want the Cabinet present?"

"No . . . yes, but only the Secretaries of Defense and Homeland Security. And I want a copy of this woman's theory on my desk in 30 minutes! Now get moving!"

. . . .

The Situation Room
1545 hours EST

Everyone stood as President Beaumont walked into the room. When she sat, everyone sat. The Seal of the President of the United States was perched on the wall behind her head. The long rectangular table was only half filled. They were silent as she glanced from face to face.

"I understand the USGS has a theory?" Clarisse asked.

"Yes, Madam President. I'm Dr. William Latham, Senior Science Advisor for the USGS. My colleague, Dr. Janice Wolf, has developed a theory of . . ."

"Then I would like to hear it from Dr. Wolf. I understand this is a 'time critical' situation."

Dr. Latham leaned back in his chair and nudged Dr. Wolf.

"She thinks this is bullshit! I can see it in her eyes," Janice thought, while clearing her throat.

"Madam President, my report indicates . . ."

"I've read the report. It looks speculative."

"Madam President, all of our work is speculative . . ." Dr. Latham interjected.

"I believe Dr. Wolf has the floor. It's her theory. I'll hear her defend it!" the President said.

"She's overwhelmed. She doesn't want another disaster on her plate. She read the report and doesn't want it to be true! How do I convince her?" Janice thought, as she locked eyes with the President of the United States.

"Madam President, if you read the report, and looked at the data, then you know what's happening. An ancient fault deep below the central United States is starting to open. When it does . . ."

56

"If it does!"

"When . . . it does . . . millions more are going to die. The heartland will be ripped in two. This will be far worse than the Great Quake on the West Coast!"

The President sat in silence, staring at her hands. When she looked up, for just a second . . . there was fear, bordering on despair in her eyes. Then it was gone, but Janice had seen it.

"All right . . . assuming this is valid . . . and the data does . . . somewhat support your theory. Where does that leave us? What are our options?"

Opinions were tossed back and forth across the table. Janice sat with her hands under the table. She was still shaking from her confrontation with the President.

"Dr. Wolf, are you only the bearer of bad tidings, or do you have something helpful to add to this discussion?" asked the President.

Janice took a deep breath, lay her hands calmly on the polished mahogany table, and remembered her dream . . . the hammer.

"We have to compress the rock at the southern end of the fault. That will stop the crack from propagating," Janice said, knowing what the response would be.

Everyone started shouting at once. Dr. Latham was talking in one ear as, once again, she locked eyes with the President.

"She's desperate. She's prepared to listen with an open mind. I can't fold now!" Janice thought.

"Gentlemen . . . Ladies! Quiet!" the President demanded.

"Explain yourself, Dr. Wolf. How could we possibly . . . compress the earth?"

Janice hesitated before beginning, "I'm not sure, Madam President. But it must be like a hammer blow. It must be powerful and precise."

Once again, the room erupted.

"There may be a way! I said . . . there may be a way!" shouted John Masters, the Secretary of Defense.

The room grew silent. All eyes were on the Secretary of Defense.

"Madam President, I'm referring to a particular asset that we have . . . above us."

"My understanding was it had used all of its . . . resources," the President said.

"Almost, Madam President! It has two remaining . . . two major assets. The system is powerful . . . and precise."

Of the people in the Situation Room, only the President and two others knew the truth about the devastating attack on the People's Republic of China. Wild theories were circulating through the media, but only a select few knew about the USS Kraken. The President placed her elbows on the table and rested her chin on interlocked fingers.

"Dr. Wolf, what is the timeline for your 'hammer blow'? How soon does this have to happen?" the President asked, while glancing over at Janice.

"Fault propagation is not an exact science. I don't . . ."

"Dr. Wolf! Hours . . . days . . . weeks . . . months? I need an answer . . . your best estimate."

Janice could feel her heart pounding in her chest as she closed her eyes and ran over the data in her mind.

"A few days . . . definitely not weeks. It's stressing now. That's why we're feeling these strong quakes all over the Central US and in the East. It will snap at a location near Pine Bluff, Arkansas, just south of Little Rock. Then the crack will rapidly propagate down to the Gulf of Mexico and up to the Great Lakes. Madam President, are you talking about using a nuke?"

"No, Dr. Wolf . . . we aren't going to nuke our own country. The Chinese have already done that. Secretary Masters, General Munford . . . Dr. Wolf and Dr. Latham will be accompanying you elsewhere. I want a strike plan developed within eight hours. You will coordinate with Director Wilkie at Homeland. Evacuations will be mandatory. Use whatever resources you need. Keep me informed. We meet back here at . . . midnight."

. . . .

The Situation Room
2345 hours EST

Janice stood in front of the mirror in the Ladies Rest Room down the hall from the Situation Room. She wanted to do nothing more than curl up on the floor and go to sleep.

"Girl . . . the bags under your eyes are starting to multiply. I'm so tired that I feel numb," Janice said, as she stared into the mirror.

"Welcome to my world!" the President said, as she watched the geologist jump.

"Madam President! I . . ."

"Sorry, I wasn't trying to sneak up on you. I come in here sometimes just to scream. It scared the hell out of my Secret Service detail the first time I did that," Clarisse said, while checking her appearance in the mirror.

Janice was still having a problem with being alone with the President of the United States.

"Do you have any children?" Clarisse asked.

"Two, a boy and a girl. I haven't seen them in three days."

"I know the feeling. I haven't seen my daughter in a week. My husband told me that he knows I'm still alive because my death hasn't been on the news."

Janice chuckled, then said, "Sounds like your husband has a real sense of humor."

"Sometimes, I think that his strength and advice are the only thing that keep me going. Are your children with your husband?"

"Yes, they're with Allen, my second husband. We've been married for three years. Hank died eight years ago . . . head on crash.

The other driver was texting. She was 17 . . . no seat belt. They both died at the scene."

"I'm so sorry . . ."

"One day at a time, but it makes being away from my kids that much harder. Without him around I feel isolated."

"I can identify with that!"

"Madam President, I'm sorry! I didn't mean to bother you with my problems."

"I need to understand what the people giving me advice are feeling . . . what their mental state is. So, it's not a problem. We all need someone to talk to. And . . . I hate 'Madam President'. I was told once that the formality and decorum were necessary. It ensured civility during times of stress. I think I understand that now, but when we're alone, please call me Clarisse."

"Janice . . . Madam Pre . . . Clarisse. Janice is my first name," Janice replied, nervous at the informality, but thrilled at the same time.

"Janice, between us two girls, how sure are you about this? The resources that I'm going to use for your 'hammer' are currently irreplaceable. We're at war with Russia, and I might need these assets in the future."

"I looked at the latest data an hour ago. The quakes are spreading southward. There's a massive piece of transpositional rock . . . a dike, that is preventing the rift from expanding to the south. North America would have split in two, half a billion years ago, if not for this formation. The Great Quake has destabilized . . ."

"Janice! Are you sure about this? Yes or no?"

Janice knew that predicting geological events was trickier than predicting the weather weeks in advance. She also knew that the President wanted an answer.

"I'm positive! A strike of sufficient magnitude, on the location I gave General Munroe, should relieve pressure on the dike. That will keep it from moving to the south, and I don't think that the rift will propagate northward. This should stabilize the continental plate . . . at least for a while."

"Then, that's what we'll do. Let's go brief the boys on our decision," President Beaumont said, as she turned and walked away.

Janice stood dumbfounded.

"Our decision?"

CHAPTER 12

USS North Carolina
North End of the California Straight
October 11, 1445 hours UTC

"So, how's she look, XO?" Captain North asked, as he and his Executive Officer sat in his wardroom.

"Rough, but seaworthy! After an 8-hour shutdown and some minor repairs, our nuclear power plant is in good shape. Reactors are back at 100 percent. The Reactor Control sailors were like everybody else. They took casualties, and there weren't that many of them to begin with. I took two sailors from the maintenance section and assigned them to the reactor group. Master Chief Ingeram wasn't too happy since they were his boys, but he got over it."

"I bet that was an interesting conversation!"

"Like I said, he wasn't too happy. We went behind closed doors . . . he expressed his opinion. I told him the sailors were still being transferred and that was it."

"Do I need to talk to him?"

"I won't even dignify that comment with a reply . . . Sir!"

"Understood, XO! You can fight your own battles. Continue your status report."

"Three more crew members have returned to duty. Possibly, four more with the next day or so. Weapons and Navigation are at 95 percent. Sonar took a beating. They are maybe back to 80 percent capability. Our stealth capability is minimal. The hull is dented and scraped clean in some places. It would take a year in drydock to make us shipshape."

"Nonetheless, our nation needs us. COMSUBLANTC hasn't informed us about US naval capabilities in the Pacific. I hope the Russians don't know how banged up we are. We normally have eight to ten fast attacks at sea in the Pacific Ocean. Another one or two in the Indian Ocean. The Carrier Strike Groups at San Diego and Bremerton, Washington are out of action. That leaves the USS Ronald Reagan in Yokohama. The Russians would want her out of the way. That would leave us with no operable carriers in the Pacific for the first time since . . . ever. Even after Pearl Harbor, we had the Enterprise and Lexington available. That was a critical failure of the Japanese attack. But even if the Reagan was at sea, I don't know how long she would last. I wonder how many Chinese subs are left out there? When they find out what happened to their country . . ."

"Do you think they would use nukes?"

"I don't know, XO. Everything I've read about their navy says they are very regimented. Even more than we are . . . if you can believe that. But if we destroyed all their command and control assets on mainland China . . ."

"What would you do, Captain . . . if you were in their position? Would you use nuclear weapons without permission from higher ups?"

"I'm not sure what I'd do. Their newest fast attack subs have cruise missiles, just like us. They are reported to have nuclear capability, just like us. If my country had just been destroyed . . . I'd want some payback."

"I don't think the politicians have gotten around to declaring war yet, but I think we're at war with Russia and China," Lieutenant Commander O'Teul said, as someone began knocking on the Captain's door.

"Enter!"

"Sorry to disturb you, Captain. But you wanted to know when we reached deep water. Sonar shows 1100 feet below the keel, but none of the terrain looks familiar. It's like things have shifted around," said Lieutenant Bottom, his head still wrapped in a bandage.

"Excellent! Let's find out if she's still a submarine or just a damn skimmer," Captain North said, as he and the XO stood up.

"Captain, I was talking with the Master Chief. Some of the crew are scared. They don't think the boat is seaworthy. They think you're going to get us killed if you take us out to deep water and dive," said Lieutenant Bottom, still standing in the doorway.

"What? I want to know who . . ." the XO began.

"XO! Jacking them up isn't the best way to handle this. We're way understaffed, and the crew that remains must all be on the same page. I can't imagine a mutiny, but I can imagine someone sabotaging equipment. In their mind, they would be saving lives. I have to convince them that the boat is reliable . . . enough, and this isn't a suicide mission."

"Sir, with all due respect, I think that's a mistake. Since when did the US Navy become a democracy? I think we should make an example of the malcontents," said Lieutenant Commander O'Teul.

"It's not a democracy, XO, but these sailors aren't servants. This is a time to lead them and convince them that our course of action is the correct one. Lieutenant Bottom, slow the boat to ten knots. Halt preparations for dive. I need to talk to the crew first."

"Yes, Captain!" Lieutenant Bottom said, as he turned and walked back toward the Control Room, followed by the two officers.

"Captain, I think this sets a dangerous precedent," said Lieutenant Commander O'Teul.

"Noted, XO, but it's my call to make," replied Captain Augustus North, as the three officers entered the Control Room.

Captain North looked around and noticed a few new faces, substitutes for the injured or deceased. He could see the fear in their eyes. Sailors talked and rumors spread. Once the fever of negativity started, it was difficult to contain. The crew members of the Control Room were extensions of his will. If they didn't believe in him, and more importantly, their boat, then he would have to rule with an iron fist. Something he was loath to do. Either way, they still had a mission.

"The boat's at ten knots, Captain. Diving preparations have been halted," said Lieutenant Bottom.

Captain North nodded, then looked around at the expectant faces turned in his direction.

"I'm going to address the entire crew, but I've decided to start here . . . with you. What we went through was unprecedented in the long history of naval warfare. Never . . . has a vessel been tossed around as violently as we were . . . and survived. Never . . . has a vessel of this size been thrown ashore onto a cliff. Never . . . has a vessel then extracted itself and returned to the sea in one piece. That all happened because of you . . . because of us. Like it or not, when you boarded the USS North Carolina, you became part of a family. I'll admit, it's not a touchy-feely family, but it's still a family. This family . . . this crew, still has a mission. We have suffered, but our country has suffered worse. Millions of our fellow citizens were murdered in their sleep. You all know that the People's Republic of China has received payback. Their government, their military, have been mostly destroyed. At the same time, the Russians have decided that this is the time for them to make a move. I know that you've heard about Alaska . . . the fighting going on there," the Captain said, as he walked around the Control Room, gauging the impact of his words on each individual.

"*They're listening, but I don't have them with me yet. I have to go deeper!*" he thought.

"I know that many of you are concerned about the status of our boat. She's a beast! She's battered on the outside, but inside she's still a killer. Under normal circumstances we'd be headed for a long stay in drydock. But these aren't normal circumstances. We're at war, and our nation needs us to keep going. You have done an amazing job in getting her back into the battle. I know what her strengths are, and I know what her new limitations are. She has a black eye and some bruised ribs, but she's a fighter. We won't be as aggressive as we once were. We'll have to be stealthy in a different way. The only thing I ask of you is that you not give up on her or on yourselves. This boat, the SSN-777 . . . the USS North Carolina, is like our country. We have all been attacked and suffered terribly, but Americans don't give up. We don't surrender. We founded this country to get away from the monarchs, the dictators of the old world. We've fought wars to defend that freedom, and to help others defend theirs. We haven't always succeeded, but we've always tried. Now, I'm not going to lie. Our backs are against the wall. We must decide if we're going to drop to our knees and meekly surrender, or if we're going to stay on our feet and get back in the center of the ring. I have to know that you are all with me . . ."

"I can see it! I've reached them, but was it enough? Will they go to war with me?" thought Captain North, as he continued his walk through the Command Center.

He stopped at the position of Petty Officer First Class Andrews, a sonar operator. The sailor reached up, touched his arm, and said, "So who's ass do we kick first? We need some payback!"

The roar of approval exploded across the Control Room. Sailors were yelling, fists were clenched, and expletives directed at the Chinese and Russians filled the air.

"At ease, you bilge trolls! Let the Captain talk!" bellowed Master Chief Ingeram from an open doorway.

"To answer Andrews' question . . . we're heading south. COMSUBLANTC says there are two US carriers drifting off southern California. They want us to go babysit them while the brass decides what to do with them. And pity any Chinese or Russian son of a bitch that gets in our way!" the Captain said, as the room erupted in cheers once again.

Captain North then went into every compartment, talked to every sailor. He gave variations of the same speech, as fit the situation. The many wounded still on board were the hardest, but even they had their internal fires relit when he was through.

CHAPTER 13

Central Intelligence Agency
Mission Center for Weapons and Counterproliferation
Office of Director Janet Davidson
Manassas, Virginia
October 11, 1345 hours EST

"Welcome back, stranger! How was your vacation?" Janet asked, as she sat behind her desk and greeted Agent Amanda Langford.

They both started laughing at the same time. Janet stood up, walked around her desk, and hugged her diminutive protégé.

"Wow, all warm and cuddly. What happened to my hardass ex-Marine boss?"

"Once a Marine . . . always a Marine! I'm just glad to see you back here in one piece. Do you have any idea what a pain in the ass it is to take someone fresh out of school and turn her into a first-class agent?"

"Even worse, if she's 'fresh off the farm' . . . or so I've heard," Amanda replied, referring to a comment made by Janet on Amanda's first day of work.

"Have a seat. You look beat."

"Just got off the red-eye from Ramstein. Civilian air traffic is shit. Almost nothing was moving. We were flying through a brown haze all the way across the Atlantic. I flew back military, in a C-141. It wasn't set up for passengers. Web seats from front to back, packed in like sardines . . . no seatbelts. It was cold, loud and filled with Army soldiers . . . infantry. Rumor was that the US is pulling out of Europe . . . coming back to defend our own land for a change. The only problem was their families. They got left behind. The soldiers with families were pissed," Amanda said, as she sagged into a chair in front of Janet's desk.

"I would offer you a drink, but that would put you to sleep in about five minutes. Why did you come in? Go back to your apartment and sleep for two days. I don't need an after-action report today."

"You ever been too tired to sleep?"

"You mean when you keep playing events over and over in your head? Yeah, I've had that a few times."

Amanda smiled. Not a real smile, but a wane one, filled with regret.

"Janet . . . I shot a man! I didn't just shoot him . . . I emptied a full magazine from an AK-47 into his back. I keep replaying the impact of every bullet. I was ten feet away. It tore him apart."

"Why did you kill him?"

"He was a monster . . . a giant. He was fighting Kate. Even with her exo-armor . . . he would have killed her . . . torn her apart like he did the Seals!" Amanda said, as tears began rolling down her cheeks.

"So, what's the problem? You're not a murderer! From what I heard, he needed killing. You saved lives, Amanda!"

"Kate began screaming as he tried to pull her arms off. I picked up an AK-47 that was lying on the ground. I didn't even look to see if the safety was off. I just walked up behind him and pulled the trigger. The weapon jumped all around, but he was so big, and I was so close, that I couldn't miss. It was like shooting a wall . . ."

Amanda paused, as her hands began to shake. Her eyes glazed over as tears continued to pour from her eyes.

"He dropped Kate and fell to his knees. His back was . . . destroyed. I could see his spine. Blood was everywhere . . . even on me. He toppled over . . . face up. Janet . . . he smiled at me as I walked up to him. I was still pulling the trigger, but the magazine was empty. I threw the weapon away. Like I . . . like I was holding a snake. When I looked back, he was dead."

"Amanda, you did what you had to do."

"But . . . I keep seeing his face . . ."

"Killing isn't easy. It's not supposed to be. That feeling of intense guilt . . . remorse . . . that means you're still human. That is your soul screaming after you've taken a life. We're not supposed to kill, but sometimes it's unavoidable."

"I froze up when he first started fighting Kate. I just watched and listened. He grabbed her by the arms and lifted her off the ground. She kicked him in the balls, but he just laughed . . . told her they had been cut off when he was a boy. That his owners had injected him with drugs and growth hormones . . . turned him into a monster. He was a slave trained to fight in a pit! What is this, the Dark Ages?" Amanda shouted, then turned and punched the wall behind the chair.

"Ow! Shit that hurt!" she said, as she shook her hand.

"Yeah, I've done that a few times myself. You feel better, as long as you don't break your hand."

"Director, I want combat training . . . whatever the Agency can provide. I want to learn how to shoot, to fight, fly a plane, scuba . . . everything!" Amanda said, while flexing her right hand.

"You'll need to put some ice on that, or it will stiffen up and be useless for a week."

"I'm serious! This mission made me feel helpless . . . more than once. I don't want to have to depend on others to protect me."

"What you are going to do is find someone to talk to. You have PTSD, and you need to learn how to cope with it. The Agency has people . . ."

"Not now . . . maybe in a few weeks. I need to sort things out first . . . on my own!"

The room grew silent as Janet watched Amanda wipe her tears away. She knew from experience that the longer Amanda delayed reaching out for help, the deeper the PTSD would settle into her psyche.

"I read the casualty list. The Seals didn't fare too well. Only one made it out alive. He's still in Germany. He'll be lucky if he ever walks again. That Chinese guy . . . Honglei . . . broke his back in three places. Whatever happened to that local woman you were with?" Janet asked, trying to change the subject.

"Marissa . . . she stayed in Germany with Relondo. He's the guy you were just talking about. When they met, it just clicked. I think she fell in love with him at first sight. He was the same way. Without her, this whole mission would have been a bust. I was stumbling around until I met her. She helped me cope with the deaths of my parents. She was the one who had the maps of the galleria, the tunnels that were the key to stopping the Chinese. We talked about her coming back here and getting a job with the Company. I never had a sister. Now I know what it feels like."

"Well, then you're lucky. I haven't talked to my sister in over 20 years. She's a die-hard lefty, and every time we would get together, we would wind up in an argument. I was at the point of wanting to punch her lights out and figured it would be a good time to say goodbye. That was during the First Gulf War. I haven't seen her since."

"I still don't know what happened to my brothers. They were both in California . . . both married, with kids," Amanda said, while wiping tears from her face."

"FEMA has set up over 200 refugee camps out west. They're still having aftershocks every day . . . bad ones . . . 6+. Things aren't much better around here. Reports and rumors are floating around about the New Madrid Fault."

"In Missouri? Didn't that open up in the early 1800's?"

"Yeah, made the Mississippi run backwards for a while. The business in California may have destabilized the fault."

"Great! Just what the country needs!"

"Nothing we can do about it. That's somebody else's problem. First thing is, you go home . . . for two days, and that is an order. If you do that, then I'll inquire into any available training courses. And, I'm going to schedule you into therapy . . . and 'no' is not an acceptable answer. We've lost a lot of people, too. Remember that agent in Mexico?"

"John Broughton?"

"Yeah, he didn't make it. His body was found four miles inland, in the desert. His lungs were full of sea water. All told, we lost over 180 of our people on the West Coast. We used to have offices in San Diego, LA, San Francisco and Seattle. The Seattle office is the only one left."

"And what's with the weather? It was snowing when I touched down. It's a little early for that."

"October 11th, and we've had over a foot of snow. It's the dust thrown up by the attack on China. Predictions are all over the place. It ranges from two weeks and the dust will settle out of the atmosphere, all the way to triggering another ice age. Average temperature in the Northern Hemisphere is down 3.5 degrees Fahrenheit. Most scientists think it's going to get a lot worse."

"Maybe I'll quit and move to South America," Amanda said, then smiled at her boss.

"The way things are going, I might go with you. Invite Marissa to come along. She sounds like my kind of girl!"

"As long as Relondo is still alive, she'll stay with him."

"So . . . two days, and that is an order. I don't want to see you until Friday morning. Work on your report, sleep, relax and eat some decent food. You've lost a lot of weight."

"But I . . ."

"But nothing! Get the hell out of my office! I've got work to do," Janet said, as she began reading a file on her monitor.

. . . .

Amanda left work and headed for her apartment. She pulled into her assigned parking space and turned off the engine. But the thought of sitting in her empty apartment held no appeal. She glanced at the time displayed on her dashboard.

"*I need some lunch . . . someplace quiet,*" she thought, as she restarted her car and backed out of the parking space.

Forty minutes later she found herself cruising the streets of Old Alexandria. The main roads were passable, but the heavy snow made the secondary roads difficult. She drove slowly down North Union Street, passing the Torpedo Factory Art Center.

"*It seems like forever ago . . . another lifetime. It all started last year in the snow,*" she thought, as memories of the sculpture, the ten-megaton device hidden inside . . . the shootout with the Siberian Tiger inside Vola's . . .

The streets were empty as she passed by Vola's Dockside Grill and Hi-Tide Lounge. Surprised that the lights were on, she pulled to the side of the road and parked. The sound of her stomach growling reminded her that the only thing she had eaten in the last 24 hours was a stale sandwich and some chips while flying across the Atlantic. She stared again at the warm glow emanating from the restaurant and exited the car. After stepping inside, she stomped her feet to remove the snow, then looked up. The restaurant was delightfully warm, cozy and nearly empty. Two couples sat at a table, lamenting the fact that the NFL season had been cancelled. One large man sat alone at the bar. Amanda just stared. Half of her wanted to turn and leave . . . this had been a mistake . . . she was exhausted. The other half wanted to run up to him and throw herself into his arms. She compromised and walked slowly past him. He was staring into a whiskey glass as if he was looking into a wishing well. He appeared as numb as she felt. She removed her coat and slid onto the bar stool beside him.

"Can't say as I thought I'd find you here," she said, while signaling the bartender.

Colonel Anthony Thompson just shook his head, as if he had been dreaming. Then he resumed staring at his drink.

She struck him in the arm hard enough that his head jerked up and a fist drew back in response. Then he turned, saw who it was, and just stared.

"It's been a while. I thought you'd be back at Ft. Bragg," Amanda said, as Anthony slowly reached forward and touched her hand as if to confirm she was real.

"I don't have a command anymore. I was relieved for dereliction of duty. Somebody had to be the fall guy for the nuclear weapon going off near Harris. I guess I drew the short straw," Anthony said, as he turned away and downed his drink.

"What? That's bullshit! You did everything you could possibly do. You got your men out of that hellhole alive!" Amanda said, while gesturing for the bartender to leave the bottle of Bulleit Bourbon whiskey and another glass.

"That's not how the Army saw it. I was slow getting to the device. I spread my forces too thin. I should have concentrated my assault on one spot and then rushed for the Fuel Handling Building. I did virtually everything wrong," Anthony said, while filling his tumbler to the brim and splashing whiskey into hers.

"That's nothing but Monday morning quarterbacking! They weren't there!" Amanda said, while picking up her glass.

"Hey . . . it gets worse. They're considering a court martial. I could wind up in prison. I'm surprised I'm not in the brig now."

"I was there! I know better! I'll testify if it comes to that. You should be getting a medal, not a prison sentence!"

"So how about you? You look worse than when I plucked you out of that bar on the North Carolina coast."

"Thanks! That always makes a girl feel better. Ever notice how we always seem to be meeting at a bar?"

"I missed you, Amanda. I don't think a day went by when I didn't think about you. Sorry . . . that was just . . ." Anthony said, as he turned sideways on the stool and stared at her.

Amanda leaned over and kissed him. It was meant to be a quick kiss, but it lingered. The more it lingered, the more reluctant she was to pull away.

"What was that for?" Anthony asked, as he gently separated from her.

"I've been . . . out of the country. I made a friend named Marissa. I told her about you. She said I was a damn fool, or something like that. It was actually in Spanish and she . . . she wouldn't tell me what she really said. I have never thought of myself as a fool. I've always been cautious . . . careful, at least until I started working for the CIA. Relationships can . . ."

She stopped talking when Anthony pulled her over, stared into her eyes, and began kissing her again.

"Amanda, you talk too much . . ."

"Maybe?"

"Do you always get the last word?"

"Uh-huh!" Amanda said, between kisses . . .

CHAPTER 14

The First Bridge
Rika's Roadhouse
Big Delta, Alaska
October 11, 1850 hours AKST

The drive down Highway 2 the night before had been nerve wracking. First Lieutenants Deion Daniels and Rico Castillo had kept their units' vehicles a quarter mile apart and completely dark. The surprise that awaited them when they reached the Big Delta State Historic Park adjacent to the Tanana River Bridge, had been unexpected. Over 200 men and women were constructing fighting positions in the dark, adjacent to the road leading south from the bridge. Both groups were shocked at seeing the other. First Platoon had spent the day installing their vehicles in ambush positions, while the two officers were in negotiations with the civilians.

"Mr. Flanagan, I appreciate your patriotism, but you're going to get all these people killed. They aren't soldiers. Some of them are as old as my parents. What do you expect to accomplish?" First Lieutenant Daniels asked, while sitting at a long rectangular table inside Rita's Roadhouse, surrounded by civilians.

"Where you from, Lieutenant?" asked Jacob Flanagan.

"Petersburg, Virginia. What difference does . . . "

"You're a black man, from a state that fought for slavery . . . just like me. I was born in Alabama. Do you know your own damn history? Do you know the history of African Americans fighting for this country . . . our country? You ever hear of Crispus Attucks? He was born in Massachusetts as a slave. He escaped and became a sailor. He was the first person killed during the Boston Massacre in 1770. He was a patriot! Over 9000 blacks fought as patriots in that war. The British had the strongest military in the world, but those men, black and white, were willing to stand together and fight. During the Civil War almost 200,000 blacks fought for the Union. That was ten percent of the Union Army. Over 40,000 died so we could all be free. So, screw the Russians! We're fighting! We're family! We have history!"

A crowd of civilians cheered the words of Jacob Flanagan. He calmed them down, and then said, "Lieutenant, we know we're outgunned. But just like you, they got to stay on the roads. The road south is lined with huge trees. We've already started notching them. When the time comes, we'll drop 1000 trees across the road. That will slow them to a crawl. We spent the last week planting IEDs beside and under the roadbed. Quite a few of these men and women are veterans. They aren't afraid of a fight."

Castillo pulled Daniels aside and said, "Deion, we can't make them leave, and they don't have a half bad plan. We just need to combine forces. Make the two plans work together."

"Yeah, you're right. That's the way to go. I'll contact the Captain and get his buy in. Get details on their plans and let them know what we're planning. Mr. Jones and our boys are planting explosives on that steel bridge right now. Everything has to be ready before sunrise."

. . . .

The Fourth Bridge
1905 hours

Captain MacLynn stood with his ROM (Radio Operator Maintainer) at an overlook just south of the fourth bridge. The sun had set 40 minutes ago, and the nightly fog was just starting to thicken.

The sky had quickly darkened and filled with stars. The brown haze that blanketed most of the Northern Hemisphere was thinner this far north . . . at least for a while. The Aurora Season began in late August and continued into April. Despite the partial haze, the sky above was filled with shimmering green bands edged with pink, gold and violet. But his mind wasn't on the light display above.

"I concur, Lieutenant. A similar problem has evolved here. These civilians are probably coordinating with each other over CB radio. It's not as organized down here, but there are probably 50 or so people meeting in a nearby lodge to talk about what they're going to do. Lieutenant Branson is keeping an eye on things. I'm overseeing the work on the bridge. Over!" Captain MacLynn said, over the backpack mounted SINCGARS Combat Net Radio carried by his ROM.

"Sir, they have limited fire power, mostly hunting rifles, but they're good with explosives. I checked out one of their IEDs. They're using 55-gallon drums filled with fuel oil, fertilizer and a quarter stick of dynamite as a blasting cap. They claim to have notched 1000 trees on the roadside leading south from here. One of them owns a store that sells four-wheelers and snowmobiles. They've got enough transport and fuel to move all of them at one time. The kids, old folks and unwilling have already been evacuated to the south. The rest of them are going to stay and fight. Over!"

"I know this is unconventional, but we must remain flexible. This whole situation is way outside anything we've trained for. I like their idea with the trees, but make sure they think it through. They need to have an exit plan. Once this starts, the Russians will call up air support. It will get real ugly, real fast. They'll have to scatter into the woods or head to the south. Have you reconned that pipe easement north of the highway? Is it passable? Over!"

"It's part of our plan and theirs. It is passable. It runs parallel to the highway for over 20 miles. The woods on the north side are thick, but we can maneuver through them. We'll be able to attack, pull back through the woods, move south a few miles and then hit the column again. Over!"

"Don't assume the Russians won't figure that out. Don't get cut off and trapped. Over!"

"Roger that, Sir! Anything else?" Over!"

"Negative! Let me know when you're set. Out!"

. . . .

The First Bridge
October 12, 0140 hours

"So, when did the light show stop?" First Lieutenant Castillo asked the Forward Observer stationed in the woodline north of the bridge.

"Like I said on the radio, LT . . . about 30 minutes ago. The fighting up north has lit up the sky since we got up here. Sometimes you could feel the ground shake. Now . . . it's gotten quiet. Whoever was fighting the Russians either gave up or got wiped out," said Corporal Juan Gonzalez.

"You heard anything from the civilians?"

"No, Sir! Two of them passed by heading north about an hour ago. They were on four-wheelers and going like a bat out of hell."

"Yeah, they were supposed to be back by now. They were going to go to the outskirts of Fairbanks and see what the Russians were up to. They were told not to get in a fight."

"Sir, I think these civilians do what the hell they want. I don't like fighting beside them. They're too unpredictable . . . too unmilitary!"

"Gonzalez, you keep thinking like that and you'll wind up an officer."

"Hell no . . . Sir! I like it where I'm at. I just do what I'm told. I don't want to tell anyone else shit!"

They both began chuckling, then stopped when they heard the high-pitched sound of small engines being pushed to their limit.

"LT . . . you hear that?" Corporal Gonzalez asked, while unslinging his M4 carbine.

"Yeah . . . and they're in a hurry!" First Lieutenant Castillo said, while unslinging his weapon.

Two four-wheelers rounded the curve a half mile north of them. First Lieutenant Castillo pulled his flashlight from his web gear and flashed the red light in a pre-arranged signal: two fast blinks . . . two slow blinks and then repeated the sequence. One vehicle flew by them without slowing down. The second four-wheeler skidded to a stop at the side of the road. The driver hopped off and removed her helmet as she ran up to them.

"You guys need to mount up and get the hell out of here! The Russians are heading south. They're probably 15 minutes behind us. I'd say 20 to 25 vehicles. Most of them looked like your vehicles, eight wheels. Only three of them had turrets on top," she said, as she shook out her long black hair.

"That's a recon company. No tanks, that's good news! Did you hear or see any choppers?" asked First Lieutenant Castillo.

"No, we were about a mile south of Eielson Air Force Base. Everything was burning . . . thick smoke everywhere. They came south out of the smoke. We got a good head count and hauled ass back here."

"Good work! That's exactly what we needed. Get back to your people. Gonzalez, get in your Hummer and head back. I'll be right behind you. I'm going to give the Captain a heads up," said First Lieutenant Castillo, as he headed for the radio inside his Hummer.

. . . .

The Fourth Bridge
0145 hours

"That's good news, Lieutenant. The long wait is over. But now comes the hard part. Remember the plan. Let the Russians pass by.

Make sure the civilians hold their fire until the column passes down to us. That will take at least two hours. We have a chance to chew up and isolate a battalion-sized unit. If we can do that, we can delay their progress to the south by at least a week. Over!" said Captain MacLynn from inside his Command Stryker hidden in the woods above the fourth Tanana River Bridge.

"Sir . . . our boys won't be a problem. They'll follow orders. These civilians . . . some of them have been drinking. All they want to do is kill Russians. I don't think they'll sit by for two hours and watch Russians drive through their land. Over!" replied First Lieutenant Daniels.

"Lieutenant, you said you had a connection with this . . . Mr. Flanagan. You can't force these people to do anything. This isn't a Civilian Affairs problem. These people are our allies whether we like it or not. Use him and other civilian leaders to control their people. If all we do is shoot up a Scout Company, we won't have accomplished our mission. The Russians can't have that many troops on the ground yet. If we can tear up an entire battalion, that will slow them down. We've got to buy some time for the Pentagon to react to this invasion. Over!"

"Understood, Sir! I'll do the best I can, Sir. I'll keep you informed as things develop. Over!"

"I've got faith in you, Deion! MacLynn out!"

Captain Dothan MacLynn stared at the handset, then placed it on the hook.

"We're back in World War II. The Russians have taken out so many of our satellites that most of our advanced shit is useless. At least the EPLRS (Enhanced Position Locating and Reporting Systems) still works," Captain MacLynn thought, as he turned and studied the screen showing the position of all his vehicles.

"We're stretched out over 150 miles of road. Four lousy rifle platoons and three Mobile Gun Systems. Everything must be perfect for this to work. Once the shooting starts, it always goes to shit . . . always! How the hell is he going to get the civilians to hold their fire

while the Russians drive by? What if the Russians stop? What if the civilians panic? Crap! I'm what-iffing myself to death. At a minimum, we'll blow the bridges. We have to blow the bridges!" he thought, as he turned and stepped out of the back of his Stryker.

Captain Dothan MacLynn was named after his hometown of Dothan, Alabama. His father and grandfather had both been mayors. His father had not been happy when he enlisted after 9/11. He had been offered a baseball scholarship at Alabama and had thrown it away. After his first tour in Iraq he had been sent to Officer Candidate School, and that had led him here, more than 20 years later, one of the oldest Captains in the Army. He had been passed over for Major twice. Retirement was only 18 months away . . . then everything changed.

He took a deep breath, trying to calm himself for the battle that might start within a few moments. His breath frosted and didn't dissipate as it drifted away. The night was getting colder, and the fog was settling in faster than normal. The bridge across the Tanana River, the fourth bridge, his bridge, was starting to disappear. It was going to be a total white out . . .

.   .   .   .

The First Bridge
0200 hours AKST

"Don't worry about us, Lieutenant. My people understand the play. Some of them aren't happy about letting the Russians just drive by, but they'll wait," said Jacob, as he and First Lieutenant Daniels stood in the treeline just south of the first bridge.

They both paused at the sound of four-wheelers crossing the bridge, headed in their direction.

"I thought all your people were back across?" First Lieutenant Daniels asked.

"They are!"

Two vehicles sped across the bridge, barely visible in the thickening fog, and turned down the access road leading toward their hidden position.

Jeremiah Jones slid off the first vehicle and stretched out his back as he walked toward them. Sergeant Bart Masterson walked behind him. A big grin splitting his boyish face.

First Lieutenant Daniels gestured for Masterson to step away.

"Where the hell have you been and what the hell have you been doing? My orders were that no one was to cross back over that bridge!" Daniels said.

"Well . . . Sir . . . we had a lot of leftover dynamite and Mr. Jones had this great idea . . ."

"So what? You decide to take off on your own . . . without consulting me?"

"LT . . . you're always talking about individual initiative . . . and thinking outside the box . . ."

"Not . . . without . . . consulting . . . me! So, what was this brilliant idea that may get you court-martialed?"

"See that big hill to the left of the bridge? It must go up 150 feet. We rigged it to blow at the same time as the bridge. That hill will slide down and block the whole road. It will take them days to dig through that shit before they even reach the wreckage of the bridge. No one will be driving this way for weeks . . . Sir!" Sergeant Masterson said, still smiling while pointed across the river at the hill barely visible in the fog.

First Lieutenant Daniels was staring at Masterson in disbelief when the sound of powerful diesel engines penetrated the fog. Both men stared at each other.

"Get back to your assigned position, Sergeant. If we live through this, I'll take a chunk out of your ass at a later date!"

"Roger that, Sir! Sorry, Sir!" Sergeant Masterson said with a smile, as he turned and began running.

"Aww . . . don't be so hard on the boy. It was the right thing to do," said Jeremiah.

"Mr. Jones . . . you're a veteran. You know I can't have my men out freelancing. They have to obey orders!"

"Lieutenant, what we have to do is kill Russians. You were off talking to your Captain, and I didn't have much time. I needed some help, and your Sergeant was nice enough to come along."

Daniels remembered his Captain's words about coordinating with the civilians, then said, "Will it work? Can you drop that hill?"

"Oh, hell yeah! They'll never know what hit 'em! The bridge and the hill . . . it'll all go at once!"

. . . .

Russian Battalion Commander
Highway 2
Five miles north of the First Bridge
0200 hours AKST

"Colonel! The Recon Platoon of 3rd Company reports they heard the sound of vehicles up ahead," said Senior Lieutenant Gennady Fedorin, over the vehicle's radio comm.

"What kind of vehicles, Lieutenant? How many? Of what type? Civilian or military? Details, Lieutenant! I need details, not panicked reports. Come back to me when you have some damn details!" yelled Colonel Popov, while standing in the open hatch of his BTR-80 PBKM Command Vehicle.

"Idiots! I am surrounded by idiots and conscripts! First, we invade the United States with no notice. Then, we are repairing vehicles while on board a damn ship. Finally, we are shot to shit while disembarking in port by an American military that isn't supposed to exist anymore! Now they send me south with an inexperienced Motorized Rifle Battalion with only two helicopters for support . . . if the fog isn't too thick . . . and if they feel like flying!" Colonel Popov said, while pounding the top of his lightly armored vehicle in frustration.

"I have to get closer. I made a mistake staying this far back," Colonel Popov thought, while opening a channel to his three company commanders.

"This is Colonel Popov. I am coming forward to 1st Company. I must see for myself what is going on. Out!"

After ordering his driver to slide to the side of the road and bypass the lined-up vehicles of his battalion, he shook his head at the minimal distance between each vehicle.

"Idiots! One of them blows up and they'll take out two more vehicles. How can we have fallen this far?" he asked himself, remembering the glory days of his youth when the Soviet Army was second to none.

"Afghanistan . . . it all started there. Then the country fell apart and we've never recovered. President Morozov is taking a desperate gamble. We don't have the forces to conquer America unless the Chinese attack has left them with nothing," he thought, as the vehicle slowly headed for the front of his unit over five miles away.

.   .   .   .

Just south of the First Bridge
0203 hours AKST

The BTR-82A Armored Recon Vehicle pulled across the south end of the bridge and stopped. The small turret containing the 2A72 30 mm gun rotated slowly to its left scanning the terrain along the shore of the river.

First Lieutenant Daniels observed the vehicle using an infrared scope. He knew this was the first test of his alliance with the civilian militia. If the Russians detected the heat signature of even one person, they would open fire using the thermal sights mounted on that cannon. Then all hope of discipline would disintegrate when the civilians opened fire. A few Russians would die, but the plan would be a bust. He held his breath as the turret began rotating in the other direction and passed over his position. A few seconds later the upper hatch opened, and a head popped out and manned an attached 12.7 mm machine gun.

Laughing could be heard as the rear ramp opened and thudded onto the roadway. A soldier could be seen walking to the side of the road. It soon became obvious that he had jumped out of the vehicle to take a piss. Two other vehicles began crossing the bridge and soon closed in on the first vehicle. After stopping, two men approached the lead vehicle. Three soldiers then began studying a map they threw on the sloped, forward plate of the BTR-82A.

"I don't believe they're using a flashlight. It's not even red filtered. Who trained these clowns?" Daniels asked himself, remembering all the tales of the ferocity and skill of the new Russian military.

After more troops exited the vehicles for roadside breaks, they loaded back up and proceeded down Highway 2. Other vehicles began to appear on the far side of the bridge, as the vehicles of 1st Company, 3rd Battalion, 8th Mountain Brigade began crossing the Tanana River and heading south.

"Captain, what looks like a Motor Rifle Company with advanced scouts are across the first bridge and heading south. Over!" First Lieutenant Daniels said, from inside his darkened Stryker.

"Roger that! Any tanks? Over!"

"Negative, Sir! So far, it's all BTR-80s. We'll keep a head count as they pass. Over!"

"Excellent work! Keep me apprised! Out!"

The parade continued by them for the next 90 minutes. The fog had grown so thick that the roadside 50 yards away was invisible. The only sign that a column of armored vehicles was passing by was the sound of the diesel engines and their heat signatures visible in thermal sights.

.   .   .   .

Side of the road
Just south of the First Bridge
0330 hours AKST

Colonel Popov had been a soldier for almost 30 years. He had been a young Junior Lieutenant the first time he fought in Afghanistan. By the time the Soviet Army withdrew, he'd been involved in more ambushes by the Fedayeen than he cared to remember. He had a similar feeling now, even though every report indicated no contact. Every report was negative. The lead recon platoon had progressed over 80 miles south. There had been no opposition. It was as if the US military was gone, and the civilian population had fled.

"Colonel, do you wish to rejoin the column? The artillery and trucks will soon be crossing the bridge. That will leave us at the back of the column," said SRLT Fedorin, from below, as he monitored the radio traffic from the rest of the battalion.

"Yes, get us back on the damn road. But something's wrong! I just feel it, but I can't see anything. Contact the company commanders. Tell them to be alert. Something isn't right!"

"Yes, Colonel! I'll let them know that you . . ." Senior Lieutenant Fedorin began, when a rifle shot rang out.

The Colonel fell back through the open hatch, semi-conscious. Blood spurted from a wound to his left arm. The Colonel's eyes were open, unblinking, as he lay sprawled on the inside of his command vehicle.

The Senior Lieutenant stared at his fallen commander, then panicked and opened the comm channel to all vehicles in the Battalion.

"We are under fire! The Colonel has been wounded! All units open fire!"

Then all hell broke loose as over 200 Russian vehicles opened fire and began shooting at everything and anything along an 80-mile path. The panic was contagious on both sides. Without being told, the

Americans returned fire, both civilians and military. Trees began falling across roads, as men waiting in the cold cranked up their chainsaws and began cutting the last few inches of previously notched trees. The First Bridge erupted on both ends. The south end fell into the water, creating a 50-foot gap. The explosion at the north end failed to bring the bridge down, but the demolitions planted by Jeremiah Jones and Sergeant Masterson dropped a million pounds of rock on the roadway north of the bridge. The last eight vehicles of the Russian 3rd Battalion were buried or swept into the river. The three MGS Strykers opened fire with their 105 mm tank guns. Careful prepositioning had given them open fields of fire on the Russians. BTR-80s began to erupt up and down the 80-mile-long column as the guns, built for US M-60 Main Battle Tanks back in the '60s, tore through the thin-skinned armor of the Russian infantry vehicles. The two M1129 Mortar Carriers opened fire with their 120 mm Soltam Cardom mortars. The Fire Support Team had established designated kill zones for precision-guided ammunition. The high-explosive mortar rounds began detonating on top of the lightly armored upper hulls of the BTR-80s. IEDs began detonating up and down the Russian column, hurling vehicles into the air and incinerating soldiers. The battle that would be known to future generations of Americans as the Four Bridge Shootout had begun . . .

. . . .

Treeline just south of the First Bridge
0340 hours AKST

"Shit, boy! There's a lot of them!" yelled Andy Moore, as more figures began running toward him and away from the carnage on Highway 2.

"Yeah, man! It's like pulling salmon during a run. They just keep coming," said Adam's best friend, Thomas Locklear, as the two men worked their bolt action, high-powered Remington model 798 hunting rifles as fast as they could.

They had grown up together, hunted together, and even been each other's best man when they had married each other's sisters. They didn't notice Colonel Popov as he crept up behind them. Two shots from his MP-443 Grach pistol . . . and he continued his own hunt. His left arm hung by a thread. He knew that he was going to die soon, but he was going to die on his terms . . . like a Russian. He had yet to see an American soldier. He couldn't believe that all this carnage had been planned by Alaskan peasants.

. . . .

"Castillo! It's Daniels! Break contact! It's time to leave. Head for the pipeline easement. We're heading for the second bridge at Gerstle River. Second Platoon will hold as long as they can. Get there or be left behind! Over!"

"Roger that! Castillo out!"

The pipeline easement ran for nine miles. Civilian four-wheelers mixed with the Strykers as everyone fled from Big Delta and made their way down to Delta Junction. From there, it was backroads all the way to the Gerstle River and the second bridge.

. . . .

The Second Bridge
0430 hours AKST

Second Lieutenant Baskin Morgan was 22 years old. He had been an officer for 14 months. Alaska had been his first duty assignment. Now he found himself commanding troops in an active engagement, defending American soil from Russian invaders . . . and he was overwhelmed.

"No! We've got to blow the bridge! If we wait any longer, the Russians will have the position!" Second Lieutenant Morgan screamed at his platoon sergeant, Sergeant First Class Malcom Scott.

"Sir! They're 15 minutes out. We have to hold the bridge for a few more minutes. First Platoon will get here! The Captain said we should wait!" replied Scott, while firing the M2 .50 cal machine gun mounted atop their Stryker.

"The Captain's not here. I'm in charge, and I say it's time to blow the bridge!"

"Sir, with all due respect. We're chewing the Russians up. We can wait a few more minutes before blowing the bridge," Sergeant First Class Scott replied, while smelling the urine running down his Lieutenant's leg.

"I'm giving you a direct order!" Second Lieutenant Morgan yelled, as he began pulling his handgun from its holster.

The Lieutenant never saw the fist that impacted his jaw.

"Yeah, I'll lose a bunch of stripes for that!" Scott said, opening fire as more Russian infantry became visible in the thick fog.

. . . .

The Third Bridge
0620 hours AKST

The Tanana River flowed down from the first bridge at Big Delta to the fourth bridge near Tetlin Junction 120 miles south. The Russian convoy had reached a point 50 miles north of the fourth bridge before the trap had been sprung. From every report received, the Russian Battalion had been devastated . . . but they hadn't stopped fighting.

"Captain, the fog's starting to thin. The sun will be up in two hours. After that, the Russians will have aircraft on top of us. When do you want us to blow the bridge and pull back? Over!" asked Second Lieutenant Branson of 3rd Platoon.

"The Second Bridge has been blown. You wait until First and Second Platoons have passed your position. At that time, you will conduct a holding action, and then blow the third bridge and pullback. Is that understood, Lieutenant?" Over!"

"Roger that, Sir! Over!"

"MacLynn, out!"

The third bridge was 50 miles to his north. It would take another hour from there for his platoons to reach his position. That gave them little time to blow the fourth bridge, disperse before sunrise, and flee south before the onslaught from the air that he knew would follow.

CHAPTER 15

Fort Wainwright Airfield
Fairbanks, Alaska
October 12, 0730 hours AKST

"When is that cursed thing going to be ready to fly?" asked Russian Major General Artur Kuznetsov, while staring out the window of his new office overlooking the Fort Wainright Airfield.

The fighting had been ferocious despite the cruise missile attack that had devastated the area. Runway repairs were still ongoing. All reinforcements and supplies were still coming in by sea. He only had two old MI-24D Hind gunships operable, and they were ineffective in bad weather, or so he had been told. The MI-24VN that sat warming up on the runway was another matter. It was designed to hunt in any weather.

"The crew is going over pre-flight checks as we speak, General. They should be airborne within a few minutes," replied his adjutant, Major Stepan Orlov.

"An entire battalion has been lost for lack of air support! Are you aware of that, Major Orlov?"

"Yes, General! A great tragedy, but we are still ahead of the timetable. We can reach the Canadian border within two days!"

"By what stretch of the imagination do you foresee this as being a possibility? The Americans are blowing up the bridges as they retreat. It will take weeks to get bridging equipment to those locations. The ground will not freeze solid for another month!"

"Sir, we only need to get past the first bridge. The Americans have left open a back door. There is another major road. It heads south and then north. It bypasses the bridges they are destroying. Here, General, look at this map," Major Orlov said, while spreading a Russian topographic map with photo overlays across a briefing table.

"We must get across the first river. That will take some days. Then we proceed to this town, Delta Junction, and south down Highway 4 until we reach Gakona. We turn north on Highway 1, which will take us all the way up to Tok and bypass the other blown bridges!"

"How far?"

"Two hundred and fifty miles! There are bridges, but they are small. The streams are shallow and rocky. Even if they are blown, it will not slow us down."

"But this last bridge, west of . . . Tetlin Junction. If they blow this one, we will still be stuck!" replied General Kuznetsov, while jamming his finger on the image of the long, steel bridge over the Tanana River.

"General, here . . . two miles west of the bridge . . . there is a small road heading south. Five miles down, it comes to within a mile of the river. The river is very narrow and shallow here. Our combat engineers can bridge the river. We bypass the blown bridge and are within a mile of the major highway on the other side! There are no other bridges all the way to Canada!"

"Do we have the bridging equipment and the engineers?"

"I've checked. The equipment is in a warehouse down in Anchorage. The equipment and the troops can be trucked up here in a day!" Major Orlov said, hoping that he had anticipated his general's questions.

"Styopa Morasivich . . . " General Kuznetsov said, using the nickname for Stepan, as he leaned forward and kissed his adjutant on both cheeks.

"You remind me of why I made you my adjutant. If this works out, I will promote you to Lieutenant Colonel. Of course, if it does not work out . . ."

"Junior Lieutenant in a Scout Platoon?" Major Orlov asked, as he stepped back and snapped to attention.

"If you are lucky! Now go make this happen! And why the hell has that damn helicopter not taken off?" General Kuznetsov bellowed.

"I will find out, General!" Major Orlov said, as he turned and ran out of the office.

"Good boy . . . and smart. He will make me famous!" General Kuznetsov said, as the sound of a helicopter taking off made him turn from the doorway.

"Tanks! That damn fool Popov ran into tanks and lost his whole battalion. He better be dead, or I'll have him shot! And that helicopter crew better be calling back within an hour reporting on how many kills they have made," the general said, as he walked over to a Mr. Coffee espresso machine sitting on a side table.

"The American General may have fled, but at least he left me this!" he said, while removing a steaming cup of espresso.

.   .   .   .

300 feet above Big Delta
0805 hours AKST

"Captain, the visibility is shit, but I can detect numerous burning vehicles," said Lieutenant Maksim Denikin from the weapon's operator position at the front of the MI-24VN attack helicopter.

The deadly craft skimmed just above the northernmost bridge crossing the Tanana River. The pilot's position was located above and behind the weapon's operator in the 57-foot-long, 13-ton killing machine.

The MI-24VN was a modern update of the venerated MI-24 that had been in production since 1973. The two-man helicopter was lighter, faster, and more maneuverable than its predecessors. It was armed with a 23 mm cannon hanging below the front of the nose and eight 9M120 Ataka anti-tank guided missiles mounted below its stubby wings. It had been specifically designed to hunt in any known combat environment. But . . . it was a rarity. Unlike most militaries across the globe, helicopters designed to support ground troops were controlled by the Russian Air Force, not the Russian Army. This decision in 2003 resulted in slow modernization and poor maintenance. Air Force generals were more focused on fighters and bombers than ground support aircraft.

"Captain, the bridge has been blown!"

"I can see, Lieutenant! Make sure that the video recorder is on. That will be a critical part of our after-action report. We are scouting, as well as killing," replied Captain Borya Vasnev.

"Target identification system identifies the vehicles as Russian. None of them are moving, Captain."

"You have the battalion frequencies. See if you can find anyone alive down there!" Captain Vasnev said, as the gunship hovered above Highway 2.

. . . .

Rika's Roadhouse
Just south of the First Bridge
0805 hours AKST

Colonel Popov lay on a wooden table. A medic had just removed the tattered remains of his left arm and stopped the blood flow. Morphine had deadened most of the pain, but he refused to allow himself to fall asleep.

"Colonel . . . we are collecting stragglers and the wounded. I have set up a perimeter around this area. Please, quit fighting it and rest. The medic has stopped the bleeding, but we need to get you to a hospital," said Senior Lieutenant Fedorin.

The groans of other wounded filled the inside of Rika's Roadhouse. Two civilians, one man, one woman, sat tied up in a corner. Both had been badly beaten after capture.

"Lieutenant! Air support! A helicopter is trying to contact us!" shouted a young private as he rushed into the building carrying a portable radio.

"Now the bastards show up . . ." mumbled Colonel Popov.

"Senior Lieutenant Fedorin, 3rd Battalion, 8th Mountain Brigade! Over!" Fedorin said, as he grabbed the radio and keyed the mike.

"Captain Vasnev, 793rd Independent Helicopter Regiment! What is your location? Over!"

"We're located one quarter mile north of Highway 2, just past the south end of the bridge. Our Colonel is badly wounded and in need of evacuation. Over!"

"Lieutenant, where are the Americans? How many tanks did you see? Over!"

"When the attack started, we couldn't see anything. Night vision . . . thermal . . . nothing! We never saw them until they started shooting! The battle lasted for about 15 minutes. Then it stopped as quickly as it started. We have two captured civilians, but no American military. The civilians were fighting with them. Over!"

"What about tanks? They must have had tanks to cause this much damage. Over!"

"My men have found only two abandoned fighting positions for large vehicles. Based on the description . . . they weren't tanks. The positions were too small and there were no track marks. I think they were Strykers, but there were reports of hearing tank fire. So, I'm not sure what we were fighting. Over!"

"Lieutenant, our mission is to find and destroy the American units that conducted this ambush. I will relay your observations to regimental headquarters. Keep your Colonel alive! Help will arrive as soon as possible. Out!" Captain Vasnev said, as he switched radio frequencies and forwarded the information provided by Senior Lieutenant Fedorin.

"Now what, Captain?" asked Lieutenant Denikin from the front seat.

"Now we hunt, Lieutenant Denikin. Now we hunt . . ."

CHAPTER 16

The Fourth Bridge
One Mile West of
Tetlin Junction, Alaska
October 12, 0859 hours AKST

Captain MacLynn stood at the overlook south of the fourth bridge. The third bridge had been blown 30 minutes ago. Three platoons and the civilian militia were pulling back to his location. First and Second Platoons had almost reached Tok, only ten miles away. Third Platoon was a few miles further back. The fog was starting to lift . . .

"All three platoons should be here in 15 minutes! No vehicle losses . . . only four wounded . . . no missing. It's a miracle! We blow this bridge, refuel, and then we pull back into Canada." he thought, as he walked back toward his Stryker.

. . . .

Northern Energy Gas Station
10 miles north of the Fourth Bridge
Tok, Alaska
0915 hours AKST

"Hey, LT! Nothing like a cheap fill up!" said vehicle driver Specialist Four Ben Simpson, as he continued to add gas to his Stryker.

First Lieutenant Daniels was pacing nervously back and forth from the road back to First Platoon's vehicles lined up at the Northern Energy Gas Station. His unit had gone the farthest north. They were running on fumes when they had reached the outskirts of Tok. Fuel had been imperative, but the fog was lifting, and he wanted to get back on the road and across the fourth bridge as quickly as possible. There were only two gas pumps . . .

"Come on, Simpson . . . hurry it up! We're sitting ducks!"

"Chill, LT! We haven't seen any Russians in over 20 miles. Baby's thirsty and 50 gallons takes a while," Simpson replied.

The mood in the platoon was almost jovial. Only two men in the platoon had been wounded, and the wounds were superficial. Soldiers were outside their vehicles taking selfies and talking about their first taste of combat. Snacks had been 'procured' from inside the gas station. The civilian militia were freely mixing with the soldiers, each side bragging about who had killed the most Russians. Then everything changed . . .

"That's enough, Simpson. Get her out of the way and let the next vehicle in here," ordered First Lieutenant Daniels.

"Come on, Sir! She's almost full . . . one more minute!"

"Simpson! I said move the damn . . ." First Lieutenant Daniels said, then spun on his heels as his heart began pounding in his chest.

"*Rotor blades . . . I hear rotor blades . . .*" he thought, as he stared back up the road.

He began walking to the north, staring into the fog. Second and third platoon vehicles had passed by five minutes ago, heading for the bridge.

"*Is it ours? Are we finally getting some help?*" he asked himself, as his hand instinctively reached for his sidearm.

The distinctive shape of a Hind gunship appeared in the mist 30 feet above the road, less than a quarter mile away . . .

"Russians!" First Lieutenant Daniels yelled, as he turned and began running back toward his platoon.

Lieutenant Castillo was standing in front of his MGS Stryker. They were last in line for gas at Pump No. 2. He was posing for pictures with his gunner in front of the vehicle, holding both hands in front of him, showing all ten fingers. He was claiming ten kills and was going to paint ten white stripes on the barrel of the 105 mm gun at the first opportunity. He was wondering what First Lieutenant Daniels was yelling about, as the first Ataka anti-tank guided missile struck the rear of his vehicle. He, his vehicle, and every person within 50 feet, was shredded by the explosion.

Daniels was thrown into the road by the concussive blast of the missile. He lay on his back, bleeding heavily from several shrapnel wounds, deafened by the detonation, as a second missile streaked over his head . . . then a third. He rolled onto his side, and watched his platoon die as all five vehicles were destroyed within seconds. The killing machine drifted by him, only 15 feet off the ground. A snarling wolf was painted across the front of the fuselage. Then the growling sound of the 23 mm cannon began, growing louder as the Russian Hind began slaughtering anything that still moved. A few civilians, parked behind the gas station, began to flee. Some were on foot, others on four-wheelers or trucks. The Russian gunship hunted them all down. Fire and smoke were everywhere. Secondary explosions shook the ground as the craft lifted away and began heading south, parallel to Highway 2 . . . toward the fourth bridge.

The Hind gunship had ruled the airspace above Afghanistan during the Russia-Afghan War back in the '80s. Then America began supplying the Fedayeen with early models of the Stinger surface-to-air missile. It was a shoot-and-forget weapon that was so simple to operate that an illiterate Afghan tribesman could operate one. The Russian Hinds were forced to retreat high into the sky after dozens of the aircraft were shot down. Their undisputed rule of the mountains and valleys of the rugged country had come to an end. That lack of close air support had led to an ignominious Soviet defeat. Historians referred to it as the Soviet Vietnam. The humiliation of that lost war still haunted the Russian military, many of whose senior officers had fought in Afghanistan in their youth.

. . . .

The Fourth Bridge
0915 hours AKST

Captain MacLynn had been on hand to greet 2nd and 3rd Platoons as they crossed the bridge. Many civilians had hitched a ride atop the Strykers. Wounded, both civilian and military, were transported to the Medical Evac Team for treatment. The reunion with his two platoon leaders had been filled with smiles and handshakes, until the dull thump of explosions in the distance reached them. A huge plume of black smoke became visible above the trees to the north.

"Lieutenants, get back to your men. This isn't over yet!" Captain MacLynn ordered, as he turned and ran back to his command vehicle.

"Lieutenant Daniels, this is Captain MacLynn. What is your status? Over!" he said into the handset, fearful of what had happened to 1st Platoon.

After two more tries and no response, he stared at the computer monitor in his vehicle. GPS and his ability to track the locations of his vehicles had disappeared a day ago, telling him that the war elsewhere continued. He changed frequency and contacted his two remaining officers.

"Lieutenants, I've been unable to contact First Platoon. We must assume they came under attack. Did you have visual on them as you passed through Tok? Over!"

"Sir, they were all stopped at a gas station. It looked like a big party. The civilians were mixed with our guys. They were all taking

100

pictures as they gassed up their vehicles. Over!" replied Second Lieutenant Branson.

"Chopper . . . chopper . . . chopper!" came over the comm net.

The sound of an explosion rocked the Command Stryker as Captain MacLynn ducked outside to see what was going on. One of 2nd Platoon's vehicles was lying on its side. Burning men were screaming as they struggled to get out of the vehicle. Other bodies had been scattered about, not moving. Troops were running around. Some were firing back across the river.

Captain MacLynn glanced across the river. A Hind gunship sat in a gap, just above the treeline. A second missile leapt from the machine as he froze and just stared. He followed the path until one of his MGS Strykers was enveloped in a fireball. The turret was hurled into the air by the explosion. He could see a man hanging from the turret as it thudded onto the ground.

"I have to act or we're all dead!" he thought, then ordered over the comm net, "Fire Support Team! Stingers! Deploy the Stingers! Kill that damn chopper!"

. . . .

The MI-24VN Hind
0917 hours AKST

"Excellent shooting, Lieutenant Denikin! Thirty degrees to your left . . . in the woodline . . . another Stryker with a tank gun!" ordered Captain Vasnev, as he guided the Hind out of the treeline and over the riverbed.

"Understood, Captain! We only have two anti-tank missiles left."

"I can count, Lieutenant! First, we take out their big guns. Then we will be a wolf hunting amongst the sheep. Our armor will protect us from everything else they have."

"Yes, Captain!" Lieutenant Denikin replied, as he lined up the last MGS Stryker in his sights.

"Missile away!"

A few seconds later, the missile impacted on the forward armor of the Stryker. The Ataka anti-tank missile had been designed to defeat a US M-1A1 tank. The Stryker ruptured like a dropped melon.

"They did not even move, Captain!"

"It's called 'surprise', Lieutenant. They thought they were safe. Now they are in a panic, and now we will kill as many of them as we can," Captain Vasnev said, as he pointed the nose of his craft toward a lone Stryker sitting by an overlook on the other side of the river.

"Lieutenant, do you see the vehicle on the right . . . the one with multiple antennas?"

"Yes, Captain!"

"That is their leader. Our last missile goes there!"

"Yes, Captain!"

"Missile a . . ." Denikin began, when the Hind jumped down and to the right, bounced off the riverbed, and began skimming across the river.

Their last anti-tank missile impacted on the riverbank beside the bridge. The Stinger that had nearly taken their lives blew the top out of a tree.

"Shit! Captain, what . . ."

"Stinger! Look for the gunners! There may be more! I got careless. The sheep still have teeth!"

Heavy machine gun fire began pinging off the side of the armored helicopter, as they hovered just off the riverbed. They returned fire with the 23 mm cannon as the pilot and weapons operator frantically searched for the source of the surface-to-air missile.

Captain Vasnev cursed as two Stingers were fired at the same time. One came from the left and one from the right. He fired the Hind's countermeasures, designed to lure the heat seeking missiles away, but he was too low. The missile on his right followed the lures, but the second missile homed in on the heat from his two turbine engines. He jerked the helicopter to the right, hoping the missile would pass them by, but it exploded near their tail rotor. The Hind began to spin, as its stability was destroyed. The helicopter landed heavily in the water, fell to its side, and slid up onto a sand bank in the center of the river. The main rotor blades bent and ground to a halt as smoke began pouring from the downed craft.

Captain Vasnev hammered the release on his restraint system and threw open the hatch above his position. He glanced at Lieutenant Denikin as he slid down the side of his wrecked aircraft. The front glass of Denikin's position was covered with blood and the Lieutenant's head was twisted at an odd angle. The canopy was bullet resistant, but not bullet proof.

"I cannot complain. It has been a good day . . . until now. They won't like it, but they will take me prisoner. The Americans are civilized. They won't shoot an unarmed pilot," Captain Vasnev told himself, as he slowly removed his service pistol with two fingers and tossed it away.

He held his hands up and began walking away from his downed helicopter, wondering how deep the water was, and if he would have to swim across to the other side. The 30.06 round entered his skull just above the left eye and blew out the back of his head. He dropped like a stone, his blood gradually mixing with the rapidly flowing river.

.   .   .   .

"Damn it! I told you not to fire! He had his hands up! He was a prisoner of war!" yelled Captain MacLynn, as Jeremiah Jones ejected a brass casing from his Springfield M1903-A4 sniper rifle.

"Two tours . . . 47 confirmed kills, all with this rifle. That's not the first Russian I've shot. Did you know that Russian officers were commanding SAM sites in North Vietnam? There was a SA-2 site just across the border near Vinh. It was a mobile unit that had knocked down quite a few of our planes. They dropped me in to address the problem. Took me over a week to track them down. They were popping in and out of a series of caves. They would stay hidden until they were notified that American aircraft were nearby. I let them all come out and set up their equipment. Then I started at the back and picked them off one by one. The Russian officer commanding the battery was next to last. "

"I don't give a shit about your war stories! That man had surrendered. He was protected under the rules of the Geneva . . ."

"Tell that to the 20 million dead in California! Tell that to the dead men of your Division in Fairbanks and Hawaii! Tell that to what's left of your damn Company. That bastard over there killed half of your men. He needed killing . . . so I killed him! It's called war, and the gloves are off! We're fighting for our survival . . . Captain! Now, why don't you go see to your men. I'm going to check and make sure our explosives are still intact. Unless, of course, you want to sit here and wait for the Russians to show up. I'm sure they'd be glad to take me off your hands!" Jeremiah said, while slinging his rifle across his shoulder and walking away.

. . . .

The fourth bridge was blown 30 minutes later. What remained of Company A, 1st Battalion, 5th Infantry Regiment, 1st Brigade Combat Team, collected their dead and limped southward into Canada. Jeremiah Jones returned to Chicken. His war was just getting started. There were more Russians to kill . . .

CHAPTER 17

The White House
The Situation Room
Washington, DC
October 13, 0830 hours EST

"So, the evacuations have been totally completed? Yes or no?" asked President Beaumont, while staring at the map of Arkansas displayed on the wall to her right.

"Yes, Madam President. We have confirmed evacuation of over 729,000 people from Jefferson Country, where Pine Bluff is located, and the surrounding eight counties. The bulk of the evacuees were from Little Rock, almost 400,000," replied Brock Short, the Administrator of FEMA.

"That seems like a pretty low number. What's the radius of the evacuation?" the President asked.

"Twenty miles, Madam President. We're lucky. The target area has pretty low population density."

"General Munford, what is the minimum safe distance from one of these kinetic weapons?"

"Ten miles, Madam President. The Impactors are ceramic-coated steel rods with a mass of over 11 tons. They strike the ground at over 60,000 mph. The explosive force is equivalent to a 300-kiloton nuclear weapon. Each impactor would leave a crater over 900 feet across and 200 feet deep. From a distance, their entry into the atmosphere will look like a massive bolt of lightning."

"Dr. Wolf, these . . . impactors are irreplaceable. Are you sure it will take both?" the President asked.

"Based on the information provided . . . yes, Madam President. It will take both. I don't think we have a choice. My seismic models are predicting a rupture within 48 hours. We have to act!"

"General Munford, are we prepared to implement this plan?"

"Yes, Madam President. The Kraken is in geosynchronous orbit 300 miles above Pine Bluff. Once you give the order to commence firing, the impactors will arrive in a little over three minutes. They will be 20 seconds apart."

"Aircraft?"

"None will be allowed within 500 miles of the area, Madam President," said Brock Short.

The President turned, stared at Dr. Wolf, and asked, "Doctor Wolf . . . you're absolutely sure about this?"

Janice felt every eye in the room staring at her as she said, "Yes, Madam President. If we don't do this, the dike below Pine Bluff will give way and the Reelfoot Rift will rupture the entire continent. We will split open from the Great Lakes to the Gulf of Mexico . . ."

President Clarisse Beaumont sighed and looked around at the somber faces in the Situation Room.

"Any more comments?" she asked, while looking at each person. Half of them were terrified. The other half were skeptical, but too cautious to comment.

"No? Then, General Munford, you have my permission to contact the USS Kraken and proceed."

"Yes, Madam President," the Joint Chief of Staff replied, as he opened a direct link to General Crowley, commanding officer of the USS Kraken.

"Lieutenant General Crowley! General Munford here in the Situation Room. The President has authorized the strike on Pine Bluff, Arkansas. Please, proceed as planned."

. . . .

USS Kraken
300 miles above Pine Bluff, Arkansas

"Understood, Sir! We will commence firing in approximately five minutes!" replied Lieutenant General Archie Crowley, from atop his command position.

The General Quarters alarm boomed through every speaker on board the gargantuan triangular-shaped space carrier. Every crew member rushed to their assigned battle station.

"General, between you and me, I hope these scientists and politicians know what the hell they're doing. We're at war with the Russians. The Chinese still have viable military resources, and we're firing our last two shots at our own country," said Colonel Larry Kerchee, the Executive Officer, while standing beside Lieutenant General Crowley.

"Are you questioning the judgement of our civilian leadership, Colonel?"

"Well, you know me, General. Even when I was a Plebe at the Space Academy, and you were a Fourth Year, I always had that questioning attitude."

"Yeah, and I remember jacking your ass up over your 'questioning attitude'. Do you need a refresher, Colonel Kerchee?"

"Negative, Sir! We're all prepared to execute the assigned mission. The degree of required accuracy is problematic, but we'll do the best we can."

"Damn! It's like threading a needle from 300 miles. They want us to hit an exact coordinate within 30 feet! Twice!"

"Yes, General . . . twice! I'm not sure that's feasible. Our simulations show plus or minus 200 yards. Our mass drivers aren't sniper rifles."

"I'm aware of that, Colonel, and I informed General Munford of our concerns. Nonetheless, we have our orders . . ."

"General Crowley, mass drivers are at 80 percent charge. We will be ready to commence firing in 90 seconds. Target coordinates confirmed. Twenty second spread between shots," said Lieutenant Colonel Patricia Howell, seated at her console one level below the command platform.

"Very well, Colonel Howell! Commence firing when ready!" ordered LTG Crowley, while reopening the link to the Situation Room.

"Madam President, we will commence firing in . . . 73 seconds. Do we still have your permission?"

"Yes, General Crowley . . . you have my permission," replied President Beaumont, suddenly realizing that she would be the first president to open fire on US soil since Abraham Lincoln.

.   .   .   .

Pine Bluff, Arkansas
0742 hours CST

Three days ago, the big news in town was Malcomb Tombs scoring 27 points on 10-of-15 shooting and grabbing 12 rebounds to lead Arkansas-Pine Bluff by Texas Southern 104-84. The people were awoken early the next morning by the sound of sirens. Soldiers and police were pounding on their doors, telling them they had to leave their homes . . . and never come back.

Today, it was a beautiful morning in Pine Bluff. The sky was mostly clear, and it was going to reach 72 degrees, perfect for mid-October. But now, Pine Bluff stood empty. The door to Country Donuts on North Blake Street was locked. The sweet aroma that brought people from all over town was absent for the first time in years. The Bible study group that always met on Tuesday mornings at Mt. Nebo Missionary Baptist Church on West 2nd Avenue was also absent. Pine Bluff High School on West 11th Avenue, home of the Fighting Zebras, was empty and silent. The only sounds in the small town were from a few stray dogs that wondered where all the people had gone . . .

. . . .

The precise aiming point provided by Dr. Janice Wolf, was just north of Pine Bluff. The First Hole of the Harbor Oaks Golf Club was a Par 4, 383 yards. There was a huge sand trap right at the front of the green. Club members called it the 'Devil's Pit'. There was an active petition to have the sand trap moved to the left of the green or removed completely. Many a triple bogey had occurred at that hole. At 0743 hours CST, the first impactor landed in the 'Devil's Pit' and resolved the issue. Twenty seconds later, the second impactor landed 30 yards away, in what had been the fairway. Five seconds after the twin impacts, Pine Bluff, Arkansas . . . ceased to exist. The combined plumes rose to over 40,000 feet. The blast was heard in New Orleans, Boston and Chicago, and felt even further away.

Deep below, the Reelfoot Rift fault's southern extension was compressed and stabilized, as Dr. Wolf had predicted. But the strain on the continent persisted, and Gaia, Mother Earth . . . would eventually have her way. She always did . . . always . . .

CHAPTER 18

USS North Carolina
Eastern Pacific Ocean
October 13, 1745 hours UTC

"Congratulations, Captain! We've reached 800 feet and no leaks! She's still as tight as a drum!" said Lieutenant Commander O'Teul, as she shook the hand of Captain North.

"That's our fourth dive, XO, and the deepest one yet! We're still seaworthy and ready for combat. We'll reach our assigned location just after midnight. Then we search for our two wayward aircraft carriers," Captain North replied.

"I heard they're calling what's left New California," said Lieutenant Bottom, while standing behind his sonar operators.

"Lieutenant Bottom! Stay on mission. We need to . . ."

"Captain . . . I lost them all . . . my family! I never . . ."

"XO, you have Command! Lieutenant Bottom, please come with me," Captain North said, as he guided the young officer out of the Control Center and back toward his quarters.

"Come in, Lieutenant Bottom . . . have a seat. We need to talk!" the Captain said, while shutting the door to his cabin.

"They're all dead . . . all of them. My parents were in San Francisco. Two brothers . . . three sisters . . . their families, all in LA and San Diego . . . all gone. My family has been in California since 1822. I read the survivor lists, hoping to see a name . . . anyone, but they're all gone!"

"Charlie, listen to me. Those reports are all preliminary. There are hundreds of thousands of people in refugee camps all over the west. It will be months before the lists are even close to accurate. Even then, people will keep showing up. We all had family and friends in California."

"Your wife is alive. I saw her name. She . . ."

"I know. I saw the list, but our oldest son is missing. We all have to wait this out and pray they'll be okay. This will destroy you if you let it! Charlie, we still have a mission. I need you. I depend on you. These young men and women are as scared and worried as we are. They all have missing family. But we must set an example. We're at war, and we are their leaders."

A soft rapping on the door broke the tension of the moment.

"Enter!"

"Sorry, Captain, but the XO says we have another sub on sonar. She wants your . . ." the sailor began, as Captain North and Lieutenant Bottom rushed out of the cabin.

"XO! What do you have? Where away?" Captain North asked, as he and Lieutenant Bottom walked into the Control Center.

"We're 112 miles due south of San Clemente island . . . or where it used to be . . . depth 810 feet. We have indication of another submarine at . . ."

"Make that two, Ma'am! We have indication of another sub!" said Petty Officer Four Audrey Poole, from her sonar position in the Control Center.

"Details, Lieutenant Bottom!"

"Yes, Captain! One minute!" Lieutenant Bottom replied, as he sat down at an empty console and studied the data.

"Two subs . . . Russian . . . Akula Class . . . one's the Kuzbass, an early model, built in 1991. The other one . . . the Gepard. It's a newer model, 2001. It's supposed to be in the Atlantic, part of the Russian Northern Fleet. They were both upgraded in 2015. Our sonar database is pretty accurate, Sir!"

"Bearing, depth and range, Lieutenant Bottom?"

"Bearing . . . 3-1-0, depth . . . 6-5-0, range 22 miles, Captain. But, that's an estimate. There's still an enormous amount of seismic noise."

"That's for both subs?" asked Lieutenant Commander O'Teul.

"Yes Ma'am, they're no more than a mile apart, same depth," replied Lieutenant Bottom.

"Sir, they're starting to rise . . . pretty quickly, too!" said Petty Officer Poole.

"She's right, but it's only one of them. I think somebody's going up for a look around," said Lieutenant Bottom.

"Captain, could they be looking for the same thing we are?" asked Lieutenant Commander O'Teul.

"Why two subs? The Russians don't hunt in pairs," said Captain North.

"Sir, another thing . . . if we can hear them . . ." Lieutenant Bottom began.

"XO, bring the boat to hover. We probably sound like a garbage truck driving around the neighborhood," ordered Captain North.

"Bring the boat to hover! Aye, Sir!"

"We can't fight this the regular way, not in this condition. I have to do this differently," thought Captain North.

"Lieutenant Bottom, let's go look at the topographic maps of this area. I'm looking for something in particular. An Army tanker would call it a hull defilade position."

"Hull what, Sir?"

CHAPTER 19

Yukon Wild Adventure Tours
Alaska Highway
20 Miles West of Whitehorse
Yukon Territory, Canada
October 13, 2115 hours PST

The large cabin sat half a mile off the two-lane Alaska Highway. A small red and white sign beside the mailbox said 'Yukon Wild Adventure Tours' with a white arrow pointing down a dirt road that disappeared in the dense forest of Alaskan Yellow Cedar. The cabin was large, two floors, with an ample front porch. Three outbuildings held everything from canoes to tents, even enough firewood for a long Canadian winter. The tourist season had dried up after the Great Quake. People were scared, and scared people didn't go on vacation. Now the Russians were coming . . .

"Do you believe this order? What the hell do they expect us to accomplish?" asked Luke Desilits, the youngest and newest member of the 4th Canadian Ranger Patrol Group (CRPG).

"Let me read it. Then Jock can tell us what this means!" said Barry Todoschuk, as he picked up the message and read it aloud.

"Proceed west up Highway 1 to Beaver Creek near the Alaskan border. Report on the presence of any foreign Russian troops. Determine numbers and composition. Report findings to 3rd Division Headquarters, Edmonton."

"Beaver Creek is over 250 miles from here!" said Alison Toews, another member of the 4th CRPG.

"Listen, all of you! The brass at Edmonton want us to scout, not fight the Russians. From everything we've heard, the Russians are almost through carving up Alaska. Their next stop is Canada . . . our country!" replied Sergeant Jock Ivan, the only member of the six-person patrol group who was Regular Force.

The Canadian Rangers were the eyes and ears of the Canadian military in the vast and sparsely populated regions of the north and far west. They were also the subject matter experts on survival in the brutal wilderness that made up most of Canada. They operated in small, mixed-race and mixed-gender patrols, armed only with the Colt Canada C19 bolt action rifle. They were all volunteers, but not considered combat troops.

"We're just in the way. The Russians are not interested in Canada. They're headed for the US!" said Luke.

"Don't be an idiot, Luke! Canada has been hiding under the American umbrella since World War II. Why do you think our military is so small?" replied Jilian Chubak, the oldest member of the group.

"Exactly! Small! We're nothing but a pothole to them!"

"Listen to me, Luke! You can walk out that door right now and head back home. I'm the only full-time soldier here. The rest of you are volunteers. You're here because you want to be here. The same goes for all of you. I can't make you stay. I can't make you obey this order from Edmonton. The Russians are invading Canada. We've been ordered to track them. I want a show of hands. Who's still a member of the 4th Canadian Ranger Patrol Group, and who's heading back to the house to hide?" asked Jock.

"Hey, do we get to vote, too?" asked Liz Rushaven, as she and her husband sat to one side of the room by the fireplace.

"Liz, this is none of our business. We're tour guides, not soldiers or rangers," said Rainer Rushaven, her husband and co-owner of 'Yukon Wild Adventure Tours'.

The Rangers had chosen Adventure Tours as a training mission site for an infantry Company of 3rd Division. The couple provided canoes and expertise in maneuvering on rivers and streams. All that had been cancelled when the Russians invaded Alaska, but the patrol had been ordered to stay put.

"She's right, Rainer, you're not military or ranger. You have no obligation . . ." Jock began.

"Yeah, but we're Canadians. Are we supposed to just sit here and do nothing to defend our country?" Liz asked, while staring at her husband.

"Liz, we're just two people . . ."

"Yeah, and there sit six more people! That makes eight! I'm just as good a tracker as you, and I can shoot a damn sight better! I'll be damned if I'm going to sit by this fireplace and do nothing while our country is invaded!"

"Listen, all of you! I'm the only one in this room with a legal obligation to obey this order. The rest of you can do what you want. But I have to know where you stand. Now, raise your hand if you're still in," Jock said, as he raised his right hand.

Five more hands were raised, some more reluctantly than others.

"Liz, Rainer, I've known you both for over ten years. I can swear you in as rangers, but that means if you follow me, you obey my orders. We're not hunting Russians. We're going to track them and report what we see."

Liz stared at her husband, then raised her right hand. Rainer sighed, looked at Liz, and slowly raised his hand.

"Woman, if you get me killed, I will come back and haunt you. Just so you know," Rainer said, as his wife leaned over and kissed him on the cheek.

"All right, the report also said there was a lot of fighting at Big Delta. American troops were fighting a delaying action, blowing bridges, and then pulling out and heading south. If the Russians are heading toward the US, they have to come down this way. The

Alaskan Highway is the only way south for large vehicles. I'm guessing that most of the satellites are getting destroyed. That's why they need 'eyes on the ground', " Jock said.

"Yeah, been a lot of 'shooting stars' the last few nights!" Liz said, as she and Rainer moved their chairs over to the large rectangular table.

"We'll leave here and head west to Haynes Junction. That's a little over 75 miles. We can get there before midnight," Jock said.

"You want to leave tonight?" Rainer asked.

"I want to be out of here within the hour. We have three vehicles. They need to all be gassed up. Liz, if you have any extra firearms and ammunition, I want to see what you've got. We aren't looking for trouble, but we still have to be prepared to fight. We were only issued 40 rounds of 7.62 ammunition for these C19s. So, if you have more, it would be appreciated."

At 2300 hours the three vehicles of the 4th Canadian Ranger Patrol Group-Reinforced, headed west up the Alaska Highway . . .

CHAPTER 20

The White House
The Situation Room
Washington, DC
October 14, 0230 hours EST

"Madam President, you must get some sleep! If you want to stay in the Situation Room, I can have a bed set up in one of the side offices," said Chief of Staff Rick Dunlevy, as he shook the president's shoulder.

"I wasn't asleep, Rick. I was just resting my eyes. Would you please get me some coffee?" President Beaumont asked, while straightening her jacket.

"General Munford, what is the . . . where is General Munford?" the President asked, as she stared at an Air Force officer sitting in his position.

"He's asleep, Madam President. I'm Lieutenant General Ian Lancaster. I have authorization to act in his stead.

"How long have I been . . . resting my eyes?"

"Approximately 15 minutes, Madam President. We've all been trying to be as quiet as possible. I was told you've been up over 40 hours. General Munford said you were the most stubborn woman he'd ever met. He meant that as a compliment, by the way," General Lancaster said.

"I bet he did. Now why am I seeing a few blank screens where my satellite images were?"

"Madam President, it seems that the Chinese weren't the only nation with anti-satellite capabilities. The Russians are systematically attacking our satellites over the Pacific and Western United States."

"They're blinding us?"

"They're trying. We are moving assets to cover the area and moving other assets to provide protection."

"Protection? What assets?"

"A flight of three Dorys has been sent from the USS Kraken, Madam President. The Russians are using their own orbital platforms, some of which have been dormant for years, and sending them on intercept courses with our satellites. The Dorys have the capability of tracking multiple targets at the same time. The details of their defensive coverage are being worked out as we speak. If this is all the Russians have, we'll put an end to our losses within the next few hours. "

"Do we have replacement satellites available to launch?"

"We had three at Vandenberg Air Force Base in California. Unfortunately . . ."

"Don't tell me . . . they no longer exist."

"The base still exists, but the launch facilities were wrecked during the Great Quake. We're looking to see if any of the equipment can be salvaged and moved to another location. Replacing the trained personnel is another matter. We're working with NASA. They have a lot of people in and around Houston. We're even looking at retirees with the proper skill sets we need."

"Is there anything I can do? Anyone I need to talk to?"

"Madam President, with all due respect, you need to get out of this bunker. We know how to fight a war. That's what the American people expect of us. That's what we've been trained to do. What we can't do is lead the nation. That's your job, and people are afraid."

"You're pretty outspoken for a Lieutenant General. Are you trying to tell me how to do my job?"

118

"No, Madam President. I'm just an American citizen who happens to be wearing a uniform. This citizen is asking his president to open her eyes and realize that our country is falling apart. After this last strike in Arkansas, the media was floating the idea that the government was attacking America. That, maybe, the government was under the control of the Russians."

"That's absurd!"

"Completely! But like I said, people are scared. They believe the last thing they hear. We'll win this war against the Russians, but I don't know if we'll still be a country after the war is over."

Clarisse rubbed her eyes, then stared at the young Lieutenant General.

"Here's your coffee, Madam President," Rick said, as he set the steaming mug on her right.

"Rick, I'm going upstairs and get a few hours sleep. Then I'm going over to the Capitol Building and talk to people. Make sure the media knows I'm going to be out and about."

"Yes, Madam President," Rick said, and with a gesture, had Secret Service personnel at her side.

President Beaumont stood up and began to walk away. Everyone in the room was on their feet. She paused and turned toward Lieutenant General Lancaster.

She nodded and quietly said, "Thank you!", then walked away.

. . . .

The Southwest Steps
The Capitol Building
0830 hours EST

"Madam President, there have been reports that the attack on Arkansas was at your order. Why are you attacking the American people?" asked Zane Davies of CNN.

"That is an absurd question. An explanation of the strike was released to the press yesterday. I'm here today to refute such blatantly inaccurate reporting."

"So, we're supposed to believe some crazy story about the continent cracking in two?"

"Zane, try being a professional for a change. Do some research. Talk to Dr. Janice Wolf at USGS Headquarters. She was the discoverer of this threat to the country. A threat which has been negated thanks to the actions of this administration. Next!"

"Madam President, how can you account for the disproportionate number of people of color who have been impacted by recent events?" asked Monique Carter of MSNBC News.

"The last time I checked . . . the Great Quake, as the media has decided to term the attack on the United States by the People's Republic of China, did not discriminate. Tens of millions have died, and you dishonor their deaths by seeking to tear apart the unity we so desperately need. Next!"

"Madam President! Candice Murray, FOX News! The disaster of the Great Quake, initiated by the Chinese, has been followed by the Russian invasion of Alaska. There are also reports of Russian aggression in eastern Europe. Is this the start of the Third World War?"

"Governments aren't in the habit of assigning titles to world events. We leave that to the media and historians. But, yes, the ongoing conflicts are of a global nature, and they seem to be spreading. Our bases in the Far East are under attack. There have been . . ."

"Madam President! Our satellite communications with our affiliates and reporters in that area have eroded over the last few days. What is happening? Are you restricting our access to these areas?" asked Natalie Davis of CNN.

"Am I? There is an ongoing battle above our heads as we speak. War is now being conducted outside the atmosphere of this planet. First the Chinese, and now, the Russians are systematically

120

attacking the satellites that are essential to the defense of this nation, and communications with your news affiliates overseas."

"What are you doing to defend our access to ongoing events?" asked Monique Carter of MSNBC News.

"Ms. Carter, what I'm going to do is defend the people of the United States. Your access to 'ongoing events' is not going to be restricted by me or my administration. We are at war, and the American people need to see that. That's your job. But, for the foreseeable future, the days of instant access to events around the world are over. The satellite assets that remain are being prioritized for fighting in defense of this country and our allies. The communication satellites of the major networks are being targeted because the Russians know that we can use your equipment to gain information useful to us in conducting this war."

"Madam President, are we losing this war?" asked Candice Murray of Fox News.

President Beaumont paused as she stood in a light drizzle on the steps of the Capitol Building. Dozens of reporters stood on the steps below her. Hundreds of people were gathering around them. Many were staring at their cell phones. Cameras were beaming her words across the world. At least, to the areas that still had access.

"Do I tell them the truth? Half of our military assets have been destroyed. No, I can't! The Russians are listening, but they already know what the Chinese accomplished. What do I tell them? Was this whole thing a mistake?" Clarisse asked herself, suddenly longing for the warm security of the Situation Room bunker.

Then she raised her head and looked down the National Mall. The Lincoln Memorial stood in the distance. She thought of the 16th President of the United States and all that he had endured. Then she began a speech that would be talked about and hotly debated in the years to come.

"In 1865, President Lincoln was elected for a second term. The Civil War was almost over as he stood on these steps and addressed the American people. The war had gone on far longer, and been more costly in blood and treasure, than any of them had imagined four years earlier. The nation had been torn apart, and he was desperate to restore a sense of collective unity. I stand here now, as a new president, appointed to this office, not elected. None the less, I am President of the United States. Our current war has just started, and already the cost has been beyond imagining. I have sought out Lincoln's words and his wisdom over the past few weeks. The speech he gave after his second inauguration ended with these words: *'With malice toward none, with charity for all, with firmness in the right as God gives us to see the right, let us strive on to finish the work we are in, to bind up the nation's wounds, to care for him who shall have borne the battle and for his widow and his orphan, to do all which may achieve and cherish a just and lasting peace among ourselves and with all nations.'*

Clarisse paused and glanced back down at the crowd below her. "My favorite photograph of President Lincoln was taken in April of 1865, ten days before his assassination. It was the eyes. The eyes that had seen so much death and destruction. I thought I understood what he was saying, but I was wrong. I understood nothing. But now . . . now I see through his eyes, and I understand the desperation he felt as the Union threatened to crumble. We are at a similar tipping point," Clarisse said, and paused.

"But, Madam President . . ." began Zane Davies of CNN.

"Be quiet! Let her speak!" said a tall, bearded man who stood beside him.

"I will not lie to you. I cannot lie to you. We the People are in great danger. The Peoples Republic of China planted 50 nuclear weapons across our country. We found 49, but the last one was detonated and caused fearful destruction in North Carolina. That same foreign power attempted to destroy us by detonating the two largest nuclear bombs ever created. We were only successful in stopping one. The Great Quake was caused by the second weapon. The Chinese have been paid back in full. Their government and military no longer represent a threat to the United States or the world. Our losses on the West Coast have been . . . horrendous. But now, we face another foreign power that is attempting to destroy us. The Russians, led by a dictator attempting to re-create what President Reagan called 'The Evil Empire', have invaded Alaska," Clarisse said, then paused.

"I told them I wouldn't lie. They need to know everything," she thought.

"Alaska is lost, and the Russians are heading south," she began, as the media erupted once more.

"Madam President! Have you led us into defeat? You're not even elected!" said Monique Carter of MSNBC.

"Be quiet, you fool of a woman! Listen to her! She's the only chance you have!" the tall, bearded man said.

Monique glared at him and began to reply when the President started again.

"We will never be defeated as long as we are willing to fight for what we believe in. Our Constitution and our Bill of Rights are more than yellowing pieces of paper! They represent what we are as a people, and what we want to become. The Founders knew their work was incomplete, but they gave us a foundation for progress. As the centuries have passed, we have corrected many of the initial flaws they left us with. We have fought amongst ourselves, sometimes literally. But in the end, we have stayed within the system the Founders created, passed new laws, amended the Constitution to make this a better nation. When outside powers threatened our very existence, we banded together and grew stronger as a result. This is another one of those times! These recent attacks, these attempts to tear down everything we have built as a people, are a greater threat than any we have ever had to endure. But . . . I believe . . . I know . . . I have faith . . . that We the People will rise from the wreckage we find ourselves in. One step . . . one step together as a unified people, is what we need. Once we take that first step, each one becomes easier. The Russian leader is a thug, a bully, another dictator who believes we are a weak people, but he is wrong! When I was young, I went fishing with my father. But the 'fish' we were after had legs, were over ten feet long and weighed 800 pounds. These creatures outlived the dinosaurs, and yet we hunted them with a hook and a small caliber pistol. I was terrified, but my father touched the side of my forehead, then touched the center of my chest, and said, 'Never forget that your real strength lies here and here!' That is true for all of us, for all Americans, for all people who refuse to bow down to the bully, the tyrant. As long as we refuse to quit, as long as we refuse to bow to a supposed conqueror, we will never lose. We will always remain We the People . . . the Americans!"

The crowd roared their approval. Even the cynics of the media felt their hearts quicken and their hands shake as her words impacted their minds and souls.

Monique turned, looking for the tall, bearded man. She felt a need to talk to him, but he had disappeared.

"He was so odd, so old fashioned. His clothes . . . like he had stepped out of the . . . no, that's not possible. That's . . . that's just . . . silly!" she told herself, as she spun and looked for him.

"He was so tall and lean. A scraggly black beard . . . and his eyes . . . so sad, yet so alive . . ."

Clarisse Beaumont, President of the United States, born and raised in Belle Chasse, Louisiana, stood on the steps of the US Capitol, having delivered the greatest speech she would ever give. She wasn't sure where it had come from, but she felt surrounded . . . not by the living, but by the spirits of those who had come before her. Others who had felt the massive weight and responsibility of the Presidency. She felt her knees buckle, then felt a strong arm lift her to her feet. She glanced up into the eyes of a man she knew only as 'Sam', one of her Secret Service bodyguards. Tears rolled down his cheeks as he fought to control his emotions.

"We've got you, Madam President. We've got your back!"

124

CHAPTER 21

USS North Carolina
Eastern Pacific Ocean
October 13, 2345 hours UTC

Captain Augustus North leaned over the plotting table in the Control Room. He swept a fingertip over the digital map of the ocean bottom, expanding and contracting the image, studying the details of the terrain.

" The Fortymile Bank . . . hull defilade . . . nice job, Lieutenant Bottom . . . very nice job. This is exactly what I had in mind. The main peak is 377 feet down, with a series of smaller peaks trailing to the south, " Captain North said, as Lieutenant Commander O'Teul leaned over the table and studied the area.

"Sir, you want us to set up here, somewhere on the north side of these peaks? Of course, that assumes the hills are still there and survived the quakes."

"Correct, XO! We're going to risk an active ping when we get to the location. That will give us a better idea of what the terrain looks like after the quakes."

"But, Sir! They'll hear us for sure if we go active," said Lieutenant Bottom.

"I hope so, Lieutenant. That's the bait. In our condition, we can't hunt them in the open like we did the Chinese boat. We make more noise going through the water than an old, World War II diesel sub. They'd be laughing while they killed us. We must lure them into a trap. We have to get them close before we fire. At least that's the plan."

Lieutenant Bottom and the XO stared at each other. They had learned that the tactics their Captain used weren't out of any textbook used at the Naval Academy, but they worked. So, they both nodded in agreement.

"We should be just north of Fortymile Bank in about 25 minutes, Captain," said Lieutenant Bottom.

"I'm going to be aft talking with our 'guests'. Let me know if anything changes," Captain North said, then turned and left the Control Room.

. . . .

Maintenance Bay

Nathan O'Malley stayed as busy as possible. The crew had been reluctant to let him touch any electrical equipment on the North Carolina, but there had been so many casualties, and his obvious knowledge was so great, they finally agreed to let him work on the repair of non-vital equipment. Master Chief Ingeram had made the final decision after observing the speed at which the man worked. The crew had given him the nickname 'Gizmo', because he could fix anything.

He was sitting at a work bench in maintenance when Captain North found him.

"Mr. O'Malley, you're up late. I haven't had a chance to talk to you or your Seal friends for a few days. I thought I'd check and see how you were doing," Captain North said, while sliding into a chair beside the work bench.

"I've found that it's better if I keep my hands . . . doing something . . . anything. If I were back home, I'd get drunk and stay drunk for a while," Nathan replied, while inspecting the threads on a component.

"I'm sorry about Mr. Padenko. I should have told him to strap in . . . I just . . ."

"Captain North . . . it was just his . . . I never thought he would . . . God, I miss him! You know, I really thought we were all going to die. When we found the cover plate over the drill tube welded shut, I knew we were screwed. I knew we couldn't get to that nuke. A few hours . . . just a few hours earlier, and I might have prevented all this. Millions of dead . . . and Jim was just one more. I feel like a useless failure."

"Listen . . . I didn't get you there on time. So that's on me. I've thought about it, but there's nothing more I could have done. I drove the crew and the boat as hard as possible. We spent a few extra hours in Pearl Harbor loading the CATs (Counter-Measure Anti-torpedo), but without them, we wouldn't have survived the attack by the Chinese sub. Would I have done things differently? No, I had to maximize our chances of survival. Maybe that was wrong. Maybe I should have focused more on getting you there faster, and not worried about my boat and crew. I don't know. I suppose I'll never know. What I do know is . . . you bear no responsibility for what happened. You were never given a chance. You had the courage to get on a mini sub with a bunch of Seals and assault a heavily defended drill platform. We didn't know the mission was doomed before you ever left. We just didn't know . . ."

"Here I am having a private pity party, thinking only about myself, and you have to keep going. You don't get to go crawl off and hide like I have."

"From what I hear, you've been a lot of help. Or, as the XO told me, you've got 'mad skills'. I guess that means you're good working with anything electrical or mechanical."

"I've fixed a few things. I think the Seals have been busy in their own way. Tremayne has been working with your corpsman. Brandon and Luis have been working with your Master Chief. He calls them 'NUB 1' and 'NUB 2' because they can't do anything but move stuff. They're like me, just trying to stay busy. I guess we've all lost friends."

"I'm sorry I couldn't get you off the boat, but there's really nowhere to go. Plus, I need your help. We're on our own. There aren't any functional ports on the West Coast or in Hawaii, so no replacements or resupply. The navy's command structure for the Pacific is gone. I'm taking orders from COMSUBLANT, out of Norfolk. We're on another mission, protecting two carriers that have floated away from San Diego. We will likely be in combat within the next day."

"Damn! More Chinese?"

"No, Russians! We've detected two subs, so far. They're like sharks smelling blood in the water. I imagine they'll sink any US vessel they come across. Somehow, we must stop them using a banged-up boat with half a crew."

"This is a piece off the forward sonar array on the sail. I guess I ought to get back to work," Nathan said, as he shook Captain North's hand.

"You do that, Mr. O'Malley. We only have about 70 percent sonar capability," Captain North replied, as he stood up and turned away.

"Hey, Captain, my friends call me Nathan!"

"Well, Nathan . . . thanks for listening."

"Do your friends call you Augustus?"

"No, they call me Captain or Captain North. Don't push your luck, Mr. O'Malley," Captain North replied with a smile, as he left the Maintenance Bay.

. . . .

The Control Room
October 14, 0030 hours UTC

"Depth 300 feet, Captain. We should be directly above the tallest peak of Fortymile Bank," said Lieutenant Commander O'Teul.

"Lieutenant Bottom, what's the latest plot on our Russian friends?" asked Captain North.

"One boat is located approximately 23.5 nautical miles on a bearing of 3-0-0. They have surfaced or are at periscope depth. The other boat has disappeared, or at least we can't find it, Captain."

"They haven't disappeared. They're hunting us. They probably have been tracking us as we plowed through the water. When did we first detect that boat, Lieutenant Bottom?"

"1745 hours . . . yesterday, Captain. That was . . . almost eight hours ago."

"One active ping, Lieutenant Bottom . . . just one."

"Sir . . . we'll see him, but he'll see us as well. Are you sure you want . . ."

"Lieutenant Bottom, one active ping!"

"Aye, Captain!"

The sound of an active sonar ping reverberated throughout the boat.

"XO, all stop! Start settling the boat. Do not blow tanks! Ease us down with the fore planes!"

"Aye, Captain!" Lieutenant Commander O'Teul said, as she rushed forward to the pilots.

"Lieutenant Bottom. Where is that Russian submarine?"

"Eight point two miles, Captain! He's on the same heading as before. He's closing in on us."

"No announcements! Pass the word . . . silent running, Master Chief!"

"Aye, Captain!" Master Chief Ingeram said, as he rushed from the Control Room.

"I shouldn't have left here. I needed this information ten minutes ago. Once again, a few minutes . . . a few hours, may make all the difference. Eight miles . . . how good is this Russian? He could be calculating a shot right now. We may already be dead and just not

realize it," Captain North thought, as the North Carolina began to settle toward the undersea peak below.

. . . .

K-419 Kuzbass
Eight miles south of Fortymile Bank

"What do you mean, they're gone?" asked Captain Taras Volkov, of the Russian Akula class submarine, Kuzbass.

"Captain, we have been tracking them for hours. A blind man with a stick could find this boat. It rattles. I'm not even sure what class it is. But suddenly, they're gone. They've gone completely silent," said Senior Lieutenant Kolya Mikhailov, the Sonar Officer.

"Have I been too cautious? We have been tracking this boat for hours. We are so close, and now the track fades away. Have I been played? How did they just disappear?" thought Captain Volkov.

"Senior Lieutenant Orlov, do we have a target lock on that boat? Yes or no?"

"Negative, Captain! The solution was close . . . another minute. What do we do?"

Captain Volkov turned away and began caressing the medal in his pants pocket. The Order of the Red Banner had been awarded to his grandfather after the battle of Kursk in 1943. His grandfather had commanded 20 T-34 tanks, part of the first defensive belt when the Germans attacked. They had faced off against the 505th Heavy Tank battalion, 50 German Tigers. Though vastly outgunned and out armored, they destroyed 12 Tigers. His grandfather had died while ramming an enemy tank. The award had come years later. Taras had been given the medal by his father as he lay dying from heavy metal poisoning. Progress in the Motherland demanded a high price from all its citizens.

"Are we still at eight knots?"

"Yes, Captain!"

"Proceed . . . close the range based on the last known position. A boat that noisy can't stay silent forever."

"Aye, Captain! Eight knots and silence!"

"Now I know how grandfather felt. It's the waiting. That's the hardest part. You must wait until the enemy reveal themselves. Then you charge and go for the throat," Captain Volkov thought, as he began studying the terrain charts of the local area.

"What is he up to, this American Captain? Why does his boat make such noise? All my information says their fleet is wrecked. Is his boat damaged or is he playing a game? I like games. I wonder if he plays chess? Should I let him see me . . . lure him into a mistake, or is he the cat and I'm the mouse?"

The sound of an active ping reverberated inside the Russian submarine.

"Captain! The American is targeting us!"

"Relax, Lieutenant Mikhailov! The American Captain and I have started a game of Cossacks and Thieves. He will hide, and I will seek to find him. He is sitting still in the water, luring me in. We will see how he reacts when the sword of the Cossack descends on the neck of the Thief.

· · · ·

USS North Carolina
0102 hours UTC

The boat creaked as it settled onto the underwater hillside known as Fortymile Bank, then lay still.

"Angle on the bow 19.5 degrees, Captain," said Lieutenant Commander O'Teul, as she braced herself against the upward tilt of the submarine.

"This is all or nothing. If he detects us sitting here, I've killed all these people," thought Captain North, as he slid over to Lieutenant Bottom on the port side of the Control Room.

"Any indications yet, Lieutenant?"

"No, Captain, but based on these readings, we're sitting between two peaks . . . in a gulley. We can only see a 40-degree arc straight ahead. We're blind to our port and starboard."

"But you can see straight ahead?"

"Yes, Captain!"

"XO, this is all going to happen very quickly. This is going to be at point blank range. Two Mark 48s . . . remove range limitations. I want them live the second they leave the boat."

"Aye, Captain!"

. . . .

K-419 Kuzbass
Three miles south of Fortymile Bank
0120 hours UTC

"Where are they, Grandfather? Submarines don't just disappear," Captain Volkov asked himself.

"Lieutenant Mikhailov, where is the American? This is not a sci-fi movie. He didn't teleport away!"

"Yes, Captain! We are listening."

"Lieutenant Borisov, have we reached those peaks yet?"

"We are approximately zero-point-five miles south of the first peak. They are coming up on our starboard side, Captain," replied Lieutenant Borisov, the Navigation Officer.

"Show me these 'peaks', Lieutenant Borisov," said Captain Volkov, as he left sonar and walked over to the plotting table.

"We are at this location, Captain. The terrain is beginning to slope upward toward this line of small hills. They are called the Fortymile Bank because they are 40 miles off the coast."

Captain Volkov stared at the topographic map of the summits as he thought, *"What game are you playing, my friend? We should be able to see you. I think you are wounded. What would I do if I were in your position?"*

"Captain, we are passing the first peak," said Lieutenant Mikhailov.

Captain Volkov stared at the map and thought of his grandfather. He pulled the medal from his pocket. The red and white silk ribbon was worn and faded. The medal bore a red enameled flag with the words 'Workers of the World Unite!' The hammer and sickle in the center were almost illegible from his rubbing the medal over the many years he had carried it.

"Dedushka (Grandfather), what am I missing?" Captain Volkov asked, as he stared at the medal and imagined himself inside a T-34 tank as the monstrous German Tigers came ever closer.

"How difficult that must have. You were very brave to have waited in your hull down position until the enemy came into a range where your gun could kill him . . . shit!"

"Hard to port! Flank speed! Now, dammit! Now!" Captain Volkov shouted, as his officers stared at him.

The Akula class Kuzbass was 362 feet long and weighed 12,770 tons submerged. It began to accelerate toward its maximum speed of 32 knots as it turned away from Fortymile Bank.

·   ·   ·   ·

USS North Carolina
0124 hours UTC

"Captain!"

"I can see, XO! Fire torpedoes One and Two!"

The Virginia class submarine shuddered as two Mark-48 torpedoes leapt from the bow of the sub. Each torpedo was 19 feet long and carried a 650-pound warhead. They quickly reached their maximum speed of 55 knots and began to home in on the fleeing Russian submarine.

·   ·   ·   ·

"Captain! Torpedoes in the water! Range 3000 meters and closing rapidly," yelled Lieutenant Mikhailov.

"Stay calm, Lieutenant! We have a few seconds to act. Lieutenant Orlov, fire counter measures. Lieutenant Borisov, take us deeper. Maintain this course."

"Aye, Captain!" came the replies.

. . . .

USS North Carolina

0127 hours UTC

"Captain! He turned sharply to port and accelerated. Did he see us?" asked Lieutenant Commander O'Teul.

"No . . . no, I don't think so. If he had seen us, he would have taken a shot. This captain is clever. He sensed or figured out the ambush. Set up two more torpedoes, XO. Send one wide to port and the other wide to starboard. He'll focus on the first two we fired. I want the second pair to slide in from either side. Get them away. Then reload all four tubes!" CAPTAIN North ordered.

"Yes, Captain! Reprogramming three and four for wide approach!" replied Lieutenant Commander O'Teul.

. . . .

K-419 Kuzbass

0130 hours UTC

"Range of enemy torpedoes, Lieutenant Mikhailov?" asked Captain Volkov.

"Fifteen hundred meters and closing, Captain! Countermeasures in the water," replied Lieutenant Mikhailov, as he felt his heart pounding in his chest.

"Where was he? Why couldn't we see him? He had to be below us . . . lying on the . . . " Captain Volkov thought, then smiled, as he remembered reading about the fixed positions his grandfather's tanks had built while awaiting the German attack.

"The American Captain settled his sub on the hill . . . on the backside, with his bow protruding upward. Then he just waited. I sprung the trap before he was ready. If we had been a kilometer closer . . ."

"Captain, the American has fired two more torpedoes!"

"Captain, the first torpedo has taken the countermeasure!" Lieutenant Mikhailov shouted, as the detonation of a nearby torpedo rocked the submarine.

"The second one, Lieutenant! Where is the second one?"

"Still tracking us, Captain!"

"Captain, what about the other two torpedoes?"

"One thing at a time! Hard to starboard! Go deeper! Flank speed! Second set of countermeasures! Now, Lieutenant!" said Captain Volkov.

The Kuzbass cut to starboard and dove deeper. The San Clemente Basin was to the west of the Fortymile Bank. The basin plunged to well over 6000 feet, far below the crush depth of the Akula class submarines.

"Do we have a location for the American submarine?"

"No, Captain! Too much noise from our countermeasures."

"Dammit! Where is the second torpedo?"

"Captain, 1400 yards! Dead astern!"

"Lieutenant Mikhailov, please count down the range to the American torpedo."

"But, Captain! We . . ."

"Count!"

"1100 yards . . . 950 . . . 800 . . . 700 . . . 500 yards!"

"Lieutenant Orlov! Full spread of noise simulation decoys! Hard to starboard and deeper!"

"Aye, Captain!"

Six MG-74 Korund noise simulation decoys were fired from external tubes. They imitated the extreme sound of a fleeing submarine. The second Mark 48 American torpedo was programmed to sort through such background noise. The standard Russian practice was to release two decoys at a time. The Mark 48 could sort through four, but not six.

The Kuzbass shook and the lights sputtered as the torpedo detonated 250 yards off their starboard side.

"Captain, we are at 2100 feet! Our crush depth is 2000!"

"Those are guidelines, Lieutenant Borisov. The Kuzbass is a tough Russian girl. I know what she can take," Captain Volkov replied.

The crew in the control room laughed or cheered, releasing some of their pent-up tension. Most of them had expected to be dead by now.

"Level off, Lieutenant Borisov. Lieutenant Mikhailov, where are the second pair of American torpedoes?"

"The noise, Captain. The background noise is still too . . . Shit! Torpedo at 800 yards . . . port side . . . 12 seconds to impact!"

"Emergency blow! Lieutenant Orlov . . . launch countermeasures . . . full spread!"

The Kuzbass lurched upward at speed, disappearing in a cloud of noisy countermeasures and discharged ballast. The Mark 48 detonated 400 yards below the rapidly ascending Russian submarine.

"Captain! The fourth . . ." Lieutenant Kolya Mikhailov began, as his eyes locked with his Captain's.

Captain Taras Volkov, veteran of 17 years of submarine service for the Russian Federation, clutched his grandfather's medal to his chest as the fourth Mark 48 torpedo struck the Kuzbass just aft of the engine room, and tore the submarine in two . . .

. . . .

USS North Carolina
0142 hours UTC

"Captain . . . sounds of a submarine breaking up," Lieutenant Bottom said, as he removed a set of headphones and smiled.

"XO, we'll stay where we are for 30 minutes. There is another Russian boat in the area. Keep the crew quiet. We'll sit and listen for a while. Good work, everyone! I'll be in my cabin," Captain North said, as he nodded toward his executive officer and left the Control Room.

CHAPTER 22

Central Intelligence Agency
Mission Center for Weapons and Counterproliferation
Office of Director Janet Davidson
Manassas, Virginia
October 14, 0845 hours EST

"Director, I know I asked for more training, but we're at war now. The Russians have invaded Alaska. They'll be in the US within a few weeks. There has to be something I can do to help!" said Amanda, as she paced in front of her boss's desk.

"My decision is final. Here's the address. They'll be expecting you at 1100 hours, sharp! Trust me! It would be prudent for you to be on time," replied Janet, as she slid a sticky note to the front of her desk.

"Krav Maga! What the hell is that?" Amanda asked, as she picked up the note.

"As I said, Agent Langford . . . do not . . . be late!"

. . . .

The Fighter's Garage
132 West Jefferson St
Falls Church, Virginia
1050 hours EST

Amanda drove slowly past the address, for the second time. She was wondering if this had all been a mistake.

"Who am I kidding? I'm five foot three, and 100 pounds on a bad day. Maybe I should just stick to learning how to shoot!"

Then she noticed two women leaving the building. One was rubbing her shoulder, but they were both laughing. They turned and walked two doors down into the brightly painted store front of 'Tea with Mrs. B'.

"Miranda would be shaking her head. Everything we went through, and I'm reluctant to walk into a training studio," Amanda said, admonishing herself as she pulled into a parking space, grabbed her gym bag and hopped out of her car.

The entry was labeled 'The Fighter's Garage'. She pushed open the door and walked up to the receptionist. The woman looked up at her as if judging her worthiness to walk into the front door of her establishment.

"Can I help you?" Basra Atkins asked.

"I've been referred here. My name is Amanda Langford. I was told you would be expecting me."

The woman rose from her chair behind the desk and looked into Amanda's eyes. Then she sighed as she walked around the counter, seemingly sizing up Amanda as she approached.

"She said you were small, but you look like you haven't eaten in a week. This will be a challenge," Basra said, as she walked up to Amanda.

"She's very small, but the scars . . . the eyes . . . this young woman has seen the wolf! She may even have been a wolf. But the wounds haven't healed . . . the wounds inside are still festering . . ."

"My name is Basra Atkins. This is my studio. Your boss, she is a friend of mine. She still comes here on occasion . . . for a refresher. Please follow me," Basra said, as she turned and walked toward a set of double doors.

"The locker room for women is on the left. Find an empty locker and provide your own lock. There are towels in the cabinet.

Your first lesson starts in five minutes. When you are dressed, come through that door," Basra, said, while pointing at a door at the end of the short hall.

The woman walked away, leaving Amanda staring at her back.

"Oh yeah, she's real chummy. Reminds me of Ms. Wilkins in high school gym class. We had to have one gym credit to graduate. She taught gymnastics. I hated it!" Amanda thought, as she entered the locker room.

Five minutes later she walked through the door at the end of the hall wearing shorts, t-shirt and sneakers. The training room was small, no more than 20 feet on a side. There were no windows. The walls were painted a bland, industrial white. A thick, blue mat filled most of the room. Basra was in the middle of the mat sparring with a man the size of Anthony, but more heavily muscled.

"Lesson number one, Ms. Langford . . . I demand punctuality. I told you to be here in five minutes. It has been six," Basra said, as she released the huge man from an arm lock and pointed at a clock on the wall.

"This is Karl Luther. He will be your sparring partner. Please step onto the mat."

Amanda's eyebrows rose as she looked at him, and then at Basra. As she walked toward the pair, the man seemed to grow even larger. He was wearing bright green, rubber body armor that extended from his crotch up to his shoulders. His head was covered in similar padding.

"Him? He must weigh 250 pounds!"

"Actually, 265. You don't get to pick your opponents, Ms. Langford, and this is your first lesson. If you have a choice between fighting and running away, what do you do?" Basra asked.

"If it's him, I'm running!"

"Good choice! Always avoid confrontation if possible. But what if you can't run away. He stands between you and any possible exit. What do you do?"

"If I have a gun, then I shoot him."

"No gun . . . what do you do?"

"Try to reason with him?"

Karl began laughing as he approached Amanda. One hand reached for her, the other was balled into a fist.

"I don't think he wants to talk. What do you do, Ms. Langford?"

Amanda began backing away.

"Karl, a demonstration!" Basra said.

Karl turned toward Basra and approached her in the same threatening manner.

"I teach Krav Maga, Ms. Langford. It was developed by Imre Lochtefeld, back in the 1930s. He was a Hungarian Jew, and those were dangerous times for people like him. Now, lesson number two! Men are arrogant. They will look at a woman like you and assume you are weak and helpless. Use that to your advantage!" Basra said, as she swept under Karl's arm and kicked him in the groin.

"Krav Maga is about ending a fight quickly. There is no dancing around or posing. This martial art is controlled street fighting. You get your opponent on the ground and finish him. By finish him, I mean kill him. If he is dead, he is no longer a threat."

Karl had doubled over after the kick. Basra finished him with an elbow to the temple. Both blows had been delivered with full force. Karl toppled over and lay still. The entire process had taken less than five seconds.

"Now what? Kill him with a blow to the nose? Drive the bone into his brain?" Amanda asked.

Karl laughed as he sat up and removed his head gear.

"Oh, my head is still spinning from that elbow! But you watch too many Hollywood movies. The nose can't be driven into the brain, but the skull at the temple is thin. That is the weak point!" Karl said, as he tapped the side of his head and stood up.

Basra paced in front of the pair, talking to herself.

Karl pointed at her as he said, "Basra's right, you know. Any man who would attack you is going to see an easy mark. You will get one chance to use that against him. The move that she used against me can save your life. A good kick in the balls will put any man down. Then you either finish him or run."

"Finish him! Never leave an opponent breathing! If they are dead, they will never come back to get you!" Basra said, as she continued to pace.

"Except in your dreams . . . isn't that right, Basra?" Karl asked, as he placed his arm around her shoulders.

"I can take my dreams. At least I'm still breathing and vertical. The dead have nothing," Basra replied, as she brushed off his arm and continued pacing.

"Now, Ms. Langford, it's your turn! Karl, attack her!"

Amanda spent the next 20 minutes being grabbed, choked and thrown to the mat. She had managed to kick Karl twice. Both were feeble attempts that wouldn't have hurt him, with or without the padding. She was sitting in the middle of the mat exhausted, watching the sweat drip from her nose and puddle on the mat. Karl was sitting to one side, looking at his cell phone. Basra was pacing again.

"Karl was a mistake. She's so tiny and she has no instinct for this. I'm 5'8" . . . closer to her size. I'm going to have to teach her personally," Basra thought, as she stared at Amanda.

"Karl, I'll take it from here. Ms. Langford, on your feet!"

"I need a break!"

"If someone is trying to kill you, are they going to stop when you get winded? On your feet! Now! Janet told me you weren't a quitter. I'm beginning to think she was mistaken. You look like dog who has been beaten into submission!"

Amanda knew she was being goaded, but the words still hurt. She struggled to her feet and stretched her tired muscles.

"Good, your pride is still there. We will take this one move at a time, and we will do it slowly. We have 40 minutes left in this session. If I see some progress, the lessons will continue. If I think you're wasting my time, this will be your last lesson. Understood?"

142

When Amanda nodded, Basra said, "Good! Now we begin again."

Forty minutes later, Amanda left the studio with a smile, after scheduling classes for every Tuesday, Thursday and Saturday. It was noon and she was starving.

. . . .

Amanda's Apartment
1240 hours EST

Amanda lowered herself onto the sofa and groaned. She hadn't been this sore since the first time she and Marissa had exited the galleria on La Palma.

"Crap! I don't know which was worse, getting choked by Karl, or kicked and tossed by Basra," she said, as she pulled the cork from the bottle of Chardonnay and filled a large wine glass to the brim.

The buzzing of her cell phone distracted her after the first deep gulp.

"All I want to do is drink, eat and then sleep. Who is bothering me?" she asked, as she leaned over and picked the cell phone up from her coffee table.

"Amanda, Director Davidson here. How did the class go?"

"That woman and her SS henchman beat the shit out of me. Are you happy now?" Amanda laughed, as she picked up the glass and slid more of the wine down her throat.

"Basra can be a taskmaster, but what she teaches will keep you alive at some time in the future. But I called about something else. I forwarded an encrypted file to your laptop. I want you to look at the data and give me your opinion."

"Great! When do you need it?"

"Tomorrow morning. Be in my office at 8 AM sharp!"

Amanda stared at her cell phone as the call was disconnected.

"Well, isn't that peachy! Let's see . . . the last time I got one of these mystery assignments, we found 50 nuclear weapons inside the United States. I wonder what this one is?" Amanda said, as she threw her cell phone on the sofa and looked around for her laptop.

She saw it sitting on a side table beside her front door and groaned.

"Maybe a hot soak, more wine, and I'll study the files," she said, as she forced herself upright and staggered toward the laptop.

1 hour later

Amanda lay back in the tub, only her face showing through the steam and scented bubbles. The file had been transferred to her iPad.

"What am I missing? Still ten more files to look at," Amanda said, while holding the iPad just above the foam.

"Hmm, what's this file? A list of component manufacturers . . . and this one is the same company that made a truck-mounted laser for the Russian Army. So what? It'll be another ten years before these systems can take on anything substantial. The systems are inefficient and would have to be upscaled, and . . . wait . . . these components are different. Is that a typo? Cylindrical glass three meters long and half a meter in diameter? Thirty of them?"

She sat up, opened the built-in stand for the iPad, and rested it beside the tub. She glanced at the empty glass and the half empty bottle. Then decided she'd had enough wine.

"Okay, Janet gave me this stuff, but I know other agents and analysts have looked at this data. Why me? What did they miss? Oh, they don't know what these are . . . these oversized cylinders. I need to do some research on weaponized lasers . . ."

An hour later Amanda was sitting in her bed surrounded by reference books, printouts, two iPads, a laptop and the remains of leftover Chinese takeout from the day before.

"Solid-state weapons require cooling. Cylinders have been discarded for slabs. Why would the Russians make a cylinder this size? Massive power source . . . kilowatts . . . no, megawatts! But the glass would deform. Slabs can displace the heat more efficiently. So why these huge cylinders?" she said, while closing her eyes and rubbing one hand through her short hair.

"My hair was so curly when I was young. I used to cry every morning before school. Everyone had straight hair, but me. Mama would just laugh as she brushed the tangles out of my hair. I miss you, Mama! I miss our talks, your wisdom. No . . . I can't go back in that hole. It's hard to climb out," she said, while brushing away the tears.

"It's 3 PM. I need some sleep. I can work on this tonight," Amanda said, as she turned off the lamp on a side table, slid in amongst the papers, books and equipment, and drifted into a restless sleep . . .

She was walking through a neighborhood. It was dark except for an occasional streetlight. The homes were closely spaced on either side of the road. None of the inside lights were on.

"What is that smell? Mama's apple pie. She's going to make Daddy get fat if she keeps baking like that. They're retired now. He doesn't need the calories."

She glanced to her right, at the squeaking sound of a front porch swing. Two silhouettes rocked back and forth in the darkness.

"Mama . . . Daddy!" Amanda said, as she tried to run up on the porch, but couldn't seem to move.

"No! No . . . this is the last place I saw them . . . on this porch. The Siberian Tigers . . . General Kung's agents had just taken the Harris Nuclear Plant. I told them to go . . . west . . . they would be safe in the mountains . . ."

The scene changed. She had forgotten how tight the tunnels on La Palma had been. She looked around for Marissa, her constant companion as they searched for the secret Chinese cave, but she was gone. Then she heard laughter. Not a happy, joyful sound, but the sound of a predator who had found its prey. She turned to run, but it felt like she was running through mud up to her knees. Then the sound, that awful, inhuman roar. She could feel Honglei's breath on the back of her neck. The Chinese pit fighter had found her. She stopped. His enormous presence hung over her like some force of nature . . . unstoppable . . . indestructible.

"It's a lie. You're a lie. I killed you in that cave. This is just a dream . . ." Amanda said, as she forced herself to turn around and stare at him.

Honglei bent down, his mouth filled with the teeth of a great cave bear. He roared . . . she screamed . . . and sat upright in bed, the image of his great, gaping maw, filled with razor sharp fangs, still fresh in her mind.

"Oh, crap! I hate that dream! Over and over . . . damn!" she said, her skin damp with sweat.

"I can never see Mama and Daddy's faces, but I can see his. Why his? I killed him. He's dead. He can't hurt me . . . he can't hurt me!" Amanda said, as she lay back down and stared up at the ceiling.

Her breathing calmed as she stared at the ceiling fan slowly turning above her.

"That's what I get for taking a nap in the middle of the day," she said, as she stared at the fan and closed her eyes, as the need for sleep overwhelmed her once again . . .

She walked into his office and it was even smaller than she remembered.

"CIA lady! What can I do for you this time?" asked Detective Angelo Morehead, as he stood up and walked around his desk.

"I need a handgun."

Angelo laughed. At 6' 10" and 300 pounds, his booming laugh shook the room.

"Well, this is what I use," he said, as he pulled the .50 caliber Smith and Wesson revolver from his shoulder holster and handed it to Amanda.

The weapon felt like it weighed ten pounds. She stared at the bullets visible in the cylinder. Each was over half an inch in diameter. Angelo took the handgun back and spun the cylinder.

"Cylinders . . . cylinders spinning . . ."

Amanda woke up and yawned, still staring up at the spinning fan blades above her bed.

"Spinning . . . spinning cylinders . . . mounted in a carousel. The heat buildup is minimized. That's what the Russians are up to! What would they do with it? What would they power it with? It would take megawatts . . . gigawatts . . . a nuclear plant!"

CHAPTER 23

Office of the Prime Minister and Privy Council
80 Wellington Street
Ottawa, Canada
October 14, 0645 EDT

"Prime Minister, you have to decide now! Either we defend Canada, or we don't. The Russians have been spotted less than 25 kilometers from the border. American troops have been blowing bridges in Alaska and fighting as they retreat, but they're done. The Russians surprised them and have eliminated most of their military assets. Our reports show more Russian forces are pouring into the state. They'll hit the border and start heading inland, then toward Vancouver and the US border," said Lieutenant General Jean Caron, Commander of the Canadian Army.

"General, what can we really do? We have lived under the American umbrella since after World War II. I must consider the long-term welfare of all Canadians. Can we truly resist this invasion . . . or is this just something to assuage your pride?" asked the Prime Minister of Canada, Henri Martel.

Lieutenant General Caron took a calming breath before replying, "Prime Minister, the 1st Canadian Mechanized Brigade Group is prepared to move on your command. We have 40 Leopard 2s and 60 LAV IIIs ready to transport by rail into the combat area. This time of year, the Russians must keep to the roads. We can set up ambushes and delay them for weeks. The Americans will defend their land and ours. They have been our close allies for decades. They will not abandon us!"

"General Caron, I'm supposed to talk with the new American President in a few minutes. We've never met, but she has a strong reputation. Look, I'll be frank. The Americans have been crippled. The American West Coast is in a shambles. Millions are dead. Their cities and infrastructure have been wrecked. Their military . . . is almost non-existent. Even Hawaii has been destroyed. I received a report that the Chinese attack has destabilized the North American continental plate . . . if you can believe that! The media has reported the US has started bombing their own territory with the same weapon systems that they used on the Chinese. Supposedly, this was to stop the continent from cracking in two. I don't know what to believe anymore! This feels like a bad Hollywood movie, except it isn't! I'll give you my decision after I talk to the American President. Have your troops ready to move, but if I don't feel that support is on the way, then we'll pull back and defend the east. I won't waste Canadian lives needlessly."

"Yes, Prime Minister!" Lieutenant General Caron said, saluted, and turned to leave the PM's office.

"And General . . ."

"Yes, Prime Minister?"

"Sorry about the comment . . . about your pride. That was uncalled for. We both love Canada and its people. I know you just want to defend your nation."

"Quite right! But you have the right to question everything. As the Americans say, 'the buck stops here' . . . at your desk. I just follow your orders."

"Very good, General, I'll be in touch."

. . . .

10 minutes later

"Prime Minister, the American president is on the line," said his adjutant.

"Well, Louis . . . this should be interesting. After this, we either go to war or we sit this one out. I pray that I make the right decision," Prime Minister Martel said, as he picked up the phone.

"Madam President, greetings from Ottawa. What do you wish to discuss?"

. . . .

1 Canadian Mechanized Brigade Group Headquarters
Building 400, Italy Crescent
Edmonton, Alberta
1030 hours MDT

"Understood, General Caron! I'll contact the Royal Canadians. Lord Strathcona's Horse will be on the move within the hour!" said Colonel William Ritchie, Commander of the 1st Canadian Mechanized Brigade Group.

"Get Lieutenant Colonel Steele on the line, Sergeant Major Ballock. The Prime Minister has given his permission for Operation Roadblock. If the Russians think they're going on holiday while driving through Canada, they are mistaken."

. . . .

Military Railway Siding
Edmonton, Alberta
1140 hours MDT

"You can yell all you want, Major. I don't work for you. I said it would take four more hours, and it's going to take four more hours!" said Emma Leblanc, as she walked away from the fuming officer.

150

"Emma, you know good and well that we'll be done in less than two hours," Logan Taylor whispered, as he walked beside his boss.

"I know, but he's an arrogant ass and I enjoy messing with him. We'll have these boys and girls on their way soon enough, but only when it's safe and by the code. Can you imagine one of these things sliding off on a sharp curve?" Emma said, while watching one of her workers secure one of the 30 Leopard 2A4 Main Battle Tanks already sitting on heavy duty flatbed railcars.

"Yeah, 50 tons sliding off would make a bit of a mess. Can you imagine the paperwork?" Logan asked, as the two laughed and continued their inspection.

"Could be worse! I was talking to Lucas over at the other loading point. They have even more vehicles. Eight-wheeled things called LAV IIIs. Sounds like a toilet!" Emma said, as the laughing continued.

"I'm glad those two are having a good time. In less than 24 hours we may be fighting the Russians!" Major Ethan Smith said, while staring at the backs of the two railway employees.

"Sir, they're just messing with us. We can go back and make sure our troops are settling down," said Captain Alice Campbell, the Strathcona's first female squadron commander and a veteran of combat in Afghanistan.

"I know, Captain, but the fact that the Russians may be driving into our country while we sit here waiting . . . is grating on my nerves."

"The Russians will still be there when we arrive, Sir. I worry more about getting attacked from the air while we're in transit. This represents almost half the Main Battle Tanks in the Canadian Army," she said, while glancing up and down the long line of railcars.

CHAPTER 24

K-335 Gepard
Eastern Pacific Ocean
October 14, 0430 hours UTC

The Russian Akula III class submarine cruised in near silence, propelled only by OK-300 retractable electric propulsors. At five knots, she wasn't getting anywhere fast, but she was invisible to any passive sonar system.

"Captain, no word from the Kuzbass. The last message we received indicated they had been attacked by an unknown submarine. We must assume they're gone, and the American is still out there. Sir, we still have a mission to complete," said Senior Lieutenant Feliks Lagunov, the Executive Officer of the K-335 Gepard.

"I don't need you to tell me my responsibilities, Lieutenant. I understand what our orders are. What I don't want is to get shot in the back by some sly American while we offload Spetsnaz onto one of their aircraft carriers," replied Captain Fyodor Bogdanov.

"Perhaps they destroyed each other?" said Lieutenant Yegor Sobol, the Weapons Officer.

"Lieutenant Aleksandrov, anything on sonar?"

"Negative, Captain! No indication of another submarine within 200 kilometers."

"How many submarines did you hear breaking up four hours ago?"

"Just one, Captain."

"So, it is probable that our adversary is still out there. But now he is completely silent. Captain Volkov told us that the enemy boat was very noisy, as if its hull had been damaged. But then the American boat disappeared, and Volkov went hunting. He didn't know that he was the prey. The Americans are very proud of their boats and how quiet they are. But now, they have no base to go to. So, repairs are impossible, but their Captain fights on."

"He lured the Kuzbass into a trap?" asked Lieutenant Lagunov.

The Captain leaned over the plotting table and began studying images of the underwater terrain in the last reported area of the Kuzbass.

"A damaged boat . . . two enemy subs . . . what would I do if I were the American? I would set up an ambush and wait. That's what he's doing right now, waiting for us to walk into the same trap!"

"Lieutenant Lagunov, reverse course. Make best speed toward the two American carriers. Two can play this game of traps and ambushes."

"Yes, Captain!"

. . . .

USS North Carolina
0435 hours UTC

"XO, we have a contact on sonar! Range 17 miles. They're making fast revolutions . . . heading away from us!" said Lieutenant Bottom.

"Seventeen miles? Did you see them before?"

"No, Ma'am! We had nothing, and then they just appeared."

"What class?"

"Another Akula! Computer is still sorting through our ID library. Wait! Here it is! It's the K-335 Gepard, an Akula III. It's the only one ever built in that variation. Super quiet!"

"Lieutenant Bottom, you have the Conn. I'm going to wake the Captain."

.   .   .   .

10 minutes later

"He's still moving away?" asked Captain North, as he sipped from the mug of thick black coffee that Lieutenant Commander O'Teul had just handed him.

"Yes, Captain, 35 knots, bearing one-three-five, toward the area where our carriers were last reported," replied Lieutenant Bottom.

"XO, have you finished the simulation with our new noise profile?"

"Yes, Captain. We're still stealthy up to 12 knots. After that we start creating a lot of turbulence as we move through the water. The faster we go, the worse it gets."

"Great . . . 12 knots . . . about like an old, World War II diesel boat. This new Captain isn't going to fall for the same trap as his friend. He's forcing us out into the open if we still want to protect those two carriers. The speed of the California Current is about four knots per hour. Based on the last known location of those two ships, where are they now, XO?"

"They were pretty close to the coast, less than a mile offshore based on the last satellite pics we received. They should be near here, near . . . the Islas de Todos Santos . . . All Saints Island, five miles off the coast of Mexico. They might have drifted into this bay to the east of the island, All Saints Bay. The current loops into the bay and then back out before heading south," Lieutenant Commander O'Teul said, while expanding the digital map with her fingers.

"There's even a decent sized harbor there. What's this city?"

"Ensenada, Captain! It would be tight, but you could park two carriers in there, assuming the harbor is still in one piece."

"How far are we from San Diego right now?"

"About . . . 37 miles, Captain? Why?"

"Head for San Diego, flank speed. Don't worry about the noise. Stay just north of Coronado Island. When we get to the eastern end of the island, slow back down to 12 knots. Then we'll parallel the coast and head south."

"Captain! The Russian boat will see us!"

"That's the point, XO. That's the point. They'll see us until we reach Coronado. I'll be aft talking with our Seal friends. You have the Conn!"

"Aye, Captain! Pilot! Ease us up off this hill. Depth four-zero-zero feet. Heading zero-eight-four! Flank speed!"

"Depth four-zero-zero! Heading, zero-eight-four, flank speed, Aye!" the pilot replied, as the USS North Carolina rose from the backside of the Fortymile Ridge, turned to port and accelerated.

. . . .

K-335 Gepard
0448 hours UTC

"Captain! Contact heading . . . due east. Range 20 kilometers! This sub sounds like a beer truck driving down Tverskaya Street in Moscow!" Lieutenant Aleksandrov said, then began laughing as he placed the sound on the speakers.

Captain Bogdanov walked over to the sonar station and silenced the speaker. Then he glared at Lieutenant Aleksandrov.

"This 'beer truck' killed the Kuzbass! If this American Captain makes this much noise it is because he wants us to hear him and see where he's going. Track him carefully and let me know when the noise disappears . . . which it will."

"Yes, Captain! Sorry Captain!"

"Captain, perhaps he's just making a run for San Diego now that he knows where we are. Even if the base is wrecked, they might be able to get supplies or just hide," suggested Lieutenant Lagunov.

"That is a possibility, XO, but I don't think so. He's up to something, but I don't know what. If he runs for port, then we have the aircraft carriers. We can sink them or board them at our leisure. Either way, we win. Bring the Spetsnaz officers up here. I want to talk to them in my quarters. It is time for some final mission plans."

"Yes, Captain!"

CHAPTER 25

U.S. Customs and Border Protection
Alcan Port of Entry
Alaska/Canada Border
October 15, 0430 hours PST

Of the 21 Strykers originally operable, only 13 remained in service. Of the 186 men assigned to Company A, 63 were dead or missing. Another 26 were wounded. Captain MacLynn was left with only two officers, little small arms ammunition, and no heavy fire support or anti-aircraft capability.

"Sir, I don't see how we can make another stand. All we've got is small arms ammo, and not much of that. The mortar section used up almost all their ammunition during the ambush and we're short on .50 cal. We used all the high explosives on the bridges. Sir, we need to pull back into Canada and wait for reinforcements," said Second Lieutenant Branson, as the three officers stood alone at the edge of the woodline north of the border crossing into Canada.

"Exactly! And, Sir, we've got lots of wounded. They need medical care! Right now! The boys aren't ready for another fight! They're shook up. This was a cluster fu . . ." Second Lieutenant Morgan began.

"Lieutenant! I know exactly what this was. It's called combat. And . . . I know who isn't ready for another fight. I know who performed well, and who had to be removed from duty!"

"I was attacked! I want that man arrested for assaulting an officer!"

"Great! I'm left with two junior officers and one of them is a coward," Captain MacLynn thought.

"That man has my full support. I've talked to him and he has witnesses. 'Weakness' during combat is unfortunate, Lieutenant Morgan. It is considered a mental condition brought on by stress . . . at least that's the Army's modern interpretation. In another time you'd have been thought of as a coward, and I would have been justified in having you shot. But now, that would be considered insensitive and uncivilized of me. Plus, it would be illegal. Therefore, you still have your command. Please take this advice in the best possible way . . . Lieutenant. Your actions will be under my constant review. For your benefit, of course. But if I decide that you are no longer able to perform your assigned duties, you will be relieved of those duties. Do you understand me?"

"I find this whole conversation offensive! I am the victim here! I was assaulted, and you won't have the man arrested. My father is a Senator. He will . . ."

"Lieutenant! I can have you court-martialed for your behavior during combat. That is what I can do . . . the most I can legally do. Your platoon may choose to operate under another, less regulated, set of rules. I would suggest that you perform your future duties to the very best of your ability. You are dismissed!" replied Captain MacLynn, as he turned and walked away.

"I'll have your head! Wait until I talk to my . . ."

"Baskin! Shut the hell up! Now you're threatening a superior officer! Listen to me! I'm your friend. We went through ROTC together, but you're wrong. You need to get your head out of your ass! Daddy's not around here. You're on your own. You made a mistake. We were all under a lot of stress. Just do your damn job!" Branson said, as he jerked Morgan by his web gear.

"Get your hand off me or you'll be up on charges, too!" Morgan said, as he stared at his friend's hand.

One mile south of the Canadian border crossing
0530 hours PST

"I said, stop, dammit!" yelled Sergeant Jock Ivan, as he stared through the front window of the 2000 Ford Explorer.

"Damn, Jock! I've been driving all night! You scared the shit out of me. I thought you saw a moose or something," said Luke Desilits as the vehicle screeched to a halt in the middle of the Alaska Highway.

Jock released his seat belt and reached into the back seat for his backpack. After removing a pair of binoculars, he resumed staring to the north.

"Turn off your headlights and pull to the side of the road."

"Jock, this is Alison. What's going on?" Alison Toews asked over the radio, from the second vehicle.

The three vehicles of the 4th Canadian Ranger Patrol Group had been driving north up the Alaska Highway for over five hours. The Canada Border Services station a few miles back had been deserted. That had spooked all of them. The government had abandoned the border, and almost every town they had driven through on the way north was dark and empty.

Jock picked up the handset and said, "All vehicles, cut off your headlights. There are military vehicles up ahead."

The little column went dark. Rainer Rushaven appeared at Jock's side window.

"Jock, what's happening?" Rainer said, as Jock lowered the passenger side window.

"Look for yourself! In the treeline . . . where the road curves to the right. I saw a light come on for a few seconds and then go out," Jock said, as he handed the binoculars to Rainer.

"Those aren't civilian vehicles. The Russians must have crossed the border. We need to get out of here!" Rainer said, as he gave the binoculars back and turned to leave.

"Rainer! Wait! I don't think they're Russian. But, I'm not sure. We'll have to get closer."

"Are you crazy? We've got to go back and contact the army, the government! Let them sort it out!"

"Rainer, we're scouts. This is why we came up here. If you and Liz want to leave, go ahead."

"We're not going anywhere, Jock!" said Elizabeth, Rainer's wife, as she appeared at her husband's shoulder.

"Let her take a look. She's got better eyes than both of us. The woman can see in the dark like a cat," Rainer said.

Liz took the binoculars, walked a few yards up the road and stopped. Jock walked up beside her and waited.

"I see two vehicles . . . four large tires on a side . . . one has a red cross on the side. I see three men behind one vehicle. One of them is smoking. They have weapons slung on their shoulders. That's all I can see from here. They could be Canadian, for all I know," Liz said, as she turned toward Jock.

"You do have good night vision. That's more than I could see. That red cross must be a medical vehicle. Do the Russians use a red cross? We'll have to get closer. Let's get everybody back to your vehicle and talk," Jock said, as he turned and gestured for Luke to get out of the Ford and follow him.

.   .   .   .

0540 hours PST

"So, we're in agreement? I'll take Aldo and Luke with me. We walk down this access road and head north. Aldo, there's another trail that cuts to the east here. You ID those two vehicles we spotted in the trees. Luke and me will approach the Canadian border station from the side. We'll scout the area, find out who these people are, and get an estimate of their capabilities. Then we'll double back, pick up Aldo, and meet back here," Jock said, as they stood at the back of the third vehicle and examined a map displayed on the lowered tailgate.

"What if we're spotted?" asked Aldo.

"Then we run for it. Don't get into a shootout. They have automatic weapons. We have bolt action rifles."

"Listen, we're all hunters. We know how to stalk prey. This is no different!" said Aldo.

"Yeah, right! I don't think I've ever had a moose shoot back!" said Luke, as the others chuckled.

"No shooting unless you have to. Understood?" Jock said, as he pointed at Aldo and Luke.

. . . .

0600 hours PST

The sky to the east was starting to lighten as the three men split up. Aldo turned down a trail that headed directly toward the vehicle with the Red Cross on the side. Jock and Luke kept heading north.

"Thirty minutes and we're going to be visible. If they're Russians, we're dead," Jock thought, as he motioned to Luke and picked up the pace.

They reached a large clearing 300 yards south of the border station. Jock paused at the treeline and began scanning the other side with his binoculars. A twig cracked as Luke settled into place beside him.

"Sorry!" Luke whispered, as Jock glared at him.

"I see six vehicles pulled into the trees nose first, maybe eight. There's a light inside one of them. Some damn fool is giving away their position," Jock whispered, as he handed the binoculars to Luke.

"Keep them. I prefer my scope," Luke said, as he rested his left elbow on his knee and assumed a high kneeling position.

161

The Colt Canada C19 had a 3-9X Leupold powered scope. Luke clicked through the magnifications while focusing on the lit interior of one vehicle.

"What an asshole! He's in there getting drunk. I can see the bottle from here. Whatever he's drinking is clear. Could be vodka! Must be a Russian officer. Should I drill him?" Luke asked, as he turned his head and grinned at Jock.

"No! Let me take a look. My scope is back in my truck . . . and I won't touch anything," Jock said, knowing how touchy Luke was about his rifle.

After Luke reluctantly handed over the weapon, Jock began studying the inside of the vehicle.

"It's some kind of armored personnel carrier, and he's definitely drinking vodka. I can't believe he's got the interior light on. This is a good scope. It must be close to 200 yards and I can read the Smirnoff label on the bottle. It's an American! I can see a US flag hanging below a computer screen. Now we have to figure out how to approach them without getting shot," Jock said, as he handed the rifle back to Luke.

"Why don't we just go back to the trucks and wait until it gets light. Then we just drive up and talk to them. We don't look military," Luke said, as he began studying the vehicles across the clearing.

"That makes sense. Let's go back and pick up Aldo," Jock said, while rising from a sitting position.

The echo of a series of shots from an automatic weapon caused them both to freeze. Each man looked at the other in the dim light, their eyes wide with fear. Jock gestured with his right hand. They slowly withdrew from the edge of the treeline and back into the dense woods. The sound of men yelling behind them caused them to break into a run. Aldo met them at the trail intersection, clutching his right arm.

"Got shot . . . my fault . . . I got sloppy. Sentry spotted me," Aldo said, as the three men began running for their lives.

. . . .

3 minutes later

"Captain! Infiltrators! The Russians must have gotten behind us! What are your orders?" asked Lieutenant Branson, as he ran up to the company command vehicle.

"I heard three shots, Lieutenant. Tell me what happened. Who shot at what?" Captain MacLynn asked, while donning his web gear and picking up his M4A1 carbine.

"A sentry was guarding the wounded. He saw a man sneaking up from the woods and opened fire. He thinks he hit the man, but the man ran back into the woods."

"Where's Lieutenant Morgan? We need everyone up and ready to move or fight. If we've been found, they may have radioed for help. It will be light in less than an hour. Where the hell is Lieutenant Morgan?" Captain MacLynn asked, as he looked around at the crowd of men.

"He's passed out drunk, Captain! I found him in the back of his vehicle with the inside light on. He had ordered the rest of the crew to get lost. He was in there with a bottle of vodka," said Sergeant First Class Scott, as he handed his cell phone to the Captain. The pictures he had taken of the drunken officer confirmed his story.

"Lieutenant Branson, Sergeant Scott, get the men ready to move. I want us buttoned up and mobile in ten minutes. Sergeant Scott, you have command of Second Platoon. Disarm Lieutenant Morgan and have him restrained. I'll deal with him later. Move!"

. . . .

The three Canadian Rangers burst from the trees and headed for their vehicle. They froze as the headlights from one vehicle blinded them.

"Halt or we fire! Shit! It's them! What happened?" shouted Jillian, as she stepped from behind her truck and lowered her rifle.

"Turn off the damn lights! They might be right behind us," shouted Jock, as he helped Aldo to the back of his truck and laid him on the bed.

"He's been shot! Get the med kit from the back seat!"

"Got it!"

"Get his coat off. Damn, he's bleeding a lot! I used to be a nurse. I'm going to need some water and some light. I can't work in the dark!" said Liz, as she opened up the first aid kit.

"Barry, Alison! Cover the road! Let me know if you see anyone coming this way!" ordered Jock.

"Be fast, Liz! We may have to get out of here quick like!"

"I know! Hold the damn light still. Where's the water?"

"I think I'm going to puke. I'm starting to get dizzy," Aldo said, while lying in the back of Jock's truck bed.

"Good, it's through-and-through! No fragments and it didn't hit bone. I need to rinse it and bandage it. You'll be okay, Aldo!" Liz said, as she rinsed the wound and handed a large bandage to Jock.

"Press hard . . . both sides. We have to start the clotting process. Then we'll switch the bandage for a clean one, and I'll wrap the wound. He's going to need stitches and antibiotics. The adrenalin from getting shot is wearing off. He's going to be in a lot of pain. Morphine would be nice," Liz said, as she discarded one pair of bloody latex gloves and put on a clean pair.

"I think he passed out. The bleeding is slowing down," Jock said, as he lifted the edge of the bandage.

"Get him in the back of one of the vehicles and keep him warm. The shock could kill him before we get him to a doctor," Liz said, as she replaced the blood-soaked bandage, replaced it with another and began wrapping the wound.

"They're coming! I see vehicle lights heading this way!" Alison said, as she came running back down the road.

164

Daylight was starting to break. The tips of the tall conifers began to glow as the darkness retreated.

"Shit! It's too late! They're coming!" Barry yelled, as headlights followed him up the road.

"Get ready to fight!" Luke yelled, as he stood behind one of the trucks and leveled his rifle.

"Lower your weapons! Don't be stupid! Those are Americans! Drop your weapons! Put your hands up!" Jock ordered, as he walked away from the vehicles with his hands empty and raised.

The huge vehicle stopped less than 20 feet away. The sound of running feet could be heard above the idling engine. Shadows appeared on either side of the road.

"Keep your hands up or I'll cut you in half!" a voice said from above the vehicle.

Jock could see a man behind the .50 cal M2 machine gun mounted on top of the vehicle.

"We're Canadians! 4th Canadian Ranger Patrol Group. We're up here scouting for Russians!" Jock shouted, as the shadows approached.

"I don't like this, Sarge! Some of them are still behind the vehicles," said Specialist Elkins.

"Relax, Collin! Mister, tell all your friends to walk into the open where we can see them. We've been fighting Russians for the last week, and we're prone to just kill anyone that we don't know," said Sergeant Masterson.

"Everyone, put down your weapons and step out front! Now, do it now!" Jock shouted, as the soldiers spread out and lined both sides of the road.

"Collin, Juan, check the vehicles and the people. We don't want any surprises. Jimmy, call the Captain. Tell him we've got armed civilians," ordered Sergeant Masterson.

"We've got a wounded man. He needs a trained medic. I've done what I could with a first aid kit, but he needs help!" Liz said, as she walked forward with her hands up.

"Lady, you take another step and I shoot. I spent two tours in Iraq. Women suicide bombers were pretty common. Tell all of your people to get down on their knees, hands on top of their heads," said Sergeant Masterson, as he shifted his aim from Jock to Liz.

"Do as he says! Down on your knees. We'll get this sorted out in a minute!" Jock said.

"Sarge! The CO is coming down here to check them out," shouted the soldier atop the Stryker.

"Roger that!"

"Sarge, there's a wounded guy in the back of the first truck. He's unconscious!"

"Eight total. Three of them are women. All we found are these old bolt-action rifles and two hunting rifles. Look at the stock on this one. It's some kind of red laminate," said Specialist Elkins.

"That's standard issue for Canadian Rangers," Jock said.

"A bolt-action rifle? That's pretty sad," said Specialist Elkins.

"Come January, when it's 25 below, your weapon will freeze up. That bolt-action rifle will still work."

"Hey, Sarge! The CO's here!"

Captain MacLynn approached and began assessing the scene.

"Sir, seven civilians and a wounded guy in the back of one of the trucks. They claim to be Canadian Rangers. Whatever that is," said Sergeant Masterson.

"I've heard of them. Are you in charge of these people?"

"Yes, Captain. I'm Sergeant Jock Ivan. I'm Regular Force. What you would call Regular Army. The rest of them are civilians. Captain, I have a wounded man. One of your guys shot him while we were reconning your unit."

"Let me see some ID, Sergeant . . . Ivan. Move slowly! We've lost a lot of friends in combat the last few days. The men are a little quick on the trigger."

Jock slowly removed his wallet and showed his Canadian Army ID and driver's license.

"Who sent you up here, Sergeant?" Captain MacLynn asked, while checking the IDs.

"Third Canadian Division, Sir. We're part of the 4th Canadian Ranger Patrol Group. Our assignment was to find where the Russians were, how many, what vehicles and numbers, and report back to 3rd Division."

"Put your hands down, sergeant. These people are friendlies! Lower your weapons!" Captain MacLynn shouted.

His troops slowly obeyed as the Canadians rose to their feet, relieved to still be alive.

"Sergeant Ivan, I'll get my medics down here. They can look after your man, but we've got a lot of wounded. We're short on everything," Captain MacLynn said, as he reached out and shook Jock's hand.

"How far behind are the Russians?"

"I'm not sure. We've blown a few bridges and we ambushed a recon battalion. Chewed them up pretty good. We pulled back and thought we were safe. Then we were hit by a Hind. That thing tore us up before we shot it down."

"Damn! Where's the rest of your Division?"

"Gone! Half the division was stationed in Hawaii, half in Alaska. Four brigades total. All were torn up. We were on training maneuvers when the Russians attacked Alaska. We got bits and pieces of information from Division before they went dark. Cruise missiles and bombers took out the airbases. Next round of attacks came after the Army bases. I was ordered to keep the company south of the fighting. When it got quiet and I couldn't contact anyone, I decided to start blowing bridges, retreat south toward Canada and then the US."

"Damn! An entire American Division? All the air bases? How the hell did that happen?"

" Tsunamis after the Great Quake took out Hawaii. I guess we never saw them coming toward Alaska. What do you think your government will do? Will Canada fight?"

"Yeah, we're not prone to getting punched in the nose and walking away from a fight. But I'll be honest. Our military is less than a tenth the size of the United States military, and most of our equipment is old or second hand. If the Russians come in force, we'll just be a speed bump."

"We're the same way. We've been beaten down and surprised before, but we'll keep fighting. You can count on that," Captain MacLynn said, as the two men shook hands again.

CHAPTER 26

Central Intelligence Agency
Mission Center for Weapons and Counterproliferation
Office of Director Janet Davidson
Manassas, Virginia
October 15, 0800 hours EST

"The first time you came up with a leap like this was your second day on the job. I thought that was a stretch, but everything you theorized at the time was correct. The Chinese had lost control of their nuclear weapons, and some crazy general was importing warheads into the US. So . . . do you really believe that the Russians have developed some 'Death Star' super weapon powered by a nuclear power plant?" asked Director Davidson.

"Yes, Director! Based on the files you asked me to look at, that's what I believe. It's either a nuclear plant or something geothermal. It must be something with a small environmental impact. There are no supporting rail or pipelines. So, it can't be oil or coal," Amanda replied, as she began to pace in front of her boss's desk.

"Amanda, there were a few irregularities and inconsistencies in the data I sent you, but I didn't see this coming. I just wanted to give you some light research. You had asked for something to do. Frankly, I glanced at the files and found it tedious reading. Now you come back with this analysis out of left field. Huge glass cylinders that rotate like the cylinders in a revolver? Then you tell me that the answer came to you . . . in a dream?"

"I know that sounds a little weird, but yes! I dream a lot. Sometimes more than I want, but I listen to my dreams. They tell me things."

"I don't see it. What are they going to shoot at? The Earth curves. The target would have to be within 25 miles or it's below the horizon. Lasers are a line-of-sight weapon. They don't curve!"

"First, I think the Russians know about the Kraken, and they are justifiably terrified of it. Second, we know the Chinese found a way of tracking the Kraken. Otherwise, they wouldn't have been able to move their satellites into such close proximity in an attempt to destroy it. Third, I think they had a grand plan to destroy both coastal areas of the US, kill the President and destroy the USS Kraken. They got two out of four. If they had succeeded in getting all four targets, we'd be in a lot worse shape than we're in right now."

"Amanda, the Russians know our West Coast bases are crippled . . . including Hawaii. They may succeed in occupying the western half of our country. I've been told that the Kraken is toothless. It's gone from being a battleship to an aircraft carrier. What I'm going to tell you next doesn't leave this office. The Kraken carries six Dorys. A fighter-interceptor with the same speed and cloaking ability of the Kraken. Two Dorys have been shot down over Alaska in the last two days, and we don't know how. They should be invisible on any known radar system. Their speed and maneuverability should also make them impossible to catch. Yet . . ."

"Yet, the Russians have shot two of them down. Director, they may have started with a small version of the weapon and then scaled it up."

"Correct! Which leads us back to your theory of them having a super laser weapon."

"We have to find out how they are detecting the Kraken and the Dorys!"

"Also correct! Can you go take a nap or something, and figure out how they're doing it?"

"Funny! Do you want me to read your palm before I go?"

170

Amanda knew she had gone a little too far when Janet glared at her.

"Normally, Agent Langford, I'd jack you up for being impertinent. My old Marine training hasn't gone anywhere. But you've earned a few 'free passes'. So, I'll let that remark go. What I want you to do is start thinking about why our super-secret invisible spacecraft are no longer invisible. Here, call this number at the Pentagon. Tell the officer who answers that I gave you the number. They will arrange for you to see any information you need to come up with a theory. I'll forward your theory about the super weapon. If it's true, the Kraken may be in danger. One other thing . . . don't miss any classes with Basra. She takes such affronts personally and might come looking for you," Janet said, handed Amanda a business card with a phone number on the back, and gestured for her to leave her office.

"Damn, that woman keeps me permanently sore. I think she just likes to throw me around. She says I bounce more than Karl."

"Very possible. One final thing! Report to Level Minus 6, Room 7 in . . . 12 minutes. You're being fitted for a handgun. Now go on, I've got calls to make."

. . . .

Room 7

Amanda exited the elevator on Minus 6. It was eerily silent, and the white walls were empty, not even a fire evacuation map. She had expected pictures of smiling faces with trophies and weapons.

"Feels more like a hospital. Did I get off on the wrong floor?" she thought, as she verified the level, and began walking down a long corridor. The only sound was the clicking of her heels on the polished concrete floor.

There were three windowless metal doors on each side of the hall. They were numbered '1' through '6'; odd on one side, even on the other. Room '7' was at the end of the hall. She knocked on the door, then entered when there was no answer.

"Great, another hallway," she said, while glancing left and right.

"More white walls and concrete floors. This place has all the personality of a morgue. No signs, I guess I'll go . . . to the right!"

"Did you know that 90 percent of the people that come down here for the first time make a right turn when they walk through that door?"

Amanda spun around and found a man walking down the hall from the other direction. He was tall, rangy, with shaggy black hair that came down to the collar of the dark gray coveralls he was wearing.

"Mike Stephanos. They call me the Weapon's Master. My official title is Director of the Weapons Training Facility. You must be Agent Langford," Mike said, as he extended his right hand.

"Yes, I was told . . . I'm Amanda . . . Langford. I'm here to . . ."

"Wow! Smallest hand I've ever seen. This will be a challenge," Mike said, as he held and examined her hand.

"Listen . . . Mike! I get enough comments about my stature. I'm here to . . ."

"I know why you're here. Don't be so damn touchy! I've got a 9mm semi that should be perfect. Follow me," Mike said, as he released her hand and turned away.

Amanda took an instant dislike for the man, but followed him, as he walked away.

"There are separate shooting ranges for pistols, combat shotguns and automatic weapons. Each weapon type has its own combat tactical range with rooms, barriers and animatronic characters. We can even simulate just about any environmental situation that exists on this planet," Mike said, while walking ahead of her.

"What? Like wading through a swamp . . . at night . . . during a downpour?" Amanda asked, trying to lighten the moment with a little sarcasm.

172

"Yeah, we've done that before. Getting permission to include gators was tricky."

Amanda couldn't tell if he was spoofing her or not.

"What's with all the concrete floors and white walls?"

"It makes cleanup easier. We occasionally use the halls for different scenarios. It can get a little messy."

"Look . . . Mike . . . I just came down here to get fitted for a handgun. I'm not interested in . . ."

"Then turn around and leave, Agent Langford. I don't just hand over weapons to untrained agents. The weapon doesn't leave this facility until I'm satisfied that you know how to use it. If I issue you a weapon, it comes with a mandatory requirement of 60 hours of training. That's for one weapon. If you wish to be qualified on multiple weapons . . . well . . . the time multiplies accordingly," Mike said, as he stopped and turned around to face her.

"Crap! Does this man blink? Why do I feel like I'm being sized up by a wolf?" Amanda asked herself, while returning his stare.

"Okay! Whatever it takes. I want the training."

He looked at her for a few more seconds. Then nodded and turned away again. Two doors and two more halls later, he unlocked a heavy metal door and stepped inside. The lights came on automatically.

Amanda blinked and stared at a room that must have been 20 feet on a side. Every wall was lined with shelves filled with pistols and ammunition.

"Over here is what you'll need. I only have two, but I think one of them will work for you," he said, while removing two cases from a shelf.

"This one is made by the European American Armory. They call it the Witness Pavona. It was specifically designed for women. The polymer frame decreases the weight. It's easy to rack and holds 13 9mm rounds. Try the fit."

The first thing Amanda did was verify that the weapon was unloaded, without a round in the chamber. She had been shooting with Anthony once, and he had taught her the basics of gun safety.

"Cute! Purple with little silver sparkles. Does it come in black?" Amanda asked, while racking the weapon and checking the size of the grip.

"Actually, it comes in six different colors, including black, but they all come with the sparkles."

"What else do you have?"

He opened another case and handed her a second handgun.

"This is a Walther CCP, concealed carry pistol. It's light, has an open trigger guard in case you're wearing gloves. It's also 9 mm, holds eight rounds. It only comes in black. How does it feel?"

"Better. I don't like the glitter of the other weapon, but the magazine capacity is a problem."

"Agent Langford, if you need more than eight rounds, you either can't shoot or you're in way over your head."

"Mike, I've been shot at, almost blown up by a nuke and killed a giant with an AK-47. Everything is over my head, and I have the scars to show it. But I'm still here. Where do we start?"

Mike smiled, then said, "Well, let's go see if you can shoot. Then I'll know what I'm working with."

. . . .

The White House
Oval Office
0820 hours EST

"No, Janet! You don't have to apologize for using my private number. I gave it to you for a reason. I only trust certain people to have the private cell number of the President of the United States. Now what do you have?" Clarise Beaumont asked.

"Madam President, I came directly to you to bypass the red tape. We may not have much time. The Kraken may be in danger of being destroyed. One of my agents has a theory that the Chinese and the Russians have found a way to track the Kraken and the Dorys," Janet said.

"Which would explain why we've lost two Dorys over Alaska."

"Yes, Madam President. Even worse, she has a theory that they have developed a laser powerful enough to destroy the Kraken. They may have used a smaller, portable version of this weapon system on the Dorys."

"Do you have any details? Or is this just a theory?"

"At this point, it's just a theory. But the agent who came up with the theory has an excellent track record with her hunches based on minimal data."

"Ahh . . . the young agent . . . Amanda?"

"Yes, Madam President . . . Amanda Langford. She discovered the Kung plan and the Chinese device on La Palma. She's very young but has proven to be tough and brilliant. I trust her instincts. She's working on verifying her theory, but that will take time."

"So, tell me about her theory . . ."

CHAPTER 27

The Fighter's Garage
132 West Jefferson St
Falls Church, Virginia
October 16, 1050 hours EST

"God, I can barely move! Why do I come here every other day just to get my ass kicked?" Amanda asked herself, as she flung open the door to her car and struggled to stand up.

She groaned when her cell phone rang. The sound of 'Happy' by Pharrell Williams, didn't fit her present mood. She pulled the phone out of her backpack and glanced at the caller as she opened the connection.

"Please tell me that you're going to have me taken out and shot. Anything is better than another beating by Mistress Basra," Amanda said, as she answered Janet's call.

"I talked to her last night. She said you're progressing nicely."

"Yeah? She just likes the sound I make as I hit the mat . . . over and over."

"Well, the cure for that is for you to learn to defend yourself. But that's not why I called. I need you back here ASAP. You have a mission, and you're leaving as soon as the briefing is complete."

"Oh, thank you, blessed woman! Your favorite whiskey is Laphroaig Scotch, right? I'll pick up a bottle on the way in."

"I appreciate the gesture, but just get your ass back here. You have a very special flight in your future," Janet said, then disconnected the call.

"Very special flight? What the hell does that mean? Whatever it is, it has to be better than another session at Mistress Basra's Torture Palace," Amanda said, as she threw her backpack into the passenger seat, suddenly feeling much better about her day.

. . . .

Three hours later
50,000 feet above the western United States

"I should have studied Russian instead of Japanese," Amanda said, as she rubbed her eyes and closed the third of five briefing folders.

The Gulfstream 550 passenger compartment was empty except for her. A flight on Janet's private jet always reminded Amanda of her parents. They had never flown, not even once. Her mother had been terrified of flying.

"I know, Mama . . . 'only angels and birds should be up above the clouds'. But, Mama, it's so beautiful, and Daddy would have loved this. I should have taken him flying . . . just once," Amanda said, as she turned and stared out the window at the desolate terrain over Arizona.

The pain of their deaths was still there, just below the surface. At least she didn't break into tears every day, but the loss . . . knowing that she would never sit with them again . . . just to talk and get her mother's sage advice . . . just to hug them. That still hurt, and she knew it always would.

She could tell the plane was descending, and quickly. Her ears were starting to pop. Glancing out the window, all she saw was dry desert and hills. The air was hazy from volcanic eruptions and the residue from the attack on China. The temperatures across the

Northern Hemisphere were five degrees below normal and were expected to get worse. The three volcanoes on the continent already erupting were projected to be joined by four others. Some things were so far beyond her control that she tried not to think about them. Her everyday life, what was left of it, was troubling enough. Her dreams were still filled with her experiences on La Palma. Honglei was always there . . . always. She woke up screaming at least once per night. Honglei was always there . . .

.   .   .   .

1100 hours PST

"Holy crap! I thought it was going to be warm like Mexico. But, it's cold here," Amanda said, as she walked down the stairs from the Gulfstream, her backpack slung over one shoulder.

Her other bag was already at the base of the stairs. As soon as her feet touched the road, the stairs began to retract back inside the plane. She stepped away as the small jet began to taxi along the road before accelerating and hurling itself into the sky.

"Thanks for the lift . . . I guess. Where the hell am I?" she asked, as she slowly turned in a circle.

There was no airport. The jet had landed on a two-lane road in the middle of a desert valley. Bone dry hills and ridges surrounded her in every direction. As the jet disappeared, the silence closed in. A true silence that very few people ever experienced.

"I should have stopped for the Scotch. She had them dump me in the middle of nowhere," Amanda said, as she opened up her suitcase and pulled out a windbreaker.

She didn't hear the craft approach as she stood up and slipped on the coat. At first, she felt it coming in her bones as a vibration. Then her feet began to tingle as pebbles began dancing across the blacktop. It wasn't like a conventional plane, appearing on the horizon and then growing steadily larger. It wasn't there, and then it was.

178

When it appeared before her, she jumped. There was a cracking sound, like lightning in the distance, and the strong smell of ozone. She just stared. It was the same feeling she had as a child standing in the middle of a field, when the sky began to darken as a thunderstorm loomed on the horizon. The same feeling of awe and wonder. But this was different, more sudden. It was just there. It hovered over the road, less than a hundred yards away, slowly drifting toward her. Each corner of the vessel glowed. Not as bright as the sun, more like a full moon. A cockpit was visible on one side. Behind that was a larger sphere. The brightness dulled as it approached.

"Oh, my God! It's a Dory!" Amanda said, as the matte-black triangular shaped vessel landed less than 20 yards away.

Amanda's ears popped once again as if a sudden pressure had departed. She could only stare, open mouthed like a little girl. As an engineer, she was fascinated by the technology. As a human, she felt she was watching something magical. The silence returned, as the glow disappeared, and the cockpit opened. She could see the pilot unlatching several physical restraints and then remove a strange helmet with several cabled connections. The pilot was a man. His face was as black as a midnight sky. The hair was close cut and gray. He stood up, then slid down the side of the vessel. He rubbed his eyes as if waking from a deep sleep, then smiled at her and walked in her direction. He was old, wrinkled, but the smile continued as he approached. He stopped and extended his right hand.

"Colonel Marcus James! You must be Agent Langford. I understand you need a lift."

"Yes, I suppose I do. But I wasn't expecting a Dory. I've been told there are only a few of them left. I assumed you would all be fighting somewhere," Amanda said, as she extended her right hand and shook the man's hand. She was surprised at how cold the hand was, even through his glove.

"Well, times are tough. They've called up the inactive reserves. I suppose, that's what we would be called."

"We?"

"I was told you have clearance, and I love telling the story. Modern aircraft live beyond their human pilots. The B-52 was the first plane to experience this. The initial design of the airframe was so durable, so adaptable, it was able to last for generations. But the B-52 was just a dumb machine. The pilots aged out and were replaced. The Dory, and the Artificial Intelligence (AI) that came with it, was something new. We didn't anticipate that the Dory, when linked with the AI and a human pilot, would become one inseparable unit. No one saw it coming. I was the first pilot. This Dory was the first, same for the AI. Over time, we became . . . one creature . . . no . . . one entity. That sounds a little less crude. If we were separated, the whole system broke down. The AI refused to communicate. The Dory wouldn't work. It wouldn't even power up. Then I got old. The Space Force wanted to retire me, but they didn't want to lose the space plane. It's worth billions," he said, as he picked up Amanda's bag and walked back toward the Dory.

"I don't understand. Why are you here?" she asked, as she followed him toward the strange craft and handed over her backpack.

"Because, I'm expendable. We all are," he said, as a hatch on the side of the craft opened, and he tossed her bag and backpack inside and secured them.

"I still don't . . ."

"The craft and the will AI die when I do. Even though they are effectively immortal, they will cease to function when I pass on. Why, no one knows, and believe me, they've been trying to figure it out for decades. But for right now, it doesn't matter. We've all been called back up to active service, despite our age. We even have the latest weapon upgrades, and it's all for you. Now, if you would," he said, as steps formed in the sloping side of the forward hull.

"You want me to climb in?"

"It's a long way to Russia. I don't think you want to walk that far. As I said, she was the first, a training vessel, the TR-4T. As such, she has two seats. I was told to render you unconscious for the trip, but

I'll give you the choice. Please take the seat on your left," he said, while offering his hand.

She looked into his eyes as she took his hand. It wasn't needed, but he reminded her of her father, and how he had always treated her mother . . . as a gentleman should treat a woman, with kindness and respect.

"No pressure suit?"

"Unnecessary. The Mercury Plasma Field Engine keeps us in a stable envelope. Without that, we'd be torn apart and splattered all over the cockpit. When I was younger, I considered flying naked once, but Artie would have none of that. She said it was unprofessional."

"Artie?"

"The AI. The first time we were coupled, she told me that she was female and that her name was Artie. She even spelled it for me. She is a little formal. She hasn't coupled with a female in a long time."

"Coupling? That sounds a little . . . "

"Creepy?"

"Yes . . . a bit . . . no offense," Amanda said, while staring down at the seat and wondering what would happen when she sat down.

"It's not that kind of coupling. In a way, it's more intense than any physical . . . interaction. The helmet links you to her . . . your mind to her mind," he said, while stepping past Amanda and sliding into his seat.

"Just sit down and I'll talk you through the process. She's looking forward to it."

Amanda looked around the cockpit. She had expected it to look like the movies: dozens of dials, levers and switches. But it was very clean. A curved screen extended from one side of the cockpit to the other. Two flat pads sat on either side of both pilot positions. With a sigh, she stepped into the cockpit and sat down.

"The seat feels stiff, like a wooden chair."

Colonel James laughed and said, "That will change. First the helmet. Reach above your head. Place your hands on both sides and she will release it. Slide it over your head and relax."

Amanda looked over her shoulder and glanced at the helmet. It was matt black. The same color as the outside of the Dory. She could see that when she placed it over her head it would completely encapsulate her head.

"How will I breathe? There's no hose in the front."

"The air comes in from the back. Your hair is short, so that won't be a problem. If you're claustrophobic . . . she'll sense that, and the next thing you'll know, you'll be asleep, and then we'll be in Russia. Go ahead, slip the helmet on."

"Oh, crap! At least I'm not bouncing around on Basra's mat," Amanda thought, as she reached up and lowered the helmet over her head.

The helmet was loose. It almost wobbled on her head. She began to make a comment when she felt the helmet begin to compress.

"Just relax! She's conforming the helmet to your head by analyzing your skull and muscle structure. You may also feel a slight vertigo. Just close your eyes and the feeling will go away in a few seconds. That's her initiating the link with your mind. I asked her to be gentle."

"With my mind? What are you . . ."

Amanda could feel her heart pounding. It was completely dark inside the helmet. It reminded her of the galleria on the island of La Palma. The vertigo was less than subtle. It hit her like a wave, or a fist, but she gritted her teeth, closed her eyes, and calmed herself with several slow, deep breaths.

"Very good! I thought I was going to have to sedate you. My name is Artie. I am very pleased to meet you."

Amanda didn't know what to say. She just sat in the dark, listening to a voice in her head.

"I reviewed all the reports about you, and I'm presently analyzing your mind. I hope you don't mind."

"Actually, I do! It's rude to just start probing around in my mind without asking my permission," Amanda said, as she felt or sensed the presence of someone else.

"You don't have to talk, Agent Langford. All you have to do is think the words," Colonel James said, or rather, thought.

"She seems anxious."

As the vertigo lessened, Amanda reopened her eyes. It was still dark, but she felt like she wasn't alone.

"You aren't alone. We are both with you. All three of our minds are connected now."

"You can read my thoughts?"

"Yes!"

"Yes, and your memories!"

Amanda began pulling on the helmet, struggling to remove it. It slowly released, and she gasped as bright daylight and fresh air struck her.

"I don't think I can do this. It's too intrusive. My thoughts are mine. My memories and pains are mine!" Amanda said, almost shouting.

Colonel James removed his helmet and glanced over at Amanda.

"I apologize. I rushed this. I forgot how disconcerting the first time can be. For me . . . it's a normal way of communicating. Artie doesn't understand your reluctance. This is her entire world, all that she knows. She has absorbed millions of lines of data about us, but understands very little. Our thought process, as human beings, is so foreign to her."

"But it considers itself a 'her'?"

"She has tried to explain it to me, and we are very close, but I don't claim to completely understand. She has . . . a kind heart . . . empathy. Most men that I have known are more pragmatic . . . more focused on the mission, the task. Even if the mission is shopping for groceries. She is, after all, a machine created by us . . . by all of us. There were male and female programmers responsible for her software. That fact has influenced what she became . . . what she is. All we can do is accept how she perceives herself."

Amanda shook her head, knowing that this philosophical quandary was beyond her. She had to focus on what she could understand. She understood her present mission.

"Colonel, how long will it take us to reach our target?"

"Agent Langford . . . in 49 minutes I can deliver you to within 1000 yards of your objective. Any closer would be too great a risk. We would probably be seen. The place we're taking you is near the naval base for the Russian Pacific Fleet. I can render you unconscious. You would not have to interact with Artie, but the aftermath would leave you . . . somewhat groggy."

"Forty-nine minutes . . . I'll just ignore it . . . think of something else," Amanda thought, as she picked up the helmet and looked at Colonel James.

"Agent Langford, do I understand that you want to proceed and merge again?"

Amanda nodded and slipped the helmet over her head. The darkness was even more encompassing. The transition even more rapid. The mind of the AI known as Artie, more intrusive . . . by far, and this time, it wouldn't let go.

"I have not interacted with a female in a very long time. I want to know everything about you. Do you mind?"

Amanda shuddered, feeling the sensation of this alien presence in her mind. Somehow, for some reason, she nodded, allowing Artie to search inside her for her deepest secrets and fears . . .

. . . .

Amanda awoke to the sound of two voices arguing. She had been dreaming of her parents, but they rarely argued, and she was concerned.

"Mama, Daddy, what's the problem?" she asked, while stretching her arms.

She knew it was almost time to leave for school and she had to hurry. Her eyes opened . . . and she was sitting in the cockpit of the Dory. It was cool, a perfect temperature. She could almost feel the spring breeze coming in through her bedroom window. Colonel James was staring at her.

"What? Where am I . . . oh crap . . . Artie . . ."

"Agent Langford, I'm very sorry! She had no right, but I couldn't get her to stop. We've been sitting here for over an hour while she connected with you, with your memories. Now she won't say anything. I think she's processing."

"I'm not processing, Marcus. I'm wondering how she lives with so much pain. I find it very distressing. I may have to isolate this data. It could corrupt my other functions."

"Artie, what you did was wrong. It was rude and insensitive. Sometimes . . . your desire for more data gets the better of you. Humans must endure painful events in their lives. Some can't . . . and end their lives. Most try to get past the pain, but it's difficult and takes time. You shouldn't . . ."

"Artie's right . . . you have to isolate the file . . . the memory of the pain . . . or it will consume you. Too bad she doesn't have a face. I need something to look at . . . something to . . . connect to," Amanda said, as she shuddered. The after effect of having someone else inside your mind was disturbing. She almost felt . . . violated.

"You failed to isolate the file. Why were you poisoning yourself with alcohol? You wanted to die. That man . . . Colonel Anthony Thompson, he saved your life. You were going to end your life. You have very strong feelings for him. Why does that make you feel guilty?"

"No, I was just drinking . . . to forget. I wasn't suicidal, and my feelings are . . . personal."

"Yes, you wanted to die. In your mind you were going to drink another pitcher of beer and then go swimming in the ocean until you reached Africa. I do not think that was possible. The

attempt would have killed you. That would be suicide. Do you love him?"

"Artie, stop it! Do you remember when my wife died of cancer, how upset I was?"

"Yes, your functionality was minimal for quite some time."

"Sadness makes humans that way. It takes us time to process painful data. Over time, the data becomes less . . . immediate. We don't forget the data. It just becomes less . . . significant, as we acquire new data."

"Like being in love?"

"Colonel, I don't think I can do this anymore. I still have a mission. You said you could drug me. I don't know how you take this," Amanda said, while looking at the flight helmet as if it were an instrument of torture.

"It's a difficult relationship. I suppose it's like having a child who's a genius. It can be overwhelming at times. I try to interject human sensitivity, but Artie has a difficult time handling emotions. They aren't just ones and zeros."

"But you've been with her for years!"

"Decades . . . actually."

"I have offended you. I can detect it in the cadence of your voice. You don't like me."

"I find it difficult . . . to like . . . people . . . that have hurt me."

"That was not my intent. I was just curious."

"Colonel, the mission!"

"Yes, Agent. Just lay back in the seat. It will feel like you're settling into a really soft bed and falling asleep . . ."

CHAPTER 28

Highway P475
Two miles south of Vulkannyy
Kamchatka Peninsula, Russia
October 17, 1145 hours PETT (Kamchatka Time)

"So, when does the trip start?" Amanda asked, while shifting her shoulders into a more comfortable position.

"Agent Langford, we're on the ground in Russia. The trip was a bit longer than expected, but uneventful. You'll find your equipment and appropriate clothing beside the vehicle when you get out. Local time is 1145 hours. There is a shelter located approximately 2000 meters to the northeast. Head for the treeline. You are expected."

"What? I just closed my eyes for a second."

"Well, actually 2745 of them."

"Colonel . . . I . . ."

"Just take a few deep breaths. It will clear your head."

"It's not that. It's . . . this. The Dory . . . you and Artie . . . it's not what I expected . . . not that I ever thought I'd . . . sorry, I'm rambling. Thank you for getting me here," Amanda said, as the hatch raised, and the bitter cold of the Kamchatka peninsula bid her welcome.

"Goodbye, Amanda. We will meet again," Artie said, through speakers mounted in the cockpit.

"Goodbye . . . Artie."

Amanda looked around, still uncomfortable talking to a ghostly voice attached to nothing. She reached out and shook Colonel James' hand, then stepped out of the cockpit and slid to the ground.

"Holy crap, it's cold," Amanda said, while slipping her feet into a pair of heavy boots.

After slipping on a full-length parka and gloves, she began walking away. There was a sharp crack, her ears popped, and the Dory was gone. Looking back, there was no sign that the Dory had ever been there. It was starting to snow.

Normal October weather on the Kamchatka peninsula meant highs in the 50s and lows in the 40s, but the weather was no longer normal in the Northern Hemisphere. Winter was coming early and was projected to be the worst in centuries. She stood and turned in a circle. Gray clouds hung thick and low. To the west she could just make out the lower levels of Vilyuchik, a stratovolcano that hadn't erupted in over 10,000 years. The peak, at over 7000 feet, was buried in the dense overcast. It was there she was headed, over 25 miles away . . . but not today.

"The tree line, up toward that intersection. I'm not expecting five stars, but I hope the accommodations are at least warm," she said, as she secured her backpack, slung her duffle bag across one shoulder, and trudged toward the red-roofed home over a mile away in the distance. As she walked down the rutted two-lane dirt road, her world began to close in. The snow thickened. The surrounding mountains disappeared. Even the tree line and the welcoming building that was her objective, began to fade away.

"Crap! Mistress Basra's is starting to look pretty good right now, and I want my long hair back," Amanda said, as the frost from her breath ran off to her right in a stiff breeze.

The snow fall increased. Soon it was over her ankles. The home in the distance had vanished. She glanced behind her and saw that her tracks were rapidly disappearing.

"Just keep going and stay on the road. Soon you'll be eating a hot bowl of borscht or whatever Russians eat when it's cold. Like

Basra says, 'Focus on the here and now. The past is gone. The future has yet to be written.' Then she'd show me a new move and throw me on my ass. Even my bruises have bruises."

She trudged on, head down against the wind, focusing on the rhythm of her steps. Glancing up, she smiled, having almost walked past the house. The powder dry snow was swirling around her as she turned toward the cream-colored building with a red metal roof. The main entrance had a green steel door at the top of four concrete steps. She climbed the steps, dropped her duffle bag, and tried to open the door. It was locked. After banging on the door several times, it cracked open. A large woman peered down at her.

"We are closed. What do you want?"

"I'd like a shot of Laphroaig scotch . . . preferably 10 years old."

The woman paused. Looked her up and down, then opened the door a little wider.

"You fit the description she gave me. Now, describe her. You know who I mean!" the woman said, her large frame filling most of the half-open doorway as the snow swirled around them.

"Six-foot-two, 180 pounds, short black hair starting to gray, rarely smiles, and has a high tolerance for pain."

"Hmm . . . she's getting fat. She used to be rail thin and could run like a deer," the woman said, then nodded and pushed open the door.

Amanda stepped into the entry, noticing that the woman was as tall as Janet and probably weighed 250 pounds. Then she noticed a man standing in the shadows on her left. He smiled as he lowered the semi-automatic pistol in his right hand.

"We were expecting you early this morning. She said you were usually very punctual. By the way, my name is Ulyana. That is Luka, my husband. We are a team, but he does what I tell him."

"I can believe that," Amanda mumbled, while throwing back the hood on her parka.

"Little one, be forewarned, I have ears like a cat, and she was correct. You would suck at poker. Your eyes tell everything you think. Disrespect me again, and I will chain you out back like a disobedient dog," Ulyana said, as she picked up Amanda's heavy duffle bag and trudged up the stairs as if it weighed nothing.

Amanda began to reply, when Luka stepped forward, placed his index finger across his lips, and shook his head. The man was tall, but very thin. He moved slowly, as if time had weighed him down. He had an easy smile and kind eyes.

"Your room is upstairs, young lady. There is a single hotplate. The food is all canned, but I think it is still good. We haven't had a visitor in a long time. Most observation of . . . things in this area, is done from . . . elsewhere. Now, please, follow me," Luka said, and followed his wife up the stairs.

The room was larger than Amanda expected. The front wall, overlooking the road, was 20 feet long. A kitchen of sorts was located just off the stairs. A bathroom, consisting of a tiny shower, sink and toilet, was on the far side of the room, separated from the main room by a curtain. The main part of the room consisted of a small, single bed, a long table, a desk and a wooden chair. The walls were painted white. Two windows looked out onto the road. The room was cool, bordering on cold. Amanda envisioned sleeping in her parka.

"She told us to expect another visitor. He is due sometime tonight. Perhaps he will be more punctual. We will see you in the morning. Then we will talk about . . . things to do," Ulyana said, while throwing the duffle bag on the table and walking away.

"Do not worry. She is like a Russian bear . . . gruff and a lot of noise, but she has a good heart," Luka said, as Ulyana stomped down the stairs.

"If you say so, but I notice that you are whispering."

"Well, I haven't lived this long by being foolish," Luka said, and winking, followed Ulyana down the stairs.

"That was interesting," Amanda said, as she hung the parka over the chair and began unpacking the duffle bag.

190

After unpacking, she stood by the window overlooking the road. The snow was falling in huge flakes. Visibility was down to 100 yards or less.

"Whoever comes in tonight better be more prepared than I was, or this mission may get delayed," she said, then turned as she heard footsteps coming up the stairs.

"I thought you could use something to warm you up," Luka said, as he handed Amanda a steaming mug.

The drink had a frothy head with a dark purple tinge. It smelled spicy and sweet.

"What is this?" she asked, took a sip, and felt her eyes water.

"Sbiten! It is a traditional Russian drink for the winter."

"Spitting?"

"No!" Luka said, and laughed.

"I am not serving you hot spit. It is pronounced with a 'B' . . . Sssbiten!"

"It's strong! I've never had anything like this. What's in it?"

"Well, I can't tell you everything, but it has honey, cloves, cinnamon, red wine and a few other things."

"There's more alcohol than red wine in here," Amanda said, while wrapping her hands around the hot mug and taking another sip.

"Well, perhaps just a touch of vodka . . . just a little. At least, just a little by Russian standards. Do you like?"

"It's perfect. Just what I needed."

"Good! I will leave you alone. Ulyana and I are still cleaning up the back room. Our next guest will be staying there. We use it as a storeroom."

"Luka, I was sent here on a mission . . ."

"Please, do not discuss such things. I don't need to know. I don't want to know. You are only a tourist who wandered up to our house in a snowstorm. If you die or you are caught, I don't want to know anything. They have ways of telling when you lie . . . unpleasant ways. Enjoy the Sbiten," Luka said, then turned and left.

Amanda watched him go, then returned to the window and watched the snow continue to fall. The snow was coming down so heavily that the road was no longer visible from the window.

"Daddy would have liked this. He loved it when it snowed. He would take all us kids outside to play. Mama just spent more time baking," Amanda thought, then remembered Artie, and how it dredged through her memories, like a child pulling things out of a toy box. She shivered, sipped more Sbiten, then sat at the small desk and opened her laptop.

"Another 'sneak in, sneak out' mission. The last one didn't go as planned, but at least we stopped the nuke. Holy crap! I'm back at another volcano," Amanda said, as she remembered the galleria on La Palma and the nightmares she was still having.

"Focus, Amanda! Our satellites above Russia have been destroyed. Old images don't show a facility of any kind on the east side of the volcano, but on the west side . . . there is this," she said, while opening a file on her laptop and expanding the enclosed image.

"This has to be the power source, but it doesn't look like a power plant. It looks like a factory. But who puts a factory this size on the lower slope of an active volcano? Crap! I've been down this trail a dozen times! It could be this . . . it could be that . . . all theories, no proof. The only thing I know for sure is this volcano was the source of the energy beam that hit the Kraken. There must be another complex built into the east side . . . underground. Great, more tunnels!" she said, while gulping the last of the Sbiten.

"A little vodka! Right! I haven't eaten all day, and now I'm getting a serious buzz. I'm starving! I wonder what's in those cans?" she said, as she turned in the chair and stared at the cans stacked on a shelf above the sink.

She found a pot, a can opener and a spoon. Now she had to choose what to heat up.

"Well, this can has a picture of a cow and this one a pig. So at least I know which animal is in here. What other options? Oh, God!

This one has a picture of a horse!" she said, longing for a can of Campbell's Chicken Noodle soup.

"Ahh . . . baked beans, some corn . . . now we're getting somewhere. I'll mix them together with the beef and make a stew. Marissa would be proud of me," she said, while remembering the smiling face of her friend from La Palma.

An hour later, she was full and lying in bed, almost asleep, when she heard boots coming up the stairs. A tall man appeared. He was still wearing a heavy white coat, pants and boots. Piercing blue eyes stared down at her as she swung her legs off the bed.

"Come, we're leaving now. If we wait any longer the snow will be so deep, we won't be able to get there for weeks."

"I just got here. We need to talk, study maps, make a plan."

"We'll plan along the way. It will take a day to get to Vilyuchik, maybe longer. Get dressed, grab your things . . . now!"

Amanda was aggravated with herself for jumping up and obeying his order. She was the agent and she didn't even know who this man was.

"Listen, I'm not going anywhere until you . . ."

"My name is Ruslan Gagarin, and no, I'm not related to the famous cosmonaut. I despise where that bastard Morozov has been taking our country. He is no better than the communists. Now he goes to war with America. I want a free Russia, a real republic, not another slave state. So . . . do you want to go find out what shot down your super plane or do you want to spend the winter eating canned horse?" Ruslan asked, while glancing at the meager rations on the shelf above the sink.

Amanda thought for about five seconds, then threw on her coat and boots, and packed her gear into her backpack. The snow was over a foot deep when she stepped out of the house. Ulyana couldn't be bothered to see them off. Luka smiled and nodded, as she turned and stared at the tan house with the red metal roof.

"Get in!"

The vehicle looked like a jeep sitting on top of a small tank. It was painted green and white. When she climbed up the side of the track system and slid through the door, she almost choked on the smell.

"Sorry, I'm also a trapper. I use entrails for bait. They are a little ripe. The scent travels much further that way. It is irresistible. I don't really notice it anymore. Close the door or we will freeze," Ruslan said, as he released the parking brake on the Uchtys ZVM 2410 all-terrain vehicle.

The inside was cramped. The vehicle was only 13 feet long and seven feet wide. There was no steering wheel. Two levers, attached to the column, were used to steer by increasing or decreasing the speed of each track. The interior was more spartan than the Strykers she had ridden in at Harris. The back seats had been ripped out to make room for Ruslan's gear and 'catches'. Amanda had to throw cans, old wrappers and trash into the back to make room to sit down.

"Ulyana called me on the radio last night. I was over 50 km south of here. 'Be here by noon tomorrow,' she said. 'A friend wants to visit the slopes of Vilyuchik.' Of course, I knew that was bullshit! No one visits Vilyuchik this time of year, not even a volcanologist. So, I knew it was a mission. I'm not an idiot. I may live in the middle of nowhere, but I know the world is going to shit!"

Amanda looked in the back of the Uchtys. Along with the cooler, scraps and garbage was a case of 'Russian Power' energy drinks. She picked up one of the drinks. The design on the black can was a medieval Russian warrior drawing his sword.

"How many of these have you had?" Amanda asked, while trying to decipher the ingredients.

"I have not had much sleep. I had to drive all night to get here. So . . . maybe six . . . or seven. I'm not sure," Ruslan said, as he reached past her and retrieved another can from the back.

"A quick stop before we head for the volcano. I will steal some of Ulyana's gas, and I have to piss," Ruslan said, as he shifted into first and drove around the back of the house.

"Great! My guide is a hunter-trapper hyped up on energy drinks. This is off to a good start. A day at Mistress Basra's is starting to look better and better," Amanda thought, as Ruslan drove around back, and started fueling the vehicle while emptying his bladder at the same time.

"Much better! Now we go!" Ruslan said, as he leapt back in the Uchtys and they sped off into the heavy snowfall.

CHAPTER 29

Slopes of Vilyuchik
Kamchatka Peninsula, Russia
October 17, 1545 hours PETT (Kamchatka Time)

For hours they followed a white ribbon through a long valley with mountain peaks on every side. The lesser peaks were attendants, servants of the great stratovolcano behind them. Vilyuchik rose into the sky on the left until it disappeared in the low hanging clouds.

"At least the snow has stopped. In another hour you will see why we can't go any further," Ruslan said, the first words he had spoken in over two hours.

Amanda had been studying topographic maps and satellite photos of the area. There was a long valley on the southern side of the volcano. She hoped to use the valley to get to the eastern side of the peak, where she expected to find the weapon system she had theorized.

"What do you mean, 'any further?' We have to go up this valley after we find the power station," Amanda yelled, over the growling sound of the engine and the clatter of the tracks.

Ruslan looked at the map, shook his head, then said, "Little lady, we will never get off the road. I am told to take you somewhere, so I do as I am told. But I will not turn myself in to the authorities and tell them that I am transporting a CIA agent."

"What are you talking about? Just drive me up the valley!"

He shook his head as if talking to a child, then grew silent, refusing to answer any of her questions. Amanda's best glare only elicited a smile. Frustrated, she returned to her files, ignoring the incredible beauty that surrounded her.

· · · ·

One hour later

The two-lane road rose up and over a steep ridge on the western flank of Vilyuchik. The constant crossbacks, no guard rails, and snow-covered roads left Amanda on edge. She and her father had slid off a highway and down an embankment after dropping her oldest brother off at Appalachian State one winter. After that, she had always been nervous driving in the snow.

"You can relax now. We are at the top. This is called the Viluchinsky Pass. The view during the summer is incredible. There are benches off to the side where couples come and kiss. Now look below. It is just clear enough to see the plant," Ruslan said, while pulling off the road and parking the vehicle.

"What? All I see is snow and mountains!"

"Then we will get out. Grab the binoculars. They are in the glove box," Ruslan said, as he slid out the door and down the side.

Amanda shuddered when she got out. The wind was fierce, and the temperature must have been in the 20s.

"This way! There is an overlook for tourists," Ruslan said, as he trudged off in the two-foot-deep snow.

Amanda followed, stretching to stay in his footsteps, until they reached a stone platform built on the side of a cliff. Then she saw the complex far below, deep in the valley. The buildings were low, only two stories, and painted a white, brown and green camouflage pattern.

"Five years ago, that was the location of the Rodnikova Tourist Base. There were half a dozen buildings and a small airstrip. Tourists used to fly in during the Summer and climb the volcano.

Volcanologists were there nine months of the year. Now it is gone. The government declared the valley a 'Closed Area' and built this place down below. If we drive further down the highway, you will see a guarded entrance, fences and many soldiers. That is why we go no further. They have roadblocks. They don't even like people driving by this area. They will stop us and ask questions, check our identity cards. I will be shot, and you will go to prison. Do you understand now?"

Amanda took the binoculars and began studying the layout of the complex. There were four large, two-story buildings set in a square. Each was over 200 feet on a side. At the center was a fifth building over 300 feet long and over 100 feet wide.

"The center building . . . that has to be a turbine building. The others must be pumping stations and steam generators. The piping is underground. But what is the power source? Still, if we take out the turbine, then . . ."

"Take out? What take out? There are hundreds of soldiers down there. I have seen tracked vehicles with missiles. We are not going down there to . . ."

They both stopped talking when the air began to hum. At first, Amanda thought it was the wind or a plane passing over at low altitude, but the volume of the humming sound increased. Then it happened . . . a sonic boom that made the ground tremble. The beam emitted from the other side of Vilyuchik lasted for over a second . . . and then it was gone. Amanda rubbed her eyes. It felt like she had stared at the sun or a welding torch. She opened her eyes and the afterimage of a streak of light was burned into her retina.

Ruslan began cursing in Russian as he knelt in the snow and began rubbing it into his eyes.

"Saint Matrona, protect us from evil. Protect our eyes from harm at the hands of this demon weapon," Ruslan prayed, as he continued to rub snow into his eyes and face.

Amanda didn't know who Saint Matrona was, but her eyes and skin were burning, and the snow helped. After a few minutes, the pain eased, and she knelt back in the snow and tried to open her eyes. The brightness of the snow was painful, but bearable.

"CIA lady, what was that?"

"My name is Amanda. That was a laser weapon, a very powerful one. I'm too late. I failed."

"They may have destroyed the Kraken. That's the only thing they would be shooting at," she thought, as she struggled to her feet and leaned on the railing while removing her camera from her backpack.

She had taken three pictures when the humming began again.

"Close your eyes! Turn away!" Ruslan yelled, as he grabbed her by the shoulders and thrust her into the snow face first.

The boom was as incredible as the first as it echoed across the surrounding mountains.

"How long was that between shots? What time did we get up here?" Amanda asked, while pushing Ruslan off her.

"Six minutes! I looked at my watch to see if I could still focus. The first shot was at 1650. The second at 1656 . . . more or less."

Amanda sat in the snow, head in hands, while thinking, *"If the first shot had missed, the Kraken would have been long gone. Which means they hit it but didn't destroy it. The second shot may have destroyed it, but if it didn't . . . a third shot in six minutes."*

"How much longer until six minutes after the second shot?"

"Four minutes! You think it will shoot again?"

"Only if they have to," she replied, as she leaned over the stone railing and began taking more pictures.

"Three minutes!"

"We wait!"

"And then what?"

"Then I forward what information and recommendations I have, and we go hide somewhere. Then we wait for a reply."

"What are you going to recommend?"

"I wish we could get to the other side of the volcano. I need to see the weapon."

"You may be little, but you are crazy. I like that! So, what recommendation?"

"Simple, destroy the turbine building. No turbine, no electricity. No electricity, no laser," Amanda said, as she picked up a handful of snow and began rubbing her eyes again.

"One minute!"

Amanda placed her camera on the rail and started the video, hoping to get a recording of the laser being activated. Two minutes later, they both turned and stared at each other.

"Your face is red," Ruslan said.

"So is yours. That beam was a mile or two away and it burned our skin. That was a lot of power," she replied, while wondering if the Kraken still existed.

A minute passed, then another. It had been eight minutes since the last shot.

"*The Kraken is either destroyed or it moved.* I think it's time for us to go," Amanda said, as the sun dipped below the edge of the cloud cover.

"I agree! That road is tricky in the dark. Sometimes you must guess at where the edge is," Ruslan said, as he began walking back toward the Uchtys.

"Are we going back to Ulyana's place?" Amanda asked, as she gathered her gear and stored it in her backpack.

"No, too far in the dark. There are some old lodges a few miles north. They are still quite beautiful and sit in the middle of a forest. They used to be full, even this time of year, but all the security has chased people away. The owner still lives there, but he stays drunk all the time. He is a good friend. We will stay there."

"Good, I need to forward all my data. Then we'll wait and see what they want me to do next," Amanda said, as they reached the vehicle, stepped up the tracks and slid in through the small doors.

"As you wish, CIA lady whose name is Amanda. I like that name, very American. It sounds like a TV star. Are you named after a TV star?"

"No, I'm named after my father's mother. She died before I was born . . . brain tumor.

My mother, she died of such a thing. She and my father lived in Pripyat in 1986. I was very young."

"Chernobyl!"

"Yes . . . Chernobyl. They were not evacuated until two days after the accident. My father, thyroid cancer, and my mother . . . I sometimes wonder when it will come for me."

"I lost both my parents at Harris. The fallout . . ."

"I am sad for you. That was not long ago," Ruslan said, as he started up the Uchtys, put it in gear and spun in a circle.

"Does the pain ever go away?" she asked.

"It was almost 40 years ago, and I never really knew them. I have a few memories . . . and some pictures given to me by relatives. I was six when she died; my father, a year after that. The pain? The pain becomes a hole . . . an empty place in your heart. It is like a bad knee or a bad back. The pain never goes away, but you learn to live with it. I think it would be worse if I had known them for . . . sorry, sorry. I am clumsy with words. I don't think before I talk. I'm not used to being around people," Ruslan said, then was silent.

"Does this place have vodka? After today, I could use a drink," Amanda said, while staring out the window at the white expanse that filled the land and the sky.

"CIA Amanda, this is Russia! If a hotel or lodge does not have vodka, it would be suspected of being a nest for foreign spies and burned to the ground," Ruslan replied, then laughed at his own joke.

"Good! Vodka always tastes the same to me no matter what the brand. Maybe you can teach me the difference."

"Ah, good lady, you have come to the right place . . ." Ruslan began, then talked for the next hour about the plusses and minuses of various brands of Russian vodka.

CHAPTER 30

USS Kraken
600 miles above the Central United States
October 17, 0450 UTC

"Colonel Kerchee, are you sure about that order?" asked Lieutenant General Crowley, as he emerged from his cabin directly below the Command Center of the USS Kraken.

Crowley was buttoning his uniform when he stumbled while climbing the stairway that led to the Command Center.

"Absolutely, Sir! Directly from the Chief of Staff at the Pentagon," COL Kerchee said, as he caught the arm of his commanding officer.

"Drop lower into the atmosphere? The Russians can track us? I need the details, Colonel! Now!" Lieutenant General Crowley said, as he shook off his XO's hand.

"Sir! He said they have some type of super laser that can penetrate our shielding . . . an upgraded version of the weapon that has been hitting the Dorys! He said we have to drop below the horizon immediately!"

LTG Crowley reached the upper level of the Command Center and paused, leaning against the railing as he continued to recover from a deep sleep.

"The sleeping pills were a mistake. I never should have taken them. I'm still groggy and I need to focus," Crowley thought, as he

turned to his XO and said, "Get me some damn coffee. Strong and black! I'll review the details of the order from my console."

"Sir, they were insistent! We need to drop lower as soon as possible. They were very urgent!"

"The Pentagon is always urgent, Colonel. I'll review the order, then we'll see if it makes any sense. We're invisible and damn near invulnerable. Whatever has taken out a couple of Dorys won't even scratch our skin," Lieutenant General Crowley said, as he plopped into his chair, opened the file with the order from the Pentagon, and began reviewing it.

. . . .

The impact of the first beam strike bored completely through one section of the triangular-shaped Kraken. The diamond coating and carbon nanotube skin that had been thought impervious, was vaporized, leaving a meter-wide hole completely through the vessel. In a ship 600 feet across, a meter-wide hole might seem insignificant. In the vacuum and cold of space, no 'leak' was insignificant.

The Kraken shuddered as it was struck. Alarms and emergency lighting went on throughout the ship. The sound of explosive decompression echoed throughout the vessel. The loss of pressure caused bulkhead penetrations to automatically seal. The ship was destabilized as primary power was severed to the Alpha power nacelle.

General Crowley and Colonel Kerchee stared at each other for a full second, before their training took over.

"Damage report, XO. Find out what struck us, where, and what systems were effected," Lieutenant General Crowley ordered, while forcing himself to sit and remain calm. He glanced at the order from the Pentagon before closing the file.

"On it, Sir!" Colonel Kerchee said, as he stepped down one level to the Systems Officers.

"Major Tall, propulsion status?"

"Alpha nacelle down from a power loss. Attempting to reroute power through secondary. Secondary down! Trying tertiary! Alpha

203

nacelle now has power. Running diagnostic. This will take some time, Sir," replied Major Andrew Tall.

"Five minutes and 28 seconds, as I remember. Let me know the results when you're complete," the XO said, as he stepped over to the Sensor Officer, Major Alonzo Smith.

"What hit us, and where did it come from, Major Smith?"

"Some type of energy weapon. I've got a penetration from Deck 5 up to Deck 1. We've been shot straight through! Emergency bulkheads have shut, but we've had losses. Two of the railguns have been damaged. The on-duty weapon crew was . . . vented into space. Their biosensors show them outside the ship. Two additional personnel were vented, and one other has completely disappeared. She must have been struck . . ."

" . . . by the beam. I get the picture, Major. Now, where did this attack originate?"

"Somewhere on the east coast of Russia. Give me ten minutes and I can give you the exact location," Major Smith said, as data continued to flood in from damaged systems aboard the ship.

"Major Tall! Propulsion status? We're sitting here waiting for another strike!" said Colonel Kerchee.

"Sir! Without a complete diagnostic of the system, I won't be able to guarantee that the Alpha nacelle will function properly. If we try to power up and it fails, then we could cause even more damage. Damage we can't repair."

"Major, if we get hit again, in some place critical, it won't make any difference!"

"Four minutes and forty-eight seconds, Colonel! Please, just wait!"

.   .   .   .

Vilyuchik Volcano
Southwest of Primorskiy
Kamchatka Peninsula, Russia
October 16, 1555 PETT

"Doctor Baranov, when will the weapon be ready for another shot? The American craft is helpless. We can finally see them visually, and on radar. They are drifting. We must not allow them to recover!" General Vova Kotov demanded, as he paced across the small control room seated hundreds of feet below the peak of Vilyuchik.

"General, you know the answer as well as I do," Dr. Pavel Baranov said, as he pointed at the large countdown timer mounted on the far side of the room.

"That is the ideal time! When can the system fire another shot?"

"That . . . is the only time, General! Six minutes and forty-five seconds from now. If we fire again before the system has cooled, we will damage the cylinders. They reach a temperature of over 2000 degrees Celsius after activation. They must be allowed time to cool. If we fire before then, they will exceed the melting point of the glass and the system will be useless, " Dr. Baranov calmly replied, while he studied data from the first ever shot of the Lightning Spear.

"Doctor, if we destroy this cursed thing, the Americans lose the high ground. This craft destroyed the People's Republic of China by itself! Do you understand what I am saying? It cannot be allowed to survive . . . at . . . any . . . cost!"

"How do you know that the Americans don't have more of these craft? It would take months for us to replace the cylinders. We must wait! Go have some tea. You make me nervous with all your pacing and shouting. In six minutes, I will punch another hole in the vaunted Kraken. Now that we can see it, we can kill it for good. The last shot was a guess based on the ionizing radiation field it emits. This shot will hit it dead center. The explosion should be quite entertaining."

"Doctor, I order you to take the shot now. Or I will have you taken out and shot!"

Dr. Baranov began laughing, then replied, "General Kotov . . . President Morozov is my brother-in-law. Do you really want to continue this conversation? I think it would be far easier for me to have you taken out and shot. Now go away and come back in five minutes!"

. . . .

USS Kraken
0455 hours UTC

"Major Tall! Propulsion status?" asked Colonel Kerchee, while standing at the Major's shoulder.

"Diagnostic complete . . . alpha nacelle operable . . . tertiary power routing stable. We can safely move, Colonel!"

"General?" Colonel Kerchee asked, as he turned toward General Crowley.

Crowley nodded, knowing that his carelessness had cost lives and damaged an irreplaceable vessel during a time of war.

"Major Baker, reduce altitude to 200,000 feet," Colonel Kerchee ordered.

"200,000 feet, aye!"

From a distance, the huge craft began to glow, as the main power core transferred energy to the three Mercury Plasma Field Engines mounted in the corners of the huge triangular craft.

"General! There is a power surge at the location detected on the Kamchatka Peninsula. I think they're getting ready to . . ." warned Major Smith.

"Major Baker! Move us now! No questions! Now!" shouted Lieutenant General Crowley.

Major Baker activated the 'Emergency Move' alarm, counted to three to give the crew time to brace themselves, and dropped the

Kraken to 200,000 feet from an altitude of 300 miles. An intense beam of energy passed through their previous location 2.47 seconds after their departure . . .

CHAPTER 31

USS North Carolina
15 miles northwest of
Ensenada, Mexico
October 15, 0500 hours UTC

"Captain, you wanted me to wake you when we were 15 miles north of All Saints Bay. What are your orders?" Lieutenant Commander O'Teul asked, as she shook her captain into wakefulness.

Captain North pushed her hands away, as he swung his legs over the edge of his bunk, and asked, "Any sign of the Russians?"

"Negative, Sir! We're still at 12 knots and heading toward the last known location of our two carriers. The water here is shallow. The depth is 310 feet and we're skimming the bottom."

"All stop, XO. Maintain silence. I'll be in the Control Center in five minutes."

"Aye, Captain! Five minutes!"

. . . .

Six minutes later

"Lieutenant Bottom, any contacts in our area?" asked Captain North as he entered the Command Center.

"Negative, Sir! We had the Russian on sonar until 26 minutes ago. Then he disappeared."

"Disappeared? Any theories, Lieutenant Bottom?" Captain North asked, as he gestured for his XO to remain silent.

"I . . . Sir . . . they may have gone out of our effective range."

"Or?"

"They . . . may have gone silent . . . and they're waiting for us."

"Or perhaps both, Lieutenant. In our line of work, predator and prey are one and the same. It's all a matter of timing. I think this Captain is luring us into his version of a trap. What do you think, Lieutenant Bottom?"

O'Teul stood silently watching. She had seen Captain North use events like this before, and she was still dumbfounded . . . amazed.

We could be dead in a few hours, or a few minutes. We don't know where the Russian is, and he's still using this as a training moment for his junior officers," she thought, as she stood by his side and watched Lieutenant Bottom struggle for an answer.

"The carriers, Lieutenant Bottom . . . do we have the present location of the carriers? They're big, they float, they should be easy to find."

"Yes, Captain! They're both in All Saint's Bay. They're about a mile apart, approximately four miles off the coast."

"Excellent! That means that our friend has his boat somewhere nearby. The Russians are waiting for us to show up and approach the carriers. Then he intends to sink us. So, what are our options, Lieutenant Bottom?"

"We have to sink him first!"

"How?"

"We have to be very quiet as we approach. Which means . . . we have to go very slowly with the condition we're in."

"And?"

"We have to find him first."

"And how do we do that, Lieutenant?"

"Sir . . . if it's an ambush, we have to figure out where the best place for that is and sneak up on him."

"All right, Lieutenant, let's look at this," Captain North said, as he walked up to the chart table and expanded the digital map of All Saints Bay.

"So where would you be, Lieutenant Bottom, if you knew we were coming from the north and you wanted to be able to cover the entire bay?"

The digital map showed the u-shaped bay with two small islands at the southern end. Lines, like those on a topographic map, showed the distance to the bottom in meters.

"I'd be here, Sir! At the southern end of the bay. Where this peninsula extends out and you have a half mile gap before you get to these two small islands. The water is over 200 meters deep and you can see the entire bay."

"So, do you think we should just cruise into the bay and approach our carriers?"

"No, Sir! We should . . . we should, go around the islands and approach him from behind!"

"Lieutenant Bottom, there may be hope for you yet! XO, maintain 12 knots. Set a course for this northern most island, All Saints Island. Keep the island between us and this location," the Captain said, as he pointed at the gap between the island and the peninsula that formed the southern half of the bay.

"Captain, how can you be so sure that the Russian sub is there?" Lt. O'Teul asked.

"Because, XO, that's where Lieutenant Bottom said the Russian sub would be . . ."

· · · ·

K-335 Gepard
Southern end of All Saints Bay
0800 hours UTC

The Gepard hovered just above the rearward slope of the Punta Banda peninsula, 510 feet below the surface of the southern edge of All Saints Bay. Captain Bogdanov was resting in his cabin reading a Russian copy of 'The Hunt for Red October' when a knock came on his cabin.

"Enter!"

"With all due respect, Captain, it's been ten hours and no sign of any American submarine. We still have an assignment! The American carriers are ripe for the taking. The Motherland needs such assets. We can offload the Spetsnaz and the specialists. Then we escort one of these vessels back to Russia. What are we waiting for?" asked Senior Lieutenant Lagunov.

Captain Bogdanov marked his place and laid the book aside as he sat up.

"Senior Lieutenant Lagunov . . . he is coming, this American. He does not play by the rules. Nor is he restricted by the training he has received. This one is a thinker, Senior Lieutenant Lagunov. That makes him unpredictable. That makes him dangerous. As I sit here listening to you question my command decisions, he is slowly approaching us. He knows where we are. Does that frighten you, Senior Lieutenant? It should! I can feel his mind as we talk. This one is a great cat, a wounded cat, but he approaches us from downwind so we can't smell him."

"Captain, this makes no sense. We are in submarines! We are not cats that can smell their prey."

"Correct, Senior Lieutenant . . . and at this point in your career you are a fool who still has a great deal to learn. When I have need of you, I will let you know. Please close the door on the way out," Captain Bogdanov said, as he picked up the book and resumed reading.

CHAPTER 32

Officer's Railcar
Prince George, British Columbia, Canada
October 15, 2130 hours PST

The railcars were old Tempo passenger cars built in the late '60s. Each coach held 80 troops. The bench seats were arranged in pairs with a small table between them. The soldiers were packed in shoulder to shoulder. Their personal gear was thrown in wire racks above their heads. The officers were in a modified version, more like a club car. The bar had been removed and supports installed for the regiment's communication equipment. The cars smelled of old leather, metal, and too many people. The railyard that dominated the northern end of the city had never seen a train quite like this one. The line of tanks, recon vehicles and troop cars stretched from one end of the yard to the other. Autos and trucks were lined up on 1st Avenue, parallel to the railyard, as citizens stopped and stared at the seemingly endless line of military vehicles. News was slow, and internet service had become sporadic, but they knew war was coming their way.

"We have to decide now, Colonel. Do we give them the entire Yukon Province and make our stand here in British Columbia, or do we proceed further? The engineer told me they will have refilled the train's diesel engines in 20 minutes. We're prepared to head further north. What is your decision?" asked Major Jacob Manx, as the regiment's officers awaited their commander's decision.

"The only orders we received, Major, were to proceed to Prince George and await further orders from Edmonton. That is what I intend to do," replied Lieutenant Colonel Edward Steele, commanding officer of the Royal Canadians regiment.

"That may be a problem, Sir. We haven't been able to reach Edmonton for over an hour. Our signals people say the comms are being jammed. It seems the further west we go, the worse the jamming gets. Contact was intermittent. Now we can't get through at all."

"Cell phones haven't worked for a week. Has anyone gotten off the train and tried a damn landline?"

Major Smith looked at one of the communications officers and nodded. The officer grabbed his hat and rushed off the train.

"Major, if the Russians want to head into the US, there are only two major roads coming down from the north, Highways 16 and 97. They intersect here, at Prince George. Canada is a huge country, and we have very limited military resources. We need to make a stand at a place of our choosing. We need a choke point where we can't be flanked. Plus, the further they have to drive, the more it will stress their vehicles. Logistics will become a major problem for them the further they go."

"You're talking about a defensive battle. Make them come to us. We have mountains to our east, and hills and lakes to our west. The terrain funnels them through here. At least for another two months, when everything will freeze solid."

"Exactly! The only worry will be air support. If they dominate the sky, then we are done for. We must have some air support. The more we talk about it, the more convinced I become that this is the place. We must keep them on this side of the Nechako River. If we can't contact Brigade Headquarters in Edmonton within the hour, then we'll be staying here. This will be where we make our stand," Steele said, as he placed his finger on the map spread out before them . . . on the city of Prince George.

. . . .

Troop Passenger Car
'A' Troop, 1st Squadron

"Quit your bitchin'! Would you rather be sitting outside in the dark and the cold, waiting for the powers that be to decide our fate? It's warm in here. The chow's good. It'll hit the fan soon enough. Now give me another card . . . just one," said Sergeant Jessica Brown, tank commander of 'Kathleen', one of the 40 Leopard 2A4 medium tanks sitting on railcars on the outskirts of Prince George.

Women had been integrated into the combat arms in the Canadian Army since 1989. The first Canadian woman killed in combat was Captain Nichola Kathleen Sarah Goddard, in 2006, in Afghanistan. Sergeant Brown had named the tank after her.

"Come on, Sarge! The Lieutenant talks to you. Where are we going? When do we get to kill some Russians?" asked Master Corporal John 'Punty' Smith, the crew's gunner.

"Be careful what you wish for, Punty. You might choke on that wish one day," said Corporal Kayla Tremblay, the crew's driver.

"The only thing I'll be choking on are the fumes of success after I've killed five Russian tanks and become Canada's next tank ace! Read 'em and weep, ladies!" said Punty, as he laid three aces and two fives on the table.

"Shit! Three hands in a row! How does he do that?" asked Private William MacDonald, the loader on the tank crew.

"It's like shooting the main gun, young Private. It takes skill and concentration," Punty said, while scraping his winnings to his side of the table.

"Luck!" said the other three crewmates at the same time, as they started to laugh.

"Just remember, Old Punty will keep you all safe when the shooting starts."

214

At 31, he was the oldest member of the crew.

"Correction! it takes all four of us doing our jobs as a team to keep us all safe! Kathleen is just 60 tons of steel without us," said Sergeant Brown, as she stared at the three soldiers who crewed her tank.

"And without her, we're just a bunch of freakin' infantry!" said Private MacDonald, as he bumped fists with Punty.

"That's right! We take care of her, and she takes care of us. Now, shut up and deal the damn cards! It's time for a comeback!" said Sergeant Brown.

. . . .

Troop Passenger Car
2330 hours PST

The poker games had shut down 30 minutes ago. The lights were off, and the sound of snoring was starting to fill the passenger car when the lights were flipped on.

"All right, boys and girls, nap time is over! The Canadian taxpayers aren't paying you to sleep. Off your asses and on your feet!" bellowed Sergeant Major Wessel, as he walked down the center of the car and shook people awake.

"Aww . . . why did it have to be the 'Weasel'? That high pitched voice is like fingernails down a chalkboard," mumbled Punty, as he rubbed the sleep from his face.

"What was that comment, Master Corporal Smith?" Sergeant Major Wessel asked, as he spun around and approached Punty.

"Nothing, Sergeant Major! Wide awake and ready to go, Sergeant Major!" Punty said, as he snapped to attention while still sitting.

"Very good! That's what I thought you said! Now get to your vehicles. The free luxury ride is over. We have a nation to defend!" the Sergeant Major yelled, as he crossed over to the next passenger car and flipped on the lights.

. . . .

U.S. Customs and Border Protection
Alcan Port of Entry
October 16, 0630 hours PST

"Captain, the Russians are no more than five miles behind us. They must have brought in engineers and forded the blown bridges. This time the advance units include tanks. They look like T-72s or T-80s. They have infantry support, and I saw several Hinds above them," said Second Lieutenant Branson, his sole remaining officer.

"Very good, Lieutenant. We can't stop them. All we can do is relay your information and pull back. Sergeant Ivan, if you have any comm with your superiors, I would suggest you tell them that Canada has been invaded. It's up to them if they wish to defend your country. We're pulling back toward the US border," Captain MacLynn said, as he shook Jock's hand.

"Thanks for patching up our boy."

"Least we could do since we shot him. Our medic said he should be okay. He was lucky. The round didn't hit bone. Make sure he takes the antibiotics," Captain MacLynn said, as he turned and walked into his Stryker.

Jock stepped back as the ramp closed and the Americans drove south.

"What have you heard from 3rd Division, Jock?" Luke asked, as the remaining Canadian Rangers circled around their leader.

"The last thing I heard was the Strathconas are coming. That was four hours ago. I haven't been able to get through since then. We're going to go with our original orders to keep an eye on the Russians. Tell Division how many tanks and troops, the usual stuff."

"Eh . . . the Royal Canadians . . . the Strathconas! Our tanks! This shit is getting serious! Looks like a real fight is getting ready to

216

happen," said Aldo, as he smiled, and looked about at the somber faces of the patrol.

"You damn fool! People are going to start dying, and we might be with them!" Jillian said, as she cuffed Aldo on the back of the head.

"Ow . . . I'm wounded! Be nice!"

"Yeah, but he's right. If the Strathies are coming, then the government has decided Canada's going to war. I hope the Americans help us, or it's going to be a short one. Now . . . Rainer, Liz, I want you to head toward Prince George. Go to every town and house along the way and . . ."

"And what? Tell them that 'The Russians Are Coming'?" Liz asked, with a groan.

"Exactly! The Russians aren't coming here on holiday. From what the Yank Captain said, Alaskan citizens put up a fight. The Russian soldiers aren't going to see any difference between them and us. They'll be shooting anything that moves. People need to know to stay out of their way."

"What if people want to fight? What do we tell them?" Liz asked.

"Tell them to start organizing. Destroy any fuel supplies along the main highway. Block roads with trees . . . anything to slow them down. It's over 1300 miles from here to Prince George. The Russians are going to find out this is a big country, just like theirs. They aren't going to get to Prince George for days. The longer we delay them, the more time the Army has to prepare for a fight. Who knows? The Americans have a big military. They may drive north and give us a hand."

"So, this is it! When this is over, we'll get together and tell war stories. We'll see who can come up with the biggest lie!" said Aldo, as they all shook hands and headed for their vehicles.

CHAPTER 33

The White House
The Situation Room
Emergency Meeting of the National Security Council
Washington, DC
October 17, 0730 hours EST

"Welcome, Speaker Jacobson, Senator Marker. I thought it appropriate that the two of you should attend this meeting of the NSC. The things that we discuss, and hopefully decide, will have a lasting impact on the nation. Speaker Jacobson, you especially are welcome. As things stand, if something happens to me, you become President of the United States," said President Clarisse Beaumont.

"Thank you, Madam President, from both of us. I believe the saying is, 'United we stand, divided we fall'," responded the Speaker of the House.

The president nodded in agreement and said, "General Munford, please update us on the latest information."

"Madam President, things are not going well. Alaska is gone. The Russians have total control of the state. They have taken all our military bases, and the major seaports and airports. Their troops continue to pour into the state. We estimate their forces at over 50,000. This includes over 200 tanks and 500 armored personnel carriers. Those numbers are continuing to grow. Within a few days they will have repaired our airbases and started stationing their air assets to support their ground forces. At present, Russian troops are entering

Canada. The limited number of hard surface roads in the northwest of Canada will restrict their movements, at least for another few weeks. The Canadians will resist, but I don't know if they'll even slow the Russians down."

"How could they move that many troops and equipment so quickly? Why didn't we see them coming?" asked the President.

"War games, Madam President . . . war games. They had a massive set of maneuvers scheduled that included use of amphibious vehicles and 17 ROLOs."

"General, what is a Rolo?"

"Sorry, Madam President! ROLO stands for Roll-On-Roll-Off. They are ships designed to transport troops and vehicles, including tanks. They have large doors. When the ship approaches the shore or a dock, the vehicles don't have to be removed with a crane. They just drive down a ramp. The largest vessels can transport 25 tanks. They had 100,000 men and over 500 vehicles near their east coast staging for these war games. It's like they knew the Chinese attack was coming."

"The Chinese and the Russians coordinating? They've done that before, but that was back in the days of the USSR. Is it possible they formed a new alliance without us knowing?" the President asked, while staring at Miller Perez, the Director of the CIA.

"Madam President, I have received no information that would indicate the Republic of Russia and the People's Republic of China have formed a new alliance. I just don't think it's possible that we would have missed . . ."

"Like we missed the PRC sneaking 50 nuclear weapons into the United States?" asked the Attorney General.

The room erupted as politicians, bureaucrats and military officers all began shouting at once.

"Enough!" the President said, as she slammed her hand on the table.

"This is not business as usual! The bickering and turf wars must stop! Now, General Munford . . . please continue!"

"Madam President, as you know, the Kraken was attacked yesterday afternoon by a weapon system previously theorized by the CIA. It was severely damaged but survived. We are looking for a surface location within the United States to affect repairs," said General Munford, as the power elite of the United States struggled to keep their focus as the bad news continued to pour in.

"Madam President, we may be at the point of negotiating a peace treaty with the Russians . . . at any terms. Our nation is in shambles, and our military . . . I hate to say this, but our military forces may no longer be capable of defending the country," said Raymond Taggert, Secretary of State.

President Beaumont glanced around the table, searching for some type of consensus. Most of her cabinet looked down at their hands or nodded in agreement.

"General Munford . . . you agree with his assessment? The two men I trusted the most to remain strong, and you two are recommending that we surrender to the Russians? Is that what I'm hearing from you?" the President asked, as she struggled to control the emotion in her voice.

"Madam President, our military forces in the west are crippled. Our naval forces in the western Pacific have been almost eliminated. We have, maybe, a half dozen attack subs left, and a few boomers. An entire fleet is trapped inside the Puget Sound! The Army, Marines, Air Force, Navy . . . all West Coast bases have been wrecked. The battle in the east hasn't even started yet, but it will be brutal. It will expand into Europe, and probably the Middle East. We can't afford to move any of our resources to the Pacific, or we may lose the East Coast. Our NATO allies have weakened their militaries to the point where they are almost defenseless. And no one wants to start a nuclear war. Unless the Russians use them first, they're off the table. The Russians think they can beat us in a conventional war . . . and they may be right. Some of our projections show them crossing the Mississippi within 90 days. At present, we don't have the resources to fight a two-front war," said General Munford.

"Then we do what we've always done. We rebuild! Surrender is not an option. If you can't get the job done, then I'll find people who can. This nation has been on a war footing before, and by God, we'll do it again."

"Madam President, you're correct. We have done that before, at a time when the nation was stable and untouched by war. But this is now . . . first North Carolina, then the West Coast, and this business in Arkansas? Millions are dead, infrastructure is wrecked, the economy has crumbled, the stock market is in a freefall, earthquakes are now a constant thing across the country. We have three volcanoes erupting in the northwest, and more are predicted to start erupting at any time. The weather, Madam President . . . even the weather has turned against us. It's mid-October, and we're having heavy snow across the northern half of the country. The attack on China drove so much soil into the upper atmosphere that it's changed the weather by blocking out the sun. It may be years before it settles out!" said Sam Murkowski, Secretary of the Treasury.

"But . . . what do we gain if we surrender to the Russians? Will they care for the American people? Will they rebuild our cities? No, all we would gain is an occupying force from sea to shining sea. Do you know what would happen then? Resistance! There are more guns in this country than people. 'We the People' would see the Russians as occupiers and start killing them. Then the Russians would start killing our civilians en masse, just like they did in Afghanistan in the '80s. No! Hell no, we don't surrender! I'm ashamed and embarrassed that you would even suggest such a thing. The resources of this nation are still vast. We must figure out how to utilize them more efficiently. Delores, I need the Attorney General's Office to help coordinate this. We are a nation of laws, and I intend to keep it that way. But we can't get bogged down in lawsuits and court delays."

"Madam President, the National Emergencies Act of 1976 gives you broad powers in times of a declared national emergency. You can call up reserves, reinstate the draft, require manufacturers to switch to wartime production. There is a list of 136 separate items that you are authorized to do. It's complicated, but extensive. This is how FDR turned the country's manufacturing base into the Arsenal of Democracy during World War II," replied Delores Bull, the Attorney General.

"Madam President, if I might suggest, come before Congress. We're beyond a national emergency. We need a declaration of war. The Senator and I will back you," said Speaker Jacobson, with Senator Marker nodding in agreement.

"Carla, thank you for your support. Then that's what we're going to do. I go before a joint meeting of Congress tonight. Let's make it at 9 PM. We're declaring war on the People's Republic of China and the Republic of Russia. I will make the case to the nation that this is a war for our very survival. I need everyone in this room to cooperate with each other. Turf wars, partisan bickering, personal differences, all must go away. If this nation is going to survive, we have to get on the same page and stay there. We meet here tomorrow morning, same time, and I expect significant progress."

"Madam President, one more thing before we suspend this meeting," said the Secretary of State.

"Yes, Raymond?"

"You must select a Vice President. I know you've been incredibly busy, but it has to happen . . . and soon, Madam President! Please!"

"I know, I know. One thing at a time. Let's get past tonight first. Then we'll talk about it tomorrow morning. Now get to work, or we may not have a nation in 90 days."

CHAPTER 34

USS North Carolina
1mile west of
All Saints Islands
Ensenada, Mexico
October 17, 0340 hours UTC

"Anything on sonar, Lieutenant Bottom?" asked Captain North.

"Two things, Sir! A pair of prop noises and some whales, Sir! Lots of whales. Sounds like they're having a party."

"Can you ID the prop contacts?"

"Computer says they're inflatable assault boats . . . small ones."

"Course?"

"I think they're headed toward the TR. The satellite pics we have showed it a mile further out to sea than the Carl Vinson."

"Shit! One thing at a time!" thought Captain North.

"How close are the whales?"

"There's a pair just ahead, about 1200 yards, same heading, about 50 feet above us."

"Interesting! Forward speed, XO?" Captain North asked, while leaning over the plotting table. He began expanding the topographic map of the ocean bottom between the southern most of the All Saints Islands and the peninsula at the southern end of All Saints Bay.

"Same as the last 14 hours, Captain . . . 12 knots. Depth 270 feet. We're skimming along the bottom . . . still on a bearing of 1-8-0. The crew is starting to get a little antsy."

"So am I, XO. One way or the other, this will be over in a few hours, maybe sooner. We'll be turning northeast in about three minutes. The more I study the topography of the ocean bottom, the more I become convinced that our friend is right here," Captain North said, as he tapped a spot on the map.

"Why there, Sir?"

"There's a ledge right here . . . 223 feet down. He's sitting right there . . . waiting for us."

"Sir? Based on what? That would put them about . . . three miles from our current position."

"You ever do any hunting, Commander O'Teul?"

"Captain, I grew up in Houston. My father ran a Nissan dealership. My mother raised five of us. The only thing I ever hunted was my little brothers . . . usually all four of them."

"Well, I grew up near Charleston, South Carolina. We didn't have a lot of money. My father repaired cars and drank. The only thing he like better than drinking was hunting. He was good at both, but he never did them at the same time. When I was about 14, he heard about a buck up in Frances Marion National Forest. People said the buck had a huge rack, over 12 points. The only problem was, it wasn't buck season yet. My father considered that a technicality that he chose to ignore. We spent two days in a deer stand. We barely talked or ate or drank. We just waited for that buck. I was desperate to leave, but he would just shake his head. Near sunset on the second day, the buck showed up. He was gorgeous. That deer fed our family for months. I hated that hunt, but it taught me patience. Start passing the word, Lieutenant. Bring the crew to combat readiness," Captain North said, as he continued to study the terrain of his underwater hunt.

.   .   .   .

K-335 Gepard
0400 hours UTC

"Captain, the Spetsnaz have reached the first American carrier. They will commence boarding within a few minutes," said Senior Lieutenant Lagunov.

"Excellent, XO! I have beaten the American at his own game. By hiding from us, and approaching slowly from the rear, the island has masked his sensors from the bay where his carriers float helplessly. Soon, they will become the property of the Russian Republic. After the addition of attack helicopters and later, Mig-29Ks, we will have mobile airfields to support our conquest of the American West Coast. The only thing left is to dispose of the American sub. I suspect he is still 10-15 kilometers away. He will have drifted far west so he can slowly approach us from the rear," replied Captain Bogdanov.

"So, we go after him?"

"Correct, Senior Lieutenant Lagunov! It is time to go hunting! Lieutenant Aleksandrov, anything on sonar?"

"Negative, Captain. There are a few whales in the area. I think it is their mating season. They are not the quietest creatures," Lieutenant Aleksandrov replied, while making crude gestures with his hands.

The crew in the control center began to laugh, until silenced by the Captain.

"Quiet! These whales, are they all clustered together?"

"Well, no Captain. They seem to have paired off. Most are in the bay. A few are to the west of us."

"Where are the closest? Quickly now!"

"There are a pair to the west of us . . . on the surface . . . six point five kilometers away. Another pair are deeper, skirting the bottom."

"How close is that second pair?"

"Three kilometers, Captain!"

Captain Bogdanov leaned on the chart table and began thinking, "*The American can hear the whales as well as I can. If he is clever, and his crew is well trained, they will be silent. Any noise he is making will be masked by the whales. He could be far closer than I thought. Or am I starting to lose my nerve? If he is that close, and we start to move, he will see us and get in the first shot. But . . . if I sit here on the bottom and continue to wait . . . What would I do if I were in his place? I would get close and flush me out! I think I have waited too long! The big cat may have my scent!*"

. . . .

USS North Carolina
0400 hours UTC

"Captain, we've reached the end of the shelf around the island. The bottom is dropping down rapidly from 300 feet to almost 1500 feet," said Lieutenant Commander O'Teul.

"Almost like falling off a cliff, XO. Let her settle, slow to ten knots. Change heading to 0-6-5 degrees. Level out at 700 feet."

"Aye, Sir! Pilot! Speed ten knots! Heading 0-6-5 degrees! Depth 700 feet!" O'Teul said, as the pilot repeated her commands.

"XO, prepare to fire a brace of four torpedoes, as we previously discussed. We're going to bracket that ledge and flush him out!"

"Aye, Sir! Four Mark 48s are loaded in tubes one through four. Bracket pattern alpha two . . . five second launch delay . . . magnetic homing."

"Captain! Contact, 0-6-7 degrees! Heavy screws! He's coming off the . . . torpedoes! Two torpedoes in the water! Range 2600 meters!" shouted Lieutenant Bottom.

"Pilot, maintain heading and speed! Dive! Make our depth 1200 feet! XO, fire all four torpedoes! Activate electronic jamming! Fire acoustic countermeasures!"

. . . .

Now they all waited . . . Russian and American. Both crews knowing that the span of their lives might be measured in minutes. The K-335 Gepard erupted from the shelf at flank speed and sped for the open water of the bay and the American carriers. The North Carolina dove and stayed as silent as possible while leaving behind a set of spinning noise makers to attract the Russian torpedoes. The shelf erupted as two American torpedoes exploded just above the previous location of the Gepard. Torpedoes three and four continued on, still hunting their Russian prey. The North Carolina dove as the sea behind her burst in anger as the two Russian torpedoes followed the multiple acoustic noise makers. The whales, come to breed and expand their dwindling population, fled the area in fear, knowing that the surface creatures were killing each other once again.

CHAPTER 35

Da Ku Cultural Centre
280 Alaska Highway
Haynes Junction, Yukon, Canada
October 17, 0730 hours PST

"I don't think you understand, Mr. Kushniruk. Your people are in a great deal of danger. The Russian military have invaded Canada. They are on their way to the United States. Our nations are at war with Russia!" said Captain MacLynn, as he sat before the Chief and Council of the Champagne and Aishihik First Nations.

"Captain, my title is Chief . . . Chief Kushniruk, not 'Mister'. Our people have lived on this land for over 2000 years. We are not at war with anyone. The Tutchone people only wish to live in peace. If the Russians come, we will greet them the same as we greeted you, in peace. You are buying fuel and food. Then you will leave. We expect them to do the same," replied Chief Kushniruk.

"Chief Kushniruk, they are here making war. I don't think they will respect the rights of your people. They will take what they want and kill anyone that resists."

"The French, the English, both came this way. They took our land, our food, our people, and tried to destroy our heritage and customs. It has taken us decades to make the government of Canada restore our rights as indigenous people. The coming of the Russians will just become another part of our long story. We aren't going anywhere. My only concern is your presence in Haynes Junction. If the Russians come, and you are still here, there will be fighting. I would like you out of this area as soon as your vehicles are fueled."

The seven council members sat across from Captain MacLynn, behind a long cedar table. In the background stood a traditional canoe over 20 feet long. It had been carved from a single cedar tree. It was carved and painted with the iconography of the Tutchone people.

"Chief . . . Kushniruk, I'm not a citizen of Canada, let alone of your tribe. I don't have the right to tell you to do anything. But I think you are making a mistake. I'm not asking you to resist. I'm just advising you to leave this area, at least for a few days, until they have passed through. You can rebuild, but people are more difficult to replace. I've lost half my men in the last few days. Whether you like it or not, war has come to your land."

"Your war, not ours, Captain. I appreciate your input, but we are staying. Now, good day! I hope your journey home is more peaceful than it has been so far."

. . . .

Kluane Lake Bridge
40 miles west of Haynes Junction
0730 hours PST

The sound of the helicopter had preceded its appearance, as the lethal hunter slowly cruised along the highway that ran along the western edge of Kluane Lake. Its twin could be seen on the other side of the lake, over two miles away.

"Shit! Now what?" Luke asked, as he stood beside Jock, hidden by the trunk of a large pine. They had driven their truck deep into the trees south of the Kluane Lake Bridge . . . and waited.

"We stay put until they move on. Those Hinds are sniffing out anything that moves. If they catch us on the road, they'll kill us. Remember the shooting from last night. Those things can see in the dark."

"I saw a small stream bed 1000 yards back up the road. We could try taking that. We head into the hills, try to get over the ridge, and then we'll . . ."

"Forget it, Luke! My truck's not an ATV. Besides, we're supposed to be getting a head count of what's coming down the Alaska Highway. We can't do that if we keep running away."

"I wonder where Barry and his team are? Did they get past us last night?"

"Knowing Barry, they're probably 10 miles north counting Russians. He's retired Regular Force. He wouldn't do anything stupid."

"I tried getting him on the radio a few minutes ago, but I didn't get anything."

"The Russians are jamming comms. Did you try Liz and Rainer?"

"No, not since last night. They were doing like you ordered, stopping and warning people to leave. They said they would be in Haynes Junction, and then head for Whitehorse. I wouldn't be surprised if they just stopped at their cabin and laid low instead."

"If it was just Rainer, you'd be right. But Liz, she'll make him keep going. Keep trying to get Edmonton or anyone east of here. We have to establish some type of comm or we're just wasting our time. Information's no good if you can't get it to someone."

. . . .

Destruction Bay
24 miles north
0900 hours PST

"Major, based on the identification we retrieved from the bodies, they were some type of scouting unit for the Canadian military . . . the 4th Canadian Ranger Patrol Group," said Senior Lieutenant Vadik Kozvov.

"Are you certain? Two women and a man? No uniforms and all armed with bolt action rifles? They look more like partisans than a military unit," said Major Grisha Semanov, commanding officer of the 6th Motorized Rifle Battalion.

"The Canadians have been hiding behind the skirts of the Americans for decades, just like the Europeans. Units like these are more like Boy Scouts for adults than combat units. These three were driving in the dark last night and heading south. I guess they didn't know our flying wolves can see in the dark," said Senior Lieutenant Kozvov, as he handed a set of identify cards to Major Semanov.

"Jillian Chubak, Barry Todoschuk and Alison Toews, all members of this . . . ranger patrol. Did you find any communications equipment, cameras, notebooks?"

"The gas tank of their truck blew up when the Hind shredded the vehicle. We're lucky we found this much. But no equipment other than cell phones."

"Playing at soldier and doing a bad job of it got them killed. If this is the best Canada has, then this will be a long leisurely ride to the American border. Then we will see what the Americans have left. How long until the tanks are refueled?"

"At least 30 minutes, but we need another hour for maintenance. Some of these vehicles are older than I am."

"One hour, no more! I want to be at this intersection . . . Haynes Junction, before noon. The APCs will need fuel by then. We will see what the locals have to share," Major Semanov said, as he pointed at a map mounted on the inside of his BTR-80.

. . . .

Kluane Lake Bridge
1050 hours PST

"Jock! I've got Liz on the radio! She and Rainer are 10 miles east of Haynes Junction. They said the US Army passed through there

231

early this morning. Captain MacLynn talked to Chief Kushniruk, but the stubborn old bastard refused to order his people out of the area," said Luke, as he handed Jock the handset.

"He's liable to get them all killed! Liz, this is Jock. Have you tried to contact Edmonton yet?"

"Yes! We told them we were evacuating people from near the highway and trying to keep an eye on the Russians. Have you seen any yet?"

"Oh, yeah! We're just south of the Kluane Lake Bridge. We've got a good overlook from up on a ridge. The Russians have been crossing the bridge for the last 15 minutes. Now write this down and contact Edmonton," Jock said, as he glanced down at the steadily rising vehicle count that Luke was marking on a note pad.

"Go ahead. I'm ready!"

"So far, we've counted 48 Armored Personnel Carriers. Most of them are BTR-80s. We have counted 24 tanks. We think they're T-80s. Then there is one vehicle we can't identify. It's some kind of truck. It's as big as a semi, with a device mounted on the front, up above the cab. The device looks more like a telescope than a weapon. There's a dish mounted toward the rear of the vehicle. It rotates about once every two seconds. My guess is it's some type of radar. I'm forwarding a picture from my cell phone. We're about two kilometers away, so the pic is a little blurry."

"I've got the data! The pic's not bad. I'll forward this to Edmonton right now."

"Good . . . that's what we're here for. Let me know if you hear anything from Barry's team . . ."

CHAPTER 36

Navigation Bridge
USS Theodore Roosevelt
All Saints Bay
Ensenada, Mexico
October 17, 0800 hours PST

"We have secured the reactor compartments and the engine room, Captain Morazovich. Two of our technicians are bringing one of the reactors online. Another technician is in the engine room. We found four sailors hiding there. After a little persuasion, they confessed they were part of the engine room crew. We are putting them to work. Sergeant Sobol will stay there with our technician to ensure cooperation. We will have power in less than an hour. The USS Theodore Roosevelt is ours! We will be prepared to sail northward in approximately two hours," said Lieutenant Barzov, as he presented the ID badge of the Senior Reactor Operator to his commanding officer, Captain Mikal Morazovich.

"Excellent, Lieutenant! All we need is propulsion for now. The Motherland will be proud of us. Our mission parameters are complete. Now we sail this vessel up the coast. Our navy will take possession and put her to good use in establishing our dominance over the United States! A pity that the Gepard will have to sink the other one, but we can't risk letting the Americans regain control of it," Captain Morazovich said, while staring out at the surrounding sea from the Main Bridge of the American carrier.

The assault on the Roosevelt, affectionately known as 'The Big Stick', or simply as 'TR', had taken less than three hours. A skeleton crew of 30 sailors and six Marines had offered little resistance for the eight members of the elite 42nd Naval Recon Spetsnaz Unit. The Marines had been ambushed and died fighting. Eleven of the sailors had been killed or captured. The remainder were hiding in the vast ship, as the Spetsnaz hunted them down.

"Captain, one problem . . . we have been unable to contact the Gepard. The explosions of a few hours ago. The American sub . . ."

"We have seen neither sub. If the Gepard was successful in sinking the American, they would have surfaced and contacted us by now. Perhaps they killed each other. Contact fleet headquarters in Fokino. Request instructions, assuming the Gepard has been sunk. Ask them . . . what are our orders?"

"Understood, Sir!"

.   .   .   .

USS North Carolina
0800 hours PST

"Captain, the nukes say they can't get the reactor back online. One of the reactor coolant pumps has been damaged. They think it's a bearing problem with the motor," said Master Chief Petty Officer Ingeram, covered in sweat after making an entry into the reactor compartment to assess the damage.

"Can it be repaired?" asked Captain North, as he leaned back against the plotting table.

"I've got our two best mechanics looking at it. If they have to pull the motor, realignment is going to be a problem with the boat at this angle."

"Nothing we can do about that, Master Chief. Keep me informed!"

"Aye, Sir!" Ingeram said, as he headed aft.

"The last thing I expected was a problem in the reactor compartment. I thought the S9G Next Generation Reactor was supposed to be indestructible," said Lieutenant Commander O'Teul.

"It was designed to last for 30 years and take a combat beating. But, being rolled over multiple times, thrown up on a cliff, then dropped back into a bay, might be a little beyond design parameters, XO."

"Plus, we've been attacked twice. The "Tarheel Boat" has taken quite a beating, but we're still here, Sir!"

"Keeled over at 20 degrees, laying in the mud at 807 feet, on battery power. We don't know if we're still being hunted or not. But yes, we're still here, XO. It ain't over 'til it's over."

"Copy that, Captain . . . copy that!"

.   .   .   .

Punto Moro Resort
Ensenada, Mexico
0810 hours PST

Breakfast was well underway as Chef Marco Argulo began his stroll along the coastal walkway outside the Punto Moro Resort. The heady scent of a cup of Espresso Mexicano mixed with the scent of the sea had cleared his head of a lingering hangover. The richness of Blue Tribe Chiapas coffee, blended with powdered sugar, cinnamon, nutmeg, cayenne pepper and heavy cream, always put a jump into his step no matter how late he had been up the previous night. But the sight that greeted him as he left the covered veranda, and entered the path leading down to the beach, left him more than a little stunned. The nose of a huge submarine was resting on the black rock of the shore, not 300 feet away.

The rising sun was at his back. At first, he thought he was seeing a beached whale, a rare, but not unheard-of sight, at their location. But the men walking along the deck told him otherwise. When one of the men began pointing at him and shouting, he dropped his coffee and ran back toward the resort.

. . . .

K-335 Gepard

"Hurry, get the divers into the water! We must know the extent of the damage. Can we conduct repairs or not?" Lieutenant Lagunov shouted, as he stared at the back of the civilian running inland toward the resort.

He turned and looked at the brightening sky, knowing that the beach would be crowded with people within an hour. Which meant that Mexican authorities would arrive soon after. The top of the bulbous, towed sonar array was just visible above the water at the rear of the sub. With a glance, he could tell it had been twisted by the explosion of the American torpedo. If the four aft rudders, or worse yet, the propeller had been irreparably damaged, the sub might be stranded.

"We couldn't run aground in some place deserted. No . . . we had to find a beach resort. Now we will become a local tourist attraction. The Mexican military will be here within a day!" Lagunov thought, as he raised a pair of binoculars and followed the fleeing civilian as he entered the resort.

. . . .

USS North Carolina
Command Center

"Lieutenant Bottom, anything on sonar?" asked Captain North, as he read the damage reports from across the boat.

"Negative, Sir! It's quiet. Not even any whales. I think they've fled the area. Probably with ruptured ear drums."

"Captain, do you still want to go ahead with the Seal assault on the TR?" asked Lieutenant Commander O'Teul.

"XO, our choices are: one, let the Russians have the TR. Two, sink the vessel with a cruise missile, or three, try to take her back with the Seals. They're willing to give it a try, but the Torpedo Sub is risky. We're at 800 feet, and the sub is rated to 700 feet. If the gaskets rupture, and they're exposed to the pressure at this depth, they'll probably die as the nitrogen begins bubbling in their bodies. I'm not ordering them to do this. I'm explaining the facts and letting them decide."

"Sir . . . they're Seals . . . they'd jump off a cliff on a bet. I'd bet their parents were on a first name basis with the local ER docs where they lived as kids," replied Lieutenant Commander O'Teul.

"Maybe so, XO . . . but I'm letting them decide."

. . . .

Crew Quarters

"Who the hell says you get to choose who goes? We're all E-6 Petty Officers First Class in the US Navy," said Petty Officer Tremayne Kelly.

"Because the US Navy says I have the senior time in grade, which puts me in command. That's who says! Luis is the only one who's ever piloted a Torpedo Sub. You're needed to help take care of the wounded," replied Petty Officer Brandon Williams.

"Screw that! I can kick the shit out of either one of you, maybe both together!" replied Tremayne, as he stood up.

"Only in your dreams, my Seal brother!" said Luis, as the two friends stared each other down.

237

"It's me and Luis! That's it! Get over it! That's my final decision," said Brandon, while continuing to slip on his wet suit.

"If you assholes get yourselves killed, I'm going to be seriously pissed at both of you," said Tremayne, as he rested a hand on each of his close friends.

"Chill, it's just a few Russians. They're used to fighting amateurs. They'll never know what hit them. You just get your lame ass back to the Sickbay where you're useful," Luis said, as he patted Tremayne on the cheek.

"Hey . . . no shit! You two be careful out there. Spetsnaz aren't amateurs! Be silent . . . be deadly!"

"All in, all the time!" Brandon said, as he fist bumped with his best friend.

"Hey, Brandon . . . one more thing! If you get your ass killed, I'm telling your mother it wasn't my fault. That woman scares me," Tremayne said, as Brandon and Luis began to walk away.

"Won't do any good! She'll kick your ass anyway!" Brandon replied, as he and Luis continued walking forward toward the Torpedo Room.

. . . .

Torpedo Room
10 minutes later

"No shit! They're going to get inside that thing and we're going to launch them?" asked Seaman Max Tourne.

"That would be correct, Seaman Tourne. Now quit jacking your jaws and verify the charge on that battery, or they won't be going anywhere," said Petty Officer Second Class Stan Longley, while pointing at the open access hatch on the side of the Torpedo Sub.

"I still can't believe someone's crazy enough to get in that thing. You'd have to knock my ass out to get me in there!" Seaman Tourne said, while verifying that the battery pack was fully charged.

"If you don't hurry the hell up and get our ride ready, that could be arranged," said Brandon, as he walked up beside the young sailor and glared down at him when he turned around.

"Son, how old are you?" asked Luis, as he walked past, glanced at the young sailor, and began stowing their gear in the storage space inside the small submarine.

"Nineteen, Sir!"

"Crap! You were 10 when I became a Seal. Now you're prepping us for a mission," replied Luis, as he turned and looked at the young man.

"Hey, Luis! I think he's got a crush on you!" Brandon said, as he verified the onboard oxygen levels.

"So, Seaman Tourne, is she ready to go?" Luis asked.

"Sir, she seems . . . she is ready . . . as far as I can . . ."

"Kid, that's a yes or no question. Plus, I'm enlisted, just like you. Don't call me 'Sir', I work for a living. Now, is it ready?"

"Yes, Petty Officer . . . she's ready!"

"Good, Seaman Tourne, very good. I'm the pilot. So, if I find a problem during my pre-mission inspection, I'll be taking a bite out of your ass. Understood?"

"Yes, Petty Officer!"

Brandon and Petty Officer Longley stood to the side shaking their heads as Luis began his inspection.

"You know we're beyond rated depth for the Torpedo Sub," said Longley.

"Yeah, we know. Captain North briefed us on the risk. We're up for the challenge. Things have been getting a little slow around here," Brandon responded, as Luis nodded that the boat was sat.

Longley just stared at him in disbelief.

"Squeeze your big ass in the back, Brandon. You're riding 'bitch' and don't adjust the seat position. I don't want to be cramped while I'm driving," Luis said, as he pointed at the rear position in the small sub.

Brandon laughed as he strapped his weapon tightly across his chest and climbed into the rear seat. The Torpedo Sub was not designed for comfort. It was like riding inside a coffin.

"I love getting in here with flippers on. It's like wearing a pair of clown shoes."

"That's what you get for being so damn big! Quit complaining and get settled, so the skilled labor can get seated."

"Hey, Longley! Thanks for getting our baby ready!" Luis said, as he fist bumped the Petty Officer.

"And, kid . . . stay chill. I don't know how you guys stand living in this boat for months at a time. I'd go crazy!" Luis added, as he climbed into the pilot's seat and strapped himself in.

"I guess it takes guts," SN Tourne replied.

The others started laughing at Tourne's bold response.

"Shit! I'm trapped in here and now he starts talking smack. You and I will have a sit down after this is over, Seaman Tourne!" Luis said, as he nodded for Petty Officer Longley to close the crew compartment hatches.

"Well, Bran . . . looks like it's just you and me. I'm surprised Tremayne didn't show up and give us a sendoff."

"Nah, he didn't want us to see him tearing up," Brandon said, as they both lowered their diving masks and turned on their air.

Their banter continued as Longley started sliding the Torpedo Sub into the Number Two torpedo tube. The talking stopped when the inner hatch slammed shut, leaving them alone together in the dark. The only lighting was the minimal glow from the instrument panel in front of Luis. The only sound was the sudden rush of water as the torpedo tube filled. Each man glanced around in the dim light, praying that the gaskets in the small submersible held.

"Hold on, Bran! This is going to be one hell of a rush!" Luis said, over their comm system.

The roaring sound and the sudden explosive thrust took them both by surprise as the Torpedo Sub was ejected from the USS North

Carolina. Luis gunned the electrical drive system and headed for their target . . .

CHAPTER 37

Torpedo Sub
Stern of the USS Theodore Roosevelt
All Saints Bay
Ensenada, Mexico
October 17, 1300 hours PST

"How much longer, Luis? I need to piss," Brandon said, as they cruised up behind the floating mass of the Roosevelt.

They were still 40 feet down and the four massive bronze alloy propellers, 21 feet across, were dead ahead, just above them.

"Mama Williams' little boy should have gone potty before we left. Just piss in your wet suit. Flooding up!" Luis said, as he began to slowly flood the interior space of the Torpedo Sub.

"Stern dock is a good idea. They'll never see us surface. Then we can climb straight into the ship."

"That's why I'm driving the bus. I'm the one with the brains. I'm going to slide back the canopy. You exit and tie the sub off to a ladder. Then we go pay our friends a visit," Luis said, as the canopy slid back, and Brandon slipped silently from the Torpedo Sub.

Five minutes later

"Okay, Mr. Big Brains, the stern dock is raised. Now what?" Brandon said, as they floated on the surface, riding the gentle swells behind the ship.

"You're the expert climber. Climb up the framework to the back porch and lower me a line," Luis said, while pointing at the steel frame folded against the stern of the ship.

"Now I'm the expert who has to help his little Hispanic buddy," Brandon said, with a grin on his face.

"It's about time you carried your weight on this mission. I heard you snoring in the back seat while I got us here."

"Just conserving my energy for the important stuff," Brandon said, while removing his flippers, attaching them to his gear, and reaching up for the lowest part of the framework.

On the third try, his fingertips locked over a piece of u-channel, and he began the ascent, pulling himself free of the water. He paused as he approached the upper platform extending from the rear of the mighty carrier, listening for footsteps or voices. The name 'Theodore Roosevelt' was painted in two-foot-high black letters, outlined in white, all along the length of the platform. Hearing nothing, he peered over the deck, searching for any movement. Seeing nothing, he slipped over the rail and into the shadows on his left.

"Luis, clear up here. I'm sending the rope," Brandon said over their personal comm, while removing a coiled length of rope from his gear bag, tying it to the rail, and throwing it over the side.

A minute later, Luis climbed over the rail and slid into the shadows alongside Brandon. Both Seals checked their silenced M-4 carbines and arranged their web gear for an assault.

"They'll have people in the engine room and on the bridge. That's where I'd be. We'll go through that hatch. Then find stairs down to Main Machinery Room 2 and Reactor Compartment 2. Both areas are in the aft end of the ship," Brandon said, as he pointed at the hatch leading from the back porch and into the Jet Engine Shop.

"They may have taken some of the crew as hostages, especially the reactor crew."

"I know . . . friendlies, but we have to take this ship back. We're at war now. If the Russians take full control of this ship, they'll use it against us. We can't let that happen. The sailors know what's at stake."

"Bran . . . they're our own people."

"Luis, if you had to shoot me to complete the mission . . ."

"That would be okay . . . momma's boy. You're a pain in my ass."

"Asshole!" Brandon said, as they slipped out of the shadows.

Five minutes later

"Damn, this place is a maze. I thought I knew where I was going, but we're getting nowhere fast. There has to be a stairway leading down to the engine room," Brandon said, as they slipped into a storeroom and shut the door.

"Don't fucking move or I'll drop you both! Put your weapons on the ground or you're dead," said a female voice from the shadows.

Brandon and Luis looked at each other. Brandon began to raise his weapon when Luis said, "We're Americans . . . Navy Seals. We're here to kill Russians and take back the ship."

"Don't move!" the woman said, as she stepped from behind a series of shelves.

The 9mm pistol in her left hand was pointed at their heads, switching from one man to the other. She was wearing a black t-shirt, running shorts, and was barefoot. The bloody t-shirt said, 'Free, Brave, Marine Corps Officer' in red, white and blue letters.

"Ma'am, I'm Petty Officer First Class Luis Santiago. The tall and ugly one here is Petty Officer First Class Brandon Williams," Luis said, when he saw that the woman was a US Marine officer.

As she stepped further into the light, they could see that she had been shot in the right arm. It was bandaged and hung loosely at her side.

"Ma'am, it looks like you've been trying to deal with the Russians on your own," Brandon said, as she stared at their faces and lowered her pistol.

244

"Second Lieutenant Ruth Mills. I lost my whole squad. They came at night. Only two of my men were out patrolling. I found their bodies this morning. They caught the others playing cards. I was in my room, down the hall. I heard shooting and ran out of my room. I got one of them, but another one got me. He was following me, but I ducked into a ventilation shaft and lost him. That was yesterday," she said, as she backed against one wall and slid to the floor.

"Watch the door," Brandon said, as he approached the Lieutenant.

"LT, you need some help. Let me look at that wound. Is it through and through?"

"Not sure, but I think it hit the bone. I bandaged it best I could, but I kept passing out. Least ways, I know the arm is broken. I can feel the ends grinding together if I move it. Hurts like a bitch. I came in here looking for painkillers but fell asleep."

Brandon could see that she was pale. As she sat there, blood was slowly dripping from her elbow.

"Luis, check outside for a blood trail leading in here," Brandon said, as he gently lifted her dog tags from beneath her t-shirt.

"*O Pos . . . same as mine. Great, a battlefield transfusion!*" Brandon thought, as he checked her pulse.

"A couple of spots, but I cleaned them up," Luis said, as he reentered the room and gently closed the door.

"She's passed out. I'm going to have to give her a transfusion. She's lost a lot of blood," Brandon said, as he stood, and began searching the shelves for medical supplies.

"Bran, we don't have time for this. I heard some noise and the ship started to vibrate. I think they're trying to get underway."

"I felt it, too, but that's good. The Russians will be distracted. This won't take long. I have to stop the bleeding first and give her one of my morphine doses. Then I give her some blood, and we can be on our way."

"Bran . . . that's a bad play. You were the one talking about the mission and whatever it takes. She's expendable!"

"I'll wake her up and you tell her that," Brandon said, as he cut off her old bandage and examined the wound.

"Shit! She got hit twice, Luis. The first one went through and the second bullet hit bone. Without a surgeon, she'll lose the arm."

"Do what you can and let's get going. Spetsnaz work in teams of eight. If she took out one that leaves seven. We have to get moving."

"Then quit yacking and help me."

One hour later

"She's kind of cute now that she doesn't have a pistol pointed at my head," Luis said, as Brandon administered a shot of morphine, gently lifted the officer from the floor, and carried her back into the shadows.

"You, dating an officer . . . a Marine officer. That would be funny. She'd be opening the door for you."

"She looks more like your type. She'd be grateful, my friend. You did save her life."

"All I did was buy her some time. She'll be dead in 48 hours without surgery. I couldn't find any antibiotics. They must keep them in the Pharmacy. I gave her all my own morphine," Brandon said, and covered her with a blanket.

"You're both on report for talking shit about an officer," Mills mumbled, as her eyes cracked open.

"Sorry, LT, but we have to go. I think the Spetsnaz are stealing your ship. They're probably painting the name of some Russian asshole on the side by now. By the way, how do you get to Machinery 2 and Reactor 2? We figure that's where they'll be, or at least a good place to start," Brandon said, as he knelt down beside her.

"That makes sense. God, it's hard to think straight! Go out, turn right . . . end of the passageway, another right . . . then left . . . stairs on right . . . down two . . ." then she passed out.

246

"Out . . . right, right, left and down two," Luis said, as he pulled Brandon to his feet.

"We have to move, Brandon. It's time to go hunting."

. . . .

They were both silent now. Any communication was with hand signals. They had found the stairwell leading downward, and a map on that elevation that led them toward Main Machinery Room 2. It seemed that even the crew could get lost inside the vast expanse of the Big Stick without a road map.

They moved in overwatch. One man moved while the other covered him . . . doorway to doorway . . . cover to cover, never knowing when the appearance of the enemy would start the inevitable firefight. The first bodies appeared in the hallway leading to the machinery room. Two sailors, one male, one female, were sprawled in positions that indicated they had tried to run. Both were face down. Both had been shot precisely . . . one bullet in the back and one in the head. The precision was noticed.

One final turn, and a glance around that corner told them they had found Main Machinery Room 2. The level of machine noise had increased as they approached. Despite the background noise, they could hear shouting.

"Don't give me excuses! Your friends tried to escape. Do you wish to join them?" the accented voice said, just down the corridor.

Brandon tapped his chest as he stared at Luis, who nodded in reply. Brandon could put a bullet in each eye of a target at 100 feet in less than a quarter second. This target was only 30 feet away. He took a calming breath, released it, and stepped around the corner. A second target had appeared. He dropped them both with two shots to the head. A sailor stood open mouthed as the two Seals proceeded down the hallway side by side, crouched, weapons at their shoulders.

Luis placed an index finger across his lips as they approached. The sailor backed against the wall and crouched down, his eyes wide and unblinking.

Luis knelt beside him and whispered, "How many?"

The sailor held up one shaking finger. Luis held his finger across his lips once more as he stood and followed Brandon into Main Machinery Room 2. The hunt continued . . .

. . . .

Navigation Bridge
USS Theodore Roosevelt
1440 hours PST

"Captain Morazovich, Petrov and his men have not called in," said LT Barzov, as he stepped onto the bridge.

"How late are they?" Captain Morazovich asked, while standing behind an American sailor steering the Roosevelt in a gradual slow turn to the north.

"Three minutes, Captain."

Captain Morazovich knew that the Gepard had been attacked by an American submarine and forced to land on the Mexican coast. Supposedly, the American submarine had been destroyed.

"We may have unwanted visitors aboard, Lieutenant Barzov. Take Sergeant Sobol with you and deal with any intruders. Warn Sergeant Kartov that we may have a problem."

"At once, Captain!" said Lieutenant Barzov, and glanced at Sergeant Sobol.

The two Spetsnaz operators left the bridge and headed for Main Machinery Room 2.

"Perhaps there are more Marines on board, Lieutenant."

"Unlikely, I found their duty roster. There was only the one squad. All are accounted for except for the officer you let escape."

"She was good. She shot Petra in the head from 30 feet. I hit her twice. I doubt if she is still alive, let alone a danger."

"Then who, Senior Sergeant Sobol, is our problem?"

"We came from a submarine. Perhaps the Americans sent us some friends to play with."

"If they came from that sub, then they are Seals. Be careful what you wish for, Sobol."

. . . .

Brandon was coughing up blood as Luis cut open his wet suit and examined the wound.

"Lung shot, Bran, and it didn't exit. I've got to seal the wound with plastic and tape it up or your lung will collapse."

"I should have gone for the head shot first. I tried to get cute with a 'double tap'. He was wearing a vest under his fatigues," Brandon said, as he covered the open doorway with his pistol.

"We all make mistakes, bro'. At least the second shot got him. Just relax while I patch you up. Takes more than one little bullet to take out a Seal," Luis said, as he sealed the wound, and pulled out a morphine injector.

"Negative! Save it. I'm still in the fight. Help me get up. There's four left. I'll rest when we're done."

"Bran, are you sure? I've got this."

"What . . . and listen to you talk shit for the next five years about how you took out a whole team of Spetsnaz and saved a nuclear-powered aircraft carrier . . . by yourself . . . because I had a flesh wound? I don't think so. I know how you roll. The story will get worse for me every time you tell it. Help me up, dammit!"

"Bet you wish you had your Iron Man suit on."

"Yeah, oh, hell yeah! I've got to get you trained on that shit. It's like being Superman!"

"Yeah, well . . . Superman, Ironman . . . whatever. There are at least four Spetsnaz left, and you're shot up. So, if you want to stay in the game, then suck it up and quit whining, or I'll send you back to Momma!"

Brandon answered with one finger as Luis helped him to his feet.

"Let's go finish this," Brandon said, sweat pouring from his face, as he holstered his pistol and replaced the magazine in his M-4 carbine.

. . . .

Lower decks

"Where is the Captain?" asked Sergeant Kartov, as his two comrades met him outside Reactor Compartment 2.

"Steering the ship. The three of us can take out 20 Marines," replied Lieutenant Barzov.

"But how many Seals, young Lieutenant?" Sergeant Kartov asked.

"As many as dare to cross our path, Senior Sergeant. I almost think you are afraid of them."

"Not afraid, Lieutenant . . . just respectful. They are very good at killing people . . . even people like us. We need to be careful. We don't know their numbers."

"How many people have you killed, Lieutenant?" asked Kartov.

"I finished first in my class at . . ."

"That would be none! This is not a simulation with blanks. If we fail, we don't get to try it again. They will step over our corpses and head for the bridge. We will have failed the Motherland."

"Then we won't fail, Sergeant Kartov. I won't allow it!" Lieutenant Barzov said, as he raised his weapon to his shoulder and headed down the hallway toward Machinery 2.

Sergeant Kartov and Senior Sergeant Sobol each stared at the other for a knowing second, before following their leader.

. . . .

Luis led the way, with the taller Brandon at his right shoulder. He discarded the slow, methodical, overwatch approach, fearing that Brandon might collapse at any moment.

Brandon could feel his heart pounding as they headed toward Reactor Compartment 2. The pain was becoming more intense with each step. He focused on his training. He kept repeating in his mind, *"Give up, give in, or give it all you've got! Give it all you've got . . ."*

What happened next is classified in military training as a meeting engagement. Both parties turned opposite corners of a hallway at the same time . . . and opened fire . . . Luis was struck in both legs but kept firing as he fell. Brandon felt bullets pass so close, that in his slowed-down mind, he began to number each one while he double tapped each Russian at the end of the hall. The battle lasted for five seconds . . .

10 minutes later

Brandon whipped out his pistol as he heard the approach of stealthy footsteps.

"Chill, Bran, it's the lady Marine," Luis said, as he lowered his own pistol.

"Didn't expect to see you up yet," Brandon said, as he returned his attention to Luis' wounds.

"My ship! My men!" she said, while walking down the hall toward the Russians piled at the far corner, pistol in her left hand.

"Nice shooting . . . head shots for the most part," LT Mills said, while nudging each body with a boot.

"That's his specialty. I'm the driver. I bet I could drive this damn carrier. Shit! Jesus, Bran, did the Navy train you in medicine at a vet school?" Luis asked, as Brandon, switched his attention to the other leg.

"Well, I'm running out of blood, and you're the wrong type. So, I either stop the bleeding or you die on this floor."

"Looks like we're all pretty well screwed!" Mills said, as she came back and sagged to the floor beside Luis.

"I still think she's cute . . . a little pale, but cute," Luis said, as he sagged against her shoulder and passed out.

"You sailors are all the same. Even when you're shot up," she said, as she checked his neck for a pulse.

"I stopped his bleeding and gave him the last of our morphine. He's a good man, a serious bullshitter, but a good man . . . and a good friend. If we can get some help, we'll all be okay," Brandon said, as he finished his work and looked at Second Lieutenant Mills.

"One minor problem, Petty Officer. There are more Russians on this ship, and we're the only Americans left alive."

"That would be incorrect. Don't shoot, we're coming out!" said a voice from the doorway leading into the reactor compartment.

The two warriors turned their pistols toward the open doorway as two Russian technicians exited the area with their hands in the air. One of them had been severely beaten based on the condition of his face. They were followed by a sailor with a wrench in his hand, prodding the Russians forward.

"I heard all the shooting and figured it was time to do my part," said Petty Officer Bassett, as he continued to push the Russians into the hallway.

"Nice work sailor. Any more Americans in there?" Second Lieutenant Mills asked.

"There were four of us nukes on board when the quake happened. We'd been working to restore reactor power for days when the Russians showed up. They put these two assholes in charge of us. I guess they're Russian navy nukes. Our Chief refused to cooperate, so they shot him. That was on day one. I had two friends try to run for it yesterday. I heard shooting."

"We found their bodies down the hall."

"Yeah, that was stupid. I told them to just wait," Bassett said, as he shoved the two Russians against the wall and glared at them.

"I'll cover them, Petty Officer. Find something to tie them up with," said Second Lieutenant Mills.

"Semper Fi and all that other Marine BS, Lieutenant. Break's over! Off your ass and on your feet!" Brandon said, as he struggled to stand up.

"You'd have made a half decent Marine, Petty Officer Williams," Second Lieutenant Mills said, while fighting to get to her feet with her one good arm.

"I appreciate the compliment, LT. After we secure these boys, let's go take back your ship."

. . . .

15 minutes later

The two Russian reactor operators walked onto the bridge of the Theodore Roosevelt with their hands tied behind their backs. Captain Morazovich stared at them as his pistol cleared his holster. The 9mm round entered his skull just above his left eye and exited the right rear portion of his skull, along with a significant amount of blood and brain matter.

"Nice shot, LT," Brandon said, as he and Second Lieutenant Mills held each other up in the doorway leading onto the bridge.

"That was for my squad."

"Now, what do we do with these two?" Brandon asked.

"I'll lock them in the brig later. Right now, we need some help," she said, and walked over to the communications console on one side of the bridge.

. . . .

USS North Carolina
1530 hours PST

"So, what's the word, Master Chief?" Captain North asked, while the two men stood outside the reactor compartment.

"Can't be done, Sir! Not with the boat at this angle."

"Great! Nose down . . . 20-degree list . . . two hours left on the batteries . . . now what?" Captain North thought, as Master Chief Ingeram stared and waited, knowing that the Captain would decide their fate.

"If the boat was upright, how long to replace the motor?"

"By the book . . . eight hours. Under these conditions, with us sitting on the bottom and running out of power, maybe two."

"Well, Master Chief, I guess we have to right the boat," Captain North said, as he turned and headed back toward the Command Center.

As he travelled back through the boat, Captain North assessed his crew as they worked or just waited. He could see fear and hope as he walked past, using precious seconds to exchange a few words.

"They're as worn out as I am, and the boat isn't in much better condition," Captain North was thinking, as he entered the Command Center.

All energy usage had been reduced to the minimum to save the batteries. Sweaty faces turned in his direction as the Captain spoke, "Lieutenant Bottom, anything from our Russian sub?"

"Negative, Sir! The last thing I heard was the sound of a bent screw. We didn't kill him, but I think we messed him up. Then he went silent."

"Akula IIIs have electric propulsors, Captain. Maybe that's why we can't hear them," said Lieutenant Commander O'Teul.

"Our torpedo detonated close enough to damage their seven-bladed prop, XO. That's a very durable piece of equipment. What else would have been damaged?"

"Their towed array sonar . . . and . . . rudders! Akulas have four rudder blades just forward of the screw. Captain, if his rudders are damaged . . ."

"Then he's worse off than we are. He can't steer his boat. He'd have to surface, XO," Captain North said, having decided on his next course of action.

"XO, prepare to dump ballast. I want a gradual rise to the surface."

"Captain, he'll hear when we start dumping ballast."

"I know that, Lieutenant Bottom. XO, take us up!"

"Aye, Captain!"

. . . .

20 minutes later

"Periscope depth, Captain!"

"Lieutenant Bottom, anything?"

"Negative, Captain! If he's out there, I can't hear anything."

Captain North exchanged glances with his executive officer. They both knew that if their theory about the Russian sub having damaged rudders was incorrect, the next sound they heard would be torpedoes heading in their direction.

"Extend the alpha photonic mast. Let's take a look around."

A pair of photonic masts had replaced the old periscope of traditional submarines. They lay outside the pressure boundary of the hull and provided a wide array of sensing data that was displayed on monitors in the Command Center.

"Captain, Master Chief Ingeram just called. His mechanics will have the new pump motor installed in less than an hour."

"Good news, XO! Now, if we can just find that Russian boat."

"Captain, look at this! It's a transmission from one of our carriers." Lieutenant Bottom said, while standing behind a sailor monitoring data from the photonic mast.

"Put it on speakers!"

"I repeat, this is Second Lieutenant Ruth Mills, United States Marine Corps, on the USS Theodore Roosevelt. This vessel needs assistance. Please . . . can you . . ." and the transmission halted.

"This is Petty Officer Brandon Williams. We need medical assistance. We have control of the vessel, but need immediate medical assistance, over!"

"Captain! The Seals! They took the ship!"

"Who is Ruth Mills?"

"How far away is that signal? Lieutenant Bottom, find that vessel. It's 1000 feet long and 20 stories high. It can't be hard to see."

"Captain, bearing 1 – 1 – 8! Range, two point eight miles," Lieutenant Bottom said, as an image of the carrier appeared on one screen.

"XO, as soon as the motor repairs are complete, get us underway and head for the Roosevelt. Lieutenant Bottom, contact that ship. Tell them we will provide medical assistance, but it may take a few hours to get to them."

. . . .

K-335 Gepard
Punto Moro Resort

"It's not just the prop, Captain. Two of the rudders are damaged. We aren't going anywhere without a tow," said Senior Lieutenant Lagunov, as he ran up from the rear deck of the boat.

"The diver is certain?"

"Yes, Captain! He's also one of our best mechanics. He says these repairs need a shipyard."

"Captain! On the shore! Tanks!" yelled one of the lookouts from the top of the sail.

Captain Bogdanov turned and began to raise his binoculars. He stopped and sighed. He didn't need binoculars to see the four Mexican army vehicles pulling off a road to his left and arraying themselves 50 yards from his sub. They weren't tanks, but the large cannon they

256

carried in turrets mounted above the six-wheeled hulls, were powerful enough to penetrate his hull. Bogdanov considered his options, then realized that he had none.

"Captain, do we arm the men and fight?"

"No, Feliks . . . we do not fight. I think our part in this war is over. We are standing on a beached whale. With all our advanced equipment, all our firepower . . . we are helpless."

CHAPTER 38

Haynes Junction
Yukon, Canada
October 17, 2030 hours PST

"Jock! What the hell? Look at the glow!" Luke said, as he and Sergeant Jock Ivan exited the utility easement and stopped their truck at the edge of Highway 1. They were two miles north of Haynes Junction.

The sun had set hours ago while they were driving backroads north of the Yukon Highway. The Russians were establishing a large supply depot near Kloo Lake. Troops, tanks and trucks continued to stream to the south. It was obvious that the Russian invasion was going to be massive. They had counted over 800 vehicles so far.

"Shit! Liz and Rainer were supposed to get people out of their way. We're heading into town to take a look around," Jock said, as he turned off the lights and headed south on Highway 1.

The clouds were thick and low hanging. It was cold, but both men had their windows down. Luke had his seat belt off and his rifle against his shoulder as they cruised toward town. Jock pulled off to the side of the road by the Kluane RV Kampground sign. He killed the engine and got out of the truck. The sky was starting to fall, and he knew it would be another cold night with thick fog. Luke appeared beside him. The two men stood silently, listening. The glow ahead of them seemed brighter as the flames were reflected from the descending cloud cover.

"You still want to go into town?" Luke whispered.

"Yeah . . . yeah, I have friends here. People I've hunted with, a few cousins. I need to see what happened."

"I don't hear anything. No vehicles, nothing in the air. Maybe the Russians have moved on."

"Let's go find out," Jock said, as he turned back toward the truck.

They drove down the two-lane highway until they reached the edge of town. Streets lights were spaced every 100 yards on the right side of the road, but the power was out. The Fas Gas Station and RV Park was visible a few hundred yards further on. The ruins still glowed. Small clumps of metal and charred wood were the only remains still visible. They drove past the Klaune Machine Works and stopped when they saw the first bodies. The building and cars still smoldered. The dead lay together in a line.

"Jesus, Jock! They were . . ."

"Executed!"

"Jock, I don't think we should . . ."

"We're going further!" Jock said, as he continued into the village of Haynes Junction, population 850.

They stopped again at the intersection of Klaune Street by the Raven Hotel. The hotel was actively burning. Dozens of bodies were stacked in the parking lot. Some must have tried to run . . . but were shot down in the street. Homes on either side of the highway were burning. As the wind shifted, the smoke swirled around the truck. Both men gagged at the smell of burning meat, knowing what that meant.

"Jock, I think they killed everybody. They rounded them up, pulled them out of their homes . . . and shot them!"

"Damn! Get your cell phone out. Take pictures, videos. We have to get this out!"

"Jock, this is war! Millions are already dead. Nobody will care!"

"They'll care about this. People need to know what's coming. We need proof. The government . . . the media . . . just take the damn pictures!"

The Russians had left, after burning every home, every business. Bodies were scattered all over town. Luke spotted a little girl wandering on a side street. She was covered with soot, her left arm badly burned. She wasn't crying, didn't talk, just collapsed as they got out of the truck and approached. They gave her water, bandaged the burn, wrapped her shivering body in a blanket and laid her in the back seat. She died an hour later while they were driving out of town. They buried her in the woods just on the other side of the Dezadeash River Bridge. They didn't talk for the rest of the night as they continued their long drive toward the south . . .

CHAPTER 39

The White House
The Situation Room
Washington, DC
October 18, 0730 hours EST

"So, the Canadians are going to make a stand here? Why this place? Why . . . Prince George?" President Beaumont asked, as General Munford continued his briefing on this new situation.

"The value of Prince George lies in its location. The city sits on a delta formed by the convergence of two rivers: the Nenchako and the Fraser. The only two roads from the northwest also meet in the city. This part of Canada has few major roads. In the US, we would call these 'major roads' . . . two-lane country blacktop. The city of Prince George lies at the convergence of Highways 16 and 97. I suspect the Russians will use both routes to get to Prince George. Highway 97 presents them with a problem. They must cross the Nechako River to get into Prince George. There are three bridges."

"The Canadians can just blow the bridges or bomb them. That seems simple enough. Then the Russians are stuck," said DHS Director Kristin Wilkie.

"True enough, Madam Director, but the Russians will have bridging equipment. The Nechako isn't exactly the Mississippi. Now, Highway 16 is even more of a problem for the Canadians. As you can see on this topographic map, it curves down and approaches the city from the southwest. There are no rivers to act as a barrier."

"So how big is the Canadian force? Can they hold the Russians?" the President asked.

"They have committed half of their tanks and one of their finest regiments. About the size of one of our battalions. Highway 97 crosses the Fraser River and heads southward, toward the United States."

"A battalion? That's nothing! What is that . . . 1000 - 2000 men?" asked Speaker Jacobson.

"Less than 1000 . . . maybe 40 old Leopard 2 tanks . . . a few dozen recon vehicles."

"What? That's half of Canada's tanks? Our reports show almost 1000 Russian tanks and APCs on the ground . . . so far!" said the CIA Director.

"That would be correct, Director Burton. The Canadian Air Force isn't much better. If . . . they commit their aircraft, they won't last more than a few days. They've kept their military . . . compact. With the US as a neighbor, and long-time ally, they saw no need to spend a great deal of money on a military they would never need."

"From their point of view, that made sense . . . until now," said Director Burton.

"I don't care. We have to help them," the President said, almost to herself. All the heads turned in her direction.

"Madam President?" General Munford asked.

"I said, we have to help them. We have to send them reinforcements!"

"Madam President, with all due respect. I'm not sure that's the best plan. We've lost tens of thousands of military personnel on the West Coast. Our bases . . ." General Munford began.

"No! You said this was a good place to stop them. Would you rather fight them on US soil? We've seen the video, the pictures. They're murdering everyone they come across. Is Prince George a good place to stop the Russians? Yes or no, General?"

General Munford stared at the huge map displayed on the wall monitor to the left of the President. He walked over and began studying the area around the city.

"There's a decent airport southeast of the city. The city also has a railway hub. First, we'd have to fly forces in from Ft. Bragg to secure the ground. Then we have the 1st Cavalry Division at Ft. Hood and the 1st Armored Division at Ft. Bliss, both in Texas. We can't transport them by air. They would have to go by rail. Madam President, if we commit those forces, two entire divisions . . . that's the bulk of our remaining armored forces in the country! I would suggest we send an initial force of one or two brigades. If we try to transport two entire divisions by rail, all we're going to do is clog up the rail system."

"The Canadians are making a stand. I promised Prime Minister Martel we would stand with them. They are our allies. We're sending help. Start with one brigade and prepare the second one to move at a moment's notice. We'll go from there as the need arises. General Simla, I expect the Air Force to provide all the help possible. Understood?"

"Yes, Madam President!"

"Madam President, the Navy may also be able to provide some support," said Admiral Mitch Richards, Chief of Naval Operations.

"I thought all our West Coast bases were destroyed, Admiral. Has something changed?"

"The bases are all damaged. Some will have to be completely rebuilt. But we do have significant forces landlocked in the Puget Sound, in Washington, that are still afloat. I'm in the process of consolidating remaining personnel in that area. It has the least amount of damage, and as I said . . . significant assets."

"Mitch, you have three carriers, but they're landlocked. The land has risen. It will be years before we can make a new channel deep enough for your carrier groups to get back to the open ocean," said General Munford.

"That's correct, General. They are trapped, but they're still afloat. They're undamaged. Two of them have full air wings aboard.

They're floating airbases . . . trapped, but functional. Their aircraft are well within range of Prince George. It's only 450 miles from Seattle. We've already started limited Combat Air Patrols over the Seattle area."

"How long before those carriers are fully functional?" asked the President.

"Fully functional . . . by the book? Weeks, maybe months. Functional enough to support combat operations in Canada . . . 48 hours," replied Admiral Richards.

"Admiral, won't the Russians figure out what's going on? Won't they come after your carriers?" asked Director Wilkie.

"Yes, Director . . . they will, but we can defend ourselves . . . for a while. Our supply chains on the West Coast have been destroyed. We'll need help resupplying from the East Coast."

"General Simla?" the President asked.

"Madam President, the Air Force is doing everything we can, but we're stretched pretty thin. Our West Coast losses are almost as bad as the Navy's. Hawaii, the western Pacific . . . all gone. We're pulling troops out of Europe as fast as we can, as previously agreed. We only have so many planes."

"Then we utilize the commercial airlines to move troops out of Europe and let the Air Force concentrate on supporting combat operations," said John Masters, Secretary of Defense.

"Can we legally do that?" the President asked.

"Madam President, all you have to do is declare a Stage III National Crisis, and the Civilian Reserve Air Fleet is ours. The agreement has been in existence since 1951."

"How many planes is that?"

"Twenty-four airlines have committed over 500 planes. Almost 400 of those are long-range, high capacity aircraft. We're not sure how many were lost on the West Coast, but at least 25 percent."

"Make it happen! Now, one other thing. What's the latest on the Kraken?"

"We had to land her in Nevada, Madam President. At the facility where she was constructed. The damage was extensive, and the craft was becoming unstable," replied General Munford.

"Can it be repaired?"

"They think so . . . in time. It may take years. One of the three Plasma Field Engines was damaged by the Russian energy weapon. The PFEs are designed to work in unison . . . as one unit. When one was damaged, it put an enormous strain on the other two. They may have sustained some damage also."

"But we still have the Dory's?"

"Yes, Madam President. But there have been losses. The Kraken held six Dorys. Two were shot down. We're still not sure how. Three more were taken out of service when the Russians hit the Kraken. We lost three pilots."

"Regrettable, but we're at war. Train new pilots."

"It's not that simple, Madam President. The pilot is linked with a very sophisticated AI. A few of our experts think the AI is . . . sentient."

"What? That's absurd!" said Director Wilkie.

"Perhaps, Madam Director, but it takes years to find a compatible pilot, and further years to train them to interact with the AI. All the Dory pilots are in their 30s and 40s. We can't just plug in another pilot. The pilots can't even switch between planes. They're bonded to a particular AI," replied General Simla.

"Bonded? They have a relationship?" asked the President.

"A deep friendship, like a set of twins. If they're separated for more than a few days, the pilots report feeling . . . anxious. The shrinks call it 'separation anxiety'."

"General Simla, how many functional Dorys and pilots do we have left?" the President asked.

"Active duty . . . one from the Kraken and three located at another base in Nevada. One training Dory was in reserve. It's the original vehicle and the pilot is way past active duty age. His services were requested by the CIA."

The President stared at Director Perez.

"Madam President, we needed to get an agent on the ground to locate the Russian weapon that hit the Kraken. All our satellites, able to assess that area, have been destroyed. We requested the use of the reserve Dory to transport an agent into the area on short notice. The agent was on scene when the weapon fired. Based on the information she provided, we know how to silence the weapon."

"A little late, Director Perez."

"Yes, Madam President. We're aware of that. We have obtained one other interesting bit of information from the Canadians. Their scouts . . . Canadian Rangers, have obtained a photo of a previously unknown ground vehicle," Director Perez said, while nodding to one of his assistants. The photo taken by Jock Ivan appeared on one of the screens.

"That looks like a weapon system! What are those cylinders for?" asked General Munford, as they all stared at the truck mounted weapon system.

"The agent we sent to Russia, predicted the existence of this system before she left. Her theory was . . . this is the first model. The one that has been tracking and destroying our Dorys in Alaska. She found data supporting the existence of a larger version. It was just a theory when she left, but . . ."

"We know what happened to the Kraken!" said General Munford.

"General Simla, back to the remaining Dorys . . ."

"We moved the remaining functional Dory from the Kraken to our Nevada base. Madam President, we need to use them carefully until we determine how the Russians are detecting the Dorys and develop a countermeasure."

"Work on a counter measure, General, but no one and nothing stays on the sidelines. We're in a war for survival. The continental United States hasn't been invaded since the War of 1812. The British burned down the White House and the Capitol Building. A thunderstorm prevented them from burning down the entire city of Washington. I don't expect any less from the Russians."

"Madam President, if we fail at Prince George, we have to keep them out of Vancouver. If they obtain a major port that far south, then their next move is into the US. The few attack submarines we still have active in the northeast Pacific can't hold Russian transports at bay much longer. The Canadians need to know that if Vancouver falls, we'll destroy the port facilities," said General Munford.

"I'll be talking with Prime Minister Martel later today. We have quite a few things to discuss. I'll add that to the list. What other divisions do we have that are still combat effective?"

"Four infantry divisions and the 101st Airborne. We've lost two full infantry divisions. The 2nd Infantry are split between South Korea and Fort Lewis, Washington. The two brigades at Fort Lewis are combat ineffective. We're working on that. The 25th Infantry is gone. Two brigades were on Oahu. The other two were lost in Alaska. We have eight National Guard divisions. Luckily, only one is located on the West Coast. We're trying to activate them, but the governors want them to stay in their states."

"You let me worry about the politicians, General Munford. Get everything activated that you can. That goes for all the services. What resources do the Russians have?"

"In 2008 they started a major reform to reduce the size of their military. They were down to only four divisions in the army. That stopped in 2013 when President Morozov took over. Now they have over 25 divisions and are still expanding. The same goes for their navy and air force. He has spent a decade enlarging and modernizing his armed forces. They can fight a two-front war, especially with our military in its present state. They are staging on the borders of eastern Europe. They have allies in the Middle East and have recently made approaches to North Korea through military liaison personnel."

"He's correct, Madam President. The State Department has received similar information through our sources. Personally, I think that Morozov is intent on turning back the clock," said Raymond Taggert, Secretary of State.

"Back to what? The USSR? Back to a communist dictatorship? They have too many oligarchs worth billions. I can't believe they would allow him to commandeer all their wealth for a new Soviet State."

"The Chinese had a lot of billionaires too, Madam President. They created a new type of communism. I think that is what Morozov is after. The People's Republic of China is . . . or was, the new model for modern communism. What his plans were before China attacked us . . . I'm not sure. Perhaps, he was just building his military to defend Russia from China. Maybe he had a deal with the Chinese to assist in the invasion of the US. He's an opportunist. He always has been. China is gone, and we're greatly weakened. He's looking for world domination."

"He's correct, Madam President. The EU has maybe 110,000 quality, combat troops ready for battle today. The Russians have well over a million. They've committed a quarter of that to the invasion of North America through Alaska. If they're successful here, they may commit more troops here, and hold off in Europe until we're finished," said, General Munford.

"I've said this before. Europe is going to have to stand on its own. That's why we're pulling our forces out."

"But . . . Madam President, we have commitments to Europe through NATO. Pulling out may encourage the Russians to attack in Europe, Madam President," said Secretary of State Taggert.

"It may sound callous, but that's to our benefit. If Morozov opens a second front in Europe, he'll have less troops to send here," said General Munford.

"This is what I want. Our focus is to remain here, the United States. Maintain all intelligence assets in Europe. Share what we find with them, but we can't afford to commit military resources. Our priorities are as follows: One, activate all resources, military and civilian, to support defense of the nation. Two, get the Kraken operable. That vessel may be the only way out of this, short of a nuclear war. Three, support the Canadian position at Prince George. It may get bloody, but if the Russians gain a major port, and start pouring more troops into the continent, things will get a lot worse. Keep me informed, especially about Prince George."

As the room began to empty, the President said, "General Munford, a word after everyone leaves."

5 minutes later

"I want a private briefing on the use of tactical nukes within the United States. I pray that it doesn't come to that, but it may become necessary. I want to understand the range of options we still have available and their impact. This is to stay between us."

"Yes, Madam President . . ."

CHAPTER 40

Queensway Tower
1501 Queensway Street
Prince George, British Columbia, Canada
October 18, 0630 hours

The Queensway Tower was the tallest building in Prince George, at 14 stories. It was situated on the southeast side of town, in an area called South Saint George. The Frasier River lay to the east, only 100 yards behind the apartment complex. Two bridges, one to the north, another to the south, were the only way across the river, and out of the city . . .

Lieutenant Colonel Steele, commander of the Royal Canadians Armored Regiment, had set up his headquarters in the top floor suite. He stood at the broad window, staring northwest across the city.

"Sir, we just received a report that the Russians are burning every town they go through. Even worse, they're killing everyone . . . no exceptions," said Major Jacob Manx, his second in command.

"That sounds like propaganda. Is the source reliable?"

"We got it from division. They received it from one of our Ranger units. It includes pictures and video from . . . Haynes Junction, up in Yukon," Major Manx said, while handing an iPad to his CO.

Lieutenant Colonel Steele was silent as he scrolled through the pictures and watched three videos.

"They don't intend to leave potential partisans behind them. They tried the same thing in Afghanistan, but not this thorough. They tried to scare the inhabitants into submission. All they did was piss them off. They don't understand Canadians. The same thing will happen here. Every hunter within 1000 miles will know it's open season on Russians and start heading this way."

"That won't help us against tanks, Colonel."

"No, but it will slow down resupply. That's their weakness. Right now, their supply line stretches all the way to the port of Anchorage. They're moving south to get to the US, but also to establish a shorter supply line."

"That same ranger report also stated the Russians are setting up supply depots along the Alaska Highway."

"That's someone else's problem, Major. We need to focus on our part. What's the status of the northern bridges crossing the Nechako River?"

"The one farthest west is four lanes with concrete and steel pillars. Combat engineers are rigging explosives to the road structure underneath. They'll be able to blow a 100-foot gap between the support pillars . . . drop the roadway into the river. The next one, for Highway 97, is two separate bridges side-by-side. Both will have to be blown the same way. The last bridge is a small, two-lane affair . . . no problem."

"What about this bridge, northeast of the city?"

"It's a combination railroad and one lane of traffic, side-by-side. That must be fun when trains cross over!"

"Major!"

"Sorry, Sir! The bridge is all steel. They should have finished rigging the explosives during the night, but I haven't received a confirmation."

"I want two ways to detonate all these bridges . . . remote and hardwired. The Russians may be able to jam a signal."

"Understood, Sir!"

"Anything from Edmonton on my request for artillery support?"

"Division is sending the 1st Regiment, Royal Canadian Horse Artillery. They left Shilo by rail around 2200 hours last night. ETA is sometime just after midnight."

"That's a dozen guns . . . M777 howitzers. It's a fine weapon. Light, fast, excellent range and accuracy, but it's towed. We have to find a good place to position them. Someplace close enough, but not so close that the Russians can find them easily."

The two officers paused as a sergeant walked in and handed a communication to Major Manx.

"Now this, is interesting!" Major Manx said, as he handed the message to Lieutenant Colonel Steele.

"It would seem the Americans aren't completely crippled. The 82nd Airborne is flying an Infantry Brigade Combat Team into the Prince George airport. The first units should start arriving 24 hours from now. That's over 4000 men! We just have to keep the Russians at bay for the next 24 hours."

"Keep reading, Sir! It gets better!"

"Damn! The 1st Armored Division is sending an Armored Brigade Combat Team by rail. I think the Americans are serious. Reinforcements will be here in less than a week."

"Twenty million dead, Sir. The Americans have never had anything like this happen to them. We felt the tremors in Edmonton. They claim it was the Chinese. Somehow, they obliterated the Chinese without using nuclear weapons. Now the Russians . . ."

"Jacob . . . we're soldiers! The Russians have jumped into this mess. They're on our land! They're murdering Canadians. Our troops depend on us. Focus on what we can control. The rest of it is someone else's problem. Our mission is to hold the Russians at Prince George until help arrives. That's all we can do!"

The sound of explosions reached into the suite and drew the two officers to the broad windows facing to the west. A Hind helicopter turned in their direction, less than half a mile away.

"Everybody out!" Steele shouted, as his headquarters staff dove for cover or fled from the room.

The Hind MI-24P attack helicopter carried a fixed, twin-barrel 30mm cannon side-mounted in the nose. High explosive rounds began tearing into the upper levels of the Queensway Tower. Screams were mixed with the sound of explosions as the men and women of the regimental headquarters were being butchered.

"They knew where we were. They tracked our transmissions. Damn, I was stupid!" Major Manx thought, as he lay in the hallway deafened by the constant explosions as the Hind continued to tear into the building.

When the firing ceased, he looked around through the acrid haze. Blood seemed to be splattered everywhere. All he heard was a high-pitched ringing in his ears. Lieutenant Colonel Steele lay down the hall only a few feet away. Manx crawled over to him, reached out, and clutched his hand. Then he saw that Steele's legs had been severed above the knees.

"Medic!" Major Manx yelled, as he rose to his knees and glanced around.

The hallway was filled with dust, bodies and blood. The cinderblock walls of the building's interior were pockmarked with huge, gaping holes. The screams of the wounded mixed with the fetid smell of the dead and dying. He looked down when the colonel squeezed his hand.

"Jacob . . . 24 . . . hold . . . for 24 hours . . ." Steele said, then sighed, as he stared up into Manx's eyes. The blood spurting from his severed legs turned into a trickle.

"Yes, Sir . . . 24 hours," Manx replied, as he reached down, and shut his friend's eyes with a shaking hand.

The battle for Prince George had begun . . .

CHAPTER 41

Beaver Forest Road Bridge
Prince George, British Columbia, Canada
October 18, 1130 hours PDT

"Somebody screwed up bad! Why the hell are we getting sent out into the middle of nowhere?" asked Master Corporal John 'Punty" Smith, as the lone Leopard 2A4 tank rounded the last turn and headed straight for the old railroad bridge five miles north of Prince George.

"First, because Lieutenant Young said so. Second, because the engineers haven't had time to set explosives on this bridge. Third, because I said so! You just shoot when I tell you to shoot! Is that understood, Master Corporal Smith?" replied Sergeant Jessica Brown over the open comm net on the tank.

"Look, Jess, I understand who's in charge, but the fighting is back there. The town's getting shelled, fighting's going on at the other bridges, and we're traipsing down an old country road . . . that's all."

"That's Sergeant Brown to you, Master Corporal! I command this tank for the people of Canada. What is your ammunition status?"

Punty rolled his eyes and looked over at his loader, Private William McDonald, while making rude hand gestures toward Sergeant Brown, seated above him in the Tank Commander's hatch. He didn't see the boot that kicked him in the back of the head. Inside the close confines of a modern tank, all the crew members were within touching distance.

"Ammunition status?"

"Yes, Sergeant! Forty-two rounds on board! Thirty rounds of Mark 829 Sabot and 12 rounds of M830A1 HEAT-MP-T. In addition, we have 4750 rounds of 7.62mm for our two machine guns."

"Hey, Sarge! I can see the bridge straight ahead," said Corporal Kayla Tremblay, the tank's driver.

"I can see it. Slow stop!" said Sergeant Brown, as she picked up her binoculars and scanned the near end of the old steel bridge.

"Nothing visible . . . still half a mile to the bridge. Where the hell are the two LAV IIIs? We were promised some infantry support," Brown thought, as she lowered her binoculars and glanced into the thick woods on either side of the narrow road.

The near constant sound of explosions to the south kept her on edge. If the Russians had already sent scouts or infantry across the bridge, they were alone and sitting in a perfect spot for an ambush.

"Protect the bridge. Don't let them get across and flank the regiment," Brown thought, remembering her final orders from Lieutenant Young.

"At least you're painted green, Kathleen. Half the tanks in the regiment are still painted for Afghanistan," Sergeant Brown said, as she reached forward and patted her tank on the top of the turret.

'Kathleen' was one of the regiment's oldest tanks. She had the square-nosed look of an old German Tiger tank from World War II. The newer Leopard A6 was sleeker, more angular. They were given to the more experienced crews.

She glanced at the bridge once more, then cursed as she jerked her binoculars back up to her face.

"Oh, shit! Gunner . . . HEAT . . . APC . . . on the bridge . . . at my command . . . " she said, and paused, waiting for the loader's response.

"Up!" Private MacDonald said, indicating that the requested round had been loaded into the main gun.

"Fire!"

Their reaction to her fire command was slow. The main gun fired two seconds late. She had been so shocked at seeing a BMP crossing the bridge that she forgot to duck. The shock wave of the Rheinmetall 120 mm/L55 smoothbore gun firing, rattled her teeth and threw her back against the edge of the tank commander's hatch. The familiar smell of cordite filled her nostrils.

The HEAT round was capable of penetrating 300mm of hardened steel armor at any distance. The lightly armored BTR-82A was one of the newer versions of the venerable armored personnel carriers first built by the Soviet Union in the 1980s. The 17-ton vehicle blew apart as the HEAT round impacted the frontal armor. The molten jet of copper, at 1000's of degrees Fahrenheit, cut through the armor, shredded the ten men inside, and detonated the stored ammunition and fuel. The vehicle jumped a foot off the ground, then settled in the middle of the bridge, as a burning wreck.

"Reload . . . HEAT!" she yelled, then paused. The burning APC was now blocking the bridge, and she didn't want to remove the barrier by blowing it apart.

"Up!"

"Let me hit it again!" Punty shouted over the intercom.

"Negative! You fire only on my command!" Sergeant Brown said, as she trained her binoculars on the bridge.

"Sarge, it's starting to move. Let me fire!"

"Negative! Wait until there's something to shoot!"

She could see the BMP begin to move and knew that another vehicle was trying to push it out of the way.

"Think, Jessica! Think! What will they do next? Infantry! They'll try to squeeze infantry past the wreck and get into the woods. Then we're in real trouble!"

"Gunner! Look for infantry through your sight. We can't let them get off the bridge! Kayla! Move out! Slow!"

"Just let the crunchies come. Kathleen's tracks could use some lubrication," Kayla replied, as she eased the tank forward, and headed for the bridge.

.   .   .   .

Colonel Petra Golubkin stood outside his BTR-82 Command Vehicle and watched as his battalion continued to stream past. He had pulled over in the parking lot of the Northwood Pulp Mill because he had to pee. So far, the flanking movement had gone well. There had been little or no enemy resistance.

"Colonel, we have a report of enemy tanks on the other side of the railway bridge. They knocked out one of our scout vehicles. The bridge is blocked," said Captain Azarov, while walking out of the right-side door of the APC.

After finishing his business, Colonel Golubkin asked, "How many tanks, and do they have infantry support?"

"Unknown, Colonel. This just happened two minutes ago. They're trying to push the vehicle out of the way and get infantry across the bridge."

"Contact Captain Kazak and tell him to pull his scouts back and send tanks to clear the bridge. He has six tanks in his motor rifle company for a reason. And tell him I want that bridge cleared in 15 minutes!"

"Yes, Colonel!"

.   .   .   .

"Driver! All Stop!" Sergeant Brown said, as the Canadian tank closed to within 200 yards of the bridge.

"Sergeant! Smoke . . . they're blowing smoke!" said Punty.

"Just watch for infantry. You've got the co-ax machine gun. Use it if you see anything."

She switched comm channels to the Company net.

"Kathleen to Strat One, over!"

After three attempts and was no reply, she switched to another frequency.

"Kathleen to Strat One, over!"

After trying every frequency in the regiment and pounding the turret in frustration after receiving no response, she thought, *"Great! We're holding the bridge by ourselves . . . and no infantry support. The APCs are backing off the bridge. That means tanks are coming next, maybe artillery fire, and we're sitting alone in the middle of this damn road."*

She glanced once more at the burning APC on the bridge and made up her mind.

"Driver! Move out! Bring us onto the bridge. I'll tell you when to stop."

"Yes, Sergeant . . . the bridge?"

"Jess, are you sure? We can't maneuver on a bridge. We'll be trapped! It's crazy!" Punty said.

"Master Corporal Smith, if you question another one of my decisions, I'll have you on report."

"But, Sergeant . . ."

"Listen up, all of you! The Russians need the bridge. We can't leave it undefended. Sitting on this road, we're fair game for artillery, helicopters or aircraft. Look at the bridge. If they use artillery, they'll risk destroying the bridge. They'll have to attack us head on . . . one at a time. This is the only way!"

"Shit! That's a good idea!" said Punty.

"That's why I'm the tank commander, Master Corporal Smith! Just obey my damn orders!"

"Yes, Sergeant!" Punty said, as the tank approached the front of the old, steel railway bridge.

The bridge had been abandoned by the Canadian National Railway back in the 1980s. The track had been ripped up and replaced with a roadway for vehicle traffic. Sergeant Brown glanced up at the

278

heavy steel beams that crisscrossed overhead, knowing their protection was an illusion.

"Driver! Stop!"

She glanced back and saw they were 30 feet onto the bridge. Kathleen's back was now covered by the steel frame of the structure. A stiff breeze was blowing from the north. The thick, black smoke from the APC's burning tires was being swept to her left. Now all they had to do was wait.

Bullets began pinging off the turret, as Sergeant Brown ducked inside her hatch and shut it. The stuttering sound of the co-ax machine gun responded, as Punty swept the area on either side of the burning Russian vehicle.

"They're trying to get infantry past the wreck, but that won't work!" Punty said, while firing several bursts.

"Save your ammo! We may be here a while," Sergeant Brown said, while peering out of her forward periscope.

.   .   .   .

Russian Motor Rifle Company 'A'
1155 hours PDT

"Captain Kazak! A single tank has pulled onto the bridge. We tried to get infantry past the wreck but couldn't do it. I lost two men to machine gun fire from the tank," said Lieutenant Levkin.

"Pull your men back. I'm sending Pimenov across with his platoon of tanks. The Colonel wants that damn bridge taken in less than 15 minutes!"

"I've seen the enemy tank. It's an old Leopard 2. It will be easy to take!"

The clanking sound of tracks interrupted their conversation as three T-72B3s pulled up to their position.

"So, I have heard the infantry is having a little problem?" Lieutenant Pimenov shouted from atop his tank.

"There's a Leopard sitting on the bridge. We've lost one vehicle already. Go have fun and kill it, Pavel!" Captain Kazak said to his brother-in-law.

"Just one tank? I have three! It's hardly sporting!" Lieutenant Pimenov shouted, then saluted and ordered his tank forward.

The T-72B3 was an upgraded model possessing Kontakt-5 explosive reactive armor that would protect it from most anti-tank ammunition. It's 125mm smoothbore main gun could kill any tank on the planet.

· · · ·

Kathleen
1205 hours PDT

"Gunner! Load Sabot! It's gotten too quiet. The next thing we see will be a tank."

"Sergeant, I have a . . . suggestion," Punty said.

"Yes, Master Corporal Smith?"

"We need to blow that APC out of the way. If I was a Russian tanker, I'd pull up to that wreck and use it as cover."

Jessica's first instinct was to tell Punty to keep his suggestions to himself. But the more she thought about it, the more she saw his point.

"Gunner! Load HEAT! APC on the bridge!"

Private MacDonald cursed as he unloaded the Sabot round, stored it, and loaded a HEAT round. It took him six seconds to exchange the 46-pound ammunition.

"Up!"

"Fire!"

The APC was sitting at an angle, with its nose pointed to their left. The first round struck the vehicle behind the second tire. The BTR-82A was flipped onto its side and thrown against the side of the bridge supports.

280

"Gunner! Nice shooting! Load Sabot!"

"Up!"

"Thank you, Sergeant!" Punty said and smiled, as he turned and looked up at Jess. The shot had to be precise, and he had placed it exactly where he had wanted. The smile fell from his face when his eyes returned to his sight.

"Tank! T-72! Firing!" he said, as he targeted the barrel on the front of the Russian tank and fired.

Armor-Piercing Fin-Stabilized Discarding Sabot (APFSDS), known as Sabot, was nothing more than a tungsten or uranium dart that used kinetic energy to penetrate armor. Reactive armor had been designed to defeat Sabot. It exploded when struck. The shock wave of the explosion lessened the effectiveness of the penetrating dart. The T-72 rocked and came to a halt as the dart struck the reactive armor and exploded.

Punty howled in glee, believing the Russian tank had blown up. He stopped smiling as he saw the turret turn in their direction. Sergeant Brown saw it at the same time.

"Gunner! Load Sabot! Tank!"

"Up!"

"Fire!"

Punty fired a second round at the same time as the Russian. The T-72B3 also fired a tungsten dart, and the Leopard was not equipped with reactive armor. The Russian dart struck the sloped glacis plate in front of the driver and skipped upward, striking the angled plate armor on the turret. It left a three-inch-deep scar over two feet long, before it ricocheted away. Punty's second shot struck the T-72B3's turret just to the right of the main gun barrel, a spot where there was no reactive armor. The autoloader was in the process of inserting another shell and propellent into the breach. The dart penetrated and hurled white-hot fragments across the turret. The propellent exploded, and the turret was hurled into the air, coming to rest atop the steel girders above the bridge.

"Reactive armor! Two more tanks! Aim for the gun mantlet beside the barrel, Punty! You brag you're the best gunner in the regiment. Prove it!" Sergeant Brown yelled.

"I am the best. I've always had the best scores on the range, but this is different. They hit us . . . we should be dead . . . but we're not," Punty thought, then smiled as he controlled the adrenalin and fear coursing through him.

The second T-72 swung onto the edge of the bridge as Punty lined up the shot.

"Thread the needle, Punty boy. Range 350 yards . . . spitting distance."

"Gunner! Load Sabot! Tank!"

"Up!"

"Fire!"

"Yes, Sergeant," Punty whispered as he fired, and time began to slow down.

He closed his eyes as the main gun ejected the spent casing, filling the turret with the smell of cordite despite the bore evacuator. He could sense MacDonald reloading another Sabot round, as he opened his eyes in time to see another flying turret. This one landed upside down on the hull of the T-72. The far end of the bridge was filled with fire, smoke and the flash of explosions, as ammunition in the two tanks he had destroyed began cooking off.

. . . .

The Russian Tanks
1210 hours PDT

"Lieutenant Pimenov! The Colonel is becoming impatient. When will you have the bridge? Over!" asked Captain Kazak from the back of his APC. He had heard the exchange of tank fire from the bridge on the other side of the plywood plant.

"It will take some more time, Captain. The Canadian tank is good . . . and lucky. I have lost two tanks. I need Second Platoon's tanks to help take the bridge. Over!"

"Is it only one tank? You had three tanks! You said it was not sporting. Clear the damn bridge, Lieutenant Pimenov! Out!"

The Lieutenant stared at the two tanks burning 40 yards to his right, cursed, then stared at the bridge. The wind was shifting, blowing the smoke west, toward the Canadian tank.

"Driver! Move forward and start pushing Mikel's tank toward the enemy."

"Yes, Lieutenant!"

"Gunner! Sabot!"

"Up!"

"Wait for my order to fire. Aim for their throat, just under the main gun. I want to see that turret flip!" Lieutenant Pimenov said, as he stared up at the T-72 turret perched atop the steel girders of the bridge.

.   .   .   .

Kathleen
1210 hours PDT

"Sergeant, the wind has shifted, I'm switching to thermal sights," Punty said.

"Understood!" Sergeant Brown replied, knowing that the burning vehicles would make his job even more difficult. She switched comm channels to the Company net, sensing their time might be running out.

"Kathleen to Strat One, over!"

After three tries, she pulled the helmet mike aside and wiped the sweat from her face. She hadn't noticed how thirsty she had become. She was reaching for water when she heard a static-filled reply . . .

"Strat One to Kathleen. What is your status? Over!"

Two minutes later the conversation was complete. She sagged and leaned back in her seat. There wouldn't be any help. The far western bridge hadn't blown, and Russians were pouring across. The fighting was at pointblank range in the streets and amongst the houses.

"What do I tell them? Do I just keep this to myself?" she asked herself, while gulping down half a liter of water.

"Sergeant, they're pushing one of the wrecks up the bridge. I can barely see the tank behind it," Punty said.

"You can only control what's right in front of you, Jess. Our fight is right here, right now . . . on this damn bridge," she thought, while staring down the bridge through her forward periscope.

She switched to thermal imaging, magnified, and thought she could see the wreck's tracks still rolling.

"Gunner! Load Heat! Target the right track of the lead tank. Disable it!"

"Understood!"

"Up!"

"Fire!"

The Heat round struck the right track return roller and blew the track apart. The vehicle began to slew to the right as the friction increased on that side. The T-72 behind it became visible in Punty's thermal sight.

"Load Sabot!" Punty yelled, fearing the opportunity would disappear.

"Up!"

He targeted the left front side of the enemy tank, below the turret and its reactive armor.

"Sharp angle . . . this has to be perfect," he thought, as he held his breath, feeling his heart pound in his chest. As he squeezed the trigger, he saw the flash of the muzzle on the enemy tank and knew he was a second too late.

The Russian Sabot struck Kathleen on the front of the right track. The track was broken, and the return roller was blown off the vehicle. The dart struck the hull behind the roller with enough residual force to crack the multi-layered armor plate and send fragments into the crew compartment.

Kayla sat in the driver's seat and screamed as her right leg was shredded by white hot bits of steel shrapnel. Smoke began to fill the interior as severed wiring and components began to short out. Punty howled in agony. His right shin felt as if someone had hit him with a sledgehammer. He glanced down and saw a splinter sticking out of his lower leg. He groaned as he forced himself to look through his sights. He could see, but the screen was blank. All the targeting data was missing.

"Targeting computer down!"

Jess looked down to her left. Will MacDonald lay sprawled on the bottom of the turret. A steady pool of blood was spreading out from his body. Kayla's screams had ceased. She could hear Punty cursing above everything else. She glanced through her periscope as her hands checked her body for wounds. She had heard that adrenaline could mask minor wounds.

The wind had shifted again. The far end of the bridge was now visible. The third Russian tank was smoking. The crew was leaping from the vehicle. She could also see infantry pass by the burning vehicles, running in their direction.

"Punty, I think Will and Kayla are dead. Can you move?"

"Piece of steel in my leg. Hurts like a bitch!"

"Infantry coming! See if the turret will turn. Try the coax!"

Punty groaned as he shifted forward and returned to his sights. He could see several moving blobs in the thermal imager. The sound of the coax machine gun began echoing inside the turret as he fired several bursts. Some of the blobs fell, others kept running in their direction.

"I'm going to open the hatch . . . get on the other gun. If they reach us, we're dead," Jess yelled, while forcing the heavy hatch upward.

She paused as the blast of fresh air filled her lungs. Then bullets began glancing off the turret and whizzing by her head. She ducked into the tank and moved over to the loader's hatch. She stood in the chair as she flung open the hatch and swiveled the 7.62 mm machine gun toward the front. She screamed as a bullet nicked her right arm.

"That burned . . . like slipping and touching the broiler in an oven," she thought, as she chambered a round in the machine gun, ducked down, and began firing at the string of soldiers running up both sides of the bridge.

Punty was focusing on the left side, so she focused on the right. Both groups ground to a halt as the two weapons began to tear up the front of both columns. She gasped as a bullet struck her in the chest. Groaning, she slid down onto the loader's seat. Her body armor had stopped the bullet, but it was hard to breathe, and she was seeing spots.

"Jess, you okay?" Punty yelled, as he glanced up at her.

She could only nod, as she pulled herself back out of the hatch. The Russian infantry were only 200 feet away. One man was kneeling, an RPG on his shoulder. She began firing as the rocket left the tube. It was so slow that she could watch the warhead coming toward them. She ducked back into the tank as it exploded harmlessly against the turret. Then she popped back up and continued firing. The infantry retreated, leaving behind a long string of bodies.

"Punty, they left! We're still alive!" she said, as she ducked back into the tank. Punty lay slumped in the gunner's seat. His head to one side. She felt his neck for a pulse, but he was gone. The floor of the tank was covered with blood.

"Bastard! You bled out and left me alone. Now what do I do?" she asked herself, as she sagged against the wall of the turret.

Everything hurt . . . she was exhausted and just wanted to go lie down somewhere quiet. Then she thought of the regiment, her regiment . . . Lord Strathcona's Horse . . . The Royal Canadians!

"Perseverance! Our motto is perseverance! It's all so glorious in the paintings and in the stories, but that's bullshit. It's just brutal . . .

killing!" she said aloud, then looked about her at the torn and blood-soaked bodies of her comrades and friends.

She groaned as she pulled herself back into the loader's chair and peeked out the hatch. Smoke was swirling everywhere from burning vehicles and burning bodies. Movement was visible at the far end of the bridge, but she couldn't see clearly.

"They're regrouping for another try. I either run or I fight," she said, as she dropped to the bottom of the turret and stared at the breech of the main gun.

It stood open. Will had died before he could insert another round. Turning, she opened the ammo hatch and pulled out a Heat round. She groaned as she stepped on Will's chest, slid the round into the cradle and slammed it into the breech. Punty was a big man, and she barely had the strength to pull him from the gunner's chair.

"This will haunt me for the rest of my life," she said, as she dropped his body beside Will's, slid into the chair, and leaned into the gunner's sight.

"No computer . . . this is like iron sights on a rifle. But like Punty said, 'This is like shooting fish in a barrel'. Only, the fish never shoot back.

.   .   .   .

The Russians
1235 hours PDT

"It's been over 40 minutes! Why am I still on this side of the river?" Colonel Golubkin shouted, as he dismounted from his APC and confronted the two Lieutenants standing behind a T-72.

"Captain, we've lost three tanks, an APC and 50-60 men. The Canadian tank is damaged, but still fighting. Our own wreckage is blocking the bridge," replied Lieutenant Okulov, commander of the second platoon of tanks.

"Where is that idiot brother-in-law of mine? He promised me this would be easy!"

The two lieutenants stared at each other. Lieutenant Okulov pointed past the curve in the road leading back to the factory.

"The medics have him, Colonel. His tank caught fire. He was badly burned from the waist down."

"I want that damn bridge. The Canadians in the town are putting up a stiff fight. We must take them in the flank. Push everything to the side. Get your damn tanks on the bridge and kill those Canadian bastards! Do you understand? Where is Captain Kazak? This is his company!"

"He died with the infantry, trying to get across the bridge."

"Shit! Captain Azarov, you are my adjutant. I leave you with this problem. Fix it!" Colonel Golubkin said, as he stormed off.

The three officers stared at the battalion commander and then at each other.

"Attach tow cables to the wrecks. Pull them off the bridge. Use smoke to cover your work. Lieutenant Pimenov, place your tanks in a tight wedge formation. Lieutenant Levkin will lead the infantry up both sides. Get every portable anti-tank weapon you have up here now. Be ready to attack in 10 minutes! Move!" ordered Captain Azarov.

.   .   .   .

Kathleen
1240 hours

Jess reloaded both machine guns, closed the tank commander's hatch, and sat there looking out the periscopes. She could fire the main gun from the TC's position. The radio was broken. Now all she could do was wait, having decided to stay with the dead. She was afraid to inject herself with painkillers. She knew that if she fell asleep, she would probably never wake up. So, she drank water, ate an energy bar, and tried to rest. Mostly, she tried not to look at her friends.

She removed her helmet and sat it in on the breech of the main gun by her knees. After pouring water over her head, she wiped her face and glanced through the forward periscope. White smoke filled the far end of the bridge. Switching to the thermal sights, she saw red-hot hulks being dragged away.

"Ahh, that makes sense. Remove the wreckage, then back at it. Somebody out there has stopped to think about this. What would I do? I'd send everything at once . . . tanks and infantry. They know we're shot up, but they're not playing anymore. Classic Russian tactics . . . attack with overwhelming force," she said, as she leaned her forehead against the hatch ring.

"Just a few more minutes, Jess . . . perseverance! Then you can get lots of sleep. Punty will have gotten some beer . . . we can play some poker and . . ."

Her head struck the side of the turret and jarred her awake. A quick look showed the bridge covered with smoke. Shells were landing every few seconds, as the mild breeze threatened to clear the smoke from the bridge. She glanced again and saw three large blocks of heat lined up at the far end of the bridge. Little blobs of heat were running past the tanks on both sides.

"Aw, Punty . . . you got four. Let's see what I can do," Jess said, as she replaced her helmet and lined up a shot on the tank on the right.

"Just hit the tracks. That will stop it and kill some infantry," she said, as she fired the main gun for the first time in over a year.

The explosion sent bodies flying into the river or into the steel superstructure, but the tank kept coming. All three Russian tanks fired at once. The first round struck Kathleen's turret and glanced off. The second struck the right track and shattered it. The third struck the left front hull and blew into the tank. Jess was shielded from most of the fragments by the bulk of the main gun and breech. Fire began to erupt around her as she scrambled out of the hatch and over to the loader's machine gun. She sat on the top of the turret, ignoring the pain and the blood that seemed to be seeping from all over her body. She screamed in rage and began firing into the smoke on both sides of the bridge.

"All right, Punty! Quit laughing at me. You were the best gunner in the regiment. I sucked at gunnery, but I was a good Sergeant . . . wasn't I?" Jess yelled, as another Sabot round struck the front of Kathleen's hull.

. . . .

Russian Medical APC
1255 hours PDT

"Good news, Lieutenant! The bridge is ours. I heard they just killed the Canadian tank. They say the turret was blown off," said CPL Debanov, one of the medics at the aid station set up inside the plywood factory.

Senior Lieutenant Pimenov lay in a morphine induced haze. One leg was gone below the knee. The other foot had been hanging by a tendon and was amputated. The rest of his lower body was covered with second- and third-degree burns. He looked into the medic's smiling eyes, nodded, closed his eyes and died.

. . . .

Kathleen
1255 hours PDT

Sergeant Jessica Brown lay semiconscious just off the eastern end of the bridge. The smoldering turret of her tank lay upside down, less than ten feet away. The hull of the Leopard 2A4, known as Kathleen, was a burning wreck, still sitting on the bridge. Main gun ammunition stored inside the hull continued to detonate, driving the Russian infantry back. Even in death, Kathleen fought on . . . until help finally arrived.

A platoon of four Leopard tanks and four Coyote LAV 3 recon vehicles were streaming down Beaver Forest Road as Kathleen held the Russians at bay. What they saw next would become part of Regimental legend. As they approached the end of the bridge, Sergeant Brown staggered to her feet, facing toward the enemy. She drew her pistol and began firing in the direction of the Russians. Her tanker's helmet was still on, but her uniform was in tatters. Burns and shrapnel wounds covered her lower body, arms and face. She only stopped when her pistol emptied and was reloading when Canadian infantry and combat engineers rushed past her.

"Sergeant Brown, please stop! We finally got here. I'm sorry it took so long," said Lieutenant John Morris.

"The bridge . . . we have to persevere . . . the bridge," she said, as tears began rolling down her face.

"The engineers are going to blow the bridge. We drove them back in Prince George. We finally destroyed the western bridge. You and your tank held the northern flank. Well done!" he said and saluted.

She said nothing, only stared at him, then turned back toward the bridge, still trying to reload her pistol, but her hands were shaking so much it was impossible. Combat engineers rushed under the bridge to place explosives. Canadian infantry and armor fought off the Russians remaining on the bridge.

Two medics appeared, forced her onto a stretcher, and ran to their vehicle 100 yards back up the road. Her last conscious thoughts before the narcotics took over, were of Will, Kayla and Punty. Her last mumbled words were . . . "We persevered . . ."

CHAPTER 42

82nd Airborne Division Headquarters
1 All American Way
Fort Bragg, North Carolina
October 18, 1930 hours

"I'm not happy about this, not happy at all, but I don't have a choice. He has friends in high places," said Major General Fred Gavin, commanding general of the 82nd Airborne Division, as Colonel Patrick Curl, commander of the 2nd Brigade Combat Team, paced in front of his desk.

"You're giving me a battalion commander whose battalion no longer exists . . . and telling me . . . that a man who was up for a court martial until eight hours ago . . . that I have to take him into my brigade right before we go into combat?"

"I can give you the number for the Joint Chief if you wish to discuss the matter with him. The order came directly from him. It was not my decision. You don't have to like it, but it's a lawful order. Lieutenant Colonel Maltun entered surgery two hours ago. He won't be fit for duty for at least a month. You need someone for 1st Squadron, 73rd Cav," said General Gavin, his patience beginning to wear thin.

"But, Sir. . . Major Griffin, the XO . . . he can take the Squadron. He's top notch."

"Yes, he is, but he's been a Major for less than six weeks. He's too green. His only combat was as an infantry platoon leader. Strykers are new to him. Besides, the charges against Thompson were bullshit. You read the report. Can you honestly say you could have done better?"

"Dammit! It's the timing, Sir. He won't know anyone in his squadron. By tomorrow, we'll be fighting Russians."

"Pat, we're soldiers. We do what we're told. We go where we're told with whomever the Army gives us. Once you walk out of this office, all this pissing and moaning will stop. Is that understood?"

"General . . . I just don't . . ."

"I said . . . is that understood, Colonel?" General Gavin said, as he rose from behind his desk.

"Yes, Sir! 'All the Way', Sir!" Colonel Curl replied, repeating the motto for the 82nd Airborne Division as he snapped to attention.

"Very good! He's waiting down the hall. Take him to his squadron, introduce him to his officers, and make sure they know you have full confidence in their new commanding officer. Is that understood?" General Gavin said, the tone in his voice indicating the time for discussion had ended.

"Perfectly, Sir!" Colonel Curl said, saluted and left the office.

Colonel Curl was still fuming when he reached the Division Headquarters waiting area and found Thompson staring out the window. As he approached, he decided that General Gavin was correct, as he always was. The time for questioning had ended.

"Lieutenant Colonel Thompson, I'm Colonel Curl. Welcome to the 2nd Brigade Combat Team," he said, while extending his right hand in greeting.

· · · ·

Headquarters
1st Battalion, 73rd Cavalry Regiment

"So, what do you think, Allen? I can't believe Division is dumping some stranger on us at the last minute! Why didn't they just give you the command? That would have made more sense," said Captain Sam Bailey, commanding officer of "D" Troop.

"Since when does anything from Division have to make sense?" asked Captain Jamal Reese, CO of "A" Troop, as the five officers waited in a meeting room beside the new battalion commander's office.

"Attenhut!" said Major Griffin, as the door opened and Colonel Curl walked in, followed by Lieutenant Colonel Thompson.

"Gentlemen, at ease. We don't have time for the usual change of command bullshit. I'll keep this simple. This is Lieutenant Colonel Anthony Thompson. He is your new CO. I have complete confidence in his ability to lead this battalion. I expect your full support and cooperation. He knows Strykers, their abilities and limitations, but he doesn't know the men of this battalion. Your mission is to fill that gap and make him successful. If he is successful, then you and 1st Battalion, 73rd Cav will be successful, and that will make me happy. Is that understood?"

"Completely, Sir!" replied Major Griffin for the group.

"Excellent! Your battalion and all their vehicles will be airborne in six hours. I'll see you in Prince George!" Colonel Curl said, then turned and left.

An awkward silence filled the room as the six officers exchanged glances.

"Normally, I'd spend the next few weeks meeting with each of you privately, visiting your units, and talking with your lieutenants and senior NCOs. But these aren't normal times. The next time the sun rises, we'll be in Canada killing Russians. Have you been briefed on the situation at Prince George?" Lieutenant Colonel Thompson asked.

"We've been told the Canadian army is making a stand at a road juncture, behind a river. We're going in to secure an airfield and rail area for 'Heavies' to come up from Texas," replied Major Griffin.

"Here's the latest info. The Canadians are holding on by their fingernails. They've lost about half their assets. They've blown all the river crossings, but the Russians are bringing up bridging equipment.

As of right now, the Russians have control of the air space above the battlefield."

"Then how do we get in without getting shot to shit . . . Sir?" asked Captain Patterson, CO of 'B' Troop.

"That's a work in progress. I've been told the air space will be secure before we arrive over the area."

The other officers all looked at each other, knowing how vulnerable they were while flying in huge, lumbering cargo jets.

Anthony reached into his briefcase and removed five thumb drives and five folders.

"Reading material, gentlemen. Included are the mission order, the warning order, the tentative plan and the current recon data. Feel free to share this information as you see fit. Each troop has specific assignments once we hit the ground. If I receive additional info, I'll disseminate as appropriate. Questions?" asked Lieutenant Colonel Thompson, as he handed out the folders and thumb drives.

"Nothing like a little light reading on a cross-country flight," said Captain Bailey, as he opened the folder.

"Hey, anything's better than being on the back of a commercial plane with all the babies. My wife had to restrain me the last time we flew out to California to visit . . ." Captain Stephens began, then remembered that his wife's relatives were probably all dead.

"Gentlemen, this is a war. The Chinese started it. Parts of North Carolina will be quarantined for decades. Millions are dead on the West Coast. The Russians have decided this is a good time to try to kick our asses. But that's not going to happen. You've all served in the Middle East or in Afghanistan. We won't be fighting insurgents. The Russians will have us outgunned, outnumbered and may have control of the air. The Canadians are defending their country the best they can. We're arriving in country to assist them and hold ground until an armored brigade from the 1st Armored Division arrives on scene. We will have to hold for two days, maybe as many as five. This assignment will not be easy. We may be outgunned, but we will not be outfought."

"So, we're just a speed bump?" asked Captain Reese.

"I prefer to think of us as . . . a roadblock . . . a big one. The clock is ticking, Gentlemen. Get to your troops and get them briefed and ready for departure. I'm headed to Brigade. I'll meet you at the airfield," said Lieutenant Colonel Thompson, who closed his briefcase and walked out of the room.

"Well, what do you guys think?" asked Captain Bailey, the youngest of the group.

"I heard the Russians have landed 20 plus divisions . . . so far. I think we're going to be lucky not to get our asses kicked," said Captain Stephens, as they all filed out of the room.

"Nice, Charlie . . . always the optimist," said Captain Bailey, his best friend and college roommate.

"Hey! Just sayin' . . ."

CHAPTER 43

Connaught Hill Park
Prince George
British Columbia, Canada
October 19, 0230 hours PDT

Connaught Hill Park was in southeast Prince George. It rose above the city affording a panoramic view of the town and surrounding hills. There were benches, tables and trails laced throughout the stately trees that covered the hillside. It would have been a glorious place to take the family for an outing. But that was for another day . . . another year.

The fighting in and around Prince George had been non-stop for over 14 hours. The population of 65,000 had been ordered to evacuate days earlier. Only a few hundred stubborn individuals remained. They now regretted that decision. Much of the city was burning from the constant shelling by the Russians. The hills on the other side of the Nechako River were barely visible through the smoke. The sound of gunfire and explosions was constant.

"Major, we have less than a dozen tanks still operable. We've finally blown all the northern bridges, but the Russians are sending infantry across the river in inflatables. We don't have enough bodies to defend the whole river front," said Captain Alice Campbell, as she stood beside Major Jacob Manx, CO of the Royal Canadians after Lieutenant Colonel Steel was killed in the initial attack on the city.

"Where are the damn Americans? They were supposed to be here before midnight. Have you heard anything from the airport?" Major Manx asked, while sitting in the back of his LAV III command vehicle on the forward slope of the hill.

"They've seen nothing, and communications are rough. The Russians are jamming our frequencies. I've had to send runners. Major, what are your orders?"

"We were supposed to hold the railyard. That's not going to be possible. Have all remaining units pull back to here, to 15th Avenue," he said, while pointing at a display screen on the inside wall of the vehicle.

"Sir, that road's almost three miles long. We can't hold that much territory."

"Captain, we'll hold this line as long as we can, then pull back toward the southern bridges. Have we finished rigging them with explosives? We'll retreat to there, cross the bridges, and then blow them."

"The two road bridges are rigged. The engineering unit that was supposed to prep the railroad bridge was lost during a helicopter attack. We don't have any more explosives."

"Damn! We'll have to . . ."

Shell fire began to erupt on the wooded hillside all around the LAV III. The lightly armored vehicle was rocked by the explosions.

"Driver, get us off this hill!" Major Manx yelled, as his crew rushed back into the vehicle. Shrapnel, dirt and tree limbs could be heard pinging off the sides as the rear ramp closed.

.   .   .   .

McMillian Creek Regional Park
0230 hours PDT

The park stood on the high bluffs just north of the Nechako River. Prince George was now laid out below him like a 3D terrain model. A brisk wind from the northwest had risen and was clearing the battlefield of the thick, smoky haze that had been obscuring his vision. His infantry looked like a child's toy soldiers as they struggled across the expanse of the Frasier River. Helicopter gunships hovered above the flowing water, targeting Canadian positions on the opposite side. Tanks, rocket launchers and artillery rained fire down on strong points, tanks and command and control hubs. The simple one and two-story homes that lined the river were burning rubble. The stately conifers and birch trees that lined the streets were shattered or burning like torches. The burning city provided more than enough light for him to see.

To Colonel General Alexander Zhurov, commander of the 5th Combined Arms Army, it was a thing of profound beauty. This campaign, this battle, was something he had longed for his entire life. Even as a boy, he had dreamed of fighting for the mighty General Zhukov as his tank armies drove the hated Nazis from the soil of Mother Russia during The Great Patriotic War, that others called World War II. Now it was finally his turn, and he relished every . . . bloody . . . second of it.

"General, you are too exposed here. At least pull back to your command vehicle. Please!" begged Colonel Vadim Borodim, his aide.

"Relax, Vadim, I am not fated to die here. I have already seen my end, and it will not be today. Besides, I need to see this personally. Unit symbols moving around on a flat screen are too sterile. From here, I can see how our men move as they cross the river . . . how they charge the enemy positions . . . sense what they are feeling. I need to know these things, Vadim. That way, I will know how far I can push them," General Zhurov said, as he raised his binoculars and resumed watching the battle unfolding below him.

·   ·   ·   ·

"Captain . . . it's the Americans . . . but they're not landing! What are they doing?" Lieutenant Basil Smith asked, as the C-17 Globemaster approached in the darkness and skimmed the 3.5-kilometer-long main runway.

"They're crazy! That's what they are, Basil . . . stark raving mad!" replied Captain Jason McGuinness, and grinned, as the huge aircraft lowered its rear ramp and disgorged a Stryker vehicle from its hold. A few seconds later, a second chute erupted from the rear of the plane, followed by a second Stryker.

A huge parachute yanked the 19-ton vehicle backward as the C-17 accelerated and leapt into the sky. Both Strykers skidded to a halt less than 50 yards apart. Each crew leapt from their vehicle, disconnected it from the platform on which it had been attached, and reconnected the vehicle to different connections on the front of the skid. Then they started their vehicles and dragged the skids and the parachutes to the side of the runway. The entire process had taken only 90 seconds. C-17s were lined up past the horizon, tail-to-tail, less than two miles apart. Each drop delivered more vehicles from the 1st Battalion, 73rd Cavalry Regiment of the 82nd Airborne Division. The Falcon Brigade was arriving . . .

"Off the runway! Get off the damn runway! Captain Stephens, align your vehicles as planned. The Russians won't let us come in unopposed!" Lieutenant Colonel Thompson yelled over the comm channel, as the second C-17 disgorged its contents.

Captain Stephens was grinning like a schoolboy as his SHORAD launcher, a variant of the Stryker, skidded to a halt in the middle of the runway. His crew leapt from the vehicle and disconnected the Stryker from the platform. His Troop possessed nine of the SHORAD variants designed to provide short-range air defense for the drop. Each was assigned a different section of the runway.

"Move it! Move it! Move it!" Anthony yelled, as he glanced at the next C-17 just over the treeline, making an approach for the runway.

They dragged everything clear, just as the huge plane dropped its rear gate and spat out its delivery. The last vehicle had just been dropped when the game changed. As the C-17 began to accelerate, and angled up into the sky, it exploded as three rockets removed its left wing. The plane spun upward, then turned downward, crashing in a massive explosion a quarter mile past the runway. The Russian Hind paused at the far end of the concrete landing strip, illuminated by the flames, as if admiring its work. Captain Stephens' Stryker, mounting the AN/TWQ-1 Avenger Air Defense System, launched an FIM-92 Stinger missile from a range of only 300 yards. The Hind's pilot never saw the missile. The resulting fireball and debris added to the chaos at the end of the runway.

"Mallet 1 to all Post Office flights, bring in the mail. Landing area hot, but security in place. Over!" Lieutenant Colonel Thompson said, after switching to the Air Force frequency.

"Roger that, Mallet 1. We've got a lot more deliveries to make. Out!" a pilot said, as another C-17 dropped over the treeline and onto the runway.

"Colonel, radar shows multiple Hinds coming in from the northwest," said Captain Stephens,

"Do your job, Captain! I've got to get the rest of the battalion on the ground and organized."

The C-17s kept coming in for the next hour. Two more were lost, one was still fully loaded. Seven Hinds were shot down by the Stingers of Captain Stephens' Weapons Troop, as they fought to protect the remainder of the battalion.

. . . .

"General, the Americans are bringing in troops and vehicles at the airport. We've shot down several of the transports, but have lost over half of our air support," said COL Borodin.

Colonel General Zhurov was seated in a lawn chair procured from a nearby house, still overlooking Prince George. The far shore of the river had been taken, and the Canadians driven back, but the cost had been high.

"Hmm, I was hoping to save the runway, but we have to slow the Americans down until the city has been secured. Switch artillery fire to the airport. Crater the runway, then switch fire to roads leading away from the airport and heading for the city. What type of vehicles?"

"No tanks . . . only Strykers!"

"Have we identified the unit?"

"Yes, General, we have the Canadian radio frequencies. They were talking about the 82nd Airborne. It appears to be a battalion-sized unit."

"Hah! Foolish! The Americans are sending a knife into a gun battle. The Chinese have really crippled them if that's all they can send to oppose us. Vadim, make sure the runways are unusable. They will have to drop their men from the sky. It will be like shooting pigeons. I hope they send the entire Division. No armor . . . Strykers only . . . and they won't have many of those!" General Zhurov said, as he stood and began clapping his hands.

"It will be a good day, Vadim! A very good day indeed! But get that bastard Bozorov to send more air support from Whitehorse. We didn't set up an airbase there for him to sit on his fat ass and play cards with his pilots!"

"Yes, General!"

. . . .

Prince George Airport
0330 hours PDT

"Yes, Colonel! The shelling started about 20 minutes ago and hasn't let up. The Russians aren't going to let us do it the easy way. Over!" Lieutenant Colonel Thompson said, while talking to Colonel Curl, commander of the 2nd Brigade Combat Team, still an hour away on a C-5A transport.

"All right, Colonel. We'll use drop zone Bravo. Shift your anti-air assets accordingly. Over!"

"Already on site, Sir. We'll do our best to keep the Russians at bay. Over!"

"Understood! How are the Canadians holding up? Over!"

"I've talked with a Canadian officer at the airport. He says the Russians have conducted a river crossing. The Canadians are pulling back to their next hold point. Over!"

"Colonel Thompson . . . hold the city. If you can't, then make sure all the bridges leading south are destroyed. Is that understood? Over!"

"Roger that, Sir! Hold the city or blow the bridges. We'll hold the city. Over!"

"See you at City Hall. Out!"

"Great! Now, how do we hold the city?" Anthony thought, as his Stryker approached the southernmost bridge leading into Prince George.

Anthony was aware that the Canadians might get aggressive when unknown vehicles approached. So, the Stars and Stripes was flying from the lead vehicle. He leapt from his Stryker and approached a young female lieutenant who was leading the unit at the bridge.

303

"Lieutenant Colonel Anthony Thompson, 82nd Airborne. Where can I find your CO?" he asked, as the young Lieutenant saluted.

"Sir! Second Lieutenant Marie Ballyard, Royal Canadians. Last I heard, he was at the Golf & Curling Club. Cross the bridge. It's about half a mile up on your left," she replied, while staring up at the tall American officer, then glancing at the long line of Strykers disappearing in the darkness.

"Curling Club?"

"Yes, Sir! Curling! It's a Canadian thing . . . Sir! Turn left when you get to Mr. PG. It's a big wooden guy over 20 feet tall."

"Mister PG?"

"Yes, Sir! You can't miss him," she said, still smiling at the sight of so many American reinforcements.

"Thank you, Lieutenant . . . and don't salute. The Russians will have snipers looking for officers," Lieutenant Colonel Thompson said, as he turned and entered his Stryker.

"Yes, Sir! Sorry, Sir!" she replied, while glancing around.

"Captain Reese, I'll lead the way. We're going to find the Canadian CO. Put three MGS behind me and follow with the rest of your company. Over!" Lieutenant Colonel Thompson said, over the command channel.

"Roger that, Colonel!" Captain Jamal Reese replied.

The MGS were a variant of the Stryker that mounted an autoloading, 105mm rifled cannon in a turret. He remembered their effectiveness during the attack on the Harris Nuclear Plant. If Russian armor crossed the river, they would be his main defense against them.

. . . .

Prince George Golf & Curling Club
0345 hours PDT

"Hey, Colonel! She wasn't kidding! Look at that thing!" said Specialist Mitch Walker, driver of the Command Stryker, as he turned left at the historic landmark.

The steel and fiberglass structure looked like a stick man made from logs. It was riddled with shrapnel hits, and singed in several places, but the Canadian flag still stood proudly in his left hand.

Three LAV IIIs were stationed around the blue, two-story building. Their guns were pointed skyward as the Americans approached. Thompson was shocked to see five battered Strykers spaced out across the parking lot. Their guns were also manned as other crew members performed maintenance on the vehicles.

"Captain Reese, spread your company out. There are too many damn vehicles clustered around here. I have to find out what's going on. Over!"

"Roger that!"

"Walker, pull up by the entry door and keep the engine running!"

The Stryker was still rolling when Anthony stepped out the vehicle's back door and headed into the building.

"Where is your commanding officer?" he asked, while ignoring the salutes of startled Canadian soldiers.

"Through those doors . . . turn right . . . big office straight ahead, Sir!" the Canadian soldier replied, while dropping his salute.

The office was a bar, a huge one, and fully stocked, but untouched. All the tables had been rearranged into a large rectangle. Maps and radio equipment were arranged to give the commanding officer as much information as possible. Anthony was impressed. Considering the amount of pressure the Canadians were under, this was very organized. As he approached, he noticed an American Captain talking to a Canadian Major. The American grinned, nodded, and stuck out his hand in greeting.

"Captain Dothan MacLynn, Alpha Company, 1st battalion, 5th Infantry Regiment, 25th Infantry Division."

"Lieutenant Colonel Anthony Thompson, 1st Battalion, 73rd Cav, 82nd Airborne. How the hell did you get down here?" Lieutenant Colonel Thompson asked.

"Fighting Russians. Those five vehicles and 32 men outside are all that's left of my company. Maybe all that's left of our Division," Captain MacLynn replied, as the two men shook hands.

"Colonel, this is Major Jacob Manx, Royal Canadians," Captain MacLynn said, as the Canadian officer approached.

"We heard you were coming, Colonel. Welcome to Prince George. I suppose you'd like to know what the hell is going on," Major Manx said, as he turned back to the map laid out on the table beside him.

Anthony could see that the man was exhausted. He looked like he hadn't slept in days. The fact that he was commanding a regiment indicated that his CO was wounded or dead.

"The Russians have gotten infantry across the Nechako River to our north. More are crossing every hour. We held them for a while, but we have no air support and their fire power was overwhelming. I've lost most of my tanks. Our casualties are over 50 percent. Your 82nd Airborne . . . I hope you're just the first wave. We need support, heavy support, or we'll be thrown out of this city by tonight. Even better, there is another Russian column approaching Prince George from the southwest. We've blown bridges, but the Russians have good engineering support. They'll get across the river eventually. All we're doing is slowing them down," Major Manx said, while indicating Highway 16, known as the Yellowhead Highway, that led directly into the southwest side of Prince George.

"The rest of the brigade will be on the ground within the next two hours. They were coming in at the airport, but the Russians are shelling that to pieces. Our backup drop zone is here, the Aspen Grove Golf Course," Anthony replied, while tapping a place on the map.

"That's five miles south of the river. Light infantry, almost no transport, I suspect. You'll have to get organized. They won't reach this bridge in force for at least two hours after they land," Major Manx replied, while pointing at the bridge the Americans had crossed less than an hour ago.

"Our orders are to hold this city until help arrives. I brought 21 MGS Strykers and over 800 men. We have firepower, and we'll fight. When the rest of the brigade arrives, we'll add three infantry battalions and artillery support. We aren't without assets, Major. We're here to help you defend your country."

"Colonel . . . Thompson, we're facing the 127th Motorized Rifle Division. That's 15,000 men. That's just the force to our north. Another division is approaching from the southwest. The lead elements are less than 50 miles away. Just what do you think you're going to accomplish with 21 vehicles?"

"We're going to kill Russians, Major Manx. The terrain is in our favor. You know that. That's why you're here. I'll move my guns south with one infantry company. We'll start here. What's this river?" Anthony asked, while placing his finger on a bridge 15 miles southwest of Prince George.

"The Chilako River, but it's small. Even if you blow the bridge, they'll be able to ford the river."

"Major Manx, we're just trying to slow them down until more help arrives. Captain MacLynn, if your vehicles and men are fit, I'll blend you in with one of my companies. It's going to take infantry to hold the city. The river to the north is keeping Russian armor out. We must keep it that way. The greatest threat is the column coming up from the southwest. If that armor breaks through, they'll butcher the rest of my brigade and everyone in this city. That's where I'm headed. The sun will be up in a few hours and we have to be in place before then. I'll have my XO, Major Allen Griffin, report to you. Try to hold this line on 15th Avenue. Good luck! I'll stay in touch," Anthony said, as he turned and left the bar.

The Canadians stared as the tall American officer left the room.

"Doesn't waste a lot of time, does he?" asked Lieutenant Morris, one of the Canadian staff officers.

"Major, he'll have his XO in here in less than five minutes. We need to plan our defense with all these reinforcements," said Captain MacLynn.

"Quite correct! We'll start here . . ." Major Manx began.

CHAPTER 44

Kamchatka Forest Lodge
Kamchatka Peninsula, Russia
October 18, 2110 hours PETT (Kamchatka Time)

Amanda leaned back in the hot tub, watching as her breath was swept away in a mild breeze. It was cold and starting to snow again. Ruslan had kept the lights in the lodge turned off. A few candles were all the light he would allow. The old, one-piece bathing suit she had found was loose, and she kept having to pull up the top. But the more vodka she drank, the less of a concern that became.

"I am surprised that Yegor still stocks the best brands of vodka. The label is in Russian, but you would call it 'Jewel of Russia'. For me, it is a bit sweet. You will like it," Ruslan said, as he cracked the seal on the fifth bottle of the evening and refilled Amanda's glass.

The other four bottles stood in a line on the edge of the hot tub, like good soldiers awaiting further orders, as the sampling continued. He had started with an ounce from the first bottle, but as the evening deepened, so did the amount of the sample.

"I always thought I had a good sense of taste, but all I feel now is the burn," she said, after tasting the latest vodka and setting the glass aside.

She ducked her head into the hot steamy water and opened her eyes. The heat and the moisture soothed the ache and sense of dryness in her eyes that wouldn't go away despite the vodka. When she raised her head, she found Ruslan staring at her.

"Do I have to worry about you trying something?" she asked, as she drained the tumbler and set the glass aside.

"Well, we are alone. There is no one around for many miles except for Yegor, and he is passed out drunk in another lodge. You are very beautiful, but I would never . . . try anything. If my babushka heard that I had treated a woman badly, she would hunt me down and remove my manhood . . . and she is almost 80!" Ruslan said, then began laughing as he refilled his own glass, drained it, and reached for a fresh bottle.

"Babushka . . . grandmother? Your grandmother is still alive?"

"Very alive! She can still drink more vodka than I can, and she is a little woman . . . for a Russian. When Dedushka died, I moved her out here from Minsk. Her friends were all dead, and the place she was living in was shit. Too much crime. It wasn't safe for an old woman. Even one as tough as her. Now she lives in Petropavlovsk, on the other side of the bay, just a few miles from here. Lots of submarines are stationed there. Dedushka . . . Grandfather, was a Hero of the Soviet Union, a submarine captain during The Great Patriotic War. There is a home for old veterans and their wives. It is warm and safe there. She is happy. So, I am happy," Ruslan said, while opening a bottle of Zyr vodka.

"This is my personal favorite. It is smooth without any funny aftertaste," he said, while offering to fill Amanda's empty glass.

"Ruslan, why do we have to kill each other? We're not so different, Americans and Russians. We both want to be free to raise our families in peace."

"Ahh . . . I have read your history. You Americans are castoffs from other places. A few, a select few, saw an opportunity for the many . . . an opportunity for true freedom. They fought for that opportunity. Even today, after all this time, you continue to fight for freedom. You argue openly about the mistakes you have made as a nation. That would never happen here. I admire that. I truly do! But Russians . . . we are not the same. We are descendants of peasants, similar to what you would call slaves. That is our heritage. We have learned how to survive under whatever regime is in power. We adapt. We thought that communism would be our salvation. At last we would be free from the master's yoke, but we were wrong. We killed the Czar, and then the Communist Party became our new master. Even today, with communism officially gone, we are still not free. Our elections are a sham. 'President' . . . Morozov is a dictator in all but title. Ahh . . . I am sorry for this . . . too much vodka. It loosens my tongue," Ruslan said, while refilling his glass.

"What you are doing with me . . . helping me? They would have you shot as a traitor. Why do you bother? You sound . . . fatalistic. As if your country is doomed by its own history."

"Ahh . . . you will meet two kinds of Russians: happy drunks and sad drunks. I am a sad drunk. I can see the greatness we would have if we ever truly became a free people. We are creative and brave. Our land is filled with rich resources. But we seem cursed by our own history. We don't have enough faith in ourselves to truly be free. Sometimes I think we are afraid to be free. It is easier to just blame someone else for your problems. That is why I am a sad drunk," Ruslan said, as he drained the glass and settled deeper into the hot, steamy water.

"Ruslan . . . I need to see the weapon in the mountain. I have to know what it is, so we can destroy it," Amanda said, as she refilled her glass from the new bottle.

"Tomorrow, little one. Tomorrow we will climb the volcano and peer into its depths. A great monster lives there. I have always wanted to hunt a monster. Just like the movies . . . I will be Ruslan the Hunter, killer of dragons!" he said, while sloshing vodka from his glass.

"To hunting dragons!" Amanda replied, as their glasses clinked together.

CHAPTER 45

The White House
The Oval Office
Washington, DC
October 19, 1130 hours EST

"I wanted to talk to you both personally. Our forces are engaged in combat activities in Canada. Specifically, in and around Prince George, British Columbia," said President Beaumont, as she sat behind the Resolute Desk.

"Madam President, we . . . already know about this. We were briefed on this yesterday," replied Senator Marker, as he and the Speaker of the House sat in the Oval Office.

"What you don't know is that we may lose this fight, and a brigade from the 82nd Airborne. The Russians are moving faster and in greater numbers than we anticipated. Our armored forces won't reach the area for at least another day."

"If we lose this battle . . . on top of everything else . . ." Speaker Jacobson began.

"The Northwest is already battered. Thousands died in the Great Quake. Power outages are widespread. If the Russians reach our border . . . they've been killing every civilian they come across. I heard they murdered thousands of people in Alaska!" Senator Marker said, the shock of the news starting to set in.

"That's an unconfirmed rumor. There was heavy fighting in and around Anchorage, but . . . that's just a rumor . . ." the President said, as a sense of hopelessness began to overwhelm her.

She looked up and noticed a tall, bearded man standing in the corner, head bowed, as if thinking. At first, she thought it was a secret service agent that had slipped into the room unnoticed. Then he looked up, and their eyes locked.

"He looks so sad and so very tired. But what else? Disappointed?" she thought, as a feeling of pity and responsibility struck her.

The shock of who he was, struck her like an electric jolt.

"Madam President! Are you all right? You've gone pale. Should we get someone?" Senator Marker said, rising from his chair.

"No! No . . . I'm fine!" she said, while rubbing her eyes.

She stared at the corner again. No one was there.

"Disappointed . . . who was . . . no . . . I'm losing my mind. God help me, I'm losing my . . . It's all right, Senator. Too much coffee and not enough sleep."

"Madam President, you need to take better care of yourself. I don't want to have to sit in that chair," said Speaker Jacobson.

"Don't worry, Carla. My husband keeps nagging me about getting some rest. I need to listen to him," the President said, while glancing back at the empty corner where the man had been standing.

"He was disappointed . . . in me! In what I said . . . about this war. We can't lose this war! We will not lose this war! We must tell the American people everything. This is their war, too! None of us are civilians anymore!" the President said, as she stood up and began pacing behind the desk.

"Madam President?" Senator Marker asked, as he turned and glanced at Speaker Jacobson.

"I said, we will not lose this war!"

"Are you thinking about using nuclear weapons?" Speaker Jacobson asked.

"What? No! At least not yet. The Russians would respond in kind. That is the last thing we would want to do. No one would want to be the first!"

"The Chinese were willing."

"And see what it got them. We aren't at that point yet. We'll stay conventional for as long as possible. We have to mobilize everything! We need to reinstate the draft!" the President said, as she continued to pace behind her desk.

"Will there be anything else, Madam President?" Senator Markle asked.

"No . . . no, start working on . . . things. I'll be back in touch. I need to think!"

"Madam President, please try to get some rest," Speaker Jacobson said, as she and the senator rose and left the Oval Office.

.   .   .   .

Out in the hallway, Senator Markle turned to Speaker Jacobson and said, "Carla, you better get ready to take over. I think she's starting to break down."

"No! She's just under a lot of stress. We all are. I've got faith in her. The people believe in her. The poll numbers show it. She's at 70 percent. Which is amazing, considering the state of the country."

"Did you see the look on her face before she got up and started pacing. It was like she saw a ghost."

"Bob, by the time we get through this mess, we'll all be seeing things!"

.   .   .   .

The President continued to pace back and forth after the Speaker and the Senate Majority Leader left. At each turn she would glance back toward the corner of the room where she had seen the figure of a man.

314

"That's twice I've seen him. the first time was on the steps of the Capitol. Now, in here . . . am I losing my mind? God, please give me the strength. Help me through this. So many people are depending on me. But he looked so disappointed. That was the look . . . disappointment! What does he expect of me? He had it easy . . . a civil war. Nature wasn't trying to destroy the country."

There was a knock on the door. Then another, a few seconds later when she didn't respond. Finally, the door opened. Her Chief of Staff stepped inside the room and slowly closed the door.

"Madam President, we've received a call from Doctor Janice Wolf, the geologist. She said it's urgent. I knew you were in a meeting, so I asked her what it was about. She said she would only talk to you."

"Rick, tell her I'll call back. Better yet, tell her I said to give you the information. I don't need any more distractions."

"Madam President, I think you should talk to her. She was scared. I could hear it in her voice. She said to tell you it was about the Reelfoot Rift . . ."

CHAPTER 46

Beverly Fire and Rescue Hall
Yellow Head Highway
Prince George, British Columbia, Canada
October 19, 0800 hours PDT

"This is the bottleneck, Gentlemen. Look at the berms created when the Canadians carved through the terrain to level the highway. Captain Bailey, position your vehicles at each berm, hull defilade. Your 105mm guns can take out a Russian tank," Lieutenant Colonel Thompson said, as he, Captain Bailey and Captain Stephens stood in the fire station, staring at a topographical map of the local area.

"That's a one-mile stretch, Colonel. If I place three guns at each berm, that's only 12 guns along the whole road."

"Look at the terrain. There isn't any way to bypass this road. If the Russians want to get to Prince George from the southwest, they have to come this way. We'll fill this damn highway up with their dead vehicles. If we can keep their choppers off your backs, you'll butcher them. The only thing showing will be your turrets and your cannon. Your light vehicle armor won't matter. We'll keep the rest on the MGS further up the road as a reserve."

"What about their choppers? Hinds are killers!"

"Place your Avenger anti-air units where you want them. They'll take care of the Hinds. Captain Stephens, your infantry company will cover the woods on either side. The Russians will try to flank Captain Bailey's guns. You two stay coordinated. When the pressure in the woods or on the road becomes untenable, you pull back to the next berm, the next position in the woods. The only thing I ask . . . is hold this damn road for as long as you can. Don't let the Russians get past you. When you have to pull back, the reserves can cover your withdrawal."

"The terrain is good, Colonel. They can't flank us . . . at least not easily. In a day their infantry can work around us. Then we're done. But for a day . . ."

"That is all I am asking of you both . . . a day . . . 24 hours. Can you give me that?"

"Hell, yeah! Sir! We'll hold the bastards off for a day. We can do it, Colonel!" Captain Stephens said, as he shook hands with Captain Bailey . . . and sealed their fate.

. . . .

McMillian Creek Regional Park
0830 hours PDT

Colonel General Zhurov had been pacing non-stop for the last 15 minutes. The Nechako River had been crossed hours ago. His infantry was progressing through the neighborhoods and businesses on the other side of the river. That wasn't his concern. His concern was the lack of resistance.

"Where are the Canadians? The Americans can't have arrived in the city yet. We destroyed too many of their transports. Americans don't like losing people in war. Their stomachs are too weak, but the Canadians are fighting for their own land. If they have pulled back, where would they make their next stand?" he thought, as he paced within the house on the ridge, that had been procured for use as his command post.

"General, we have received word that the Americans are in the area. Despite their air losses, they are still coming," said Colonel Borodin, as he handed new reports to his commanding officer.

"Define in the area! What are their numbers? What are their dispositions? Is this intelligence or rumor? How many vehicles reached the ground, and what types? Are you a Junior Lieutenant or a Colonel?" general Zhurov yelled, as Colonel Borodin snapped to attention.

"General! Approximately one brigade from the 82nd Airborne. The first wave consisted of Strykers in battalion strength. They secured the airport long enough to land. They have now abandoned the airport and are continuing to land additional infantry at another location. We have been unable to ascertain that location due to intense fire from the ground. Based on their communications, it is somewhere to the southeast."

"Better! General Mulnatov will have his division approaching from the southeast by now. Get me his exact location and status. His breakthrough is critical. The Americans will rush toward us, toward the city. Then we will have them pinned between the hammer and the anvil. This Brigade of the vaunted 82nd Airborne will cease to exist. That will send a message to Washington and to Moscow. We cannot lose this battle . . .

.   .   .   .

Prestige Treasure Cove Hotel
2005 Caribou Highway
0915 hours PDT

Sergeant Jessica Brown awoke in luxurious surroundings . . . and in a great deal of pain. She was lying on one side of a plush, king-sized bed. The surrounding furniture was a rich, brown leather. The room was painted a pale yellow. Tasteful art decorated the walls. The aroma of the leather blended with the smell of ointments, urine and her own feces. Blurred faces rushed past as her eyes cracked open. She shuddered and flinched, as memories of the battle flashed into her consciousness.

318

"Where? No! Where am I?" she mumbled, as she tried to sit up, and found herself linked to tubes, medical devices and wrapped in bandages.

"Please, don't move! You're safe . . . at least for now. Your wounds have been treated. Mostly shrapnel wounds and some minor burns. You're bruised all over, but nothing is broken. I'm sorry about the pain, but we're running out of narcotics. I left some Tylenol on the table. I'll give you some after I make my rounds," the medic said, as the room shuddered from the impact of nearby artillery fire.

The last thing she remembered was standing in front of the bridge, reloading her 9mm pistol. The Russians were still coming across the bridge. Her tank was destroyed. Her friends were dead. Now, she was lying in a bed.

"Where am I? What's happening? Is it over? Did we win?" she asked.

"Sergeant, we're in a hotel. All the wounded are being brought here. You'll get a roommate soon. The fighting is still going on. I don't know how long we'll hold out. I heard that the Americans have arrived, but I haven't seen any. It may just be a rumor," Combat Medic Dan Mitchell said, as he checked her blood pressure.

Another artillery round landed nearby. The building shook. A section of tile in the ceiling shifted and fell to the thickly carpeted floor. Screaming could be heard outside as the medic rushed from the room.

"I have to get out of here. We're still fighting," Jessica said, as she looked at the needles inserted into her left hand and began pulling them out.

Throwing them aside, she sat up and swung her legs over the side of the bed. Bandages sheathed her legs and other arm. Every limb ached as she stood up. Her head felt as if someone had punched her repeatedly.

"Clothes? Where are my damn clothes?" she asked, then stared at a pile of bloody fatigues thrown into one corner.

She stared down at herself, shocked to see herself naked except for bandages, then chuckled, remembering a scene from Bride of Frankenstein, one of her favorite old movies.

"All I need is a white streak in my hair," she mumbled, as she staggered into the adjoining bathroom and stepped into the shower.

She turned on the water and gasped as the cold stream shocked her into wakefulness. The wounds had been wiped clean, but the rest of her was filthy. The bandages peeled away as she rinsed the grime of the battle from her torn body. The moans of pain seemed to come from someone else as she cleaned herself with her own hands. Stepping from the shower, she left bloody footprints as she dried herself and walked back into the room. She stood in front of the mirror and almost cried. Her torso had been protected by her body armor, but her legs and arms seeped blood from numerous small puncture wounds. Part of her just wanted to crawl back into the bed and go back to sleep. She began dressing in her old fatigues. They smelled of cordite, sweat and blood. After tying her boots, she stood erect. Everything hurt. The room shook once more. Screams could be heard from the hallway. Sergeant Jessica Brown glanced in the full-length mirror and ran her fingers through her short, wet hair.

"A little messy, Sergeant Brown . . . but this will have to do," she said, as she tucked the bottle of Tylenol into her pants pocket, opened the door, and reentered the war.

. . . .

Prince George Toyota
2772 Recplace Drive
0945 hours PDT

Jessica gulped down two more Tylenol as she fought through the pain tormenting her every step. She had found a black beret in the parking lot and felt much better being 'in uniform'. The crack and thunder of gunfire and explosions could be heard to the north, and she began walking in that direction. A familiar shape caught her eye as she crossed the Yellowhead Highway, searching for some cover as artillery shells began to randomly fall across the area.

"*Tanks at a car dealership? Leopard tanks . . . repairs or staging?*" she asked herself, as she tried to run, and instantly regretted the attempt.

Two Leopard tanks were tucked up against the side of the Toyota dealership, just outside the maintenance bays on the southern end of the building. They were obviously different models, but both were in one piece. As she walked up, she could see that the engine covers were removed from the back deck of one of them. Two soldiers were immersed in their repair efforts.

"Does it work?" she shouted.

One soldier looked up and stared, while wiping his hands on a rag.

"Shit! Are you wounded?" Corporal Liam Morris asked, as he leapt off the back of the tank and walked toward her.

"No . . . yes, but no, I've been treated and released. Is this tank operable?"

"Not for hours. She took a rocket in the ass. Nothing we can do about the hole. We'll have to pull the engine. We've got one more replacement in there," he said, while pointing inside the dealership maintenance shop.

"How about that one?" she asked, while gesturing toward the second Leopard sitting on the other side of the rollup doors.

"That one's fine. It had a broken track. Tension wasn't set right. We've been working on that piece of junk for months, even before this war started. It's an old Leopard 1A3. It was sitting on a pedestal in Edmonton, in front of Brigade Headquarters. That's why it's painted in winter camo, all gray and white. We were ordered to get it working in our spare time. That was a joke! It took us months to get that thing combat ready. It was dragged along as a spare. Now, she's fueled and armed, but no tankers. Jimmy and me were talking about taking her out to the fight ourselves, but neither of us are gunners. We can both drive but we're mechanics, not tankers."

"So, all we need is a gunner?" Sergeant Brown asked, as she stared at the white tank. The lines were different than 'Kathleen', more angular, more brutal.

"Yeah, but . . ."

"Where is your sergeant . . . officers?"

"Dead or wounded. We're all that's left of our maintenance platoon. Some Captain came by and took everybody else."

"Well, Corporal . . . Morris, it looks like you and Jimmy are coming with me. Who's the better driver?"

"Me . . ."

"Crank her up. Tell Jimmy to get in the turret. He's the loader. I know where to look for a gunner. This is a direct order from a Noncommissioned Officer. Now, move!" Sergeant Brown yelled, as the man just stared at her.

He ran toward the tank after gesturing for Jimmy to join him.

"Now if I can just climb up there without passing out," she thought, while walking toward the tank.

. . . .

Prestige Treasure Cove Hotel
1010 hours PDT

"I need a gunner! Who can still walk and see?" Sergeant Brown shouted, while walking down the first-floor hallway of the hotel.

"What the hell are you doing? These people are all wounded," a doctor asked, as he walked out of a room.

"So am I, but this is a war . . . in Canada . . . our Canada! I need a gunner! Who's got the guts to get back in the fight?" Jessica shouted.

"Sergeant! I am a Captain in the Canadian Army. I am ordering you to leave this place immediately. Better yet, you need to be in a bed. Who the hell discharged you?"

"I did, Sir! I still need a gunner!" she shouted again.

A tall blonde-haired man walked out of one of the rooms. His left arm was in a sling and the hair had been singed from the left side of his head, but both blue eyes were focused as he walked toward them.

"I'm a gunner. Damn sure can't load, but I can shoot and I'm good at it. You got a tank?" Corporal Jackson Wills asked.

"Sitting outside with a driver and a loader. You willing?"

"Help me climb up there and into the turret. Then I'm good."

"We'll help each other. I'm Sergeant Jess Brown. The loader is a mechanic. You may have to talk him through loading."

"Mechanic? Hell, why not? The rest of my crew is dead. I'm tired of sitting around here and waiting for the Russians to walk in and kill us."

"Same here, that makes us double lucky."

"Or unlucky," Corporal Wills said, as they walked away from the fuming doctor.

CHAPTER 47

Northern Slopes of Vilyuchik
Kamchatka Peninsula, Russia
October 19, 0830 hours PETT

The snowmobile was making good time as Ruslan headed up the valley. Fresh snow from the night before left the terrain pristine. The sky was cloudless and a deep blue. The cold was intense. Amanda would have enjoyed the journey, holding onto Ruslan's broad back, except for her massive hangover. She had already forced him to stop twice so she could empty the contents of her stomach. All she wanted to do was lie down in the snow and sleep.

"How much longer?" she shouted, over the noise of the speeding machine. Ruslan seemed to be enjoying her discomfort.

"Five hours!" he replied, as they plunged deeper into the canyon.

"Holy crap! Five hours . . . I'll be dead before then. I am never drinking again," she thought, as the noise and endless vibration churned her stomach once again.

She glanced around Ruslan's wide body. Jagged cliffs rose on either side as the valley closed in. At the far end was a solid white wall. It reminded her of the ice wall in Game of Thrones. There was a gleaming spear, a spike . . . something that rose from the valley floor to the peak of the white wall. Her vision began to blur, and she closed her eyes. She awoke after the first bounce; the thick snow having cushioned her fall.

Ruslan jerked her to her feet and thrust a flask up to her lips.

"Here, drink this. It tastes like shit, but it will keep you awake and calm your stomach."

She gagged but swallowed the foul-tasting mixture.

"What is this?" she asked, as she pushed the flask away.

"A secret elixir of mine. It starts with my favorite energy drink, Russian Power. Then a shot of vodka and over 20 secret ingredients. Hah . . . I sound like a TV commercial. One day I will market this drink. Russians will love it. I will become very rich and have a dacha near Moscow. Here, drink some more. You are lucky you didn't hit a rock when you fell," Ruslan said, as he thrust the flask forward.

Amanda drank some more. It was foul tasting but soothed her roiling stomach.

"It tastes like crap. You should add some honey."

"Honey! That is an excellent idea. I will cut you in for five percent. Now, we have to get going. It is still a long way, and it is going to get very cold tonight. We must reach the cabin before dark," he said, as he replaced the cap on the flask and tucked it inside his heavy coat.

"I thought you said it was only five more hours!"

"Five hours of riding . . . then we walk," he said, while patting the snowshoes strapped to the side of the snowmobile."

. . . .

5 hours later

Amanda stood in the cold, staring upward. The white wall was just that, a cliff face at the end of the valley that went straight up for over 300 feet. The valley floor at its base was curved, sloping steeply upward on either side. A wide groove had been cut into the center of the wall. As Amanda stared in amazement, she could see that the groove had been cut by a waterfall. The water had frozen solid in the bitter cold and glistened like a glass sculpture almost 300 feet long.

The base of the frozen waterfall was over 50 feet wide, disappearing in a pedestal of thick snow.

"In the summer, people used to come here to hike and eat. Russians love to eat. People were even married here, with the falls roaring in the background. Now, no one comes. We would be arrested if they found us in this valley. So come, Agent Amanda from the CIA. The easy part is over. We hike up that path. The first hour is steep, but after that, not so bad. Then we rest in the cabin and wait for daylight," Ruslan said, as he pointed to a narrow trail through the rocks leading away to the left.

And so, they climbed. The first half mile was through a twisting path between fallen boulders. Amanda remembered the treacherous descent down the cliffside on La Palma, and the terrifying ascent in the dark after fleeing from Honglei. Ruslan seemed surprised that she did not complain and was able to keep up with his pace.

"You are strong for being so little, Agent Amanda. You have been hiking before. You know how to place your feet," Ruslan said, as they rested on a dry outcropping of rock, drank water and ate dry energy bars concocted by Ruslan.

"So, you made these, too? Is there vodka in it?" Amanda asked, while chewing on the tough mixture of meat, chocolate and some kind of binder.

"I tried that. It would never set up unless I froze it."

"The meat is strange. What is it?" Amanda asked, instantly regretting the question.

"A secret blend with spices. Some of it is fox, some muskrat, and we have very large nutria around here," Ruslan replied, then laughed as Amanda spit a mouthful onto the snow and stared at it as if it was going to start moving.

"Nutria are rats!"

"The chocolate was my best idea. It cut down on the gaminess. It is Hershey's, real American chocolate, a lot of sugar," he said, and laughed again, as Amanda rinsed out her mouth with water and glared at him.

326

"You have a very good stare. A woman needs that to warn a man he has gone too far. If we were married, I would be a little bit afraid of you."

"How much longer?"

Ruslan glanced upward, then said, "The top of that ridge. Then we put on snowshoes for two miles. Maybe it is three. I don't really remember. I hope the cabin is still there. It has been a few years since I have been up here."

"What? You don't know if the cabin is still there? We'll freeze!"

"No, Ruslan will not let that happen. We will burrow into the snow like the animals, and huddle together," Ruslan said, and winked as Amanda stared at him in disbelief.

"There it is again . . . that glare. It is really good. I pity the man you marry. He will spend half his life in fear!"

Amanda thought about Anthony, the afternoon and evening they had spent together. She forced the memory from her mind, as Ruslan stored the 'food' in his pack and began climbing again.

. . . .

The remainder of the day was one long nightmare. They crested the peak, donned snowshoes, and descended into a smooth valley of deep snow. Without the snowshoes, they would have been up to their hips. Progress would have been impossible. As is, they still sank in over six inches. Each step became an effort, and after an hour her legs were burning, and she was gasping for breath. Ruslan's face was red, as he turned and settled into the snow.

"Here, drink some of this. I know it tastes bad, but it will keep us going. Keep it. Tuck it inside, against your body. It tastes better when it is warm. And do not ask how much longer. You are like my little nephews and nieces on a long drive through the countryside. We get there when we get there," he said, as he handed her a flask of his secret potion.

327

"I didn't know you had any family. Why do you live alone?"

"There are many things you don't know about me, Agent Amanda. Get up. Easy part is over. Now we go uphill again!"

Amanda looked around. They were sitting in a huge bowl filled with snow. The terrain sloped upward in every direction. The sun was sliding toward one set of peaks. Darkness was coming and they had to hurry. Ruslan had been right. The easy part was over. The ache in her thighs spread over every muscle in her body. She followed in his wake as he plowed a path upward through the deepening snow.

The sun slowly sank below the ridge behind them. Shadows began to lengthen, as the cold intensified. The hills above them seemed so far away. Ruslan turned to the north, toward a cleft in the ridge. A snow-covered trail appeared that cut through the rim. An hour later, they rested in the darkness, both too exhausted to talk.

"Don't worry. I won't ask. I'm too tired," Amanda said, as she sipped from her flask, using the foul liquid to wash down the even fouler meat and chocolate bar.

"I must be getting delirious. I'm beginning to like the taste of this stuff," she told herself, after taking another sip to wash down the chewy meat.

She stored the flask inside her coat, then tilted her head back and sighed, wondering if she would be able to stand. She looked upward. It was a moonless night and cloudless. The galactic rim was rising to the east. The swirling pattern of billions of stars was crisper and more vibrant than she had ever seen. The high elevation, combined with the complete lack of artificial light pollution, allowed even the faintest stars to glisten in the deep blackness of the night sky.

"Yes, it is amazing. Some nights we will have an aurora. It is usually green, but I have seen pinks and blues swirling up there with the stars. It can be so beautiful that it makes me want to weep. Russians can be very emotional."

"Not exactly the image that the rest of the world has of you."

"Well . . . the rest of the world is wrong, Agent Amanda. Have you read Dostoyevsky, Tolstoy or Solzhenitsyn?"

"No, I'm not really much of a novel reader. I stick to technical journals and . . ."

"Ahh . . . then you know nothing about us, other than what you read in your journals and briefings. These men will make you weep. They will give you a glimpse into what it is like to be Russian."

They both sat in the snow as the night deepened and the temperature fell. Each alone in their memories, as they stared upward at one of nature's great wonders . . .

．　．　．　．

The timber cabin was solid, but very small, only 15 feet on a side. The front door was covered in a snow drift. Amanda collapsed while they were digging. Twenty minutes later, Ruslan dragged her inside, shut the door, and began building a fire in the fireplace. The floor and hearth were stone. A pair of bunk beds sat against one wall. Firewood was stacked beside the beds. He pulled the mattresses from the beds and lay them, and her, beside the fire. After moving more wood beside the fireplace, he lay down beside her and fell asleep.

She dreamed of Wrightsville Beach in North Carolina. The sun was warm on her face as she dug her heels into the hot sand.

"I can't fall asleep. I'll get sunburned. I need to roll over," she thought, as she opened her eyes and turned onto her side. Ruslan's bearded face shocked her into wakefulness.

She sat up and groaned. Every muscle ached. After throwing more wood onto the fire, she stood and staggered around the cabin stomping her feet. Despite the warmth of the fire, her breath was frosting, and her feet felt frozen.

"This was crazy. We still have no idea where the weapon is. It could be miles away, buried in one of these peaks. That walk almost killed me. No food or water. What was I thinking? What was he thinking?" she said aloud, as Ruslan flipped onto his back and began to snore.

"Great! That'll start an avalanche, and we'll be buried alive. I thought the galleria on La Palma were bad, but this . . . freezing to death or hibernating with a Russian bear. Mama, what has your little girl gotten herself into?" Amanda said, as she threw more logs on the fire, and lay back down beside Ruslan.

His snoring reminded her of the equipment her father used to operate on the farm. She fell asleep dreaming of the old farm that no longer existed, the taste of fresh strawberries, blueberries and the smell of honeysuckle blooming in the moist heat of a North Carolina summer . . .

. . . .

The sound of the helicopter was muffled by Ruslan's loud snores. The impact of the boot that kicked open the door was not. Amanda rolled toward the fireplace as the fighting commenced. Two men dragged Ruslan from the floor and began beating him with the butts of their rifles. A third figure stood to the side, ignored the beating, and stared at Amanda as she scurried toward the fireplace and her backpack.

"Agent Langford, it is a pleasure to meet you. My name is Dominika Bobrova. My friends call me Mistress. My enemies refer to me as 'That Bitch'. Your reputation precedes you. I hope we can be friends," the tall woman said, as she pointed a pistol at Amanda's head.

Amanda's hand rested inside her backpack, on the grip of her new pistol, the 9mm Walther CCP that Mike Stephanos had reluctantly given her less than a week ago. She knew one round was chambered as she flicked off the safety with her thumb.

"Remove your hand from the backpack. I really don't want to kill you. We just need to talk . . . girl to girl."

"She is a killer! Don't trust anything she says!" Ruslan yelled, as he threw one man against the wall, grabbed his weapon, and turned toward Dominica.

She dropped Ruslan with one shot to the chest. The pistol returned to point at Amanda's head.

"Don't force me to kill you. Remove your hand from the backpack. I will not ask you again."

Amanda knew that the woman would kill her. She thought of her parents and how nice it would be to see them again. Then she thought of Anthony. She slid her hand from the backpack and stared as Ruslan sagged to the floor. He glanced at her . . . for a few brief seconds . . . and then he was gone. His dreams, his ideas, his dacha near Moscow, all vanished with one shot.

"He was a stupid little man. We have been tracking him for quite some time. Ulyana is one of my people. Did you think we would let you wander around our country unnoticed? We don't know how you arrived here, but we will find out. We always do. It would be better if you just tell me what you know. Otherwise . . . the pain comes next. Though, I must admit, I hope you are stubborn. I enjoy such things. It is one of my pleasures," Dominika said, as the two soldiers grabbed Amanda and bound her with tye-wraps.

CHAPTER 48

Carriage House Apartments
The 15th Avenue Line
Prince George, British Columbia, Canada
October 19, 1530 hours PDT

As the Russian infantry withdrew from the area, their artillery shells began to rain down on the complex like rain. The 15th Avenue line had held throughout the day. The Carriage House Apartments were at the left end of that line. Fifty Canadians held the buildings on the right, facing the city. The buildings on the left were held by Alpha Company, 1st Battalion, 325th Infantry, 82nd Airborne. One other unit defended the area. They all called it the 'Ghost Tank'. They knew it was Canadian, but it was different. All the other Canadian tanks were painted in the desert camo of their last deployment to the Middle East. This one was unique. It was painted gray and white. Black kill stripes decorated the barrel of the main gun. It was a convention that had not been practiced since World War II. Each broad band represented five kills. Each narrow band represented one enemy kill. The Ghost Tank had two broad bands and two narrow ones, indicating 12 kills. This tank had come and gone during the day. Every time they were threatened with being overrun; the tank reappeared. When the threat was gone, it disappeared into the haze and smoke of shell fire and burning buildings.

"I don't know how, but the bastards are getting tanks across the river. That last one was a T-72, not some damn infantry BMP. My Javelin glanced off the turret. The Ghost Tank killed it. This place is haunted!" said Spec 4 Jackson Bowles, as he lay back against the remains of a stone retaining wall at the edge of the apartment buildings.

"You're full of shit! I saw the kill! It was an M-1. One of our tanks!" said Private First Class Logan Murrow, as he took a swig from his canteen.

"Asshole, we don't have any tanks up here. There's lots of Russian tanks, and a few of the Canucks, that's it. Whatever you think you saw . . . it wasn't one of ours. Now shut up and reload the Javelin. Next time, aim for the tracks or shoot them in the ass," Spec 4 Bowles said, as he peeked over the wall and peered into the haze that filled 15th Avenue.

The Canadians had been falling back when the Americans arrived. Bolstered by their presence and additional firepower, the resistance had stiffened, but at a cost . . . and the cost was rising.

.   .   .   .

Apartment 102
1550 hours PDT

Captain Jamal Reese had just finished meeting with his platoon leaders, when Captain Alice Campbell walked into the basement apartment.

"Glad to see you're still with us. That last push was the roughest yet. If they get more tanks across the river, we're done. What's this crap I keep hearing over the comm net about a 'ghost tank'? It has to be one of yours," Captain Reese said, as he offered Captain Campbell a chair.

"It's one of ours. I don't know who's in it or who's telling it where it's needed. It's an old tank we brought along as a spare. Lord

Strathcona's Horse are running out of horses," she replied, as she accepted a drink from Jamal's canteen.

"So, what can I do for you? Or did you just want to chitchat?"

"I need some of your firepower. We're tankers. We stripped what we could from our tanks, but we're not trained as infantry. I need your help."

"I've got one platoon across the four-lane highway to the west. The Russians are working their way through the neighborhoods and the surrounding hills. We're holding three of these four apartment buildings. I can give you a weapons squad. They have two Javelin gunners and two M240B machine guns. Sergeant Miller! Take the Captain to see Lieutenant Riley. He'll be pissed off, but tell him I said to send his weapons squad to the Canadians."

"Thank you, Captain Reese. I owe you one."

"You don't owe me a damn thing. We're in this thing together. If you fail, we're all screwed. Keep in touch. Miller, make sure she has our frequency."

. . . .

Beverly Fire and Rescue Hall
Yellowhead Highway
1620 hours PDT

"Major, the Russians are working their way around our left flank. Once they get to University Way, they can head south to Tyner Boulevard and cut off the American troops in the southwest. The Americans will be attacked from two directions. They won't have a chance," said Sergeant major Wessel, as new information was assessed and added to the paper map being used to keep track of their collective forces.

"Major Griffin, we have a problem. If we leave my Canadian troops and your Alpha Company at their present locations, they'll be cut off and eliminated within a few hours. We need to make a decision," said Major Smith, CO of what remained of the Strathconas.

"My orders are to hold the 15ᵗʰ Avenue line."

"Are your orders to commit suicide?"

"My orders are to hold this city until the heavies arrive. We have an armored brigade heading up here by rail. We can't let the Russians get past us and start heading to the south. If that brigade gets caught while they're still on railcars, it will be a massacre. We are going to hold this city until reinforcements arrive," replied Major Griffin, as he locked eyes with the Canadian Major.

"I admire your tenacity, but that won't keep us alive. We need to preserve our forces for as long as possible. I would . . . suggest . . . we give ground gradually and consolidate our forces . . . while continuing to hold the city. We can't afford to lose entire units."

"Like you've lost yours?"

"Listen, you hoser! We've been . . ." Sergeant Major Wessel began.

"At ease, Sergeant Major! Our American ally . . . misspoke. We're all under a lot of pressure. Isn't that correct, Major Griffin?"

Griffin knew that he had more than 'misspoke'. He had let his own fear of failure overwhelm him. The Colonel had left him in charge of the city and more than half of the battalion's forces. The remainder of the brigade was still making their way northward from scattered drop zones. They wouldn't reach the two main bridges for another three hours. They couldn't be met by Russian tanks. The city had to be held.

" My apology, Major. I did misspeak. This intersection, down south of the city. the Russians would come out here. That's where they would cut off our forces to the south, correct?" Major Griffin asked.

"Correct."

"These two bridges crossing the Fraser River, on the northeast side of the city. We blow them. Then we fall back to this north-south road . . . Ospika Boulevard . . . and Massey Drive and 20ᵗʰ Avenue. They go east to the Fraser River. We're defending half the territory and half the frontage. That way we can consolidate our remaining forces and still keep the one bridge crossing the river to the south open."

"We'll need to evacuate that place we're using as a hospital, Sir. Other than that, the plan looks pretty good. We can hold that line for a while longer and still have a way out if we need it," said Sergeant Major Wessel.

"We'll start getting some reinforcements from the south within the hour. I'll reinforce the hinge between us and our southern forces. Then we'll start funneling troops into the city. We know how to fight in urban terrain. We've had a lot of practice," Major Griffin said, as the three soldiers nodded in agreement.

.   .   .   .

The Berms
Yellowhead Highway
10 miles southwest of Prince George
1700 hours PDT

The berms were natural rolling features in the terrain heading southwest from Prince George. Modern highways no longer followed the flow of the land. They cut through the hills to make as straight and level a road as possible. The berms were the residue of old road construction projects from the 1980s. They were staggered on both sides of the Yellowhead Highway, 10-20 feet high and 300 feet long. 'New construction' was converting them into fighting positions for MGS Strykers of 1st Battalion, 73rd Cavalry Regiment of the 82nd Airborne.

"Not so damn deep! We're fighting from these positions, not hiding! The turrets must clear the top of the berm! And take that American flag off the antenna! You trying to advertise our location?" yelled Captain Bailey, as his Stryker crews continued to insert their vehicles into their new fighting positions.

He went from position to position, adjusting each location. Trying to imagine every possible approach the Russians would use and making sure each vehicle's field of fire would cover all areas.

"Captain, one of my men has an idea. Look at all these concrete road barriers. Right now, they're set up as guardrails to protect the drop off on that side of the road. What if we hook a tow cable to them and drag them into the middle? There must be 200 of them," said Sergeant Baker, as Captain Bailey approached his dug in position.

Captain Bailey turned and stared at the long line of barriers on the left side of the road.

"I like it. I'll send some of our infantry brothers down here to help. Jumble the barriers up. Make it hard for even a tank to get over them. If nothing else, they'll expose the thin armor on their bellies as they crawl over."

. . . .

Preparations began as the sun began to set. Two hours later, over 100 barriers had been dragged onto the road, forming an erratic obstacle over 100 yards deep. The plunge off the side that the barriers had shielded led into a steep ravine. The work continued.

"Any word from your scouts?" Lieutenant Colonel Thompson asked, as he and Captain Bailey stood at the first berm. The two-lane highway led downhill and curved to the right, disappearing less than a half of a mile away.

"They're positioned at a bridge two miles west of here. When they start to hear vehicle noise, they have orders to blow the bridge. The river isn't much more than a big creek, but it will slow the Russians down for a while."

"That's what we have to do, Captain . . . slow them down. We must delay them for at least two days. If our heavies aren't here by then it will be . . . entertaining. Anyway, I like the way you used the concrete road barriers. The Russians will play hell getting over those. If you add a few of their tanks to the pile, that would be even better."

"We'll add more than a few, Colonel. Our problem will be their artillery and the Hinds. The tanks will grind to a halt here. Then they'll try to get infantry around us. We've got that covered. Then they'll try to blow us out of the way. That's what I'd do. I'd back off and let the artillery and choppers remove us."

"The Avengers should keep the Hinds off you. The artillery is another problem. Make sure your men dig deep. Once the artillery starts falling, you'll have to wait it out. Brigade is setting up our artillery now. That's 18 M777A2 howitzers with a range of over 14 miles. Once they start shooting, we'll be able to shoot back. Like I told that Canadian Major, we didn't come here toothless. The 2nd of the 319th AFAR is a good unit. Counter battery fire is one of their specialties."

"Colonel, any info on how far away the Russians are?"

"My guess . . . they'll come pay you a visit some time tonight. My best guess . . . around midnight. That should be to our advantage. They can see in the dark just like us, but they don't have the combat experience of operating in low light. The Canadians say the fog and mist will settle in around 10 PM. It won't burn off until two hours after sunrise. The Russians will have trouble coordinating their actions in this mess. I guess we'll have to give them some training," Lieutenant Colonel Thompson, said with a smile.

"Hell yeah, Sir! We'll train the shit out of them!"

.   .   .   .

Prince George Toyota
2772 Recplace Drive
1945 hours PDT

"If this keeps up, we're going to have to put an extension on that barrel. That make 14 kills," said Corporal Wills, as he painted two more black kill stripes on the Leopard's gun barrel.

"Well, you didn't lie when you said you could shoot, Corporal Wills. You're almost as good as my last gunner," Sergeant Brown said, as she grimaced, and handed another Sabot round up to Corporal Morris

"I would help, Sarge, but you know . . . wounded arm. So, who was your gunner? I might have gone through gunnery school with him," asked Corporal Wills, as he stepped back to admire his artwork.

"John Smith, but everyone called him Punty."

"Punty Smith! That asshole! The only thing better than his aim was how much he loved himself. I finished second to that prick, and he'd never let me forget it. Sixteen other gunners in that class, and you'd think I had finished last rather than second. He used to brag that he could place two shots in the same hole at 1000 meters. That was bullshit! But damn, he was good. I'll give him that. How many kills did he get before he . . .? Sorry! Now I'm being the asshole."

"We got five. He made Ace before he bled out," Sergeant Brown said, remembering the feel of the sweat on Punty's neck as she checked for a pulse.

"Damn! That puts you near 20 total kills. That breaks the record of Radley-Walters during World War II. He only killed 12."

"Yeah, but you've personally shot 14."

"Well, to be honest, we've only killed six tanks today. APCs don't count for the record, only tanks."

"Hey! I know I'm just a Private, and just the loader, but shouldn't we be getting on with this?" asked Barnes, after sticking his head out of the tank.

Jess stared at the six remaining shells standing by the tank and sighed.

"Right! Let's finish this and fuel up. This war's not waiting on us," Sergeant Brown said, as she hefted the 47-pound shell upward, and handed it to Corporal Morris. She could feel wounds open up as she lifted the shell. Her blood mixed with her sweat as the reloading continued.

"Where to next, Sarge?" asked Corporal Wills, as he struggled to climb the tank with one arm in a sling.

"Check the comm while we're finishing up. Make sure you check the American frequencies, too. Find out where we're needed," Sergeant Brown said, as she paused, placed two more pain killers in her mouth and washed them down with a swig of water.

.   .   .   .

Connaught Hill Park
2010 hours PDT

Colonel General Zhurov was back at the stone wall overlooking Prince George from the ridge north of the Nechako River. The sound of fighting from the city had subsided. The sun had set two hours ago, and the temperature was dropping rapidly. Two battalions of infantry had been chewed to pieces getting across the waterway and establishing a foot hold on the far shore. Another two had been mauled during repeated assaults into the city during daylight hours. Those units were being relieved by another four fresh battalions. His engineers had been able to complete three temporary pontoon bridges across the river. Two had been destroyed by artillery fire. The third had been damaged but was under repair.

"Borodin! When is that damn bridge going to be useable? The Canadians and Americans are dug in like ticks. My infantry must have tank support to dig them out," General Zhurov shouted, as the first flakes of another snowfall settled on his thick, full-length coat.

"The engineers have taken a lot of casualties, General. The resistance has been stiffer than anticipated."

Alexander Zhurov was far from a patient man. His first instinct was to take out his pistol and shoot his aide, but he restrained himself. Competent aides were hard to find.

"I trust they are being reinforced?"

340

"Yes, General. Their commanding officer, Colonel Kapov, is on the scene, personally directing repairs. Reinforcements are arriving as we speak, but we are having a traffic problem. Everything is backed up due to the loss of all the bridges."

General Zhurov fumed but held his temper in check. He released energy by pounding the top of the stone wall as he paced back and forth.

"And where is General Mulnatov? His units were expected to arrive from the southwest hours ago?" General Zhurov growled, as he stopped in front of his aide.

"They are also having bridge problems, General. The last bridge between them and Prince George was blown as they approached. They are bringing up pontoon bridges . . . but the traffic backup is causing delays."

"The roads, forests, hills . . . the Canadians were clever to choose this place to make a stand. It is very congested. I must be patient and keep the pressure on them. Damn! I should have kept more artillery forward. The Americans will send more than one airborne brigade. This is how they operate. The airborne holds the ground and waits for reinforcements . . . other units . . . armored units. If I allow this to go on too long, the opportunity will be lost. We can't get to open terrain and into the United States until we get past this damn city!" General Zhurov thought, as he resumed his walk along the stone wall.

"Colonel Borodin! Shift artillery fire from the city and onto the highway north of the bridge Mulnatov is stuck behind. Start chewing up that road and the surrounding area. The Americans will be there waiting for him. Let's see if they like the taste of Russian steel! And where is my damn air support!"

"Yes, General! I'll find out, General!"

. . . .

The Summit Lake Resort consisted of a series of small cabins and a general store supplying overpriced consumables. The area had been bulldozed clean when the Russian artillery battery had moved in. The wreckage had been pushed into the once pristine lake. The bodies of the few, full-time residents floated amongst the debris.

The young Lieutenant was very excited as she ran toward the command vehicle of Battery 'A', 1st Company, 305th Artillery Regiment.

"Captain, I have received a fire order from brigade!" said Junior Lieutenant Dinara Astakov, as she rushed up to the back of the BTR-80.

Captain Alex Yegorov frowned as he stared at her smiling face.

"Why are you always smiling, Junior Lieutenant Astakov? Our mission is to kill the enemies of the Russian Republic, not to enjoy ourselves," asked Captain Yegorov, still ill at ease with the recent decision to allow women into the combat branches of the Russian Army. Even worse, was the decision to saddle him with what he considered an extreme burden. The attractiveness of the young officer had not been lost on his men.

"Exactly, Captain! I have never fired our rockets at a real enemy . . . only in training. It will be exciting! I have heard that our troops are meeting a lot of resistance. This is our chance to help them. We've been sitting here all day doing nothing."

"Have you ever seen what our rockets do to a human body, Junior Lieutenant?" Captain Yegorov asked, as she handed him a copy of the fire order.

"No . . . but I have read about the crater size, and the effect on buildings and vehicles of different types. Our 122 mm rockets are very effective at . . ."

"Bodies are shredded. The entrails are the worst. They look like long links of sausage when the abdomen is ripped open and they burst out. The smell, even in the cold, is something that you will never forget . . . Junior Lieutenant Astakov. This request we have received is at our extreme range. This will decrease our accuracy. I hope that our units aren't too close. Lieutenant Bakov! Process this order!" Captain Yegorov said, as he handed the paperwork to his second in command.

. . . .

The Berms
Yellowhead Highway
10 miles southwest of Prince George
2030 hours PDT

"So, what do you think of our chances?" Captain Reese asked Captain Bailey, as they stood outside Bailey's MGS Stryker.

"They'll come riding up the road in a wedge formation . . . probably T-72s or T-80s. They'll pause on the other side of our concrete barriers, and then my boys will start killing them. You just keep their infantry off our asses and things will work out just fine."

"You make it sound real simple."

"It is, Jamal! Kill onto others, before they kill onto you!" Captain Bailey said, as both officers stared down the darkened highway through infrared scopes.

"You ain't right, Sam . . . not even close," Captain Reese said, as they shook hands and he turned to leave . . .

The first 122 mm rocket landed a quarter mile down the road, 50 yards shy of the concrete barriers and the American positions. The second and third rockets landed in the middle of the pile. Dozens of barriers were shattered or hurled into the sky by the massive explosions. The first salvo of 16 rockets covered an area 400 yards across.

The two American company commanders were standing together at the rear of the first berm. The last rocket landed 30 feet behind them. Both were killed instantly, leaving the conduct of the battle to a collection of Lieutenants . . .

. . . .

Aspen Grove Golf Course
4545 Leno Road
Headquarters 2nd Brigade Combat Team 82nd Airborne
2035 hours PDT

LTC Thompson stood inside the clubhouse receiving a final mission brief from COL Curl, when a Staff Sergeant rushed into the room.

"Sorry, Colonel, but something's happening west of here. The horizon is lighting up like the 4th of July."

Thompson and Curl stared at each other.

"Go on, Thompson. Call me when you find out what's happening. Remember, forward elements of 2nd Battalion are at the Highway 97 bridge and entering Prince George. If we need them to peel off and head southwest, I need to know soon!"

"Roger that, Sir!" Anthony said, and rushed from the room.

He sprinted the 50 yards to his Stryker, sitting parked beneath a tree near the First Tee. It was beginning to snow as he yanked open the rear door and stepped inside. His crew jumped as he shut the hatch and said, "Crank it up. We're heading out. The fighting has started. Head up 97, cross the bridge, then pick up 16 heading south. Move!"

He picked up the handset as the vehicle roared into life and began to move. After verifying the correct frequency, he said, "Roadblock, this is Big Bird. Over!"

After two repeats, he switched frequencies.

"Woodman, this is Big Bird. Over!"

344

He switched frequencies after every two attempts but received no reply. His frustration building, he slammed the handset into the holder, donned his CVC (Combat Vehicle Crewman) helmet and climbed into his position in the hatch. The cold air calmed him down as the Stryker sped up Aspen Golf Course Road.

"What the hell is going on? Are the Russians blocking transmissions? We're supposed to be safe against that. So, what's going on? Why no reply?" Anthony thought, as he switched to platoon frequencies in the Weapons Troop.

"Roadblock 2, this is Big Bird. Over!"

Static filled the response, but it was clear enough.

"Big Bird! This is Roadblock 2. We're under heavy rocket fire. Can't contact Roadblock. Three vehicles burning. Over!"

"Roadblock 2, this is Big Bird. Hold your positions. Expect imminent contact. Over!"

"Roger that, Big Bird! Out!"

Anthony switched back to brigade headquarters, stared at the handset, and said, "Falcon, this is Big Bird. Over!"

"Big Bird, this is Falcon. Over!"

"Roadblock is receiving heavy rocket fire. I'm requesting some counter battery assistance. Over!"

"I'll see what I can do. They're still setting up, but I'll put in a personal request. Over!"

"Roger that! All assistance appreciated. Over!"

"Maintain contact, Big Bird! Falcon out!"

Anthony switched back to the Roadblock and Woodman frequencies, but neither company commander was responding. He switched to the platoon frequencies and listened. Most of these soldiers were young and had never been under artillery fire. They weren't panicking, but they didn't sound organized either.

"Do I request that Falcon turn one of the battalions to the south? But if I do that, I'm bleeding reinforcements away from the city when the Russians are coming across the river to the north. But if the south collapses, then the Russians will drive up the highway and take

them in the flank," Anthony thought, as his Stryker sped past rows of stately conifers that lined the road exiting the golf course.

Parachutes, rigging pallets and equipment were everywhere. The snowfall was growing heavier as the final units of the 2nd Brigade Combat Team organized themselves and headed toward Prince George. Before his Stryker crossed into the woods leading to Highway 97, he saw units of the 2nd Brigade's artillery setting up on the open field of the Driving Range. The M777A2s had an effective range of 15 miles. Nineteen miles if they used 'base bleed' shells which extended the range.

"I have to see for myself. I can be there in 20 minutes," he said, as his vehicle turned left onto Highway 97 and sped past long lines of infantry marching north along both sides of the highway.

. . . .

815 Adams Road
Summit Lake Resort
2045 hours PDT

Lieutenant Dinara Astakov found herself weeping as the last of the 122 mm rockets left the launch tubes of her BM-21 Grad. The smell of propellent and the thrill of combat had affected her emotionally. As a little girl, her grandfather had told his stories of fighting the Germans near Leningrad. Now she understood the fire in his eyes as he told of salvos of Katusha rockets raining death on the hated Nazi invaders of Mother Russia.

"It is such a beautiful thing to see . . . and hear . . . and feel," she said, as she began to exit the cab of the six-wheeled truck.

Her six-man team was already in the process of reloading the 40-round launch system mounted on the back of the vehicle. They were offloading ammunition from the resupply truck when the first American counterbattery round arrived. The six Russian vehicles were arranged in a line 50 yards apart. That was the way they always lined up. It was doctrine, and the Americans knew that.

The 155mm Excalibur ammunition fired by the American M777A2 Howitzer was designed for extended range and precision. Three of the rounds were airbursts, three of the rounds were impact. The six guns of Charlie Battery fired three salvos at the Russian battery, 18 rounds in all . . .

Junior Lieutenant Dinara Astakov awoke to find herself outside her vehicle. She had no memory of leaving the cab. Her ears were ringing as she staggered to her feet and looked around in the thick haze. She screamed as one of her rockets cooked off and went streaking across the lake, exploding as it struck a tree. Burning vehicles were scattered across a wide area. Bodies and parts of bodies were everywhere.

"What . . . what happened? Where is everyone?" Dinara asked, while turning to her right and tripping over something at her feet.

It was a torso . . . with no head, no arms and only one leg. It was blackened and burned. She backed away but tripped again and fell. Something had wrapped around her feet. Her vision was blurred and the pain in her head was becoming sharper by the second.

"A rope! Who has left a rope lying around? It's a safety hazard. Someone is going on report," she said, as she sat up, reached toward her feet and pulled the rope.

"Not a rope . . . sticky . . . a cable?" she asked, as she pulled and felt a sharp pain in her abdomen.

She screamed, then toppled onto her side. The snow began falling again. Each flake came into focus as it settled gently before her, attempting to cover the blood-soaked ground.

"Captain Yegorov was correct . . . the smell is terrible," Junior Lieutenant Dinara Astakov said, blinked twice, began choking on her own blood, then closed her eyes forever . . .

. . . .

The Berms
Yellowhead Highway
10 miles southwest of Prince George
2105 hours PDT

First Lieutenant Pace Atkins sat huddled inside his MGS Stryker waiting for the next salvo of rockets to land. The bombardment had lasted less than ten minutes, but the chaos and fear it had caused, still remained. His driver had started yelling after the third explosion rocked the vehicle. His screams of defiance were his way of enduring the terrifying bombardment. Atkins chose to try and focus on his platoon of four vehicles. He didn't understand why two of the icons, representing two of his vehicles, had disappeared from the flat screen image of their location.

"Four Alpha 2, this is Four Alpha 1, over!"

Neither Four Alpha 2 nor Four Alpha 3 was responding. Four Alpha 4 was 30 feet to his right, dug into another section of the second berm. His other two vehicles were further down on the other side of the road, 50 yards away. His view through his optics was obstructed. Something had been thrown onto his vehicle.

"Four Alpha 4, this is Four Alpha 1. Do you have a visual of Four Alpha 2 or Four Alpha 3? Over!"

"This is Four Alpha 4 . . . all I see is smoke from their location. Wait . . . I'm seeing something moving on thermal . . ."

"Four Alpha 4, this is Four Alpha 1. What are you seeing? Is it our men? Over!"

"Negative . . . further down the road . . . three hot spots. Shit! Computer says they're . . . T-14s . . . Armatas. LT . . . LT, the Russian tanks are here!"

The T-14 Armata was Russia's latest tank. The three-man crew was housed inside an armored capsule inside the hull. The turret was entirely occupied by the autoloader and ammunition for the 125mm smoothbore cannon. It was considered a 5th Generation tank. The vaunted American M1 tank of Gulf War fame was, in comparison, an antique.

"Roadblock, this is Four Alpha 1. Enemy tanks approaching! T-14s! Over!"

"Four Alpha 1, this is Roadblock 2. Roadblock is down. I have the Troop. Engage the enemy! Over!"

"Roadblock 2, I've lost two vehicles, over!"

"Four Alpha 1, this is Roadblock 2. Do your damn job, Lieutenant! Out!"

The Russian artillery began to fall again as three Russian T-14 tanks advanced up the Yellowhead Highway. The rolling barrage was timed and coordinated based on the GPS locations of the lead tanks. Five of the 12 MGS Strykers were destroyed by the initial bombardment. Four more died in the follow up. The remaining three MGS Strykers fought back. Hits were made on six consecutive shots before all the MGS Strykers were destroyed by the T-14s. The M900 105mm APFSDS-T round fired by the MGS was incapable of defeating the Kontakt-5 explosive-reactive armor of the T-14. Thirty minutes after the initial Russian bombardment, most of the Weapons Troop and Alpha Troop of 1st Battalion, 73rd cavalry Regiment, 82nd Airborne, had ceased to exist . . .

.   .   .   .

Connaught Hill Park
2200 hours PDT

Colonel General Zhurov had retreated from the stone wall overlooking the Nechako River and Prince George. The biting cold and heavy snow had begun to penetrate his old bones, and he had not slept for over 30 hours.

"General, perhaps some hot tea?" Colonel Borodin asked, as he removed Zhurov's heavy coat and handed it to an aide.

"That would be good . . . and some food. I want an update, then two hours sleep. Two hours, Borodin! No more! Understood?"

"Yes, General!" Colonel Borodin said, as he pulled back a heavy wooden chair and gestured for the general to sit down.

"What have we heard from General Mulnatov? Has he gotten over that creek or are his men still afraid to get their boots wet?" General Zhurov asked, as he settled into the chair with a sigh and stared at a mug of hot tea.

"They have crossed the river and are progressing up Highway 17. I think it's called the Yellowhead Highway."

"Borodin, you are not a tour guide. Have they met the Americans? What resistance are they facing? Ahh, the tea is very good. Hopefully, your answers will keep me in this good mood."

"The road was blocked with concrete barriers. American M1128 Strykers and infantry were dug into the terrain by the road hoping to ambush our tanks. Our artillery took care of both problems. Spetsnaz had been over the river in the darkness and identified the dug in positions. The American artillery conducted some counter battery fire against our artillery units, but our losses were insignificant."

"I have not fought with Mulnatov before, but his reputation as a tactician is excellent. He knows how to use his tools effectively. I trust he is proceeding up the highway?"

"Yes, General! Debris is being cleared and he is proceeding northward. He says his lead units will reach Prince George by 0300," Borodin said, as a plate of cheese and bread was placed in front of the general.

"Excellent! I'm starving. Remember, no more than two hours sleep! I want this business finished by sunset tomorrow. It is time to head south and pay the citizens of the United States a visit."

. . . .

Anthony's Command Stryker was racing southward when he ordered the driver to pull over.

"Colonel, I keep trying, but no one is answering. I can't get hold of either troop, not even at the platoon level," said Sergeant Matthews, on the vehicle's internal comm.

Anthony stared at the southern horizon. The intense booming noise and flash of combat had ceased. There was only a faint glow, barely visible as the rate of snowfall increased. He switched frequencies to brigade, then paused, wondering if he was wrong.

"No, they're gone . . . all of them. The roadblock is gone. I tried to use them to fight tanks in a standup battle. But what choice did I have? We had to buy some time. Did I sacrifice all those men for 15 minutes? I have to know for sure," Anthony asked himself.

He switched back to the vehicle comm and said, "Take us south. All lights off, infrared only. Stop if you see anything."

"Roger that!" the driver said, as the Command Stryker pulled back on the road and sped southward.

"Falcon, this is Big Bird, over!" Anthony said, after switching back to brigade.

"Big Bird, this is Falcon. What is the status of your mission? Over!"

"Falcon, this is Big Bird. Unable to contact Roadblock. Intense sound and visuals have ceased. Am proceeding southward to determine status. Suggest moving assets as previously discussed. Over!"

"Proceed with caution. Am taking suggestion under advisement. Stay in touch. Falcon out!"

10 minutes later

"Slow down! We're coming up to a curve. Our Roadblock positions started a mile down the road," Anthony ordered, dropped down into the Stryker, and shut the hatch.

He activated the Iron Vision display on his helmet. Now he could see outside the vehicle in any direction. The system was brand new. Only command vehicles had the asset. The system was linked with multiple video feeds mounted on the outside of the vehicle. He was literally looking through the vehicle at the surrounding terrain in all directions.

The Stryker eased up to the curve. Every infrared scope on the vehicle was searching for anything warm, anything moving.

"Sergeant Matthews! Two o'clock, at the treeline, just past the Petro-Canada gas station . . . 120 yards. It looks like two of ours from the profile," Anthony said, as he magnified the image.

"All I see are two red blobs, Colonel. Are you sure? It could be Russian infantry."

"Negative! One of them is wounded. Driver, take a right onto the paved road. Pull up by those men."

"Roger that!"

The Stryker pulled up beside the wood line. The ramp dropped and a three-man fire team exited with Anthony right behind them.

The two soldiers dropped to the ground, one barely conscious, the other exhausted.

"He's lost a lot of blood. I've got a tourniquet on his leg, but he needs help. I don't think anyone else is coming. Colonel . . . it was bad. First, the artillery, then tanks. The troop comm said we were facing T-14s. I heard reports of direct hits on their frontal armor, at less than 300 yards, with no effect."

"Load them up! Let's get out of here! Head back north!" Anthony yelled, as the wounded were carried into the back of his Stryker.

Thirty seconds later, the ramp closed. The vehicle spun in a circle and headed north.

1814 Hoferkamp Road
Prince George
October 20, 0040 hours PDT

Jeremiah Jones had spent the last 10 days hunting Russians. He had arrived at his present location, an abandoned home overlooking the Nechako River, only yesterday. The back deck of the two-story home sat on the edge of a steep cliff, giving him a panoramic view of the river front. He had set up his shooting position there. He had killed 14 Russian officers, at ranges from 500 yards to over 1000 yards in less than eight hours, all along the river front. Some had been on the shore. Some had been in midstream. The sound of explosions and gunfire had been everywhere. He had only missed once, and he attributed that to his age and dimming eyesight. Now, he was hunting bigger game.

The cold had chilled him to the point where he had to retreat from the porch and back into the living room. He sat by the gas fireplace warming his bones and cleaning his Springfield M1903-A4 sniper rifle. It was the same rifle that had given him 47 confirmed kills in Vietnam. He knew that the Russians were becoming suspicious. Officers were becoming hard to find. Snipers never stayed in the same position for long. That was a basic tenant he had been taught in sniper school decades ago and had never forgotten. It was a rule he had never violated, until now. The Russian officer he was hunting was old. He was waited on by junior officers. He paced behind a low stone wall and watched everything unfold below him. Jeremiah had learned all this in the 20 minutes he spent tracking this new target. He was fascinated. He knew the man was someone important. He had lined up the shot and was processing through his breathing sequence, when the target had turned and disappeared. So now he waited. He knew the man would reappear. It had been over two hours. Every few minutes he would stand, cross to the sliding glass doors and focus his binoculars on the stone wall only 300 yards to his right.

. . . .

Connaught Hill Park
0105 hours PDT

"General, it's time to wake up! I have some fresh tea," Colonel Borodin said, as he turned on the lights in the bedroom and gently shook the commanding officer of the 5th Combined Arms Army.

Colonel General Zhurov rubbed his eyes as he swung his legs over the side of the bed. His freshly polished boots were just to his right. His jacket, freshly brushed, hung from the back of a nearby chair.

"What time is it, Borodin? What is happening?" General Zhurov asked, while slipping on his boots.

"Other than no air support, things are going well. General Mulnatov is beginning his march toward the city, and our troops are reporting decreased resistance inside Prince George," Colonel Borodin replied, as the general stood and was helped into his uniform jacket.

"No air support? Did I not tell you to order that idiot Bozorov to get his damn pilots to support us?"

"Yes, General. But he claims that the snow is so thick that it is not safe for his pilots to fly."

"That effete bastard! My soldiers are dying, and his pilots are afraid of a little snow? I want to go back to my wall to see things for myself. Then, we will come back here, and I will personally inform that prick of his upcoming execution!" General Zhurov said, then drank down half a mug of tea and threw the rest across the bedroom.

. . . .

354

Jeremiah Jones was staring through the sliding glass doors when the two Russian officers appeared at the stone wall. One of them was yelling. His hands gesturing toward the river and then pointing up in the air. The other officer seemed to be at parade rest, quietly waiting for the outburst to subside. Jeremiah's heart began pounding, which surprised him. He was used to controlling his emotions in such situations.

"Come on, boy. You're not that damn old. Just execute the shot. Just like the old days. Verify the range, windage, temperature, humidity. Then control your breathing . . . relax and squeeze," he told himself, as he threw on his jacket and proceeded outside into the bitter cold.

He had placed the weapon outside after cleaning it. The optics and the weapon needed to adjust to the ambient conditions before the shot. He picked up the bolt-action rifle and settled into his prone shooting position. After verifying all his settings, he placed the cross hairs of his 20-power scope on the chest of the older officer. He was pacing and the younger officer kept obstructing his sight picture. The glare from the burning city provided just enough ambient light.

"This may have to be a double, but what if they're wearing body armor?" Jeremiah said, as he reached into his pocket and verified the presence of three more rounds.

He removed each round from his pocket and laid them beside him on a linen napkin he had found in the house. Each round lay parallel to his rifle. Each round was precisely one inch from the next. His Springfield bolt action rifle was single shot. Each round had to be placed on the loading platform by hand and slid into the chamber by the bolt. This disrupted the sight picture, but after 10,000 rounds of practice and application, it was as instinctive to him as breathing.

· · · ·

Connaught Hill Park
0114 hours PDT

"Borodin! It is . . . 0114 hours. I expect us to be . . ." General Zhurov began, when his aide's head exploded, splattering the general with blood and brain matter.

The young Colonel was thrown into his arms by the force of the bullet. Colonel General Alexander Zhurov hesitated for one second, his arms holding the twitching corpse, before lunging to his left. The lunge caused the bullet to enter his right eye rather than his left. Both Russian officers were dead before they hit the ground. Command and control of the 5th Combined Arms Army was thrown into disarray . . .

. . . .

Jeremiah Jones wrapped his two remaining bullets in the cloth napkin and returned them to his pocket. Then he packed up his gear and walked out of the abandoned house. He knew from experience that the ridgeline would soon receive unwanted attention.

CHAPTER 49

Eastern Slopes of Vilyuchik
Kamchatka Peninsula, Russia
October 20, 1830 hours PETT

Amanda awoke to find herself lying in a bed in a tiny room. There was no pillow or blanket, only a thin mattress covered in stained, gray vinyl. She sat up and swung her legs over the side. She was barefoot and the concrete floor was very cold. Her breath frosted. She was wearing dark green one-piece coveralls that zipped up the front. It was two sizes too big. She noticed that she was wearing nothing beneath the coveralls.

"Where am I? What is this place?" she asked herself, as she stood up, staggered, and sat back down. Her head was swimming.

She focused on her surroundings, while rolling up the sleeves of the coveralls, which extended past her fingertips. The cinderblock walls were a teal green for the bottom five courses, then switched to a sea green. The room was 12 feet long and six feet wide. The door at the far end of the room had a small, screened-glass window and a narrow pass-through slot a foot up from the bottom. A small table with a round built-in seat was mounted on the wall across from the bed. To the right of the door was a toilet with a sink mounted above it, all built as one unit. You had to straddle the toilet to use the sink. There was no lid. Everything was steel and bolted in place. There were no sharp edges. A single fluorescent was mounted in the ceiling, over 12 feet above her head.

"Holy crap! This is worse than the cabin . . . industrial chic. At least the cabin was cozy. This is a prison . . ." she thought, then remembered the shocked look on Ruslan's face as he died.

"Poor, Ruslan . . . with all his plans. He tried to protect me. He should have just surrendered. Now, I'm stuck in a Russian prison. Janet is not going to be happy about this. I can hear the lecture now," she thought, as she pulled her cold feet under her thighs and leaned back against the wall beside the bed.

A face appeared in the window, then disappeared. A few minutes later, another face appeared, and the door opened. A tall, thin woman stood in the doorway, backed by two soldiers. It was the woman from the cabin.

"Ahh, Miss Langford . . . finally awake. The drug you were given was a bit much for someone of your . . . small stature," the woman said, as she walked into the room and shut the door behind her.

The woman stepped over to the bed and sat down beside Amanda. She stared straight ahead, then cocked her head, as if listening to something. She turned and smiled. It was not a pleasant smile. She had thin lips, a long face, and overly large green eyes. She wore no makeup. Her light blonde hair was close cropped, too short to grab. Amanda decided the face was almost . . . reptilian.

"I told them to confine you while I dealt with other . . . business. But this is a bit much, I must admit. It looks like you have been captured and are locked inside a prison. Tourists aren't treated like this! Ahh . . . but you aren't a tourist, are you? Nor a geologist . . . nor a mountain climber. So, what were you doing in a tiny cabin in the middle of nowhere, Miss Langford? Having a fling with your friend, Ruslan?" Dominika Bobrova asked, as she slid closer on the bed, her eyes level with the top of Amanda's head.

Amanda knew she was being baited. She also knew there was no point in denying anything. Her belongings, her laptop, her cell phone . . . everything had been thoroughly searched and analyzed by now.

"If you contact the American embassy in Moscow, I'm sure arrangements can be made. We just have to reach a mutual . . ." Amanda began.

"You seem to misunderstand the situation, Agent Amanda Josephine Langford. You work for Director Janet Davidson, at the Mission Center for Weapons and Counterproliferation, located in Manassas, Virginia. Your office is on the third floor. Your view is of the parking lot, far inferior to the view your boss has on the seventh floor. You live alone in a small apartment. You had a pet fish named Rambo. He's dead now. You failed to stop the detonation of the Chinese device at the Harris Nuclear Plant. Because of that, your parents died a gruesome death from radiation sickness. You tried to drink yourself to death, but failed at that, thanks to . . . another friend. Now, you are attempting to become a real secret agent, by taking classes in the Jew martial art and learning to shoot. But deep inside, you fear that you just don't have the 'Right Stuff'. Have you noticed yet that everyone around you seems to get killed? Could it be that they try to protect you, but all you are is a little a farm girl who has gotten way out of her depth! By the way, there is no American embassy in Moscow, nor in any Russian city. The time for talking has passed . . . with one exception. Soon, you and I will talk again. Then, you will tell me everything you know. Enjoy your stay. If the accommodations are not to your liking, call room service," Bobrova said with a disdainful sneer, as she stood up and walked toward the door.

The door opened. She turned back, glanced at Amanda, then said, "Rest up, my little friend. My conversations tend to be lengthy, exhausting and quite painful."

The door closed. A shutter slid across the outside of the small window with a clang. Amanda choked back a sob, determined not to let the woman's words demoralize her.

"But it was true! Everything she said was true!" she thought, as the light was turned off, and she was left alone in the cold darkness.

CHAPTER 50

The White House
The Oval Office
Washington, DC
October 19, 2330 hours EST

"Doctor Wolf, I apologize for the delay. I had so many other pressing matters. Please, come in and have a seat. Would you like some coffee or tea?" President Beaumont asked, as she gestured toward a sofa and coffee table in the middle of the Oval Office.

Dr. Janice Wolf held a thick folder and her laptop against her chest as she shook hands with the President of the United States. She had been waiting outside for most of the day as an endless parade of politicians, officers and foreign dignitaries came and went from the Oval Office. The President looked as exhausted as Janice felt. She had gone over her data dozens of times. Her conclusion and its impact hadn't changed in three days.

"Madam President, thank you . . . no . . . I'm fine. No, I'm not fine, but we have to talk. You must know what's going to happen. We failed . . . well, we didn't fail, but it won't hold . . ." Janice began, then stopped as her folder slid to the floor, papers going everywhere.

"Janice, please call me Clarisse. Do I need to get a doctor? Are you sick? We're all exhausted. Maybe this can wait for you to get some rest."

"No! It can't wait!" Janice snapped, as she slipped from the sofa onto her hands and knees and began collecting the spilled papers.

"Doctor Wolf . . . Janice . . . what's happening? Just sit, try to relax and talk to me."

Janice looked up, embarrassed, and piled the papers on the coffee table as she sat on the sofa.

"The Reelfoot Rift . . . it's going to open, and there's nothing we can do to stop it."

"I remember you telling us that it would happen someday, but you said that would probably be in 1000 years or longer."

"I was wrong. The impactors fired from the Kraken worked, but the strain on the continent's bedrock is too great. The rift is going to split open," Janice said, as tears began to slide down her cheeks, relieved at having finally said the words to the only person that mattered.

"How long do we have?"

"Days . . . no more than a week. The strain is enormous. It can't hold for long. The North American continent is going to split in two."

"Why? What has changed?" the president asked, as her heart began pounding in her chest. She saw motion in the corner of her eye. The specter had reappeared, standing in a far corner, as if observing.

"Madam President . . . Clarisse . . . there are geologic features called plutons, deep reservoirs of solidified magma that formed beside the Reelfoot Rift. They are faults of a sort, magma uprisings from below the shallow crust that never reached the surface. The Devil's Tower in Wyoming. That's a pluton that has been exposed by erosion. These structures are ancient, hundreds of millions of years old and massively heavy. The ones beside the Reelfoot Rift have shifted because of the Great Quake. Their immense weight is causing subsidence on the western side of the rift. This is going to cause the rift to elongate . . . and open. When this happens . . ."

"Our country splits in two . . ."

"Yes, Madam President . . . our country splits in two. The size of the seismic disturbances will be similar to the Great Quake, but worse. As powerful as that series of quakes were, the West Coast bedrock was already severely fractured, especially in California. The

East Coast is relatively fracture free in comparison. The quake, and the extent of the shaking, will be felt over much longer distances. The entire East Coast will feel a series of 7s or 8s. These quakes may go on for an hour or longer depending on how long it takes the rift to open and then restabilize. It will be devastating . . ." Janice said, as the President rose, then sat beside her and squeezed her hand.

"Janice, show me everything. I need to see the data for myself," the President said, as she glanced at the specter once more.

"The face . . . that look . . . can a ghost weep?" she asked herself, as Janice opened the folder and began talking.

CHAPTER 51

Fraser River
23 Miles South of Prince George
October 19, 2200 hours PDT

"Two hours! You said it would take two hours to construct that damn bridge! My tanks have been sitting here for almost five hours!" shouted Brigadier General Frazer Walrath, commanding officer of the 1st Armored Brigade Combat Team, 1st Armored Division.

"General, that's two hours during daylight operations in dry weather. It's 28 degrees, snowing heavily and dark as hell. Plus, the current is stronger than anything we've ever practiced in. I've already had four casualties from hypothermia. My troops are going as quickly as they can! We'll be done by midnight," replied Lieutenant Colonel Rob Broadwater, commanding officer of the 16th Engineer Battalion.

The Improved Ribbon Bridge (IRB) consisted of a series of floating sections that were placed in the water and pushed into position by boats. The sections were then mechanically linked together to provide a roadway for military vehicles.

"All right . . . two more hours! My lead vehicles will hit that damn bridge precisely at midnight, and it better be ready!" General Walrath said, as he held two fingers up in front of Broadwater's face and stormed off.

"So, what did 'General Warpath' have to stay this time? More words of encouragement?" asked Major Lynn Wright, XO of the 16th Engineer Battalion, as she walked up to her boss.

"I don't blame him. I'd be pissed, too. We're behind schedule, and from what we're hearing, the 82nd and the Canadians are getting pounded. Maybe we should have chosen the narrow ford instead of here."

"Negative, Sir! Then we'd be carving a trail through two miles of dense forest . . . across hills . . . and in a blizzard. Once we get across here, it's 400 yards to a paved highway. Remember, he chose not to use the bridge. That bridge downstream was perfectly usable."

"Yeah, but then we had a 200-mile road march to get to Prince George. The tanks would arrive on the scene and run out of gas. We all make choices, Major. He has to live with his. We just have to get this damn bridge finished."

"And hope the Russians don't know we're coming," she replied, as she knocked on her helmet.

CHAPTER 52

Beverly Fire and Rescue Hall
Yellowhead Highway
Prince George, British Columbia, Canada
October 20, 0430 hours PDT

"I don't know what happened, Colonel. The Russians were pouring across the river. Tanks, troops, artillery raining down, then it all stopped. We were getting ready to abandon the 15th Avenue line and pull back to the southern bridge. The wounded have already been evacuated to the south. Then . . . they just stopped. It was like they received an order to just hold in place," said Major Manx, as he and Major Griffin stood over a map of Prince George, giving a situation brief to Colonel Patrick Curl, commanding officer of the 2nd Brigade Combat Team, 82nd Airborne Division.

"Between us, we were down to 300 effectives covering a three-mile front. We were getting low on food, ammo and water. Colonel Thompson is scraping together walking wounded, supply and maintenance people and trying to hold Highway 16 to the south. The two Troops we had down there were wiped out. We wouldn't have lasted another day," said Major Griffin, as Major Manx nodded in agreement.

"Well, the respite has allowed the rest of the brigade to cross the river. 3500 men can hold some ground, especially in a city. I've got one battalion headed south to link up with Lieutenant Colonel Thompson. Another one will start reinforcing your lines in the north.

All we have to do is keep the Russians at bay until the 2nd Armored arrives," Colonel Curl said.

. . . .

Canadian Tire & Gas
5000 Domano Boulevard
0430 hours PDT

"So, how many tanker trucks did you find?" Lieutenant Colonel Thompson asked, as the two officers stood outside the propane distribution center in south Prince George.

"Three! Each one contains over 10,000 gallons of liquid propane. I guess they were getting ready to make deliveries to local distributors when the city was evacuated. They were all parked out back, gassed up and ready to go," replied Captain Matt Vinson, CO of Headquarters Troop. His logistics and training support soldiers were now front-line troops, and the last untapped resource left in the battalion.

"That's a four-lane highway bridge. If we place those trucks underneath and denotate them, will they take down the bridge?"

"Colonel, 30,000 gallons of liquid propane underneath that overpass will rip it out by the roots. I used to be a firefighter. One of the most feared things we were trained to fight was a bleve from a loaded propane or gas tank. The explosion is awesome! Anything within 1000 feet is cooked. We place some C-4 on each tanker, link them together, then . . . boom! No bridge!" Captain Vinson said, while throwing his arms into the air and smiling.

"I think you missed your calling, Captain. You should have been in EOD. Get the trucks moved. You have 30 minutes to set them up."

"Roger that, Sir!" Captain Vinson said, as he turned and ran off.

"With all due respect, Colonel . . . that young man is disturbed in the head. Did you see the look on his face as he described the explosion? How the hell did he wind up leading a Headquarters Troop?" asked Sergeant Major Alton Schmidt.

"The needs of the Army, Sergeant Major. The needs of the Army. We go where they tell us to go. Now, where is that Canadian tank commander? She and her crew have a part in this plan."

. . . .

The Russians
Yellowhead Highway
2 miles southwest of Prince George
0530 hours PDT

"Lieutenant, what in the hell is going on? We have been sitting here for hours. Why are we not advancing up the highway? The Americans and Canadians don't have anything that can touch us," asked Senior Sergeant Radoslav Yolkin, from the driver's position in the lead T-14 Armata.

"Shut up, Rado! Just because you won the 2022 Tank Biathlon in Moscow doesn't make you anything special. Just drive the damn tank," said Senior Sergeant Vasilik Gribov, from the gunner's position.

"You are just jealous, Vasilik. Your tank finished second. You almost lost to the Chinese, thanks to your poor shooting."

"Poor shooting! I missed one shot in three days. It was a faulty round!"

"Both of you, shut up! You sound like a pair of schoolboys arguing over a football match. Senior Sergeant Yolkin, run a system check on our communications! Senior Sergeant Gribov, run a Main Gun diagnostic! Now!" ordered Senior Lieutenant Burien Vetrov, tank commander, regretting the presence of two such primadonnas inside his tank.

The two experienced tankers stared at each other and nodded. The lieutenant was a favorite in the brigade. His family connections were said to extend to General Grigory Gerasimov, the highest-ranking officer in the Russian military. As such, they understood the rules of the game.

The crew layout of the T-14 was unique. The three crewmen sat side-by-side in an armored capsule located in the front of the vehicle. As such, they were like cosmonauts trapped beside each other within arm's reach for hours. Personality conflicts often came to the fore. But collectively, they felt invulnerable. Their armored home was separated from the explosives-laden turret and the fuel stored near the rear-mounted engine compartment.

"Yes, Senior Lieutenant! At once, Senior Lieutenant!" they both said with a knowing smile, then proceeded to complete the unnecessary checks the Senior Lieutenant had ordered.

10 minutes later

"Senior Lieutenant Vetrov to all tanks! We have received orders to advance. We continue to be the tip of the spear. Wedge formation! We will lead in 'Molotok' (Hammer)! 'Shotina' (Brute), stay on our left flank! 'Grom' (Thunder), stay on our right! Speed 25. We are heading for the center of the city. This is the final push. Stay in formation! Kill anything that isn't Russian! Vetrov, out!"

The three tanks began to move in the darkness. All were using their night-vision and infrared-vision devices. Behind them came the remainder of the 59th Motorized Infantry Regiment led by the 124th Tank Battalion and 75 T-90A's. Helicopter support was due to arrive at sunrise, but that wasn't for another 90 minutes. The snow continued to fall and was projected to increase as the day went on.

20 minutes later

"Vasilik, have you seen any Canadian girls yet? I hear they are like Russian women, solid with a big chest," Radoslav said, as he drove the Hammer up the four-lane highway.

Vasilik laughed, then said, "Always with the women. I bet you're still a virgin!"

"My friend, you would lose that bet. I grew up in a little farming village. Did I ever tell you about Ursula Magyar? I was only 12 and she was 15 going on 25. Her family worked with mine during harvest time. We were in the barn storing hay one day, when . . ." Radoslav began, as they drove onto the Southridge Avenue overpass.

. . . .

Captain Vinson was standing on the roof of the Walmart Prince George Supercenter when the three tanks reached the center of the overpass. He lowered his binoculars and reached for the detonator sitting at his feet.

"Time for a little payback, Ruskies," he said, as he flipped the cover from the trigger and detonated 30,000 gallons of liquid propane sitting beneath the overpass.

The bridge disappeared. Three 47-ton Armata tanks were flipped through the air like toys. The Hammer rotated once in the air, then landed upright on the side of an earthen embankment. Falling bridge debris and burning propane enveloped the vehicle. The three-man crew, strapped in their seats and inside their armored capsule, survived the explosion.

"Rado! Get out! Open the damn hatch! We're burning!" Vasilik yelled, as he threw off his harness and began climbing over his crewmate and grabbing for the hatch lever.

"I'll get it! Quit stepping on me!" Rado yelled, as the red emergency lighting filled the small fighting compartment.

"No! Don't! The fire will . . ." Senior Lieutenant Vetrov yelled, as Rado grabbed the lever and cracked open the hatch . . .

All three men began yelling, as a thin red line formed at the hatch boundary. The line turned into a white-hot demon, with a smiling face. The hatch was wrenched open, as if grabbed by a fiery hand. Rado's head and torso burst into flame as he howled and tried to crawl away. Mercifully, their collective screams only lasted for a few more seconds. Their lungs and flesh were seared by white-hot fingers that began cleansing the interior of the tank . . .

. . . .

The Ridge

The 'Ghost' sat on a ridge that rose to the left of the Yellowhead Highway. They were only 200 yards from the long column of Russian tanks crossing below them. They had been in position for 15 minutes when the overpass exploded.

"Holy shit! That American Colonel wasn't kidding. That was the 'Mother of All IEDs'!" Sergeant Brown said, as she ducked down and shut the hatch of the Leopard tank.

"So, Sergeant Brown, are we going to continue to admire the American's work, or are we going to participate as requested?" asked Corporal Wills, from the gunner position.

"Gunner! Tank! Load Sabot! Flank shot on the rearmost tank!" Sergeant Brown yelled.

"Up!"

"Fire!"

. . . .

The Russians

The two columns of Russian tanks, spread across the highway, were in disarray. Lieutenant Colonel Maosovich, commander of the 124th Tank Battalion, had been riding with the lead tank platoon 100 yards behind the T-14s. He had been enjoying the view from his open hatch, as his armored juggernaut marched toward certain victory. He envisioned a promotion and the accolades that would surely follow. His head was removed by a section of flying guardrail.

Russian tanks began firing in all directions, but there was no enemy to be seen. Some rushed forward, others backed up. Individual company commanders fought to regain control as debris and fire rained down on their vehicles. One T-90 was crushed when 'Grom' crashed down on its turret. The resulting massive explosion spread burning fuel across the highway, adding to the chaos. Then the tanks of the 124th Battalion began to explode . . . one by one . . . as the Ghost worked its way up the column, from rear to front.

. . . .

The Ghost

Tracer fire began pinging off the front of the Ghost's turret, as the barrel of the main gun swung to the left to engage the next target. If Sergeant Brown could have viewed her position from the Russian perspective, she would have seen a line of 12.7 mm tracer rounds ricocheting from some steel item up on the ridgeline. The steel item . . . was her tank. The tracer fire was identifying the latest tormentor of the Russian tankers.

The first Sabot round soared over the Ghost, as did the second and the third. The fourth blew a chunk out of the fold in the ground they were hiding behind. Only the front of their turret was visible from the highway down below, but more Russian tanks were firing in their direction as their officers regained control of their units. The fifth round glanced off the mantlet of the main gun, rocking the tank.

"Sarge . . . I think they've got us! That one hit the turret!" shouted Corporal Wills, as he hit another Russian tank.

"Keep firing!"

"They're turning our way! No more flank shots! I'm hitting their reactive armor. We're not killing them!"

Another Sabot glanced off their turret. Followed immediately by another!

"Sarge!"

"Shit! Driver, back up, pivot left. Get us out of here! We're moving to a new firing position!"

. . . .

The Russians

"Take a deep breath, Major. Tell me what is happening," Lieutenant General Mulnatov said, while sitting in the back of his command vehicle, three miles south of the ambush.

"An IED, General! They blew up this bridge. We lost the T-14s! Then an ambush from the ridgeline above the highway! They have tanks up there. The lead tank company was decimated!" Major Alov said, while pointing at the flat screen map across from the general.

"IEDs? They are getting desperate if they're using IEDs. The 117th Motor Rifle Battalion is next in line. Get them off this highway and onto . . . here, Westgate Avenue. Head south, then east on Cathedral. We need to bypass the fallen bridge and then turn north."

"But what if there are more ambushes, General?"

"Young man . . . that is why we have tanks and guns. We kill them. Fight through any ambushes. Penetrate the center of the city. if we split them up into small pockets, we have them. Don't give them time to form another line of resistance."

"Yes, General!"

. . . .

Canadian Tire & Gas
5000 Domano Boulevard
0630 hours PDT

"Colonel Thompson, I just heard from Major Griffin. The Russians are attacking again from the north. Griffin and the Canadians have been reinforced by the rest of the brigade. They're going to try and hold the 15th Avenue line. They don't know how long they'll be able to hold. The Russians are flanking them to the west and tanks are coming down Tyner Boulevard. If we wait much longer, we'll all be trapped!" said Captain Vinson.

"It'll be light in less than an hour. Then their air support shows up. Where the hell is the 1ˢᵗ Armored? Where is our air support? So far, we've seen nothing!" Anthony thought.

"Sir! What are your orders?" asked Captain Vinson.

"We hold until the 1st Armored gets here, Captain."

"Sir, what if they don't make it?"

"They'll make it. Just hold every block, every building as long as you can!"

"Roger that, Colonel!"

"They have to make it or we're all dead," Anthony thought, as Captain Vinson turned and walked away.

. . . .

1455 Blackwater Road
3 miles south of Prince George
0630 hours PDT

Samuel and Marsha Robinson stood at the bay window of their small, one-floor home, staring in disbelief. It had snowed over a foot last night, but that wasn't what woke them up. The road in front of their house was filled with gigantic vehicles. M1A2C tanks and Bradley Infantry Fighting Vehicles disappeared in both directions.

Their two young sons had rushed to the front door and were going to run outside in their bare feet, until admonished by their mother. Now the boys just stood at the door, staring through the glass in blissful wonderment.

. . . .

"All right, gentlemen, that's it. Any more questions?" asked General Walrath, while sitting in the back of his command vehicle alongside his seven battalion commanders.

"It will be light in an hour, General. What about air support?" asked Lieutenant Colonel Tucker Knight.

"Colonel, you get your tanks in position. Let me worry about air support. Remember . . . 0650 kickoff. Colonel Knight, go straight up Blackwater Road. Your work will be up close and personal. Colonel Moore, use your speed. Get your tanks on line as you're coming across the open fields. You'll be taking them in the flank while they're strung out on Yellowhead Highway. Colonel Bush, your cavalry regiment will swing to the left along the creek. When you come out of the woods, you'll be within 200 yards. Use your TOW missiles on your Bradleys to take out their tanks. Then go to work on their infantry vehicles. Place your Linebackers here to provide air cover. Their Stingers will be able to cover our entire front. If Russian Hinds show up, which they probably will, take them out. Colonel Garcia, once everyone's in position, I'll want a walking barrage all along the length of that highway from north to south. I'll tell you when to cease fire as I track the vehicle movement of our troops. The Russians outnumber us three to one, but they're stretched all along this highway for ten miles. We have to crush this three-mile section. Then we'll address the rest of them. Get moving!"

. . . .

"Dammit, Colonel! We have to retreat. We have to head for the bridges or we're going to be massacred!" Major Griffin said.

"Major Smith, what are the Canadians going to do? I can't order you to retreat or to stay," Lieutenant Colonel Thompson asked.

"We came here with 40 tanks and an equal number of APCs. I've got one troop of four tanks holding a bridge to our north with some infantry support. Fighting in the city has chewed up everything else. We have a few APCs and one or two tanks left. That's it. Our casualties are over 60 percent. I think it's time we . . ." Major Smith began.

"Colonel! 1st Armored . . . they're here!" shouted Second Lieutenant Russell, as he ran into the office that had become the temporary headquarters for the battalion.

"Calm down, Lieutenant. Tell me what you know. Is this a rumor?"

"No, Sir! It just came in on the brigade channel. The 1st Armored Division is attacking from the south."

"When? When are they attacking?" asked Major Smith.

"Now, Sir! Right now!"

"Well, gentlemen . . . I guess we're going to hang around for a while. Get back to your troops!"

. . . .

Yellowhead Highway
Four miles southwest of Prince George
0650 hours PDT

Lieutenant General Leonid Mulnatov stepped out of the back of his BTR-87 command vehicle and relieved himself on the side of the road. Tanks, trucks and armored personnel carriers continued to stream past as he stood by the guard rail. He glanced up and smiled. Broad fields stretched out to the south. The heavy snow overnight had left them pristine all the way to the far tree line. The clouds were lifting, and the sun was already starting to peek above the horizon to his left. It would be a cold day, but clear.

"Ahh, what a beautiful day. This battle is almost over. A dozen Hinds will cycle in and out all day and help eliminate any final pockets of resistance. Imagine, an entire brigade of the 82nd Airborne massacred! I'll have to send out an order that we don't want any prisoners. That would just slow us down. With Zhurov gone, I will pick up the pace. He was a lover of set-piece battles, a plodder. With a little luck, this battle will put a third star on my shoulder!"

The death of Colonel General Zhurov left Mulnatov in charge of the 5th Combined Arms Army. His mind was already drifting onto the next battle. It was time to head south for the US border. He looked to his left and saw the comforting sight of dozens of armored vehicles slowly streaming up the highway, heading north toward Prince George. To his right, an identical sight disappeared a mile down the road as it curved out of sight.

The sound of heavy fighting to the north was music to his soldier's ears as he finished up and began walking back to his vehicle. The distinctive crack of the 125mm guns of his tanks mixed with the thumb and rattle of explosions and machine gun fire. The first indication that things weren't going as planned was the sound of heavy caliber artillery impacting to the north. He turned and stared, wondering if one of his officers had requested artillery support. The sound continued to increase in volume and frequency until the first explosion detonated on the highway one mile up the road, just where it curved out of view. Huge explosions were walking down the highway in his direction as he ducked into his vehicle, closed the door, and picked up the handset.

"This is General Mulnatov to all battalion commanders! Get off the highway. Enemy artillery is focusing on the highway!" he said, as the nose of his vehicle lifted off the ground.

A few seconds later . . . it was time for another change of command in the 5th Combined Arms Army.

. . . .

"A" Company, 2nd Battalion, 37th Armored Regiment
Blackwater Road
0655 hours PDT

The artillery fire had just lifted as the M1A2C tanks of Alpha Company approached the intersection of Blackwater and Leslie Roads. The Yellowhead Highway was less than a quarter mile away, around one more bend in the road. Smoke, the smell of cordite and burning diesel filled the air. The sound of gunfire and exploding munitions was constant.

Lieutenant Colonel Tucker Knight ordered his M1A2C tank to halt just past the turnoff to Leslie Road. He didn't need to look back to see what was happening. His orders during the Final Mission Brief had been explicit.

"Captain Davis, take Alpha Company to the right down Leslie Road. Take the next left onto Birchill Crescent. This will bring you into their flank. Prosecute the attack with extreme aggression! Work your way north."

Unlike other battalion commanders, Lieutenant Colonel Knight was leading from the front. He felt this was a time for instantaneous reaction. He needed to see things for himself and not through the eyes of a flat screen. Such tools were useful, but he felt his fellow commanders were becoming overly dependent on what he considered electronic toys.

The 14 tanks of Bravo Company lined up behind him. Charlie Company was turning to the left in a line formation. Each tank was plowing through the narrow line of trees beside the highway. The sound of snapping pines was audible above the chaos as the 70-ton tanks made their own path toward Yellowhead Highway.

"Patience . . . patience . . . 60 seconds, then advance. We all hit them at the same time," Knight thought, as he ducked into his tank and shut the hatch.

"The toys do have their uses," he said, as he watched all the tanks of his battalion moving on a flat screen display. Each tank was represented by a red wedge.

"Driver! Forward at 20 mph! Gunner! Load Sabot! Prepare to engage the enemy!"

. . . .

20 Miles West of Prince George
0700 hours PDT

The flight of six Mi-24D Hinds had been late taking off. They were due over Prince George five minutes ago, but Captain Andre Kuznetsov wasn't particularly worried. The mission brief was to support the removal of enemy infantry from buildings. All his choppers were armed with four UB-32 rocket pods. Each pod was capable of firing 32 S-5 ground attack rockets. Combined with the 12.7 mm Yak-B Gatling gun mounted beneath the nose, they were perfectly armed for attacking infantry in soft buildings.

Captain Kuznetsov guided his Hind 200 feet above the long line of Russian vehicles on Highway 17, the Yellowhead Highway. It was a beautiful day for flying. The clouds had finally cleared, and the view was gorgeous. The white terrain, vast forests and mountains reminded him of home. He missed his wife and his children, but duty to Mother Russia took precedent over everything else.

"Bear Flight, this is Bear 1. We will be over target area in five minutes. Remember, enemy targets will be marked with green smoke. Be careful with your fire!"

"Bear 1, this is Bear 4! All I'm seeing in the distance is black smoke!"

"Bear 4, that is a sight you will tell your grandchildren about. That is the might of Mother Russia coming to . . ." Captain Kuznetsov began, when his helicopter and two others exploded.

"Break . . . break . . . break! Enemy aircraft!" Bear 4 shouted, as the A-10 Warthog streaked overhead. It had attacked from behind them.

The Hind Mi-24 was armored to withstand an impact from a .50 cal bullet, but the depleted uranium, armor piercing 30 mm rounds from the GAU-8 autocannon mounted in the nose of the Warthog were designed to kill a tank. The GAU-8 rate of fire was 65 rounds per second. The Hinds were shredded like paper. The wingman of the first Warthog finished the task. The flight of six Hinds was destroyed in less than a minute.

. . . .

A-10 Warthogs

"Vengeance 2, this is Vengeance 1. Let's start sweeping the road. Look out for SA-19 Grisons. Their surface-to-air missiles will make for a bad day," said Captain Mike Seabeck, as his aircraft started a strafing run on the Yellowhead Highway. Tracer rounds were heading everywhere as the ponderous antique continued its deadly run over the column of vehicles.

The A-10 Thunderbolt II, nicknamed the "Warthog" for its ungainly appearance, was past obsolete by US Air Force standards. Designed in the early 1970s, it was slow, low tech and brutally effective. Its simple design, robust construction and ease of maintenance made it a favorite of pilots and maintenance personnel.

"Vengeance 3 . . . Vengeance 4 . . . this is Vengeance 1. When you arrive on station, follow Highway 17 to the west. This Russian column goes on for miles. ADA (Air Defense Artillery) fire is thick! Good hunting! Over!"

"Vengeance 1, this is Vengeance 3. Understand there's no limit on hunting Russian bears this season. Over!"

"Roger that! Out!"

The A-10s of the 354th Fighter Squadron were stationed at Davis-Monthan Air Force base in Arizona. The base had escaped the Great Quake with minimal damage. It was the location of the largest aircraft boneyard in the world. Thousands of aircraft, some dating back to the 1950s, were stored at the base. The fact that A-10s were stationed there wasn't lost on the pilots. Once again, they had to prove their worth.

. . . .

"A" Company, 2nd Battalion, 37th Armored Regiment
US Army
Yellowhead Highway
0730 hours PDT

Lieutenant Colonel Tucker Knight pushed open the hatch on his M1A2C tank, reached forward, and chambered a round in the .50 cal M2 machine gun mounted outside the hatch. He had ordered a halt to the shooting when no viable targets remained, but there was no point in taking chances. Destroyed and burning Russian vehicles were scattered across all four lanes of the highway. Hundreds of bodies were mixed among the destroyed vehicles. Three of Alpha Company's tanks were wrecked. Four more were crippled. The fighting had been at point-blank range for tank warfare. Tank crews were trained to fight at ranges up to two miles. This brutal fight had been at 200 yards . . . or less. His heart was still pounding in his chest as he tried to assess the situation.

The reports from his company commanders had been the same. Surprise had been total. The Russians had grown used to having air superiority. When it disappeared, their tightly packed columns of vehicles had been easy prey for the gruesome firepower of the A-10s. Knight glanced up as an A-10 flew low and slow over the highway, the 'grinning shark' painted on the nose clearly visible. The A-10 had also run out of targets. The plane wagged its wings, and turned to the west, hunting fresh prey.

"All companies . . . consolidate your gains. Ensure that enemy effectives are rendered ineffective. Push prisoners across the highway and into the fields. We'll contain them there. Continue offensive operation toward the west. Destroy any enemy forces still operable," Lieutenant Colonel Knight ordered over the battalion network.

. . . .

50 miles West of Prince George
Altitude 15,000 feet and descending
0745 hours PDT

The flight of four Russian SU-35s had been scrambled from their new home at Eielson Air Base in Alaska after the appearance of the American A-10s over the Prince George battlefield. Armed with short-range R-73 air-to-air missiles and KAB-500 bombs, they were intent on reestablishing Russian dominance in the air.

. . . .

180 miles South of Prince George
Altitude 25,000 feet
0745 hours PDT

The F-35 Lightning II had a very difficult childhood. By 2014 the development program was $160 billion over budget. First flown in 2006, the US Navy declared its first F-35Cs ready in 2019. The finished product was overly expensive, complex, and difficult to maintain. It was also the most lethal multirole stealth combat aircraft ever built. At least that was the thinking before the existence of the Dory became common knowledge.

"Bulldog Leader to Bulldog Pack. Looks like we've got another pack intruding into our air space. Over!"

"This is Bulldog 2. My Targeting Computer identifies them as Russian Su-35s . . . four each. One for each of us. We'll be within range in 30 seconds. Over!"

"Bulldog Leader to Bulldog Pack. Do not fire! I repeat, do not fire! They can't see us. Let's get a bit closer. Fire only on my command. Out!"

Four AIM-120D AMRAAM air-to-air missiles were fired 90 seconds later. The AIM-120D had a flight time of just over one minute from 60 miles out.

. . . .

The Su-35s

"Major Yolkin, enemy missiles have targeted us" said First Lieutenant Grinin.

"Relax, Lieutenant. I can see. Locate the aircraft that sent us these presents. We have at least one minute to decide our response."

"Major, I'm seeing nothing. These missiles came out of nowhere."

"I concur, Lieutenant . . . probably F-35s. If it was a Dory, we wouldn't be having this conversation. Descend to 500 feet. Prepare to release countermeasures. Target the southern half of the city. Then head north. We will warn our next flight. Let them handle these stealthy American bastards. We will help our comrades on the ground and then go back to base."

. . . .

And so, the battle for Prince George went on for the remainder of the day and into the long night. Each side kept reinforcing their forces. The Russians were not amateurs in the Art of War. More importantly, their losses in men and material meant little to their leaders. The only thing that counted was victory, and so the killing continued. But soon, everything was to change . . . for the entire planet!

CHAPTER 53

The Lincoln Bedroom
The White House
Washington, DC
October 21, 2215 hours EST

She couldn't remember why she had come up to the Lincoln Bedroom. The feeling of wanting to move . . . to do something . . . anything, but be President of the United States, had overwhelmed her. So, she had left. Now, she stared at the report still clutched in her fingers. The pages drifted to the plush carpet as a floorboard creaked, pulling her attention away from the horrible numbers and facts. Every detail showed a nation on life support, and it was going to get worse if Dr. Wolf was correct. Far worse than anyone could imagine.

The evacuation of the Mississippi Valley had begun. Every state from Louisiana to Michigan was being emptied by Presidential decree. Renewed calls for her impeachment had started within two hours after the evacuation order went public. Half of her White House staff had resigned in protest. Her Chief of Staff had pleaded for her to reconsider. All she could think about were the tens of millions of lives that would be lost if they weren't evacuated. Her head was on the chopping block either way.

Lincoln had never used the room as a bedroom. Instead it was his cabinet room and study. It was here that he signed the Emancipation Proclamation. At that time, the walls were covered with maps of the ongoing Civil War. Now she could feel his presence as she walked over to the ornate rosewood bed and sat down.

"*All I want to do is go to sleep and never wake up,*" she thought, as she closed her eyes, and lay back on the tall bed, her feet dangling off the floor.

She felt a sudden chill. Then she heard a voice . . .

"I hated this room and all the maps. They reminded me of my failures, all the death and fracturing of the Union. The Emancipation Proclamation was the only thing I ever did up here that left me feeling satisfied. I knew it wasn't the end, but I had begun the healing. At least, that was my hope. Let me tell you, there were more than a few people who thought I was insane to do it in the middle of a war. I told them if we don't do it now . . . then when? Slavery had to go! I wish I could have been around for a few more years. Maybe things would have gone better after the war.*"*

Clarisse heard the voice and froze, her heart pounding in her chest. She refused to believe it was real. She just lay on the bed, staring up at the ceiling, afraid to move. Then she felt someone close by and sat bolt upright.

"Sorry, I didn't mean to startle you. They told me you had come up here. I'm worried about you, Clarisse. So is Denise. Our little girl doesn't understand any of this. I've tried to explain it to her, but she just shakes her head, as if it was just part of a bad dream," said Paul Beaumont, as he walked up to the bed and sat down beside his wife.

"Paul . . . I think I'm going crazy. I just laid back on the bed and closed my eyes . . . for just a second. Abraham Lincoln began talking to me. I heard his voice."

"Babe, you're exhausted. You're not eating right. All you do is work 18-hour days."

"More like 20!"

"Yeah, more like 20, and you wonder why you're hearing voices," he said, as he put his arm around her and pulled her closer.

"Paul . . . I've seen him before . . . more than once. I've seen his sadness and fatigue . . . in his face, not in a painting. I think he's trying to . . . I don't know . . . comfort me, counsel me . . . something," Clarisse said, as she leaned into his shoulder and grasped his hand.

"Well, the White House is supposed to be haunted. That's common knowledge."

"I don't believe in ghosts . . . or I didn't. I wonder if I can talk to him?"

"Clarisse, if you tell anyone other than me, about you and 'Old Abe', they'll place you in a straitjacket, and haul you out the back door in the middle of the night."

"You'd let them haul me away like a piece of furniture?"

"Well, I'd get a receipt and visit you at least one a month!"

"My hero!" Clarisse said, as she elbowed him in the side.

"Have you had anything to eat today?" Paul asked, as he dodged another elbow.

"Coffee this morning . . . a doughnut, later I think."

"And you wonder why you're hallucinating? You're eating like a 19-year-old college student cramming for finals."

"Paul . . . it was real! I heard him!"

"Hey, back in the day I'd say let's go on a midnight run to Jack-in-the-Box. But how about we go to our bedroom and call room service. I hear they make a mean turkey sandwich downstairs. That, and a few hours of sleep, and you'll feel like a new woman," Paul said, as he held her hand and stood up.

He sat back down when the room started to shake. He stared at her with wide eyes, surprised to see tears streaming down her face.

"No! Please, God . . . no! Paul . . . Dr. Wolf was right! It's started. The Reelfoot Rift . . . the New Madrid Fault . . . it's opening up!" she said, as the heavy furniture began to dance across the floor.

They both fell back on the bed and held each other as the shaking continued . . . and grew worse. She squeezed his hand and pointed toward a far corner of the room.

"Paul . . . he's here!"

Paul Beaumont stared in amazement at an apparition that could only be Abraham Lincoln. The man was tall, thin, wearing black trousers, suspenders and a white shirt, unbuttoned at the collar. Apparel he would have been wearing while working in his private office in 1865.

The apparition seemed unfazed by the shaking as he took two steps toward them and halted, before saying, **"You two better leave while you can. Stay strong, Madam President. The nation is going to need you. The pain and the suffering are going to get worse . . ."**

The image faded. Paul and Clarise stared at each other, as the room tilted and jumped. The sound of items crashing to the floor, fracturing plaster and splintering wood, shocked them both into action. Paul grabbed her hand, and together they bolted from the room. Multiple Secret Service agents met them in the hall and whisked them away.

. . . .

Memphis, Tennessee
2110 hours CST

"For those of you who are still with us, this is Ernie Coleman, reporting from the WMC-TV Action News 5 chopper. We are hovering 1000 feet above the Mississippi, just west of downtown Memphis. It's a strange sight. I can only see one or two sets of headlights down below. Memphis Light, Gas and Water has secured power to the entire metropolitan area. Regional One, Baptist Memorial and Methodist University Hospitals are dark. Normally they're lit up like Christmas 24 hours a day. The only light is from a full moon.

Personally, I think this administration has made a fatal mistake. The financial cost of evacuating the Greater Memphis area must run into the tens of millions. And for what? The wild theory of a lone geologist that the continent is going to crack in half? HG Wells caused a panic back in 1938. I think this debacle will make that look like . . ."

"Ernie . . . shit! Ernie, shut up and look down below. Something's happening!" said Macklin Reese, the chopper's pilot.

"Dammit, Reese! I'm live! You get paid to fly the damn . . . oh hell! The ground is moving. It's falling away. That's not possible! Are we still live? Dan, that camera better be recording this! This will go global! Folks . . . at this point, the Mississippi is almost half a mile wide, and it just disappeared. The bridges, the Memphis-Arkansas Bridge . . . Interstate 55 . . . they're all gone. A little further north . . . the Hernando de Soto Bridge, almost a mile long . . . I just saw it fall into a black crevasse. Harbor Town is gone! Downtown Memphis . . . is . . . sliding down into . . . I don't know. As I look to the south . . . it's the same . . . like a big crack in the earth. It's spreading . . . cutting through the bends in the river. Now what? Dammit, I'm live! The studio? What about the studio? Where the hell are you going?"

The chopper flew to the east. The western half of Memphis had vanished, and the WMC-TV Action News 5 station along with it . . .

. . . .

Montrose Harbor
Lake Michigan
Chicago, Illinois
2140 hours CST

"Relax, Sheila. In about two days all these idiots are going to come streaming back into the city. They're going to be tired, hungry and pissed, because of this 'chicken little' bullshit! I packed champagne . . . some eats. We can cruise up the coast and watch the stars. It's cold, but I'll keep you warm," Lance Jakobson said with a wink, as he steered his new 242 Limited S Yamaha 24-footer out of the Montrose Marina.

"Are you sure, Lance? My parents, my brother and sister, they all headed toward Cedar Rapids. Our grandparents still live there."

"What we have, Sheila, is a President who has hit the panic button. Believe me, I'm a life-long Democrat. I love having a female President. But this one? She's completely incompetent! I don't know who she's been listening to, but all she's done is make things worse since she was sworn in. Hell, she wasn't even elected! We should have held another election. That's what we should have . . ."

"Lance! The water! Why is the water shaking?"

"Duh! We're driving in a boat. It's supposed to . . . shit!" Lance said, as the nose of the boat began turning toward the south. He steered to the north and accelerated, but he was caught in a strange current . . . a very strong current. A rumbling noise became audible as the small boat picked up speed.

"Lance . . . look!" Sheila said, while pointing to the south at the majestic skyline of downtown Chicago.

Five buildings were over 1000 feet tall. Another 30 were over 600 feet tall. As the couple stared in disbelief . . . they all began to tilt and fall into Lake Michigan.

"No! It's not possible!" Lance said, as he turned back to the north and pushed the throttle forward. But the current was accelerating. It was as if the lake had turned into a river and was rapidly flowing to the south . . .

. . . .

Pierre Part, Louisiana
2140 hours CST

It had been a rough day hunting gators. Jacob Broussard stared at the 38 tags in his hand and sighed.

"Two damn days left. How the heck did Marie expect me to just drive away 'cause the President says the country is going to crack in half. Prices for hides are already down. If I have to eat the cost of these tags, we'll be eating beans all winter long. That's what I get for marrying a girl from Oklahoma," he said, as a swell lifted his Gator Trax hunting boat and set it back down.

He looked around, surprised because he hadn't heard another boat approaching. He peered into the darkness while continuing to sip from a mason jar of cousin Pierre's 'special brew'. His boat was drifting in the Avoca Island Cutoff, a narrow channel that penetrated an isolated part of the swamp. He had just finished hanging bait for the next day's hunting and had decided to stop for a sip.

Then the wind picked up and the boat began to shudder. At first, he thought a gator might have bumped the bottom of the boat. Jacob had lived in the swamp for almost 30 years. He knew every sound, every creature, all the tricks of 'Mère Nature', or so he thought. Then suddenly, the varied sounds of life in the swamp grew silent. He had never heard such silence. The swamp was never quiet. Then, he heard a new sound, a ghostly moaning coming from . . . everywhere.

When his boat tilted forward, he dropped the mason jar and grabbed his rifle, sure that a huge gator was attacking his boat. Then he glanced at the trees. Everything was tilting, as the water began to swirl and rush in different directions. The silence ended, as the swamp screamed around him. Not the sound of life, but snapping, cracking, the sound of rushing water and tearing earth. Then his world turned upside down . . .

. . . .

10500 Mt. Sunapee Road
Reston, Virginia
2340 hours EST

Dr. Janice Wolf sat in her home, alone with her thoughts in her darkened office. The only light came from the two 24-inch monitors on her desk. An empty bottle of 2017 Caymus Cabernet Sauvignon sat beside the printer. It was the last bottle of a case that had been an anniversary present from her husband, Allen. He had left for Chicago over eight hours ago to find his parents. All the flights were full or cancelled after the president's order of evacuation. He had decided to drive. She had begged him not to go, but now she was alone. The kids were upstairs asleep. The front yard of their two-story brick home was full of leaves. Rick was supposed to rake the leaves tomorrow. A rake wouldn't touch their yard for a long time.

The power had died after the first great shock. Her whole-house generator had kicked in and she was linked with satellite data from multiple sources. She had turned off all the lights in the house, not wanting visitors.

"Unbelievable! It really is unbelievable. It looks like Edgar Cayce was correct. The North American continent is splitting down the middle," she said, as she stared in disbelief at the satellite images and drained the last of the wine from her glass.

"Whiskey on wine . . . mighty fine. Where does he keep his whiskey?" she asked, as she stood, and walked away, as two streams of tears poured down her face . . .

CHAPTER 54

Ministry of Defense Building
22 Frunzenskaya Naberezhnaya Avenue
Moscow, Russia
October 22, 0700 hours MSK

Russian President Vladimirovich Morozov was sitting in his study, deep below the Ministry of Defense Building. He had slept very little the previous night. The war in Canada was not going well. The Americans had been able to mobilize troops far more quickly than his advisers thought possible. He had hoped for a quick campaign that would force the Americans to capitulate. After the fighting at Prince George, both sides had been bloodied. The invasion would have to be reinforced, something he had wanted to avoid. Europe still had to be pacified. A knock at the door interrupted his brooding.

"Whoever the hell it is . . . bring me some tea!" President Morozov shouted, as the door slowly opened.

"I will have your aide bring us both some tea," General Grigory Gerasimov said, as he nodded to the aide, stepped into the room, and closed the door.

"You have nerve showing up. I'll give you that! I am not happy with you, old friend. Things are not going well . . . not well at all!" President Morozov said, while glaring up at the commanding general of the Russian military.

"There have been a few bumps, Vovich, my old comrade, but it is a war. And before you touch that button on your chair and have me thrown into prison . . . everything has changed while you slept," General Gerasimov said, as he slid into a chair across from the fuming president.

"You always have been a mind reader. Now what has changed that will save your life?"

General Gerasimov relished the moment and let his answer wait while he smiled at his friend of 30 years.

"I will have you shot before . . ."

"America is no more, Mr. President. What the Chinese started, Mother Nature has finished. The United States of America has split apart."

"They have political strife, but they will never . . ."

"Physically! The nation is now in two pieces. It happened less than four hours ago. I could feel the earth shaking here . . . on the other side of the planet. A geologist told me that an ancient flaw in the crust of North America was destabilized by the Great Quake on their West Coast. The United States split down the middle from the Great Lakes to the Gulf of Mexico!" General Gerasimov said, and began to laugh and slap his thigh.

"Are you serious? I remember the briefing, but it was supposed to be 1000 years from now . . . if ever. The damage . . . the deaths. Their infrastructure! They are finished!" President Morozov shouted, as he leapt to his feet.

"So, what do we demand, Mr. President? Total surrender? Alaska, of course! Seven million dollars for 500,000 square miles of territory. Emperor Alexander II was an idiot! Do we even want the West Coast? It is a mess. The ground will be shaking for years. Volcanoes! Yellowstone may blow up! Perhaps we should just leave them alone to rot."

"No, Grigory . . . we will not leave them alone. They must be crushed and removed from the world stage. Assume nothing. Despite their political differences, they are a resilient people. Despite being torn in half . . . they will resist! Keep up enough pressure in Canada to force them to divert resources in that direction. But now . . . now is the time we finish the business that should have been addressed after the Great Patriotic War. We . . . you and I, my old friend . . . are going to resurrect the Soviet Union. We will complete the consolidation of all of Europe and Asia under our banner. We will have a new flag, Grigory. It will be the flag of our Russia, the new, ever-expanding Russia, combined with the Hammer and Sickle of our illustrious past. We will not make the mistakes of that idiot Brezhnev and the traitor, Gorbachev. Joseph Vissarionovich Stalin . . . he knew how to run a country. He will be my model, old friend. One of my favorite quotes of his goes, ' Everyone imposes his own system as far as his army can reach'. We are going to take everything and reach everywhere, old friend. For starters, it is time to move into Western Europe. Grigory, my Russian bear who is now a fox, I want our tanks on the west coast of Spain in 90 days . . ."

To be continued in

BROKEN UNION – WAR IN THE EAST

Made in the USA
Columbia, SC
06 August 2019